TERROR TALES OF
THE WEST COUNTRY

TERROR TALES OF
THE WEST COUNTRY

Edited by

PAUL FINCH

First published in 2022 by Telos Publishing,
139 Whitstable Road, Canterbury, Kent CT2 8EQ,
United Kingdom.

www.telos.co.uk

ISBN: 978-1-84583-208-7

Telos Publishing Ltd values feedback. Please e-mail any
comments you might have about this book to:
feedback@telos.co.uk

British Library Cataloguing in Publication Data.
A catalogue record for this book is available from the British
Library.

TABLE OF CONTENTS

COPYRIGHT INFORMATION

THE DARKNESS BELOW
Dan Coxon

You asked so I'll tell you, but you won't believe a word of it. You'll read the reports and assessments, the opinions of doctors and social workers, and you'll take their theories as facts. And yet my story – the story of someone who lived through this, and lost his world because of it? That, you'll dismiss as fantasy.

So be it. You don't have to believe me. Just listen.

That year was Angie's choice. The previous year had been mine: two weeks in the Lakes, days spent hiking and a spot of night fishing. More than our fair share of rain. It might be that the rain swayed her, turned her mind to the sunny Southwest. Maybe she simply had her eye on a cream tea or two. If I ask her now she won't even tell me.

Somerset. Even the name is evocative, isn't it? The end of summer, hay baled in a sun-baked field. Long days, warm nights. A cold pint of cider in a country pub, condensation pearling on the glass. Yes, I can see the appeal. Even now, after all that happened, I can feel its tug, a promise of balmy days in the great outdoors. We forgot that it has its dark places too. That some things like to hide from the light.

It was Kirstie who suggested Cheddar Gorge. She liked the name, I think – when you're nine, every meal comes with a side of cheese. We saw a leaflet in a Tourist Information stand, an image of the caves, the stalactites glistening wet like something from another world. She snatched it into her hand and pointed at it.

'Can we go here? This looks so awesome. Can we?'

Angie and I shared a glance, but it only took a second. Of course we could. Like her older brother, Kirstie spent most of her time glued to a screen, playing cheap mobile games that baffled me with their blocky graphics and homemade music, or watching strangers playing those same games on YouTube. That she wanted to go to an actual attraction, Cheddar's infamous Gough's Cave, was rare enough to raise our eyebrows.

'We can do that,' I said with a nod. 'It might be fun. I went there when I was a boy.'

Luke grunted, simmering with thirteen-year-old angst, but I let it pass. One child was on board: I counted that as a win.

I hadn't considered how much the gorge would have changed. In my head it was still a twee parade of gift shops pincered between steep cliffs, the caves little more than a hole in the rockface. I think even the tickets were tiny paper chits spat out by a hand-operated machine. I should have realised how out of date I was. After we'd sat in traffic for ten minutes, the kids grew restless. Kirstie kicked the back of Angie's chair over and over, until she snapped and shouted at her to stop it; Luke, meanwhile, huffed through his nose at every poorly parked car, and made unhelpful comments about how we should have gone to Wookey Hole instead. He was probably right.

Finally, having scraped around a few tight corners, we found a car park tucked behind a Chinese restaurant. A group of bikers had kicked down their stands, six-packs of lager at their feet. Angie wasn't comfortable, so we hustled the kids out of the car and told them to wait by the bin as we unloaded our bags and hats from the boot. Luke was watching them with interest, I could see. Not for the first time, I wondered if he'd begun experimenting with alcohol. We allowed him a glass of wine at Christmas, but he hadn't asked for more, and we had felt it was best not to bring it up. He'd discover it in his own time.

The bikers paid little attention as we gathered our things, and Angie herded Luke and Katie up the road. The shops from my childhood had multiplied like mould; now they stretched along both sides of the narrow street, cafes and gift emporiums rubbing shoulders with fudge shops and boutique cheesemongers. The pavements were barely one person wide, and we had to walk single file, the kids sandwiched between us like they were still toddlers. From my position at the back I mentally urged them to stay tucked in close to the wall. More than once I imagined one of them slipping, our world exploding in a collision of steel, blood and bone. The one time I'd told Angie about these mental flashes she'd looked at me like I was broken.

At the caves I'd expected a guide, but once we'd paid for our tickets we were told there was a self-guided tour, with headsets included in the price. The kids snapped their headphones on with something approaching glee, and once they were cocooned in their audio bubbles the bickering stopped. I told myself that half an hour of silence was worth the entry fee.

I don't know when Luke wandered off. I've come back to this moment time and time again, at first as things started to unravel, then later when the police questioned me, trying to place a timeline on my story. I should have been paying more attention, but I was distracted by the audio commentary, and the rare experience of being buried under a hundred feet of rock in an Aladdin's cave of sensory wonders. Have you visited Gough's Cave? No? Then you should, if you're to understand what it was like. Not only the strange shapes formed over millennia as the water dripped through this underground hollow, but the textures, the play of electric lights across random patterns bringing to life hunched figures, gaping mouths filled with needle-thin teeth.

Did you know that the show cave – the portion open to the public – only accounts for a quarter of the network? I looked that up later that evening, when I was trying to make sense of it all. The rest is flooded and only accessible to divers, but sometimes, depending on the height of the water table, other caverns open up, often for a matter of hours. Passages that have slumbered underwater for a thousand years might drain for an afternoon, laying bare rocks that have not been seen by human eyes for centuries – and who knows what else lies down there with them.

The last few summers have been dry, haven't they. The water table was low. We should all have taken greater care.

I'd reached a stopping point in the audio commentary, and the headset was digging uncomfortably into my scalp. I pressed pause and slipped it off my head. I could see Angie ahead of me and Katie next to her, the pair of them examining a large stalactite that stabbed down from the ceiling like the tooth of a buried monster, a single droplet sparkling at its tip. There was no sign of Luke. Looking behind me I saw only a shadowy cluster of strangers, old enough that I took them to be a coach party of pensioners. There was no way our son could have disappeared among their number. He must be ahead.

Skipping one of the commentary points, I hurried forward to catch up with the girls. I still couldn't see Luke. Tapping Angie on the shoulder, I signalled for her to lift her earphones.

'Have you seen Luke?' I asked, trying to keep a note of panic from my voice. 'Is he in front, do you know?'

She shrugged, but I noticed her eyes darting around the dark corners of the cave. 'I thought he was back there with you. He hasn't fallen behind?'

That must be it, I thought. Of course it must – the self-guided walk was a simple straight line up the cave system and back, there was nowhere else for him to go. Still, I signalled that I was going back to look for him and left them to their stalactite and the commentary.

How long did I wander up and down that cave, searching each face for our son? It felt like hours. The first few minutes passed quickly, then the realisation crept slow and cold that he wasn't anywhere obvious, and this might be more than a simple telling-off for wandering away from his family. I reached the entrance without any sign of him, then doubled back; when I caught up with Angie again, this time with panic in my eyes, she abandoned the audio too and we both marched ahead, calling his name.

It didn't take long for other people to take up the call. It was the parents most of all, I noticed – the people like us. They knew what it was like to lose a child, or imagined it at least. The kind of dream that would wake them in the middle of the night, alert and sweating. What had happened to us might happen to any one of them.

Luke's name echoed up and down the cave network, and each time I heard it my heart constricted a little tighter. One of the cave stewards had been directed to us by another family, and he was asking questions, taking down details on a clipboard that shook in his hand. Then we heard a shout from up ahead, louder than the others.

'Here! Over here! We've got him!'

I don't remember the rush to find who had spoken, the frantic panic to uncover what had happened, whether he was traumatised, or injured, or worse. Those moments are gone, although I assume they lasted little more than a minute, the four of us – Angie, Kirstie, myself and the steward – pushing through the crowd.

'Here! I just saw him sitting there … He's here. Your son?'

Finally, I saw Luke. He was sitting against the wall of the cave, clutching his headphones. He looked up and smiled at us, blowing his fringe away from his face in a way that I hadn't seen him do before.

'Hey Mum. Dad. What's all the fuss?'

I took a breath before I said anything. Anyone who has ever lost a child – even for a few moments, in a supermarket, or among the lights and bells of a fairground – will tell you that your heart races faster than you can keep up with, your breath catches in your throat. For that period of time, whether it's hours or seconds, your entire world shrinks to a single dark tunnel, leading you towards whatever fate awaits you at the other end. Most of the time it will be your child, puffy-faced and streaked with tears, but otherwise healthy and alive. Other times it won't.

Sucking breath back into my lungs, I held out a hand. Luke clasped it and I pulled him to his feet. I expected his usual sullenness – was preparing myself to give a lecture on manners, and responsibility, and not giving your father a premature heart attack – but was surprised when his face bloomed into a grin. His hand felt hot, and I dropped it as he spoke.

'I guess I gave you all a fright. Sorry about that. These stupid things broke –' he waved the headphones in front of us, '– and I was trying to get them working again. Short connection, I think. A loose wire. You should ask for a refund.'

We all turned to the steward, who gave us a bashful look before leading us back to the cave entrance. There were forms to fill out and sign, a health and safety requirement whenever anyone got lost in the cave network, plus they offered us return tickets for any date in the next two months. I couldn't imagine we'd want to, but I took them anyway. Maybe Kirstie would be so offended we'd cut her excursion short that we'd have to do it all again.

While Angie and I ticked, scribbled and signed, Kirstie and Luke sat on two chairs in the corner. I half expected we'd have to separate them, but they stayed quietly engaged in something on their phones, occasionally exchanging a word or two. It was only when I heard laughter that I paid attention.

'Everything okay over there?'

Luke just nodded, and his sister wafted her hand at me, shooing me away. 'Kid stuff,' she said, 'nothing for you to worry about, *Dad*.'

The last word was drawn out so that it sounded like a sheep bleating, and it set them laughing again. I'll admit that I was a little affronted at being the butt of their joke, but I'd take that over squabbling and simmering teenage aggression every time. If they were laughing at me at least it meant they were happy.

The health and safety forms asked a question about injuries sustained during the 'incident', so at the risk of provoking more laughter, I turned to ask Luke again whether he was okay. As I did, he looked up at me and I caught sight of his eyes for the first time since we'd lost him.

I don't know if you have kids – I doubt you'd tell me either way – but if you do then you'll back me up when I say that every parent knows their child's eyes. I'm not just talking about the colour – although that's part of it, no matter how muddied the brown or hazy the grey – but also the spark within them, that unfathomable glimmer of life that distinguishes us from a mannequin. It's more unique than even a fingerprint, that porthole onto another world that exists only inside their head; what some may still call the soul. More than anything else, it's the purest expression of who they are, the life they have lived so far, and who they may one day become.

In Luke, it was gone.

My first thought was that it was a trick of the light, my own eyes struggling with the fluorescent strips after the murk of the caves. But the more I stared, the more I was aware that it wasn't me – it was him. His eyes looked dead and cold, more like marbles or glass beads than living tissue. If there was anything behind them it was so far from the Luke I knew that it barely seemed human at all.

I must have stared for a while, as Luke suddenly said, 'What is it, Dad? Have I got something on me? You're staring like you've never seen me before.'

I could have said something then. But how do you tell your son that the light has gone out in his eyes, that you barely recognise him anymore? Instead I said, 'You didn't bang your head, did you? In the cave, I mean?'

It sounds ridiculous now, telling it to you. Maybe I should have told them all what I saw, or what I didn't see: the departure of my son's soul and its replacement with … what? He was still walking and talking, still interacting with us and his sister, in some ways better than he had done in years. They'd have thought I was mad.

Luke shook his head. 'No, nothing like that. The headphones broke so I sat down to fix them, like I said.'

13

I turned back to the form and ticked the relevant box. I didn't tell anyone about the hollow that had opened in my stomach. There was something wrong with my son – but I was so incapable of expressing what it was that the thought went unspoken, swallowed down and festering inside me like rotting meat.

The sunshine hit us like a spotlight as we headed back to the car. I walked behind the others, watching. I can't tell you what I was looking for. I simply knew that something was different, something was *off*. I can honestly say that I only wanted the best for my wife and my children. You must believe that.

I saw something in Luke, as we passed the gift shops and cafes, that I'd never seen before. The way his feet rolled slightly when they hit the ground, the reflexive scratching at his chin, the almost imperceptible squaring of his shoulders when he saw a pretty girl heading his way ... they were all there, in plain sight but small enough to escape attention. Had they been there before? I couldn't say. I don't believe I'd looked at him so closely since he was a toddler. They might have been classic Luke, an integral part of who he was, and who he was becoming. Our children are constantly changing before our eyes. But from time to time, as we walked beneath the towering cliffs of the gorge, I'd see something different in him, something alien. A lopsided smile that lifted one corner of his mouth, an edge of malice in it. A hand clenching into a fist, unprovoked, only to relax again. These I didn't recognise as being typical of our son. These were something else, although I didn't know what.

I was so engrossed in watching him that I didn't hear when Angie called my name. I think she said it twice, but it may have been three times or more before I broke out of my trance. I'd barely recognised the name as referring to me.

'I'm sorry?' I said, taking my eyes from Luke. 'Thoughts elsewhere – what did you say?'

'Kirstie wants to buy something from the gift shop we

passed earlier. A dragon or something?' She turned to Kirstie as she said this, who nodded. 'I said we'd take a look, if that's alright with you. She still has some holiday money left.'

The shop was poky and crammed with every conceivable knick-knack and bauble, most of them only spuriously connected with the caves and the gorge, if at all. Kirstie had seen a diorama of sparkly miniature dragons in the window display, and while she chose one Luke spun a stand of keyrings, setting them clattering over and over again. Eventually I'd had enough.

'Can you stop that?' I said, reaching out to steady the stand. 'It's annoying the other customers.'

'There are no other customers, Dad.' He didn't bother to look around to confirm this. 'It's only us.'

'Well it's annoying me, then. If you're bored, find something to look at. Don't they have any books?'

Luke looked at me like I'd just suggested he should join the priesthood, then he held out his hand. 'Give me the car keys and I'll see you back there. At least then I can listen to some music while I wait. Plus this place stinks of incense, doesn't it?'

Angie looked at me and shrugged. We'd been trying to encourage him to take more responsibility lately, quelling our natural tendency to micromanage the kids, and I couldn't think of any good reason why we shouldn't let him wait in the car. I still felt the urge to watch him, but I knew how paranoid it would sound.

'Fine.' I dropped the keys into his hand. 'You sit in the back, though. And only the radio, nothing else.'

Luke pocketed the keys, swivelling to leave. 'Yes boss. Roger-roger.'

Kirstie took almost ten minutes to decide, eventually settling on a glittery pink thing curled around a crystal ball. By the time we made it back outside I was worried about Luke again.

'Do you think he'll be okay?' I muttered to Angie as we hustled back through the crowds to the car park. 'He can't have got into too much trouble in ten minutes, can he?'

'Of course not,' she laughed, 'you just need to trust him. He's a good kid.'

We were both wrong. We heard the laughter and shouting before we turned the corner of the Chinese restaurant. The bikers were still gathered around their Harleys, a sweaty huddle of leather and buckles. In the middle of them stood Luke, a can of lager in his hand, tilted to pour its contents down his throat. His eyes found me as I shouted and ran over, but he didn't stop. By the time I swiped it out of his hand the can felt about a quarter full.

'What the hell do you think you're doing?' I aimed this at Luke, but then I turned to include the smirking faces of the biker gang. 'He's thirteen, for fuck's sake. Who gave him this? I should call the police on the lot of you.'

Someone mumbled something about minding my language, which brought another round of snickering. Then a bearded man stepped forward, his face so close to mine that I could smell the beer and tobacco on his breath.

'Before you go accusing anyone, talk to your son. He walked over here, bold as anything, and helped himself to our beer. Now, I don't know what you teach your children, and I don't much care, but if you get the cops involved then you'll find that's officially what they call "stealing". We didn't give him a thing. Your call, but everyone here will back me up.' He smiled, his teeth yellow and crooked. 'So, why don't you just get back in your middle-class pussywagon,' this provoked another hoot of laughter, 'and get out of our faces?'

I turned to Luke, but he shrugged. 'What he said. You don't want to start something you can't finish, *Dad*.'

While we'd been having this exchange Angie had bundled Kirstie into the car, using her keys to open the doors. Beard wasn't backing up, so after a couple of beats I turned, placing a hand on the back of Luke's head to guide him to the car door.

'Come on. Let's get you home, we'll talk about what happened there.'

It was only once we were in the car, Kirstie sobbing in the back seat as Angie tried to talk us all down, that I realised I was still holding the near-empty can of lager, half-crushed in my fist.

Did you know they've found prehistoric remains in Gough's Cave? They don't mention it on the audio tour. A wide variety of human bones, dating back to fourteen thousand years ago. The so-called 'Cheddar Man' is the most famous, but there have been many others, too many corpses to piece together from all the bones and skull fragments.

You have to dig a little deeper for the juicy parts. A large number of the bones – *human* bones, remember – show cut marks, where crude tools were used to strip the meat. Others show teeth marks, and some of the longer bones have been cracked open and the marrow sucked out. To date they have unearthed three skulls, hollowed out and shaped to form bowls. These early men, these Cro-Magnons – they were cannibals. Best guess, they ate human flesh as part of a ritual, hidden in the darkness beneath the surface of the earth, where even the sun couldn't see them. Who knows what they worshipped down there, or what they hoped to bring about. Who knows if they succeeded.

I dug all this up that evening, at the rental cottage. Kirstie had retreated to her room as Angie and I cornered Luke in the kitchen and quizzed him on what had happened, what he'd done, and what the hell he'd thought he was up to. Angie gave him the lecture on growing up and taking responsibility, but I was barely listening. I watched his face. He still looked like our son, didn't he? But the change I'd noticed earlier, the deadness behind his eyes, was still there. He appeared unmoved by his dressing-down, shrugging and half-smiling at times, as if he found it all funny, this incident that had so violently derailed our family outing. But even when he smiled, the laughter never made it as far as his eyes.

It's like he's wearing a mask, I thought to myself, as Angie

17

raged and pleaded beside me. *Or something else is wearing a mask. A Luke mask, that looks and sounds like our son.*

At that moment a shiver ran through me. It must have been visible in my face, or my hands, because Luke turned to look at me. He didn't wait for a break in Angie's sermon before he spoke.

'Is something wrong, *Dad*? You don't look well.'

I shrugged off the question – for Angie's benefit more than mine or Luke's – but he was right. Something was very, very wrong, and the feeling remained with me throughout that evening and into the next day. Something had happened to our son when he was lost down there in those caves, the site of who knew what kind of savage and violent rituals. Something had happened and he was no longer who he used to be. Luke was gone, and someone else was now in his place.

There was another casualty of the incident in the car park. We didn't notice until later that evening when the kids were in bed, Angie reading her book in the fading light from the cottage window. It was only when she reached into her bag for her glasses that she discovered the paper bag with Kirstie's dragon in it. Reaching inside, she swore, then held it out for me to see. Someone must have dropped it or sat on it in the confusion, because the pink resin statue had snapped cleanly in two.

'She's going to be heartbroken,' Angie said, scrunching the bag up with the broken dragon still inside, then pushing it down into the waste basket. 'She spent long enough choosing it. We can give her the money back, but I'm not sure how much that'll help.'

'Why don't we drive back there tomorrow?' I said, almost without thinking. 'You guys can take a walk up the gorge, and I'll run along to the shop and see if they can replace it. I'm sure they won't mind making another sale. If we're clever about it, we won't even have to tell her.' My initial thought was that it would save us an hour of tears, but then another thought followed: I would be able to revisit Gough's Cave, see if I could make any sense of what had happened to our son.

We almost got away with our subterfuge. Both kids were up late the next morning, sleeping off the adrenaline of the day before, and Kirstie didn't ask about the dragon statue. My suggestion that we should drive back to Cheddar Gorge was met with predictable resistance, but no more than any other suggestion I'd made.

'Why are you dragging us back out there?' Luke asked through a mouthful of toast, the marbles of his eyes staring through me at the wall behind. 'Didn't we all have enough fun yesterday?'

'There's some paperwork we forgot to sign at the caves,' I lied, a line Angie and I had decided upon in bed the previous night. 'I can run along and deal with it while you three take the path up to the cliff top. I shouldn't be too far behind.'

He shrugged, then stood and walked back to his room, still chewing, his dirty glass and plate abandoned on the table.

It was as we bundled our coats and bags into the car that he brought it up. He hadn't spoken a single word to us since his sudden departure from breakfast, and I'll confess that I'd spent my time avoiding him too. Kirstie got into the back of the car first, and as Luke followed her in he said, quite loudly, as if to be sure that we heard, 'What happened to that figurine you bought yesterday, sis? Your dragon? I've not seen that since we got home.'

Angie slammed the car door a little too hard as she got into the passenger seat, and I winced. I couldn't bear to look at the confusion and sadness on Kirstie's face.

'Mum?' she asked. 'Have you still got it?'

There was silence for a beat or two, then Luke said, 'I'm sure she has, don't you, Mum? Why don't you show Kirstie?'

'Don't pick on your sister,' I said, sliding into the driver's seat and taking care not to slam my own door. 'And don't be ridiculous – your mum doesn't have it with her here, and we're not unlocking the cottage again just to find it. We'll give it to you when we get back later. Now, buckle up.'

Looking in the rear-view mirror, I could see Luke smirking.

He knows, I thought. *He knows it's broken and he's doing this on purpose. Which means he either overheard us last night, or ...*

It seemed ridiculous to suggest that Luke might have intentionally broken the resin statue, but then I reminded myself – this person in the back seat wasn't Luke, not anymore. This was someone else, staring out through the eyeholes in Luke's skin.

For whatever reason the gorge was quieter than the previous day, so we didn't park behind the Chinese restaurant again. I was unreasonably grateful for that, as if the car park itself were to blame for what had happened. Instead we were able to snaffle a spot in front of an ice cream parlour, closer to the caves and within only a minute or two of both the gift shop and the path up to the cliff top.

I was reluctant to part ways with Angie and Kirstie once we were out of the car, mainly because it would mean leaving them with Luke, but our plan left me with no other option. Hurrying along the main street, I stopped at the gift shop first, explaining the situation as best I could to the bored-looking woman behind the counter. They didn't have a duplicate of the dragon on display, but after describing it to her she went out back to their storeroom, returning with an identical one – and another for the shelf – several minutes later. She took extra care to wrap it in several layers of tissue paper this time, and I made sure to handle it gently as I jogged along to the caves.

It was soon clear they had no answers for me, though. The steward who had taken our details yesterday was nowhere to be seen, and both members of staff looked at me blankly while I explained what had happened. I stopped short of vocalising my suspicions about Luke, but I told them I had some questions about the caves, and whether they were safe. Had any other areas been open yesterday that he might have stumbled into? Should we be concerned that he had drifted away from us for so long?

Their responses were barely more than a single word, and

their looks told me they were more concerned by my reaction than his. On the way out I glimpsed an information board with two blurred images of the bone fragments I'd seen online, one of them bearing scrape marks caused by Cro-Magnon teeth.

It may not have been far to the clifftop walk, but I was already out of breath as I started up the steps in the rock face. The morning's wisps of cloud had dissipated and it was a bright and clear day, everything sharp in the sunlight. The paper bag containing Kirstie's dragon knocked against my side as I raced up the steps, sometimes taking two at a time, and I realised suddenly that I was supposed to leave it in the car. How else could I explain the fact that I had it with me, when we'd told her it was back at the cottage? It was almost enough to make me turn around, but then I thought of Luke left alone with the girls – not *our* Luke, but whoever this new imposter was, leering out from behind his smile – and I quickened my pace as much as I was able. I couldn't believe I had been so reckless.

Rounding a corner, I saw them. They had already reached the top, where a wooden viewing platform overhung the edge. Angie was hanging back, looking at something on her phone; Luke and Kirstie were leaning over the railing. He had his hand on her back, and as I mounted the last set of steps he looked up and saw me. Luke grinned, winked at me, then pushed her.

I barely had time to think as I barrelled up onto the platform. Kirstie had somehow managed to keep from toppling over the side – saved by the solid wooden barrier, no doubt – but I knew what I had seen. Without thinking I dropped the paper bag and grabbed the boy who used to be Luke with both fists, pushing him against the railing. His mouth opened wide, but the surprise failed to reach the dark pools of his eyes.

'What the hell are you doing?' I yelled, flecks of my spit anointing his face. 'You leave her alone!'

Not-Luke looked genuinely flustered. His hands scrabbled at me, trying to wrench himself free, but his strength was no match for mine. I had already lost one child. Nobody was going to keep me from protecting my daughter.

'Dad —' he said, the words half-choked from him as I

pushed him back harder against the wooden railing. 'I didn't—'

And then with a final heave he was gone, over the edge, tipping backwards and tumbling head-first down the steep cliff-side, his arms hitting rocks and branches as he tried to find something to grasp onto until, finally, with an almighty *crack*, the back of his skull hit a rocky protrusion and he stopped struggling, falling the rest of the way as limp as a doll.

There was silence for a moment, then Angie and Kirstie started screaming.

I felt unnaturally calm. I had done what needed to be done. He had posed a threat to my family, and while I mourned the son I had lost, the bundle of muscle and bone that lay at the foot of the cliffs was no longer him. Something took him from us that day in the caves, I reminded myself, as I sat and waited for the flashing lights to come. Our Luke was already gone.

As the officers led me away, I spotted the paper bag with the dragon statue still in it, lying on the wooden decking of the lookout. They wouldn't turn back for it, though, and nobody listened to my entreaties. It's probably still there, if the foxes haven't stolen it. That's what hurts most of all – knowing that after all she's been through, poor Kirstie is still missing her dragon.

I've had a lot of time to think, sat here in this cell, and so many other cells and holding rooms that I've lost count. I have no doubt that I was right. Something lurked down there in those caves, an ancient force that only wanted a vessel to allow it back into this world. Something vast, and black, and unfathomable. But as I stare into the mirror at night, searching my own face for a spark of life, for that unique flame that makes me who I am, I sometimes wonder if I ever came back from the caves at all.

UNTO THESE ANCIENT STONES

The West Country lies at the mystical heart of England. Its pastoral landscape is planted thick with rural legends and studded with the relics of civilisations now entirely vanished from history. The lore of this place goes back to time immemorial. According to myth, this is the Summer Land, and entrances to the faerie realm still lurk behind the tranquil facades of woodland pools, at the backs of caves or in the gnarled faces of age-old trees. King Arthur, they say, ruled this land from Cadbury Castle, the original Camelot, while Jesus himself walked amid the limestone ridges of the Mendip Hills, his uncle, Joseph of Arimathea, later planting the Glastonbury Thorn and watering it from the Holy Grail. But there are terror tales here too. In 'The Hound of the Baskervilles', Arthur Conan Doyle was only mining a long-standing Devonshire tradition that phantom hounds roamed the wilds of Dartmoor, while mysterious hill figures hint at the one-time presence of pagan gods and warlike giants.

West Country horror can be found in truth as well as fable. Placid though it seems today, this realm was once a cradle of revolution: the Prayer Book Rebellion (1549), the Pitchfork Rebellion (1685), and so on, all of which were put down with extreme blood and fury, events from which a plethora of ghost stories now descend. In fact, so rich is this region in eerie superstition that it remains the only part of the British Isles to spawn its own supernatural drama series, West Country Tales, *screened on BBC2 in the early 1980s.*

But if there is no doubt that the West Country is the focal point of mysterious Britain, the focal point of the West Country is Stonehenge.

Now regarded as a British cultural icon, and without doubt one of the most famous prehistoric monuments in the world, the mere sight of Stonehenge, two rings of standing stones, one inside the other, several connected by doorway-like lintels, is sufficient to evoke a sense of wonder, awe, and – maybe, yes – a vague tremor of unease.

An unforgettable scene in Jacques Tourneur's classic horror film of 1957, Night of the Demon *(an adaptation of the equally classic M R James short story, 'Casting the Runes') sees the hero of the piece, John Holden, motoring down to the West Country and comparing the symbols scrawled on an ancient parchment with those carved on one of the uprights at Stonehenge. Needless to say, in reality there are no such carvings at Stonehenge, but film audiences were easily persuaded, such is the air of menace and mystery that surrounds it.*

In truth, the only things we really know about Stonehenge are what the archaeologists tell us, and much of this data is fairly prosaic.

The monument occupies a site in a central location on the Salisbury Plain in Wiltshire. The circle itself is obviously now a ruin, but well-preserved and instantly recognisable. It is believed that construction, which might have taken several centuries (because some of the monoliths are 13 feet tall, seven feet wide and weigh about 25 tons!), was completed no later than 1500 BC, which would place it firmly in the Bronze Age, long predating the Celtic peoples of Ancient Britain who have often but inaccurately been associated with its creation. Stonehenge itself sits in the midst of numerous other Neolithic and Bronze Age sites, which suggests that it may once have been part of a much vaster religious complex, while the fact it is oriented towards the rising sun at the time of the summer solstice has reinforced the theory that it might have been a form of calendar or even a primitive means by which to track the movements of stars and planets.

But just because there is much that is mundane about this arcane site, that doesn't mean there aren't mysteries here too, not to mention stories that are decidedly eerie.

For one thing, no one really knows how Stonehenge was built. The colossal size of the stones would surely have posed a mammoth challenge to a society that didn't even know the wheel let alone machinery, especially as some of them, the bluestones, were somehow transported to Wiltshire having first been quarried in the Prescelly Mountains of South Wales, over 200 miles away.

Disturbing rather than simply mysterious is the evidence that human sacrifices once occurred here. Although the druids, the religious leaders in pre-Roman Britain, had nothing to do with the building of Stonehenge, it's quite possible that they made use of it, and though we know very little about the druids themselves as they and their followers wrote nothing down, they were described by Julius Caesar as regular practitioners of human sacrifice (it is Caesar who provides one of our very few eyewitness accounts of actual 'wicker man' burnings).

John Aubrey, a philosopher and archaeologist of the 17th century, proposed that the druids made Stonehenge into a centre of sun-worship and that a series of 56 holes he discovered surrounding the site had once been deemed doorways to the underworld, and were thus used to collect the blood of sacrificial victims as an offering to the gods. Other eminent scholars, such as Inigo Jones and William Stukeley, echoed this. It might have remained a sensationalist theory were it not for the discovery in the 1960s of a child's skull, neatly cloven in two by a blow from an edged implement, at nearby Woodhenge. Quite clearly, human sacrifices were indeed carried out here at some point in history.

That on its own would perhaps not be so shocking, but there are additional, even more frightening tales that make Stonehenge a place of folkloric significance in modern times. To start with, there are several ghost stories. Both Stonehenge and the other great prehistoric West Country site, Avebury (some 40 miles north), have allegedly played host to ethereal dancing figures on moonlit nights and the sound of unearthly music. In 1786, a sailor called Gervase Matcham was tramping across Salisbury Plain with a friend, when a ghostly form came out of the henge and fell into step alongside him. The sailor broke down and wept that he had murdered a young boy, and that this was the lad's spirit. He confessed, not just to his friend but to the authorities, and was hanged the same year, even as he walked to the gallows weeping and begging the forgiveness of a person no one else could see.

There are various potential explanations for all these curious events, but fewer for something that happened in 1971. At that time, the stone circle was still accessible to the general public (it only gained legal protection in 1982), and so, that August, there was nothing to stop a bunch of dope-smoking hippies building their camp right in the middle of it. This wasn't to everyone's liking and a local farmer, who had been disturbed by the visitors late that night, called the police. When a lone officer arrived to liaise with the farmer, a furious storm commenced and the stone circle was struck several times by lightning.

The two men then described an intense blue glow emanating from the heart of the henge, so fierce that it dazzled them, and hearing terrible screams. When the storm had abated, as quickly as it had begun, they ventured over there and found only burnt and smoking tent pegs, with no sign of the tents themselves or the people who had been sleeping in them.

As no one actually knew who this group had been, it proved impossible to contact relatives or even commence a search for them. But it's a fact that, even though the story made the news, no one came forward to claim that they had been part of that group or to explain that everyone was safe and well.

Theories as to what happened range widely. Some believe the hippies were just trouble-makers who didn't practice what they preached and failed to clean up their camp. Others that they were literally incinerated by the lightning. But some are more esoteric. One New Age explanation holds that Stonehenge, like other sacred sanctuaries, was built at a convergence of ley lines, straight but invisible tracks lying not just across Britain but the whole world, along which clairvoyants and psychics have allegedly detected the passage of all kinds of unknown energies, and that because of the powerful electrical storm, some kind of implosion or vortex was created. Others reflect older beliefs, namely that Stonehenge was built to honour eldritch celestial powers, in other words the gods, and that it was owed far more respect than those pot-smoking campers had shown.

The mystery is only one of many that has never been solved here. And no one expects that it ever will be. Stonehenge, that timeless monument to an age long lost, is notorious for keeping its secrets.

OBJECTS IN DREAMS MAY BE CLOSER THAN THEY APPEAR
Lisa Tuttle

Since we divorced twenty years ago, my ex-husband Michael and I rarely met, but we'd always kept in touch. I wish now that we hadn't. This whole terrible thing began with a link he sent me by e-mail with the comment, 'Can you believe how much the old homestead has changed?'

Clicking on the link took me to a view of the cottage we had owned, long ago, for about three years – most of our brief marriage.

Although I recognised it, there were many changes. No longer a semi-detached, it had been merged with the house next-door, and also extended. It was, I thought, what we might have done ourselves given the money, time, planning permission and, most vitally, next-door neighbours willing to sell us their home. Instead, we had fallen out with them (they took our offer to buy as a personal affront) and poured too much money into so-called improvements, the work expensively and badly done by local builders who all seemed to be related by marriage if not blood to the people next-door.

Just looking at the front of the house on the computer screen gave me a tight, anxious feeling in my chest. What had possessed Michael to send it to me? And why had he even looked for it? Surely he wasn't nostalgic for what I recalled as one of the unhappiest periods of my life?

At that point, I should have clicked away from the picture, put it out of my mind and settled down to work, but, I don't know why, instead of closing the tab, I moved on down the road and began to discover what else in our old neighbourhood was different.

I'd heard about Google Earth's 'Street View' function, but I'd never used it before, so it took me a little while to figure out how to use it. At first all the zooming in and out, stopping and starting and twirling around made me queasy, but once I got to grips with it, I found this form of virtual tourism quite addictive.

But I was startled by how different the present reality appeared from my memory of it. I did not recognise our old village at all, could find nothing I remembered except the war memorial – and that seemed to be in the wrong place. Where was the shop, the primary school, the pub? Had they all been altered beyond recognition, all turned into houses? There were certainly many more of those than there had been in the 1980s. It was while I was searching in vain for the unmistakable landmark that had always alerted us that the next turning would be our road, a commercial property that I could not imagine anyone converting into a desirable residence – the Little Chef – that it dawned on me what had happened.

Of course. The Okehampton by-pass had been built, and altered the route of the A30. Our little village was one of several no longer bisected by the main road into Cornwall, and without hordes of holiday-makers forced to crawl past, the fast food outlet and petrol station no longer made economic sense.

Once I understood how the axis of the village had changed, I found the new primary school near an estate of new homes. There were also a couple of new (to me) shops, an Indian restaurant, wine bar, an oriental rug gallery, and a riding school. The increase in population had pushed our sleepy old village slightly up-market. I should not have been surprised, but I suppose I was an urban snob, imagining that anyone living so deep in the country must be several decades behind the times. But I could see that even the smallest of houses boasted a satellite dish, and they probably all had broadband internet connections, too. Even as I was laughing at the garden gnomes on display in front of a neat yellow bungalow, someone behind those net curtains might be looking at my own terraced house in Bristol, horrified by what the unrestrained growth of ivy was doing to the brickwork.

Curious to know how my home appeared to others, I typed in my own address, and enjoyed a stroll around the neighbourhood without leaving my desk. I checked out a few less-familiar addresses, including Michael's current abode, which I had never seen. So *that* was Goring-on-Sea!

At last I dragged myself away and wrote catalogue copy, had a long talk with one of our suppliers, and dealt with various other bits and pieces before knocking off for the day. Neither of us fancied going out, and we'd been consuming too many pizzas lately, so David whipped up an old favourite from the minimal supplies in the kitchen cupboard: spaghetti with marmite, tasty enough when accompanied by a few glasses of Merlot.

My husband David and I marketed children's apparel and accessories under the name 'Cheeky Chappies'. It was exactly the sort of business I had imagined setting up in my rural idyll, surrounded by the patter of little feet, filling orders between changing nappies and making delicious, sustaining soups from the organic vegetables Michael planned to grow.

None of that came to pass, not even the vegetables. Michael did what he could, but we needed his income as a sales rep to survive, so he was nearly always on the road, which left me to take charge of everything at home, supervising the building work in between applying for jobs and grants, drawing up unsatisfactory business plans, and utterly failing in my mission to become pregnant.

Hard times can bring a couple together, but that is not how it worked for us. I grew more and more miserable, convinced I was a failure both as a woman and as a potential CEO. It did not help that Michael was away so much, and although it was not his fault and we needed the money, I grew resentful at having to spend so much time and energy servicing a house I'd never really wanted.

He'd drawn me into *his* dream of an old-fashioned life in the country, and then slipped out of sharing the major part of it with me. At weekend, with him there, it was different, but most of the time I felt lonely and bored, lumbered with too many chores and not enough company, far from friends and family, cut off from the entertainments and excitement of urban existence.

Part of the problem was the house – not at all what we'd dreamed of, but cheap enough, and with potential to be transformed into something better. We'd been jumped into buying it by circumstances. Once Michael had accepted a very good offer on his flat (*our* flat, he called it, but it was entirely his investment) a new urgency entered into our formerly relaxed house-hunting expeditions. I had loved those weekends away from the city, staying in B&Bs and rooms over village pubs, every moment rich with possibility and new discoveries. I would have been happy to go on for months, driving down to the West Country, looking at properties and imagining what our life might be like in this house or that, but suddenly there was a time limit, and this was the most serious decision of our lives, and not just a bit of fun.

The happiest part of my first marriage now seems to have been compressed into half a dozen weekends, maybe a few more, as we travelled around, the inside of the car like an enchanted bubble filled with love and laughter, jokes and personal revelations and music. I loved everything we saw. Even the most impossible, ugly houses were fascinating, providing material for discussing the strangeness of other people's lives. Yet although I was interested in them all, nothing we viewed actually tempted me. Somehow, I couldn't imagine I would ever really live in the country – certainly not the practicalities of it. I expected our life to continue like this, work in the city punctuated by these mini-holidays, until we found the perfect house, at which point I'd stop working and start producing babies and concentrate on buying their clothes and toys and attractive soft furnishings and decorations for the house as if money was not and could never be a problem.

And then one day, travelling between the viewing of one imperfect property to look at another, which would doubtless be equally unsatisfactory in its own unique way, Blondie in the cassette player singing about hanging on the telephone, we came to an abrupt halt. Michael stopped the car at the top of a hill, on one of those narrow, hedge-lined lanes that aren't even wide enough for two normal sized cars to pass each other without the sort of jockeying and breath-holding manoeuvres that in my view are acceptable only when parallel parking. I thought he must have seen another car approaching, and taken evasive action, although the road ahead looked clear.

'What's wrong?'

'Wrong? Nothing. It's perfect. Don't you think it's perfect?'

I saw what he was looking at through a gap in the hedge: a distant view of an old-fashioned, white-washed, thatch-roofed cottage nestled in one of those deep, green valleys that in Devonshire are called coombs. It was a pretty sight, like a Victorian painting you might get on a box of old-fashioned chocolates, or a card for Mother's Day. For some reason, it made my throat tighten and I had to blink back sentimental tears, feeling a strong yearning, not so much for that specific house as for what it seemed to promise: safety, stability, family. I could see myself there, decades in the future, surrounded by children and grandchildren, dressed in clothes from Laura Ashley.

'It's very sweet,' I said, embarrassed by how emotional I felt.

'It's exactly what we've been looking for,' he said.

'It's probably not for sale.'

'All it takes is the right offer.' That was his theory: not so much that everything had its price, as that he could achieve whatever goal he set himself. It was more about attitude than money.

'But what if they feel the same way about it as we do?'

'Who are "they"?'

'The people that live there.'

'But you feel it? What I feel? That it's where we want to live?'

I thought about the children – grandchildren, even! – in their quaint floral smocks, and nodded.

He kissed me. 'All right!' he cried, joyously, releasing the hand-brake. 'Let's go!'

'Do you even know how to get there?'

'You've got the map. Direct me.'

My heart sank. Although I had the road atlas open in my lap, I never expected to have to use it. Michael did not understand that not everyone was like him, able to look at lines and coloured patches on a page and relate them to the real world. His sense of direction seemed magical to me. Even when the sun was out, I had no idea which way was north. On a map, it was at the top. In the world, I had to guess at right or left or straight ahead.

'I don't know where we are *now*,' I objected. 'We need to stop and figure it out.'

Fortunately, we were approaching a village, and it offered parking space in front of the church, so that was easily done. Michael had no problem identifying which of the wriggly white lines was the road we'd been on, and where we'd stopped and seen the house, and with that and the location of the village we were in, he was able to perform some sort of mental triangulation that enabled him to stab a forefinger down on a blank place within the loops of spaghetti representing the nameless country roads. 'There,' he said with certainty. 'It's got to be there. An OS map would show us exactly, but anyway, it shouldn't be hard to find. We'll just drive around until we spot it.'

We drove around for the next two or three hours. Round and round and round. The same route, again and again, up and down the narrow roads, some of them like tunnels, they were so deep beneath the high-banked hedges, until I was dizzy, like a leaf swept away in a stream. Deep within those dark green lanes there was nothing to see except the road ahead, the deep, loamy earth with roots bursting through on either side, and the branches of trees overhead, through which I caught pale, gleaming shards of sky. The house remained hidden from view except when Michael drove up to higher ground, and found one of the few places where it was possible to see through, or over, the thick, ancient hedgerows that shielded nearly every piece of land from the road.

There it was, so close it must be just beyond the next curve of the road, yet forever out of our reach. The faint curl of smoke from the chimney inspired another yearning tug as I imagined sitting cosy and warm with my dear husband beside a crackling fire. I could almost smell the wood-smoke, and, closer, hot chocolate steaming in a mug.

I was hungry, thirsty and tired of stomping my foot down on an imaginary brake every time we met another car. There was a chill in the air as afternoon began to fade towards evening, and I wondered if we'd be able to get lunch anywhere, and made the point aloud.

He was impatient with my weakness. 'We'll get something afterwards. Surely they'll invite us in for a cup of tea when we get there. They can't have many visitors!'

'If we could find that house by driving around, we would have found it already. You've already taken every turning, and we've seen every farm-yard and tumble-down shed and occupied house in the whole valley.'

'Obviously we have missed one.'

'Please, darling. It'll be dark soon. Look, we need to try something else. Why not go to Okehampton and ask an estate agent?'

'So now you're assuming the house is for sale.'

'No. I assume it was for sale some time in the past and will be again in the future, and it is their business to know the local market. It's a beautiful place. We can't be the first people to have asked about it.'

'No, but we will be the ones who get it!'

No one knew the house in the offices of the first two estate agents, and the man in the third one also stated there was no such cottage in the valley where we claimed to have seen it – that area was all woods and fields, he said – but there was something in his manner as he tried to fob us off with pictures and details of ever more expensive houses located twenty miles away that made me think he was hiding something, so we persisted, until, finally, he suggested we go see Mr Yeo.

Mr Yeo was a semi-retired property surveyor who had been in the business since before the War, and knew everything worth knowing about every house in this part of Devon. He lived still in the village where he had been born – Marystow – a name we both recognised, as it was one of the places we'd passed through a dozen times on our futile quest. So off we went to find him.

He was an elderly man who seemed friendly, happy to welcome us in to his home, until Michael revealed what we had come about, and then, abruptly, the atmosphere changed, and he began to usher us out again. The house was not for sale, we would not be able to visit it, there was no point in further discussion.

'But surely you can give us the name of the owners? An address to write to?'

'There b'ain't owners. He's not there.'

I thought at first 'he' referred to the owner, unused to the way that older inhabitants of rural Devon spoke of inanimate objects as 'he' rather than 'it'. But Mr Yeo made his meaning clear before sending us on our way: the perfectly desirable house we'd seen, nestled in a deep green coomb, did not exist. It was an illusion. We were not the first to have seen it; there were old folk and travellers' tales about such a house, glimpsed from a hilltop, nestled in the next valley; most often glimpsed late in the day, seemingly near enough that the viewer thought he could reach it before sunset, and rest the night there.

But no matter how long they walked, or what direction they tried, they could never reach it.

'Have you ever seen it?'

Mr Yeo scowled, and would not say. ''Tis bad luck to see 'im,' he informed us. 'Worse, much worse, to try to find 'im. You'm better go 'ome and forget about him. 'Tis not a good place for you'm.'

Michael thanked the old man politely, but as we left, I could feel something simmering away in him. But it was not anger, only laughter, which exploded once we were back in our car. He thought Mr Yeo was a ridiculous old man, and didn't buy his story for an instant. Maybe there was some optical illusion involved -- that might explain why we hadn't been able to find the house where he'd expected it to be -- but that was a real house that we'd seen, and someday we would find it.

Yet we never did. Not even when Michael bought the largest scale Ordnance Survey map of the area, the one for walkers that included every footpath, building and ruin, could we find evidence that it had ever existed. Unless he'd been wrong about the location, and it was really in a more distant coomb, made to look closer by some trick of air and light ...

Even after we moved to Devon -- buying the wrong house -- we came no closer to solving the mystery. I think Michael might have caught the occasional glimpse of it in the distance, but I never saw it again.

I shouldn't pretend I didn't know what made Michael's thoughts return to our old home in Devon, because I had been dreaming about it myself, for the same reason: the Wheaton-Bakers Ruby Anniversary Celebration. We'd both been invited -- with our respective new spouses, of course -- to attend it at their house in Tavistock in four weeks' time. I didn't know about Michael, but I had not been back to Devon in over twenty years; not since we'd sold the house. The Wheaton-Bakers were the only friends from that period of my life with whom I'd kept in touch, although we saw each other no more often than Michael and I did.

I'd been pleased by the invitation. The party was in early October. David and I had booked a room in an inn on Dartmoor, and looked forward to a relaxing weekend away, with a couple of leg-stretching, mind-clearing rambles on Dartmoor book-ending the Saturday night festivities. And yet, although I looked forward to it, there also a faint uneasiness in my mind attached to the idea of seeing Michael again, back in our old haunts; an uneasiness I did not so much as hint at to David because I could not explain it. It was irrational and unfair, I thought. My first marriage had not worked out, but both of us, or neither, were responsible for that, and that failure had been come to terms with and was long in the past. There was no unfinished business between us.

When the weekend of the party arrived, David was ill. It was probably only a twenty-four-hour bug (it was going around, according to our next-door neighbour, a teacher) but it meant he couldn't consider going anywhere farther than the bathroom.

I should have stayed home and tended to him, like a good wife – that is what I wish I had done. But he insisted I go. The Wheaton-Bakers were my friends. They would be sorry not to see me. We wouldn't get our money back for the hotel room – that had been an internet bargain. And he didn't need to be tended. He intended to sleep as much as possible, just lie in bed and sweat it out.

So I went. And I did enjoy myself. It was a lovely party; the Wheaton-Bakers were just as nice as I remembered, and they introduced me to other friendly, interesting people, so I never felt lonely or out of place for a moment. Michael was there, but he'd been seated at a different table, and struck up conversations with a different set of people, so although we'd exchanged greetings, we'd hardly done more than that. It was only as I was preparing to leave that he cornered me.

'Hey, you're not leaving!'

''fraid so.'

'But we've hardly spoken! You're driving back to Bristol tonight?'

'No, of course not.' I told him where I was staying.

'Mm, very posh! I'm just up the road, nylon sheets and a plastic shower stall. Want to meet and have lunch somewhere tomorrow?'

I was happy to agree. We exchanged phone numbers, and he offered to pick me up at my hotel at ten. 'If that's not too early? It'll give us time to drive around a bit, see how much the scenery has changed, before deciding what we want to do.'

There was a familiar glint in his eye, and I was suddenly

certain he meant to take me back to look at our old house, and maybe one or two other significant sites from our marriage. I didn't know why he felt the need to revisit the past like that – the past was over and done with, as far as I was concerned – but I didn't say anything. If he needed to go back and see with his own eyes how much time had passed, to understand that we were no longer the people who had fallen in love with each other, then perhaps I owed him my supportive, uncomplaining companionship.

Anyway, I thought it would be more fun than going for a walk by myself or driving straight back home.

The next morning, I checked out, and left my car in the car park. There was no question that we'd go in his: I remembered too well that he'd always disliked being a passenger. His car was better, anyway: a silver Audi with that new-car smell inside, soft leather seats and an impressive Sat-Nav system. Something by Mozart issued softly from hidden speakers as we headed down the A386 before leaving the moor for the sunken lanes I remembered, winding deep into a leaf-shadowed coomb.

'Remember this?' he asked, as the car raced silently along. It was a smoother ride than in the old days.

'I'm glad they haven't dug up all the hedgerows,' I said. 'I was afraid Devon might have changed a lot more.'

He frowned, dissatisfied with my answer. 'Didn't you click on that link I sent you?'

'Yes, I did. I saw our old house – didn't I send a reply?'

He shrugged that off. 'I thought you might have explored a bit more widely. Not just the village, not just the street view, but moving up and out, looking at the satellite pictures.'

'It's a busy time of the year for us, with Christmas coming. I don't have much time to play around on the internet. Although I'm sure it's very interesting.'

'It's more than just "interesting". You can see things that aren't on other maps. The aerial shots – do you remember how we had to go up to the top of the hill to see it?'

I understood. 'You're not talking about our house.'

'You know what I'm talking about.' He touched the screen of

his navigation system and a calm, clear female voice said, 'You are approaching a cross-roads. Prepare to turn right.'

'You found it?' I asked him, amazed. 'How?'

'Turn right. Follow the road.'

'Satellite view on Google. I zoomed in as much as I could – it wasn't easy to get a fix on it. Street View's no good – it's not on a road. But it's there all right; maybe not in exactly the place we kept looking for it. Anyway, I have the co-ordinates now, and I've put them into my system here, and – it will take us there.' He grinned like a proud, clever child.

'How, if it's not on a road?'

'Prepare to turn left. Turn left.'

'It will take us as close as it can. After that we'll walk. Those are good, sturdy boots you have on.'

'Take the first turning to the right. '

'Well done, Sherlock,' I said. 'Just fancy if we'd had GPS back in those days – we'd have found it, and … do you think they'd have accepted our offer?'

'Bear left. At the next crossroads, turn right.'

Despite the smoothness of the ride, as we turned and turned again – sometimes forced to stop and back up in a *pas-de-deux* with another Sunday driver – I began to feel queasy, like in the old days, and then another sort of unease crept in.

'Haven't we been along here already? We must be going in circles,' I said.

'And when did you develop a sense of direction?'

'Prepare to turn right. Turn right.'

The last turn was the sharpest, and took us off the road entirely, through an opening in a hedge so narrow that I flinched at the unpleasant noise of cut branches scraping the car, and then we were in a field.

There was no road or path ahead of us, not even a track, just the faint indication of old ruts where at some point a tractor or other farm vehicle might have gone, and even they soon ended.

'Make a U-turn when possible. Return to a marked road.'

Michael stopped the car. 'So that's as far as she'll take us. We'll have to rely on my own internal GPS the rest of the way.'

We got out. He changed his brown loafers for a pair of brilliant white sports shoes that looked as if they'd never been worn, took an OS map out of the glove-box, and showed me the red X he had marked on an otherwise blank spot. 'And this is where we are now.'

'Why isn't it on the map?'

He shrugged.

I persisted. 'You must have thought about it.'

He shrugged again and sighed. 'Well, you know, there are places considered too sensitive, of military importance, something to do with national security, that you're not allowed to take pictures or even write about. There's an airfield in Norfolk, and a whole village on Salisbury Plain —'

'They're not on maps?'

'Not on any maps. And those are just the two examples I happen to know. There must be more. Maybe this house, or the entire coomb, was used for covert ops in the war, or is owned by MI5, used as a safe house or something.'

My skin prickled with unease. 'Maybe we shouldn't go there.'

'Are you kidding? You're not going to wimp out on me now!'

'If it's so secret that it's against the law —'

'Do you see any "No Trespassing" signs?' He waved his arms at the empty field around us. 'It's a free country; we can walk where we like.'

I took a deep breath, and thought about that airfield in Norfolk. I was pretty sure I knew the place he meant; it was surrounded by barbed wire fences, decorated with signs prohibiting parking and picture-taking on the grounds of national security. It was about as secret as the Post Office Tower. I nodded my agreement.

It was a good day for walking, dry and with a fresh, invigorating breeze countering the warmth of the sun. For about fifteen minutes we just walked, not speaking, and I was feeling very relaxed when I heard him say, 'There it is.'

Just ahead of us, the land dropped away unexpectedly

steeply, and we stopped and stood gazing down into a deep, narrow, wooded valley. Amid the turning leaves the golden brown of the thatched roof blended in, and shadows dappled the whitewashed walls below with natural camouflage. If we hadn't been looking for it, we might not have seen it, but now, as I stared, it seemed to gain in clarity, as if someone had turned up the resolution on a screen. I saw a wisp of smoke rise from the chimney, and caught the faint, sweet fragrance of burning wood.

Michael was moving about in an agitated way, and it took me a few moments to realise he was searching for the best route down. 'This way,' he called. 'Give me your hand; it's a bit tricky at first, but then I think it should be easier.'

I was suddenly nervous. 'I don't think we should. There's someone there.'

'So? They'll invite us in. We'll ask how long they've had the place and if they'd consider selling.'

I saw that the notion of an MI5 safe house was far from his mind, if he had ever believed it. He wasn't even slightly afraid, and struggled to comprehend my reason for wanting to turn back.

'Look, if you want to wait for me here ...'

I couldn't let him go by himself. I checked that my phone was on, and safely zipped into my pocket, and then I let him help me down to the first ledge, and the one after that. Then it got easier, although there was never anything as clear as a path, and on my own I'm certain I would have been lost, since my instinct, every time, was to go in a direction different from his. He really could hold a map in his head. At last we emerged from a surprisingly dense wood into a clearing from which we could see a windowless side wall.

I fell back and followed him around towards the front. Pebbles rolled and crunched gently underfoot on the path to the front door. I wondered if he had a plan, and what he would say to whoever answered the door: was he really going to pretend we were interested in buying?

Then I looked up and as I took in the full frontal view, I

knew I had been here before. It was the strongest wave of *déjà vu* I'd ever felt, a sickening collision between two types of knowledge: I knew it was impossible, yet I remembered this visit.

The memory was unclear, but frightening. Somehow, I had come here before. When my knock at the door had gone unanswered, I'd peeked through that window on the right, and saw something that made me run away in terror.

I could not remember anything of what I had seen; only the fear it had inspired was still powerful.

Michael knocked on the door, then glanced over his shoulder, impatient with me for hanging back.

I wanted to warn him, but of what? What could I say? I was in the grip of a fear I knew to be irrational. I managed to move a little closer to Michael and the door, telling myself that nothing could compel me to look through that window.

We waited a little while, but even after Michael knocked again, more loudly, almost pounding, there was no reply. I relaxed a little, thinking we were going to get away with it, but when I spoke of leaving, he insisted, 'Not until I find out who lives here, what it's all about. There is someone here – I can see a light – look, through that window '

I moved back; I wouldn't look.

'I think I can smell cooking. They're probably in the kitchen. Maybe a bit deaf. I'm going to try the back door. You coming? Suit yourself.'

I didn't want to stay, but wanted even less to follow him around the back, so I waited, wrapping my arms around myself, feeling a chill. The sun didn't strike so warmly in this leafy hollow. I checked my phone for the time and was startled to see how much of the afternoon was gone. I wondered if I should call David to warn him I'd be late, but decided to wait for Michael.

I didn't like to keep checking the time because it made me more nervous, but at least five minutes had passed when I felt I had no choice but to walk around to the back of the house to look for him.

I had no sense of *déjà vu* there; I was certain I'd never seen the peeling black paint that covered the solidly shut back door, or the small windows screened by yellowish, faded curtains that made it impossible to see inside.

'Michael?' I didn't like the weak, wavering sound of my voice, and made myself call out more loudly, firmly, but there was no reply. Nothing happened. I knocked as hard as I could on the back door, dislodging a few flakes of old paint, and as I waited I listened to the sound of leaves rustling in the wind; every once in awhile one would fall. I felt like screaming, but that would have been bloody stupid. Either he had heard me or he hadn't. Either he was capable of reply – could he be hiding just to tease me? – or he wasn't. And what was I going to do about it?

As I walked back around to the front of the house I was assailed by the memory of what I had seen when I looked through the window the last time I was here – if that had ever happened. I'd seen a man's foot and leg – I'd seen that there was someone inside the house, just sitting, not answering my knock, and the sight of some stranger's foot had frightened me so badly that I'd run away, and then repressed the memory of the entire incident.

Now I realised it must have been a dream that I recalled. It had that pointless, sinister atmosphere of a bad dream. Unfortunately, it now seemed like a precognitive dream.

Nothing had changed in front of the house. I got out my phone and entered the number Michael had given me. As I heard it ringing in my ear, I heard the familiar notes from *The William Tell Overture* sounding from inside the house. I clenched my teeth and waited. When the call went to his voice-mail, I ended it and hit re-dial. Muffled by distance, the same tinny, pounding ringtone played inside the house, small but growing in volume until, once again, it was cut off by the voice mail programme.

I knew what I would see if I looked through the window, so I didn't look. I wanted to run away, but I didn't know where to go. It would be dark soon. I had to do something.

The front door opened easily. Tense, I darted my gaze about, fearful of ambush although the place felt empty. To my right, I could see into a small, dark sitting room where an old man sat, or slumped, in an armchair.

He was a very, very old man, almost hairless, his skin like yellowed parchment, and appeared to have been dead for some time. It would have been his foot I would have seen if I'd looked through the window: his feet in brand new, brilliantly white sports shoes. But even as I recognised the rest of the clothes – polo shirt, jeans, soft grey hooded jacket, even the phone and car-keys in his pockets – I clung to the notion of a vicious trick, that someone had stolen Michael's clothes to dress an old man's corpse. How could the vigorous fifty-eight-year-old that I'd seen a few minutes ago have aged and died so rapidly?

I know now that it is what's left of Michael, and that there is no one else here.

I am not able to leave. I can open the door, but as soon as I step through, I find myself entering again. I don't know how many times I did that, before giving up. I don't know how long I have been here; it seems like a few days, at most, but when I look in the mirror I can tell by my hair that it must be two months or more.

There's plenty of food in the kitchen, no problems with plumbing or electricity, and for entertainment, besides all the books, there's an old video-player, and stacks of videos, as well as an old phonograph and a good collection of music. I say 'good collection' because it might have been planned to please Michael and me, at least as we were in the '80s.

Having found a ream of paper in the bottom drawer of the desk in the other parlour (the room where Michael isn't) I decided to write down what has happened, just in case someone comes here someday, and finds my body as I found his. It gives me something to do, even though I fear it is a pointless exercise.

While exploring the house earlier – yesterday, or the day before – I found evidence of mice – fortunately, only in one place, in the other sitting room. There were droppings there, and a nest made of nibbled paper, as if the mouse had devoted all its energy to the destruction of a single stack of paper. One piece was left just large enough for me to read a few words in faded ink, and recognise Michael's handwriting, but there was not enough for me to make sense of whatever he was trying to say.

THE HORROR AT LITTLECOTE

One of the true cause célèbre *ghost stories of English history comes to us from Littlecote House in Wiltshire. The tragedy at the heart of this case occurred in the 16th century, but while the actual facts are difficult to establish for certain, there is much anecdotal and written evidence that these events genuinely happened.*

And they make for grim reading.

The tale is set in 1575 and centres around a certain Mother Barnes, who was a midwife in the Berkshire village of Shefford. Late one night she was accosted in her own cottage by hooded intruders, who said they had a job for her to do, for which she'd be amply paid so long as she knew to keep her mouth shut afterwards. Too frightened to do otherwise, the old woman consented, and was then blindfolded, placed on a horse and led for several miles along quiet country lanes and finally into a silent building. When the blindfold was removed, she found herself in a very fine chamber. Estimating that it was 12 feet high and many yards across, she assumed that she'd arrived among gentlefolk, though there was little gentleness on show. The only other people in the room were a young woman, whom the midwife deduced was a serving girl, who was pregnant and in the latter stages of labour, and a fierce older man who was evidently of knightly stock, though his presence terrified her.

Mother Barnes set to work and a baby was eventually delivered, but before it could be handed to its grateful parent, the fierce man snatched the child and flung it onto the hearth, which he then stoked into a furious blaze. The shrieking servant girl was led away as the child was consumed by flames.

Mother Barnes was appalled for all kinds of reasons, not least because she assumed that she would die next. However, this didn't happen. The knight gruffly departed, his hooded servants returning, paying the midwife handsomely, replacing her blindfold and leading her back the way she had come. They didn't notice that the midwife, who was determined to see justice done for this crime, had cut a length of material from the bed-curtain and pocketed it. Nor did they notice that she was counting the steps on the way down to the courtyard.

Once she'd returned to her village and her mysterious escorts had galloped off into the night, she told her husband, who advised her to keep it to herself. In his words, these were the doings of the nobility and it would serve no purpose to anger them.

The midwife took her husband's advice at first, but could not shake from her mind the grotesque thing she had witnessed. Bent on locating the scene of the crime, she wandered the roads around her village for days, trying to remember anything she could about the blindfolded journey. In due course, she crossed the border into Wiltshire and came to Littlecote House, home to the celebrated 'Wild' Will Darrell, a local MP and soldier who would later go on to do good service during the Spanish Armada crisis.

Everything now fell into place for Mother Barnes. The time it had taken to reach this spot from Shefford seemed roughly to approximate the time it had taken that fatal night. In addition, Wild Will was known as a rakish man who was capable of violence. He also had a reputation for drinking and fornication. It didn't require a great leap of imagination to conclude that he had been disposing of a child that he himself had got upon one of his household maids.

Here, the details of the story become hazy.

Tradition holds that Mother Barnes took the curtain clipping to the local magistrate, a certain John Popham, and that further investigations, based on the observations she had made, proved beyond doubt that Littlecote House was the scene of the crime. Unfortunately, we now know that Popham was only appointed magistrate in that district in 1602, which either means the original date of the incident is wrong, or it was some other local official, or presumably that Mother Barnes waited a full 27 years before she reported it, which seems unlikely. Either way, it casts some doubt on the truth of the tale.

There is certainly no official account of Judge Popham ever having brought Will Darrell to trial, though village gossip held ever afterward that he did, or at least was planning to, only for the wealthy Darrell family to ply him with such generous bribes that he finally dropped the case.

However, scraps of intriguing evidence remain. For example, the Wiltshire antiquarian, John Aubrey, writing less than a century later, claimed that Littlecote House passed to Judge Popham after Darrell's death (which it undoubtedly did) in reward for his refusal to prosecute, while a letter dated 1578 (possibly connected to the curtailed enquiry) and preserved in the Longleat archives to this day, was addressed to the brother of a woman believed to be Will Darrell's mistress, demanding to know the whereabouts of her children as 'the report of a murder of one of them is increasing foully, and will touch Will Darrell to the quick'.

Of course, once the murder mystery ends and the ghost story begins, we must rely solely on rumour.

Darrell died in 1589. He was still an active man, aged only 50, but his body was found with a broken neck in woodland close to his home. It would seem that he'd fallen from his horse. A skilled equestrian, no one could understand how this had taken place, though wagging tongues insisted that when in his cups, Wild Will had confessed several times that he was being haunted by the apparition of a burning child. The story then took hold that he'd been confronted by this grisly spectre while out riding, and in his reckless efforts to rein his beast away, had been struck by a low-hanging branch. The sight of his death is still known today as Darrell's Stile.

Littlecote House itself, meanwhile, had also become the scene of ghostly activity. No one seems to know what happened to the young mother who lost her child (who may or may not have been the one referred to in the Longleat letter), but we must assume that she didn't live long, because within a few decades stories were rife that a sorrowful girl in a blood-stained shift was to be seen walking the manor's passageways at night. Even in very recent times at Littlecote House, now a hotel and leisure centre, visitors have described being approached by a dishevelled young woman, white-faced and tearful, who asks if they have seen her baby.

More frightening still, it's also been said that, on the eve of the death of the heir to the estate, Wild Will himself will ride up to the manor house door in his coach and four, the horses neighing, hunting hounds baying, hammer on the woodwork and demand to be admitted. And indeed, this actually seems to have happened in 1861, when Francis Popham, the six-month-old only child of the then owners, was sick and apparently dying. His nurse, having sent a message to call his absent parents home, was drawn to the front door late at night, having heard a coach and horses arrive and a thunderous knocking, and assuming that this was they, only to open it and find nobody there.

In the early hours of the following morning, young Francis died.

THE WODEN JUG
John Linwood Grant

*Scrape and scramble; inside the pantry and under the damp sheets.
Whisper and chitter, eyes in the angles, claws in the corners, always
the dull-dark – ready, so ready.*

Close, so close …

Somerset, 1978

My paternal grandmother, Eunice Margrave, lived to be
ninety-seven years old, a formidable relic of Victorian England
and a great source of both wisdom and prejudice. Curiously,
she had a strong dislike of the West Country, which she never
explained. I remember her refrain, often shared when that
region came up in conversation:

Caught in Cornwall
Suffered in Somerset
Died in Dorset

Her views on Bristol I will spare you, as the language she
used caused me to be banned from her house for a month. I
should not, perhaps, have repeated it in front of my parents –
not when I was only nine.

So when I found myself on business in that city of fat
waistcoats and lean dole-seekers, Grandam Eunice was often
on my mind. Bristol is, much like Liverpool, a place of such
historical contrasts that one's head can spin – a place of slave
manacles and Masonic handshakes, you might say. But it has
its attractions, attractions which include a small restaurant on
the edge of the St Pauls District, *Le Bon Couteau*, where cheap,

wholesome French and Caribbean cuisine sit easy with each other.

My guest there, on one particular warm August night, was Margaret O'Leary, a St Pauls sculptor. Margaret, a thin and vociferous Irishwoman, was employing new techniques with the local Dundry stone – with some success. I rather liked her, but there was something off about her that night, a distracted note to her conversation. In the end, I gave in.

'A man, a woman; a block of stone that won't play nicely? Or, if you're having trouble with the studio rent, I could –'

'Ah, Jaysus, it's none of them usual fellers. It's a thing I was coming across, the other day. Stuck at the back of me mind, it did.'

I waited for more, and if my heart rose at the very modest bill presented whilst we drank our coffee, it sank a little when she continued.

'You know of witch-bottles, do you not, Justin?'

I knew of them. They turned up on the antiquarian rounds now and then. An old practice – bottles and jugs, buried in walls or under hearths, as supposed protection against curses and sundry country annoyances. I'd never given them much thought.

'In passing,' I said. 'I did value some jugs once used for the purpose in Sussex, last year, as collectable items. Their bearded faces amuse me; their purpose doesn't.'

Margaret squinted at me. 'I'm thinking this isn't your ordinary witch-bottle. It has me itching. And then I thought to meself – wasn't Justin involved in that affair at Kemberdale ...?'

I winced. It did sometimes seem that my lot was to be drawn towards unnatural events, regardless of my own preference for a nice wine bar and a catalogue of Venetian glassware. Or simply a nice Venetian.

'Margaret, I am a rapidly ageing queen, slightly too thick of girth. I really don't need to be caught up yet again in –'

'You'll not be coming with me tomorrow, then, when I go Dundry way to call on the woman who was finding one of them?'

My coffee stared at me.

Of course I would.

My Irish temptress – in matters strange, not in any carnal sense, of course – drove at a speed which was suited to neither the lanes of her Cork youth or the byways of Somerset. As tractor drivers swore, and delivery vans swerved, she explained how she had been visiting several small quarries earlier in the week. And it was when she had paused at the sole tea-shop in Dundry village, that she encountered Mrs Judith Wheeler.

'You wouldn't have known her from a fighting cock,' said Margaret, swerving round an alarmed bicyclist. 'Calling such names, she was, demanding to know who had been at her hens and defacing her property. And while I like a bit of fire, she was in a state.'

In short, Margaret ordered a pot of tea, and offered the woman a neutral and sympathetic ear. My friend half expected to get her own mouthful, but instead, the woman burst into tears and began to talk …

'I told her about you on the phone this morning, and is it not better to let a cat catch its own mice?'

Which meant that she wanted me to hear Mrs Wheeler's story directly from the source.

We parked without completely destroying a stand of hollyhocks; Margaret was out of the car before I was sure it had stopped, and rapping on the cottage door.

If I had expected a termagant with rolling pin in hand, I received an awkward wave from a slight, pale-cheeked woman, and the indication that I should come in. So I levered myself from the car, and joined them.

'Justin Margrave.' I bowed, and kissed her hand.

Mrs Wheeler – Judith, please – ushered us in to the parlour, and asked if we minded tea with lemon, as the milk had turned again.

'You've found what you believe to be a witch-bottle, I understand.'

She glanced at Margaret. 'My father did,' she said, in a voice which had only a touch of Somerset in it. 'Many years ago.'

If that were the case, why was the thing suddenly of interest?

'Did you want it valued? If Margaret here hasn't warned you, I'm a critic and valuer – sculpture, ceramics, other fine art if I'm in the mood. Surprisingly trustworthy, they say, for one of my kind.'

'Mr Margrave, I don't know *what* I want. I daren't keep it; daren't sell it, and daren't open it – not a third time.'

A third time? Witch-bottles commonly contained all manner of things – urine, menstrual blood, iron nails, spit, hair and herbs. Whatever 'flavour' was popular in that neck of the woods. Opening them once was usually enough.

The tea, made with concentrated Jif lemon juice, was painful. I tried to smile.

'May I see the item?'

Margaret looked relieved, seeing that I had been hooked; Judith went to a rather fine Regency cupboard in the corner. A simple silver cross had been hung on the brass handles, the chain looped through both handles. She removed that, her hands trembling slightly, and brought out a stoppered stoneware jug, which she deposited on the coffee table.

Some witch-bottles were simply that – glass bottles filled with all sorts of superstitious muck – but Bartmann jugs were a well-recorded alternative. This was at first glance typical of the late seventeenth century. Salt-glazed stoneware, with a surface like polished orange-peel, the colour muted to a pale russet. About nine inches tall, it had the usual bearded face at the neck, though there was something ominous about the mask on this one – rather than being an obvious application, the face seemed to flow from the body of the vessel.

Why did it bother me? This was *like* the usual Bartmanns – but was it?

Candle-wax had recently been melted over the thick cork stopper, sealing it in place. Sitting back without touching it, I considered her nervous expression.

'The vast majority were simply used for wine, beer, or other liquids,' I said. 'The Rhineland potters produced them by the thousand. Why would you assume this is a witch-bottle?'

'Because there's *things* inside it, which clatter if you jiggle it. And because They want it. They … hate it.'

Um. 'They' was said clearly, with a capital T. It sounded like the language of the isolated countryside, the folklorist, the aspiring Wiccan, and the slightly deranged. Into which category did my hostess fall?

'Why do you say "They", Judith?'

Witch-bottles were made to avert supposed curses, spells of misfortune and so forth. To stop a daughter's cramps, and relieve the sores on a plough-ox. To keep away a witch – rather obviously.

'I … it just feels like that. I hear … whispers.'

She seemed quite genuine. When some yobbish youth on a bleak housing estate grabs your arm and asks if you know anything about early Byzantine iconography, you stop to listen further. And when a sensible-seeming woman like Judith Wheeler offers a story like this …

Oh Margaret. Why did I linger over coffee in the restaurant; why did I stay long enough to let you drag me into this sort of thing? I shot her a rather venomous look.

'Judith, I want you to tell me the whole story. If you keep anything back, then I am Bristol-bound, and home in London by this evening, settled in my comfortable study. Do you understand?'

She nodded.

'It began with my father …'

Jethro Wheeler had a disappointing war. Asthmatic, he was refused by the Army, and of limited use on the farms. But he was first in the Local Defence Volunteers, and then the Home Guard. Dundry, Chew Magna, Norton Malreward and many other small settlements were all on the flight path of the German raids over Bristol – and they suffered for it. Not as badly as central Bristol, but Dundry caught it a number of times, and there was always the worry of worse.

From the tower of St Michael's Church on Dundry Hill, to the flattened peak of Maes Knoll, Home Guard lookouts watched for the bombers, and for German gliders bringing paratroopers or infiltrators.

To their North, Bristol burned.

Yet the gliders did not come, and they could do nothing about the bombers; watch duty on Maes Knoll was long, and tedious. Each time he was on duty there he bicycled out, wheezing, and sat next to a small shed put up for them, watching the night sky. The other man with him usually dozed off, but Jethro didn't like to report that.

One night in 1941, after the luxury of a small piece of chocolate, Jethro went wandering around the knoll. A single German bomb had fallen nearby the previous week, probably a Heinkel getting rid of the last of its load after a run over the city, and the side of the tump, the highest point, was scarred by the explosion. Perhaps he wondered if there was a keepsake there; perhaps it was idle curiosity. Whatever the reason, he took up a spade from the shed, and poked around in the hole, his torch picking out fragments of burned and twisted metal ...

Until the light reflected off something rounded, honey-brown, and intact.

The skies were clear, the Germans elsewhere. He got down on his knees, and with a piece of bomb casing he scraped away the soil until he could lift this odd object from where it must have been resting for many years. He knew Maes Knoll was old, and had hoped for something Roman, but this didn't fit the bill. A beer jug left by a Victorian farmhand?

The vessel swished and clinked. Beer didn't clink.

So he tugged at the thick cork, and slowly, very slowly, it came free ...

Judith shook her head.

'I was fourteen, Mr Margrave, when he told me. He only talked about it because I'd discovered the witch-bottle in our air-raid shelter, buried under a loose plank. He was mad with me when he found out, and took it away to hide elsewhere.

'I pestered him and argued for a week, until he explained where it had come from, but he'd never say what happened when he opened it, just that he stoppered it again quick, and brought it home to keep it out of others' hands.'

'Maes Knoll is ...'

'An Iron Age hill-fort,' said Margaret. 'A few miles east of here. Nothing terribly spectacular, an elevated triangle of land with a mound on the top at one end, the "tump". They say it's the near end of Wansdyke – you know, the one which stretches from Wiltshire to here.'

I knew Wansdyke vaguely, though not that it came so far west. An Anglo-Saxon boundary earthwork, broken in places. Later than Maes Knoll, which must have fallen out of use well before the dyke was dug.

'When my dad went into a care home, end of last month, I found the jug again. It was buried with a load of scrap metal under the old chicken run. I was digging, thinking I might use the run for potatoes, and there it was, cork and all. Well, I put it in the backroom, thinking I might get someone to look at it – one of them museum blokes.

'Then early last week, I decided to tidy the jug up, get the soil off. I swear I'd hardly touched it when the brush seemed to twist in my hand, like, and clean knocked the cork out ...'

She shuddered.

'Did I get a fright? The smell, for one, like my Nan when she was in her last days, all bedpans and suchlike. And a touch of winter, though it was July. I even thought I heard voices, as if they came from far off, but now I don't know. Fair made me shiver, and I pushed that stopper right back in. Since then, nothing's been right. The house feels off; milk turns, the hens won't lay, and someone's been outside, scraping along the walls – like with a knife, scoring the plaster.

'At first I put it down to Bill Roughton's kids – bad'uns, the lot – and that was when I met Margaret here, and she asked me what was bothering me. The jug came to my tongue, and I told her of it, right out.' She looked directly at me. 'Margaret said you might be able to help. Are you a man who knows about … these things?'

I stood, and went to stare out of the window. A chicken pecked at the sparse grass in the front garden; a cat on a large log watched me watching the chicken.

'I really am an art critic. But I've come across some strange things in my time …'

'Ah now, these are the Summerlands, full of mysteries,' said Margaret.

'Pshaw, as the writers used to say. Don't smear this with faux-Celtic nonsense – you'll be lecturing me on King Arthur, Avalon, and Tír na nÓg next.'

The sculptor reddened. 'Justin –'

'Mythology doesn't bother me, Margaret. It's what lies behind the myths I don't like. There are truths that don't tend to suit us.'

I went and picked up the Bartmann jug. Moving it around, you could certainly hear the swish of liquid and the muted clatter of harder objects, loose inside. And there was that broad, crude face. When I looked more closely, it was clear that it had only one eye. There was no obvious damage – it had been made that way, which was certainly not usual for its kind.

'You could have it, if you like, Mr Margrave,' said Judith.

I did not like, yet I was caught, unable yet to leave this mystery – if such it was – to its own devices.

'Might I borrow it until tomorrow? There are people I can speak to. I'm staying at the Royal.'

She assented gladly; I took the witch-bottle, told her not to worry, and that I'd find out what I could. She seemed a little easier when we left. As we did so, I glanced at the limewashed plaster outside.

The scratches around the front door were deep, and to my untrained eye, they looked like claw marks.

Soon Margaret and I were back in Bristol.

'I'm going over the water to see me da in Kinsale for a few days,' she said as she deposited me outside the Royal. 'Will I leave you to it, then?'

I assured her that I would ferret up anything of use, and keep Mrs Wheeler informed.

'Good fortune, then, Justin.' And she sped away, choking every pedestrian in the area with exhaust fumes.

In my room, I placed the jug on the writing desk, and stared at it. The Bartmann style had been copied at a number of English potteries from the late 1600s on, though I'd only seen examples from Derby and Staffordshire myself. Some clays worked better than others; there would be variations in the tone of the salt glaze, and in the devices on them – this jug had nothing but the wild, bearded, one-eyed face.

The theory behind filling a bottle full of your urine or whatever was, as far as I could remember, fairly simple. Either the contents lured in the offending witch and trapped her 'power' there, or they acted as a general charm, stopping the witch from having any influence over a particular person. Why such a bizarre act would work, I couldn't imagine.

I made a few calls to a ceramicist friend, an antiquarian in Bath and so on, but came away from them little wiser – except for the phone number of a contact who might be of use, and from another person, a thought about my one-eyed friend.

'End of Wansdyke, eh?' said Archie Crane, a London 'dealer' who, whilst being very irritating, was also reasonably experienced. 'Obvious connection, old boy.'

'Which is?'

'Odin, Woden. Wansdyke is Woden's Dyke. You know, the chap who gave his eye for knowledge, hung on a tree and so on?'

A witch-bottle made to invoke Odin, or warn him off? That

was a new one on me. So I drank half a bottle of something which might once have visited Burgundy briefly, and fell asleep.

Tumble and scurry; scritch at the doors, and scratch at the keys. Chitter and whisper, down past-ways and thin-ways, peer through your dead hopes and out of the half-world, into the night-place, free of the day.

Hungry. Hungry for child-fat and sorrows; parched for the rattle of life in its leaving.

They are almost here, and They must play ...

Margaret rang me at the Royal, the next morning.

'I'm off up to the ferry, but that witch-bottle, now – I was saying it was trouble, wasn't I? Well, there's the Divil abroad, and bad fortune laid on many a hearth round here. It's in the local papers, when you're looking for it. Sure, I haven't the Sight, but Mother of Mary ...'

'Coincidence. The more you read these rags, the worse life seems.'

'Ah, I don't know, Justin, I don't know.'

When she rang off, I looked at my notes. With some reluctance, I picked up the telephone again and arranged to meet the local contact who'd been recommended to me. After which I went – with equal reluctance – to hire a car.

Beth Trethick was a short, round woman, maybe thirty years old, with tangled black hair and heavy eyebrows above hazel eyes. In corduroy trousers and a worn khaki army jacket, she was waiting on the roadside by Maes Knoll – waiting for me to rattle up in my car.

'Good of you to come,' I said. I knew she was from Trowbridge, the other side of Bath.

'Choice is as choice does,' she said, which told me nothing.

We strolled towards the knoll. Margaret was right – the knoll was scenic, but not spectacular. It rose from surrounding ditches like an enormous misshapen burial mound, most of its flat top about fifty feet above us and the 'tump' another twenty or so feet higher, one small mound on the back of its mother.

'Might I ask why you did come? Are witch bottles an area of yours?'

I had given her the gist of the matter on the phone.

'I've never seen one. But the rest, what's in the air … it feels wrong. The land here isn't happy. And then I got your call.'

The climb was steeper than I'd expected; when we reached the base of the tump, I abandoned any shame and sat down on the grass, breathing heavily. To the north, the sprawl of Bristol lay in hazy sunshine.

'I don't suppose you feel like explaining what's going on to an innocent soul like myself?'

Thick eyebrows arched. 'An "innocent soul", Mr Margrave?'

'A figure of speech.'

'You mean a lie.' But there was a faint smile there as well.

'Art is a lie that makes us realise truth, at least the truth that is given us to understand.' I returned her smile. 'Picasso said that, the year I was born. But in Spanish, of course.'

She joined me on the grass.

'It's not a witch-bottle. Or, it is a witch-bottle, in its way. But it wasn't made to keep away the muttered curses of some mean beldam or local busy-body. It's a warding against something worse. I wasn't sure what, until we met today.'

'I haven't shown the jug to you yet.' I had returned it to Judith Wheeler before driving out to Maes Knoll.

'The wind is wrong. I felt it as soon as I came near Dundry. They've been playing, in their fashion, waiting for the moment. One of you will weaken, or be clumsy. You'll show the jug to a colleague, who – too curious – will open it before you can speak. You'll turn it on its side, and the wax will crack; Judith Wheeler will go to bury it once more, and trip, drop it. They'll be gathering to make that moment, now the jug can be felt. It's how They work.'

We were back in the land of Capital Letters.

'I wish someone would tell me who "They" are.'

She didn't answer.

A bird sang; a tractor crawled past the car on the road below.

Few people would call me an impatient man, but at times, I grow tired of those who act as if they have mysteries hidden behind their ears. And I remembered a time, in Abbot's Elk, when I had used words I did not know, standing barefoot in the blush of a Spring dawn …

'I have caused the Greenway to be run,' I said, perhaps a little theatrically. I would have suited the stage, I think.

Which got those eyebrows working.

'I wasn't told you had the Cunning,' she said, her voice softer.

'I haven't.' I held up my hands – look, nothing up the sleeves. 'But let's say I've blundered into this sort of thing before. Not quite *this*, obviously.'

'Okay. I don't know exactly what we have here, but I can smell the Children of Angles and Corners on you. Do you know of Them?'

I shook my head.

'It's hard to explain, unless you've been taught, shown. "They" are something dark, ancient, known from the first days that people ever strode these hills and valleys. They foster still-births and dying cattle; ruin lives and weaken bridges; They delight in our misery, suckle on our failures.'

'Actual creatures? Monsters?' I didn't know quite how much of this to swallow.

'If you like, but trust me, definitions won't help you get your head around Them. How does a tuna describe a shark? They live – exist – askew from our lives, until They find a way through. Older than monsters, we say of them.'

'So this isn't about tricksters like pixies, or brownies, those sort of folk?'

I watched her face twist between derision and sheer horror at my ignorance.

'No,' she settled for, very clipped.

'And the jug, the witch-bottle?'

'The Children are vengeful, mercurial. They know the Old Ways, and they like the weak spots of the land, so places rich with myth suit them. Like this area. That's where Their name comes from – Their crooked pathways, Their ways into the World. So, what age would you say this jug is?'

'It's typical of the 1680s, 1690s. Severn Valley clay, I'd say. Probably made as a single item, not one of a batch. It may be unique. There's no record of another "Woden" jug that I can find. A ceramics expert might – especially if the jug was chipped – be able to look at the material used, and give it a more exact place of origin.'

Beth thought a moment.

'You want my best guess?'

'It would be better than mine.'

'Then I'd say that someone, centuries ago, was troubled by Them, and had the jug made for a single purpose – to keep the Children far away,' She gestured to the tump. 'They chose to put it in a beacon place, an ancient place. Look at the view Maes Knoll commands. There must have been a lot of worrying things going on at the time, to try such a thing.'

Her comment woke a few brain cells.

'War?'

She frowned. 'They love any form of strife. It draws them. "War brings the woe-mongers", as we say. Why?'

'Well, look – there was the Monmouth Rebellion ravaging Somerset in 1685. The jug could easily have been fired around that time.' I knew my history, at least. 'Chaos and uprising, ending in bloody battle at Sedgemoor – and a fair number of hangings.' I warmed to my theme. 'And then, when it was exposed, another war. 1941.'

'Buried in one war; unearthed in another. That would suit Them. And the charm must be so much weaker than once it was. Did a bomb fall on Maes Knoll, exactly where the jug was hidden, just by accident? I wonder who might have brushed a harassed German bombardier's mind, over thirty years ago?'

I got to my feet.

'What does Judith Wheeler do, then? Break it apart, bury it

once more? Or let me sent it to some dusty museum far away, and let it be forgotten?'

'That's a hard one. They have the scent of you now, and of the Wheeler woman. Who else has seen it, been near it?'

'My friend Margaret. She's left for Ireland. Oh, and Judith's father. The chap who found and opened it.'

'Their contact with him would be Their first touch in this part of the country for many years. Their first whisper of opportunity. I say that, but don't think of Them as people, with the same basic thoughts and motivations. The Children are as "wrong" and unlike us as anything you will ever meet. They'll peel the fat from under babies' skins, drown family pets, and drive people to suicide – simply for idle amusement.'

The cynic in me wondered at that. I'd known people who … well, never mind.

She might have heard my thoughts.

'It doesn't stop at single incidents, Mr Margrave. It doesn't stop until They're sated, if They come in numbers. You've heard of those deserted Medieval villages that the archaeologists find from time to time?'

'Emptied by the Plague and the Clearances, yes.'

'Not all of them. Some were ruined and emptied by another evil.'

Was that possible?

I was quiet the rest of the way down.

Somehow my new acquaintance had found a bus to get her near Maes Knoll – a magickal act in itself, given rural services – and so she had no transport. I said I'd drive her to Judith Wheeler's house, to see the Woden jug 'in the flesh'.

If I puzzle you, I should admit that I already had a rudimentary acquaintance with Beth Trethick's kind of knowledge. She and her ilk were said to be the people of small magicks and the old ways – the Cunning, basically, which only means 'knowing'. In storybooks, the wise ones, the hedge-wizards, and counsellors. The ones you went to when you really believed that a witch was out to get you, or that some malign influence possessed your life.

Almost every village in these Isles would have had one once, though he or she may have been called a herbalist or a healer. Everything I knew suggested that they were the real version of people who sold crystals from over-priced shops at Glastonbury, and put on Marks and Spencer robes to cavort in the woods. And poor, harassed Justin, when he wasn't try to decipher a dusty wine label, or admiring a Hepworth in the galleries, believed in calling on whatever might be useful when times grew hard.

For I had picked up those 'rags', as per my conversation with Margaret earlier in the day, and I was no longer so sure about the state of things. I had even been in brief contact with a newspaper editor I knew. The reports were true. If you could lay misfortune like a blanket across a stretch of countryside … house fires in Winford, with no apparent cause; tuberculosis from nowhere around the Nortons, in cattle and men; a rush of tranquilliser prescriptions in Dundry, and a sudden spate of fights, illnesses, paediatric emergencies, in half a dozen other villages.

All reported since a woman near Dundry dug up the Woden jug.

Judith Wheeler was not well.

We found her pale, shaken, lying on the sofa in the parlour, with her arm in a sling. The front door had been open, a woman in a District Nurse's uniform nurse just leaving.

'I was lucky,' said Judith. 'Mrs Grainger, the nurse, was cycling past. She heard me cry out.'

Judith had been cleaning the Welsh dresser in the kitchen when she heard faint voices at the back of the house. As she turned on her steps, the dresser, well settled in its place, made a cracking noise, tipped forward and caught her shoulder. It almost fell right on top of her.

Beth gave me a Look.

'My best china's broken.' Judith shifted uncomfortable, favouring her arm.

'Better than your neck,' I said.

I went into the kitchen, and the dresser lay there, the upper portion almost split in two. Oak needed help to break like that. When I reported this to Beth, her cheek twitched, a tic below her left eye.

'Where is the jug?' Snapped out at Judith.

'The … the witch-bottle? Under the stairs. You can go and see if you –'

Beth dragged it out and set it down in the hallway, examining it out of Judith's sight. Which didn't take long.

'I don't think there's any doubt. Mr Margrave, I need to protect this place; you need to find out what happened that night in 1941.'

'Is this about my dad?' asked the injured woman when we rejoined her. I felt a bit sorry for her, and tried to form a reassuring smile.

'I need a little more information, Judith, that's all. Do you have the address of the care home?'

She pointed to the cupboard, where I found an address book. D for Dad. The place was almost in Bristol, and on this side of the city.

'Is he, um …'

'He gets confused. But he has his good days. If you're going, tell him I'll be over on Friday, all being well – don't mention this silly fall.'

'Ms Trethick will look after you.' I hesitated. 'You can rely on her.'

Cars these days have too many gears, and the one I'd hired had less of them by the time I reached the Elmtree Nursing Home. It was as if the damn thing were fighting me all the way, and I wished I'd had time to hire a driver as well.

Elmtree was a large Victorian villa, converted into a facility which was hard to negotiate. Former servants' stairs and corridors confused my hurried brain, but a cleaner guided me to Jethro Wheeler's room. He looked a lot like his daughter.

'Mr Wheeler, hello. I'm Justin, one of Judith's friends.'

He peered at me from his chair, watery eyes only half-focussed.

'Judith's not here.'

'I know. She sent me to have a chat with you.' Close enough to the truth. 'About the war.'

'You a reporter?'

'Yes,' I descended into bald-faced lies. 'We're doing a series ...'

Jethro Wheeler had a bent frame – he must have been in his eighties – but a strong voice. I teased him into the open with a few remarks about the air-raids, and he was soon spouting easily. Like many of us as we age, past excursions were clearer than recent weeks, and he had no problem giving chapter and verse as to that night on Maes Knoll – up to a certain point.

'You opened the jug,' I said. I said it twice, because he had gone silent.

'You ever had rats, Mr Margrave?' came the eventual response. He spoke with a Somerset burr, with 's' almost a 'z'.

'As pets?'

'In your house, under it, round it. That was the way of it. Like having rats in your head. And small, thin voices ... Cork in one hand, jug in the other, and the smell of it, like all the piss and droppings ever made by all the rats there ever were ...'

He jerked in his chair, as if surprised at what he'd been saying.

'You a reporter?'

'I'm Judith's friend, remember?'

'I still hears Them, smells Them ... like rats, you know?'

I thought of folk songs, of deals made with shadows; the beat of the bodhrán and a warning refrain ...

'Did They offer anything, ask you to do anything?'

'Can't say They did.' He narrowed his eyes. 'But I could feel Them, prying, looking to find a way into me. I corked it damn fast, and buried it where They couldn't go – and I have ways.'

He fumbled under his blanket, and brought out a large, crude iron nail, four or five inches long.

'I'll prick Them, if They come,' he said, his loose dentures grinning.

And that was all I could get from him.

Back at the Royal, I showered and went down to the front desk to add a day or two on to my stay. There was a message for me, from Gareth, one of Margaret's Bristol friends:

Accident at Holyhead before the ferry left for Ireland. Margaret in Valley Hospital. No need to call – doctors say minor stroke, or seizure. Recovering well, sends her love.

Judith, and now Margaret. I did not think that Beth Trethick would call these accidents.

Insane though it might seem, I was beginning to believe in the Children of Angles and Corners.

The scrape and the scratch of it, claws on the door-step, eyes in the angles and paws in the dark; mutter and murmur, gape at the green-rings, push through the moss-banks where hate cuts the air. The oh-so-sweet honey of death-beds and fever cots, sharp from the sorrow-bound, weak and resentful. And the warding at large, torn from its high seat, borne from its safeness, back in the hands of the stupid and small ...

Coming, coming ...

'He buried in the air raid shelter,' I said to the Cunning-woman. 'And I've had a look at what's left of it, in the back garden. Corrugated iron. And there was scrap iron in the second hiding place.'

Beth nodded. 'Iron has power. Enough to bother Them. Then his daughter moved it, and They came back. They want to be here, amongst us.'

'Why?'

'To foster anything that hurts, and worries, and divides. It's what They feed on. Misery and distress. Any other harm They cause it for pleasure. Your friend Margaret – what happened to her was for fun, simply because They had touched her, even briefly. If allowed, They'll be a scourge on all the lands around here, until They're sated.' She gave me a sharp look. 'And don't be fooled by small starts, Mr Margrave. There will be deaths.'

I didn't have much choice but to believe her.

'Have you a plan?'

Judith was asleep in her bedroom upstairs, and we could speak freely. I'd reassured her that her father was fine, and safe. He was certainly a lot less worried than I was.

Beth paced the parlour, her boots leaving smears of soil on the carpet.

'I'm an accounts clerk for Woolworth's, Mr Margrave. I like puppies, and a few beers. The Cunning comes from family blood and history; some of the time, it makes me more scared than complete ignorance would. I'd rather this were someone else's problem. And it's eating into my sick-leave. My boyfriend's not too pleased, either.'

'You sound almost human.'

We grinned at each other, and she sat down. Her dark brows came together.

'But as for plans … Are you strong, Mr Margrave?' she asked.

'I wouldn't be the first person to turn to if you wanted furniture moving. That Welsh dresser —'

'No, no. I was thinking about will, and stubbornness. Such people deal better with the Children. The uncommitted and indecisive tend to fall by the wayside. Because I have an idea, but we would need someone strong at the heart of it.'

That didn't sound promising. 'Go on.'

'The best we might do is to renew the ward, the single purpose of the jug – which means someone must be the bond-maker, the key. Better than starting from scratch. But Judith's too vulnerable and confused. Besides, Woden is a male figure. It pays to stick as closely to the original making as possible …'

'And dear old Justin is to hand.'

'It's you or her father, really. Men who know of the jug.'

It was tempting to volunteer the old chap from the care home, but the sad ghost of my conscience must have been hovering nearby.

I agreed to do it.

I always kept a travelling bag with me, and so I stayed at the house, along with Beth. There were fresh claw marks on the outside plaster; a chicken had been gutted, messily, on the edge of the lawn, and the rest of the hens had fled, as had the cat. Hardly surprising.

When we weren't talking, we could hear Them – voices slightly too far away, nasty voices. Not words, more an insidious feeling of threat and malice which ran along your nerves and swirled inside the caverns of your brain.

Like radio waves from a foreign country, whispered in a foreign tongue.

'They're calling out from the Half-World. They would sound much louder, be more of a threat, if I hadn't raised my own wards around the house.'

Beth was on the sofa; I was propped in an armchair, surround by cushions.

'Such as?' I was curious.

'Such as a Cunning-woman might know. I'll share trade secrets some other time, Mr Margrave.' She paused. 'Do you ever think about your name?'

'Justin?'

'Margrave. A walker on, or protector of, the borders. Lord of the Marches – Mark-graf. And here we are talking about touching the Half-World, a true borderland.'

I sighed. 'I'd rather not go there, to be frank. It interferes with my digestion. But speaking of names, why Woden – does that have some significance? Are the Cunning Folk pagans?'

'We're pretty much anything we want to be. Atheists, even – as long as we touch the land, and remember the Old Ways.' She scratched her armpit, and thought a moment. 'I imagine our predecessor, whoever he or she was, chose to have Woden on their jug because the Children would recognise the name, and its resonance. These were Anglo Saxon lands once. And with Woden's Dyke being here, yes, it must have seemed particularly appropriate.'

'Reasonable enough.' My back hurt. I wasn't built for

sleeping in chairs. 'So where do we do this? And when?'

'It will have to be on Maes Knoll. And as tomorrow is Wednesday ...'

'Yes?'

'Wodensday, Mr Margrave. Might as well draw on what we can get.'

She was tired, as was I.

I had one last question, prompted by the sight of that eviscerated chicken. There might be dogs, or foxes, or some such animal around, but still ...

'How dangerous are these creatures, physically?'

By asking that question, I saw that I had fully and finally bought into Beth Trethick's interpretation of events. Oh dear, oh dear ...

'The Children?' She pulled a blanket over her and stretched out. 'Who knows? I've never faced Them. But I hope that Woolworths will miss me if it all goes wrong.'

A reassuring note on which to go to sleep.

Wriggle and writhe, the Half-World is opening; hungry, so hungry...

We did not tell Judith Wheeler what we were going to do. In the morning I helped put the dresser back up, and as I cleared away broken dinner plates, I went on about the ways wood could warp in the heat and damp of a kitchen. And I said that, although I gave no credence to talk of it bringing misfortune, I would take the jug away that night. Just to settle her mind.

When she said she might walk up to the village, Beth and I encouraged her. Fresh air, a little exercise. In her absence, we made our preparations. Or Beth did, and I listened.

'No iron on you. We want Them to focus solely on you and the jug, whilst I do what I can to keep you standing. No crosses, religious symbols, anything which might bother Them. No talismans, amulets, or similar paraphernalia.'

'Do I look like a man of paraphernalia? Unless They object to hand-made Italian shoes and a rather nice Art Deco silver tie-pin.'

'Lose the tie-pin, Mr Margrave. Just in case.'

I checked all my pockets, removing keys, loose change and one of the iron nails I'd purchased in Bristol.

'I am ritually naked,' I announced.

She looked out of the parlour window.

'Dimpsey soon.'

'I'm sorry?'

'Dimpsey. What we say in Somerset – that time when dusk is almost upon us.'

Judith returned not long after, and the three of us had a light tea together. Gammon ham and fresh bread. I talked about some harmless art finds from my past, adding a few poor jokes, trying to keep Judith at her ease.

When she was up in her room for an early night – she was still a little shaken from her fall, I think – Beth and I took the jug out to the hire car.

'I would have liked to have the rooks with us,' she murmured. 'But this has to be done at night, which is not their time.'

I could feel the jug now, like a leaden weight in my hands, and with 'dimpsey' came the voices once more. In some ways, it was more annoying that they were too low and distant to make out – you kept trying, straining, to catch something intelligible. Rat-scratches on the air.

The Children were under the floorboards of our world.

We had a fifteen, twenty minute drive to the east – not the crow's distance, but further because we had to curve round by the small village of Norton Malreward. The radio in the hired car crackled a lot.

'And in local news, a number of sheep have been found dead on pasture land near Dundry South Quarry. Police say that the bodies bear some signs of a dog attack, but are not ruling out human agency ...'

'Not animals, nor human agency,' said Beth, turning the radio off. 'They are growing confident.'

Near Norton Malreward we parked and walked west, up through the farmland to reach Maes Knoll. We both had decent flash-lights. What else Beth had in her backpack, I couldn't guess.

A full moon pierced the country darkness, showing the way but setting more shadows than felt comfortable.

'So, is the moon a friend of ours?' I picked my way across a boggy ditch; I'd never worn a pair of hiking boots in my life, but was beginning to consider their value more seriously.

'It's the moon,' said Beth from ahead of me. 'It can be used, for good or ill.'

At last we were on solid grassland, the slope up the side of the knoll.

Maes Knoll looked larger, more important now. Were the wights of Iron Age warriors watching our approach, wondering why we dared their fort? Or was it rabbits? More comforting to think of rabbits crouching under the bushes, simply annoyed to have their suppers disturbed.

As we reached the main heights of the knoll, there was a chill wind where there had been none before. Around us, Somerset slumbered, a patchwork of fields, woods and villages; to our North, Bristol was on fire with street-lights and motorway lights, shop neons and hotel displays. I thought of Jethro Wheeler standing where I stood, a war around him.

And I could hear Them clearly at last.

Out from the gore-grass, up from the mire; tumbling, laughing, with mouths agape. Flesh to tear, bellies to rend – out from the corners, through every angle; here for the blubber-man, his soft flesh waiting.

We are coming, coming …

'Try to hold on until the right moment.' called out Beth, her tangled black mane loose in the breeze.

The right moment. The Children had to be there, in our world, when I renewed the witch-bottle, for it to work, Beth said that I needed to know what I was binding, that this was no time for vague moves. As I stepped away from her, making myself alone and obvious, I felt Their presence on the other side of a wall of icy air -- and They felt me, reaching out from the Half-World to enter my thoughts.

Where They found something They could use, and unlike Jethro, I couldn't just slam the cork straight back in, seal the Woden jar.

Waiting, waiting …

They tugged at my past, at the Margraves who had been, the ones who were weak and lonely. They brought back all the small hatreds I'd encountered, week after week, month after month, whilst growing up; the weaknesses in me and the blows I'd taken. Half-forgotten but never forgiven, from shameful gym sessions and showers after rugby; late nights in unlit alleys, the sound of those who scorned me. Fat Margrave – queer boy, shirt-lifter, loser …

> *'You touched him, I saw you, your hand on his arse.'*
> *'A kicking will teach you.'*
> *'Kiss her, you bum-boy. She wants you, she wants you.'*

A callous stranger, a kindly desk sergeant …

> *'Get along home, son. And steer clear of them woods, there's some bad'uns up there.'*

My parents, stiff, distant, always muttering in the other room, always sighing as they spoke of me to 'decent' people. The voices we collect, and cannot un-hear. And now these other Children, finding me ripe, undefended. I was weeping, shivering in the cold, half-propped against the side of the tump -- but to my own surprise, I was also angry.

How dare They?

I think I snarled, or as good as did so, and I held the Woden jug up in my left hand – *left-hander, sinister, hello sweet-heart.* With my right hand, though my fingers didn't want to obey me,

I twisted the cork, snapping the wax, and I pulled.

Ahhh, opening, opening …

They were there.

And They were beautiful. Beth Trethick had lied to me.

Out on the razor-edged winds, out of the Half-World, with the border no longer guarded. Tall, slim figures, wreathed in gossamer, princes of air and darkness – I could not count them, or turn from the light of their long, slender limbs and Their perfect faces.

The Children of Angles and Corners, with eyes of moonlight.

I knew I should shatter the jug forever, and let Them play here, on Maes Knoll and Dundry Hill, in the gentle meadows and broad fields; Their places, barred to Them by envious lesser souls. The Cunning was no more than sly obstruction and control, and the Cunning-woman, only a few paces away, was a small, mean creature …

In that moment, an accident of the breeze brought a stench to my nostrils, the rotting, rat-piss stench from the jug, and with that came another memory – Bainley, proud prefect and school golden boy, as he forced my head down over the urine-slick toilet bowl, as he fumbled all the while with my zip and trouser belt. Bainley, who was as beautiful as the Children – but only on the outside.

'Justin!'

But I didn't need Beth to spur me on. I thought of 'Bonny' Cheyvis, and the razor he took to his wrists after one of his failed affairs; my dear friend Helene, her sculptures unfinished, a shovel-load of barbiturates in her half-finished Bacardi and coke. Of those who had lost entire careers over one ill-chosen night of love, one newspaper photograph, and how I had survived, even prospered.

Of how difficult it was to be human – which these creatures were not.

'Look at Them, Justin.' Beth was on her knees, Their pretty

fingers tearing at her clothes, her hair, her skin. Blood ran from one corner of her mouth as she wove steel wire between her fingers, pattern after pattern, the iron-tinged glamours that were helping me stand firm. 'LOOK AT THEM!'

All glamour fled; illusion fell.

When people talk of something being indescribable, they do not usually mean it. They mean that some basic verbal skill had temporarily failed them. I could describe the Children, but I choose not to.

You must settle for whatever terrible memories you yourselves have – malice and anger distorting a woman's face, a man's cheap, bullying rage; the warped pleasure of a damaged child as it hurts anything, anyone, it can grasp – and the slobbering greed of those who already have too much.

These things are only part of the Children of Angles and Corners, wrapped in stick-limbs and claws, outlined by harsh, triangular gashes in the night which might or might not be their cruel mouths.

Beth, of course, had not lied.

They bore down on me, trying to stay my right hand and claw the jug from me; They drove me back against the tump, but I had seen Them now. I had judged what They were.

I thrust out the jug, not trying to shield it.

The Woden jug, on Woden's Day.

'Third, High, and Just-as-High.' A memory of eddas and verse I had read over the years. 'He knew you, hung on a tree to be sure of what you were.'

On the Bartmann jug, surely crafted for only a single purpose, the one-eyed face was alive in the moonlight – or it suited me to believe that. The salt-glaze writhed; I bit down on the inside of my cheek until the blood came – a somewhat more difficult and painful act than I had anticipated. The Children shrieked and swirled, and a crooked claw lashed at my face, connected, but I was too busy to pay attention.

I spat blood into the open neck of the jug.

'Margrave!' I yelled into the storm of Them. 'Border-Lord. So do fuck off, the lot of you!'

My right hand arced and drove the cork back into the jug with all my strength.

Time is malleable, ductile, whatever you want to call it. That moment twisted and lasted, one half-second stretched so long and thin …

A man and a woman, both bloodied, stood alone on Maes Knoll, on a warm August night. There was ice in Beth's hair.

'Are They …?' I said, putting the jug down on the grass.

'Yes.' She had lacerations across her face and the backs of her hands. The steel wire formed some sort of cat's cradle between them. Its purpose, she'd said, was to give me purpose, stop me from being wholly dragged into Their illusion. It seemed to have worked.

'I feel like –'

Four figures coming up the slope, tall, dark.

'More trouble,' I moaned.

'No.' She managed a hoarse laugh. 'The Cunning Folk of the Southwest, come to finish things. They were ready in case we failed.'

'Only four of them?'

'That's about all we have between here and Salisbury. We're not what we were, Mr Margrave.'

A woman who must surely have been in her nineties; a teenage girl, and two very ordinary looking men. Even the old woman would top Beth Trethick by eight or nine inches. They had spades over their shoulders.

'They'll bury the jug deep under the turf, and place Words in the soil of Maes Knoll, that no one digs here by accident or purpose. Magpie and mole will keep watch for us, so we're not caught unawares again.'

Beth ushered me down the mound, back to the car.

'They know what to do – they don't need us.'

'The accidents, the illnesses …'

'Will stop. And everyone will forget them, given a week or two.'

'It isn't only here, though, is it?'

'Some other day, some other place, anywhere where the night

is thin, They will try to enter again. But we've done what we can for today. Don't bring me down, Justin.'

It seems I had been permanently promoted from being merely Mr Margrave.

At Judith Wheeler's house, we let ourselves in with the spare key, splashed our cuts with antiseptic, and fell asleep in our parlour-bedroom. The armchair was far more comfortable this time.

I didn't tell Margaret the truth. Partly because she didn't need to know, and partly because she was a gossip – as am I – and giving her the full story, whether she believed it or not, would cement me into a role I didn't want.

'How was Dundry, then?' they would ask in the galleries and dining rooms, and smirk, or lean forward, eager. There were enough stories about me in circulation already.

We dined at *Le Bon Couteau* towards the end of August, and I listened, sipping a decent Bordeaux, as she told me that the doctors could find nothing wrong with her.

'Over-work,' I said.

'What happened about that witch-bottle thing?'

'Oh, some people who know their stuff better than I do took it off Judith's hands.'

'But all them goings-on around Dundry –'

'Sometimes a fish is just a fish, Margaret. Maybe someone upset a black cat, or broke a mirror. Anyway, I gather it's quiet in those parts now.'

She looked disappointed, and made up for it by ordering a huge plateful of profiteroles, dripping with a dark chocolate sauce. I would have joined her, but my waistline had suffered enough from another few days of West Country cuisine. The dessert waiter was a tall, rather striking man in his thirties, very attentive, and I might have given him my card, except for one thing – there was a tattoo just visible beneath his rolled-up shirt sleeve.

It depicted a broad, bearded face, with only one eye …

AND THEN THERE WAS ONE

A picturesque island off the south coast of Devon. It's tidal, so sometimes you can cross over from the mainland quite easily, though on occasion there are wild seas roaring around it and whoever's there may be marooned for days. The island possesses only one habitation, a large, privately-owned mansion filled with mysterious but exotic Art Deco features. You only go there because you've been invited to a weekend party by a couple you've never met before, a certain Ulick and Nancy Owen. When you arrive, the other guests say the same thing. They've no idea why they've been invited either. What's even stranger, the supposed hosts of the party, the Owens, are not present, and the staff have no explanation for this.

The next thing of course, you are cut off by the sea. At which point the situation takes a turn for the genuinely eerie. To start with, there are ten of you, and yet at the same time there are ten lifelike figurines arranged in a circle on the main dining table. Moreover, in each guest bedroom there hangs a selected portion from a popular children's nursery rhyme, and in each case the section of rhyme appears to carry a direct threat, because it describes an untimely death.

It isn't long after this when the murders begin, and a horrifying awareness dawns that you aren't here for a party at all. But to be slaughtered by a maniac.

This isn't a real-life scenario, of course. Nor is it the first act to a modern day slasher movie. It's actually the opening stanza to what is still the best-selling crime novel of all time. Agatha Christie's seminal And Then There Were None *was published (originally under a different title, which we don't mention these days) back in 1939, and since then over a hundred-million copies have been sold. It's been adapted for stage, screen and radio multiple times, and has spawned a host of imitations. You may wonder what any reference to it is doing in a horror anthology like this, though in truth the original book is probably as close to horror as Ms Christie's novel-writing ever took her, containing numerous extremely dark elements, and I don't just mean the weird nursery rhyme or the figurines being smashed one by one as the murders occur.*

You may recall that the guests on Soldier Island, as it is named in the book, have all been invited there to be punished for crimes they are perceived to have got away with in the past. One of these, for example, Antony Marston, ran over and killed two young children while driving at ridiculous speed, and as a result, dies by drinking whiskey laced with poison. Another, Lawrence Wargrave, a judge, persuaded a gullible jury to find an innocent man guilty of murder, thus sending him to the gallows, and later pays his own debt to society by being tied up and shot through the head from pointblank range.

Screenwriter, Sarah Phelps, when adapting the novel for the BBC version of 2015, expressed surprise at how cold the tone of the novel was, and how violent the deaths.

But the main reason it belongs in a book like this is because the location chosen for And Then There Were None *is based on a real place, Burgh Island – again off the south coast of Devon (Bigbury Bay) – where a real murderer once hid out, the champagne-sozzled party crowd of the 1920s and 1930s always ready to chance the darkness, the wind and the sea-spray with storm-lanterns, as they searched the coves and caves for his ghost.*

But that isn't the only similarity. The thing that really caught Agatha Christie's imagination when she first visited Burgh Island in the 1930s was the hotel there. An Art Deco masterpiece called the Burgh Island Hotel, it still operates in the 21st century, but so famous and exclusive was it in the early days of the 20th that it attracted a very racy set. Noel Coward, Edward and Mrs Simpson, Lord Mountbatten and King Farouk are all said to have stayed there regularly, while during the build-up to D-Day, Winston Churchill took General Eisenhower there, so they could draw their plans in private.

It was this fantastical but remote place, occasionally populated by celebrities, some of whom were rumoured to have led scurrilous lives, that gave Christie the basis for a truly terrifying tale. 'But what about the real story?', you may ask. 'Who was the killer who genuinely lurked on Burgh, and whose reign of terror was so infamous in his day that his evil spirit is still said to dart from one hiding place to the next, both down on the rocky shore and even in the precincts of the Burgh Hotel itself, just waiting to leap out on the unwary?'

His name was Tom Crocker, and he lived in the 14th century. By reputation he was a thoroughly wicked individual. No crime, it is said, was too vicious to be attributed to Crocker and his band of desperadoes. To start with, they were bandits and highwaymen. The Devonshire of the Middle Ages was not the hub of tourism that it is today. It was a bleak, faraway place. The few villagers there scratched a living from difficult ground, the fisher-folk were at the mercy of the Atlantic, and communications in general were very poor, the majority of roads little more than unmade moorland paths.

Crocker and his band stalked all of these, regularly attacking and robbing travellers, and if they resisted, killing them. As their hideout was on Burgh Island, which was approachable only by a sandbar that often was flooded by the sea, they also indulged in smuggling, piracy and wrecking, the latter offence involving the displaying of lights on stormy nights, confusing ship steersmen and thus luring them onto the rocks. Goods were then looted from the wreckage, and any survivors slain where they were washed up.

If Crocker thought the remoteness of the south Devon coast would protect him forever, he was wrong. When England's warrior king, Edward III, learned that many valuable vessels were going down in Bigbury Bay to the benefit of a local robber band, he sent a company of soldiers, who stormed the island. Crocker's band fought back but all were cut down, their leader then secreting himself in one of the many zawns or sea-caves on Burgh. These were searched for days before he was finally located, though rumour had it that he slit several throats before this was done (hence his reputation as a creep-about killer, making him an ideal inspiration for And Then There Were None*).*

When finally captured, he was led shouting and struggling to the nearest coastal outcrop, and hanged on a hastily-erected gibbet, where his body swung for months until the gulls picked it down to the bones. The time-honoured Pilchard Inn occupies this spot now, and, as previously mentioned, is only one of several venues on Burgh Island where Tom Crocker's gruesome pecked-to-pieces ghost is still said to appear.

CHALK AND FLINT
Sarah Singleton

The ruin in the wood appeared only on certain days.

At least, it seemed so. She found it three times.

The wood, a lingering remnant of low-growing oaks on a high spur of the downs, ran up and down and up, across a deep valley on the scarp face overlooking the vale. Despite the underlying chalk, its two diverging paths were boggy in winter, with pockets of sucking mud, which were gold-oak-leaf-patterned at the end of November. Stripes of wild garlic and bluebells in spring, bright protrusions of fungi in the autumn. But only a few acres, all told – an awkward, often sunless patch of land too troublesome to cultivate, the soil interrupted by surprising springs and numerous, deep-bedded sarsen stones: a kind of flinch, a hunched shoulder on the smooth roll of the downs. Despite annual forays by the more adventurous bluebell photographers, and visits from summer dog walkers, it retained an atmosphere of secrecy. So it seemed to her -- sensing the wood's resistance to visitors. From the outside, that hunch of trees was opaque, costive. On the path, the air seemed to tighten as you stepped past the oak pollard at the boundary.

She found the ruin the very first time she entered the wood. This was early spring. On the lower ground the first flush of hawthorn buds brightened the hedgerows but otherwise the land was still bleak, bare and washed out, with gusts of biting wind and acres of mud. Her walk, mapped out in advance, had gone wrong and it was by mischance she found herself, already tired by cold, at the foot of the long holloway leading up the scarp face from the vale into the wood.

It was one of those moments. The hill looked so long and steep, and she was so cold and exhausted, that the urge to cry was almost overwhelming. But she gave herself a talking to. You're just tired, get a grip. All that sort of thing. She started to sing aloud – this often helped. It was one of her walking regulars, *Cold blows the wind tonight, true love…*

The path ran straight up the scarp face, a curved white gutter on the hillside with hawthorn and blackthorn arched over, making a tunnel. Here and there, the odd bead of a berry clung on – sloes and haws, dried and withered by winter. Trickles of water flowed along the wheel ruts. Half way up the slope a robin was singing, high above her head.

Sometimes, on a long walk, energy ebbed and flowed. Reaching the top of the hill, and entering the hem of the unexpected wood, she was no longer tired. Her route home led straight on, and down, but the wood on the left of the path seemed to offer itself – an invitation of low oaks in coats of bright green moss, seeming to bow, rising in an undulating slope to a pinnacle of the hill not quite in sight. Was there a path? Yes, there, a breach in the low bare earth-bank at the edge of the wood, its ditch lined with last year's grey leaves. This breach allowed a walker onto a track of smooth-flattened soil, perhaps an animal path. It wasn't entirely straight, under tree, over knuckles of flint embedded in the ground. The first tips of garlic leaves pierced the surface. The rusty ghosts of last year's ferns still clung on the branches of some of the little oaks: swoop branched, twisting, stumpy – oaks from a picture book, a fairy tale.

The tiny path, incised by hooves of deer, wandered up the hill through the trees. Above the canopy of bare branches, a buzzard called.

The embedded flints began to look like little people – a head, the rise of shoulders, a huddle of them standing together in a group. A green leaf spotted with black was a frog, momentarily, before her right boot. It happened sometimes, this shift, mostly when she had been walking a long time, always when alone. The moss shone; last year's leaves shifted under her feet.

And there it was, on a mound within the wood, a tiny ruin, half tumbled, half standing, four walls and half a roof. Beyond it, trees continued to rise, up and up to the summit of the hill, so the ruin seemed, from a momentary perspective, to be framed by a circle of trees, of wood.

An old gamekeeper's cottage? She had found one before, in a wood closer to home, more ruinous than this, almost entirely gone except for a rectangle of low walls, a buried bath tub and gas cooker, overwhelmed with rhododendrons. Sometimes she spotted the remains of old farm buildings, tiny barns or collapsed animal enclosures, always fascinating and worth a poke around.

She stepped closer. The trees seemed almost to close behind her, barring the way back (she was in that state of mind, suggestible). The walls of the ruin were built of chalk blocks, chequered with squares made up of field flints. The chalk, porous and friable, was crumbling away. The flints were obdurate. A doorstep remained, and a beam across the top, though the door was gone. The single room had a broken floor of sarsen stone and dirt. The remaining one third of a thatched roof pitched towards the earth, a blackened mass of decayed straw and moss, of fallen leaves and dead weeds – but mostly the space inside the walls was open to the sky. An empty window, and at one end opened a large fireplace with a mass of sticks and twigs in a pile on the hearth. The chimney was blocked, no light visible, corked, mostly likely, by a nest, or generations of nests, from which this mass had fallen.

Pushing at the fallen twigs, seemingly bound by weeds and web, her boot encountered something solid. She pushed again, and this heavy object shifted slightly, with a scraping sound, stone against stone. Intrigued (some treasure?) she rootled around and observed it was another flint nodule, a large one, needing two hands to lift. It was pleasingly knobbled, four or five rounded sprouts at the compass points, a smooth hole in the middle like a single eye. The nodule had been sliced along one side, exposing the dark grey, glassy-smooth interior.

What an interesting little person you are, she thought, remembering the huddles of flint beings in the wood. She weighed it in her hand, this lump of flint, turned it around, lifted it to peer one-eyed through the hole. Take it home? No. It was too heavy to carry. Above the old fireplace was a recess in the wall of about the right size. She set it there, like some kind of patron saint.

Beyond the ruin, the cold wind blew. She sat on the doorstep for a time, leaning on the wall. She closed her eyes and stilled her thoughts.

Listen, she thought. Listen.

And an hour passed. Her phone jumped in her pocket, like a small animal. Sixteen texts and three voice mails. Seeing them, the flare of angry light in the darkening wood, her throat, heart, guts squeezed into one long tangle. She struggled to her feet. How long would it take to walk home? But it didn't actually take long, indeed not long enough. The path seemed to unroll in front of her. There it was, her home, the warm golden eye of the cottage where she lived. Lower Kennet Cottage, standing beyond the stone bridge, beneath which the chalk river flowed. The perfect rural residence, like something from one of those country magazines she used to read so avidly. Her home, Nick's home, like, indeed, something from a fairy tale.

'You're Janice,' he said, with a smile that, yes, made her weak at the knees. He was out of her league, she saw instantly, with a sinking of the heart and a quiver of insecurity.

They first met in a Costa franchise at a motorway service station, half way between Leicester and Marlborough. This was not a romantic destination they joked then, and later. A November day of squally rain, a miserable drive to the meeting, the tables crowded with damp, miserable travellers. But a first meeting had to be somewhere accessible and public.

Internet dating is a numbers game, Janice had been informed by her best friend Emma. And Janice knew her numbers – she was a six out of ten on a good day. In the mirror she saw someone short but a little heavy-set, with pale, almost waxy skin, a miserly portion of lustreless, brown hair, and eyes a touch too closely set together. Now some people overcome mediocre looks with an illuminating smile, but Janice could see her smile was slightly lopsided, making her lips thinner and her eyes almost disappear. So on her dating profile pictures, she didn't smile. Instead, she stared out with a calm, almost indifferent expression. Janice did not use any kind of filter or choose a flattering angle: she imagined seeing the flash of disappointment in a potential suitor's eyes if she turned out to be even less attractive in real life than photographs proposed. No – best be up front about the quality of the goods on offer.

Internet dating is a numbers game: Janice specified potential partners should live within a twenty-mile radius of Oadby. Nick, however, ignored her boundary. He lived over a hundred miles away in Wiltshire. But there was something about her, he messaged, some quality of kindness and gentleness evident in her profile that caught his attention.

Janice turned up half an hour early, afraid of traffic and of keeping him waiting. Nick arrived exactly on time. He spotted her across the noisy tables and, with a smile, made his way through the crowds, keeping his gaze on her all the while, till there he was beside her, still smiling, holding out his arms as though he would scoop her up and embrace her, hold her to him, gather her up. But Janice only held out her hand to shake, overwhelmed and heart-aching.

She had assumed Nick's photos had overplayed his looks but in fact he had undersold himself. His number was eight, maybe eight-and-a-half: he was taller than she expected, lean and wide shouldered, with a head of energetic dark hair and a handsome angular face. Yes, out of her league by a country mile.

It was a devastating realisation. They'd been messaging for a couple of weeks and she had enjoyed it, allowing herself the fantasy of a connection, a romance. Emma had warned her that if she was contacted by someone with potential, a meeting In Real Life had to come soon, to test the seriousness of the offer – to check the imagination before it ran too far ahead. Four was the number this time: four weeks.

Janice scanned Nick's face for clues of disappointment but

his smile did not waver. After the handshake, he went to fetch them both coffees. In the queue he kept glancing over, still smiling. He looked so pleased. In fact, he seemed delighted. When he returned with the drinks, Nick took off his thick woolly jumper and for one eternal moment his dark pink tee shirt was pulled up, revealing a stretch of smooth, taut stomach with a narrow wedge of hair that draw a dark line from the top of his jeans to his belly button. With a laugh, he yanked the shirt down again but inside, Janice seemed to deliquesce. It was extraordinary, the contradictions in these overwhelming feelings: desire and despair, hope and the dread. She waited for him to make a polite excuse and leave, for the glance at his phone, for the call that took him, gratefully, far from this encounter.

They exchanged preliminary pleasantries about their journeys and all the while Janice's stomach seemed to somersault. She could hardly keep a tremor from her voice, unbalanced and on the back foot, intimidated by just how attractive he was. Then he put his elbows on the table, leaned slightly towards her, and said:

'So. Tell me something about yourself I don't know.' He held her, in his sunny, intense gaze, the smile softened, but still on his face.

'Oh. I don't know – I mean, what can I say?' What an idiot. What a useless fool.

'What about your family? Tell me about them.'

'Well, there's not all that much to say. I'm an only child. My Dad's a teacher, like me. My parents split up ten years ago, when I went to university. He's remarried now. He moved to France with her, to Brittany. She's okay I suppose. I go over and see them occasionally. And my mum ...' she took a little gulping breath and looked at the surface of the table. 'My mum died last year. Quite suddenly really – she had cancer.'

She looked at Nick again, waiting for him to respond with an awkward but necessary phrase of sympathy, for him to change the subject, or to use her admission of bereavement as a take-off point for a speech about a loss of his own. She was also afraid it might put him off, just how alone she was, bereft of an ordinary family, that he would back away. But he did not do any of these things. Instead, he seemed to study her face with enormous care, and then he said:

'That must have been a terrible shock. I am so sorry. Tell me what that was like for you – I mean, as much as you feel comfortable sharing. I appreciate it must still be very raw, to lose your mother like that.'

Janice's mouth opened. The noise and bustle and fug of the services seemed to recede into the distance. When had anyone ever spoken to her like this? Even Emma, who for years had unloaded every minor worry and trouble on Janice in long, exhausting monologues, had urged Janice to 'buck up' and 'dump the self-pity' as soon as her mother's funeral was over.

They spent three hours in the café. Janice talked and Nick listened. Whenever she tried to stop, afraid she was boring him, anxious she was being selfish, he urged her and prompted her to continue.

And he listened.

He focused his attention on what she was saying. He asked her questions, wanting to understand better.

It was astonishing, the relief she felt, the healing power of his listening. He did not try to advise her or offer solutions, nor did he offer parallel experiences of his own. Never, in her whole life, had Janice experienced this kind of interest and attention. It was as though the long, bitter thorns of loss were drawn from her breast, as though the poison was released from the wounds.

Afterwards, driving north along the motorway she was elated and ashamed all at once. How could she have talked about herself so much? How bored he must have been! She did not expect ever to hear from him again. And in some way, this did not matter too much. Just the experience was something she would never forget.

But he did call again. When she apologised for talking too much, he laughed good naturedly and told her not to worry, it was fine, and there would be plenty of time for him to talk about himself in the weeks and months to come, don't you worry.

Janice was happy. She had never been so happy, so richly alive. She could not believe what was happening, that this could be real. He was so attentive, texting or calling every day. He came to stay for weekends in Oadby, and they went on adventures to Wales and Devon. He sent white roses to her school, and when she was sick in January, a delivery of artisan soup and bread. They did not have sex for three long months, him wanting to be sure, he said tenderly, that she was sure. By the time this happened, in a boutique hotel on the Cornish coast, she was so burnt up and tortured with longing that every touch, every caress, was such a violent pleasure she felt he had branded himself upon her forever.

After nine months, he proposed. When she finally called her father, and told him over the Internet, he was delighted to see her so happy but wondered aloud, was this all a bit fast? How well did she know him, really, wasn't he a bit too good to be true? But the question glanced off, impelled as she was by the intensity of a first consuming passion, by feelings that were carrying her along with all the heat and sparks and impetuous fury of a runaway steam train. She had never felt like this before; shouldn't she follow her heart, she said. And it irritated her too, coming from the father who had moved abroad with his new wife, leaving her alone.

In December Nick and Janice were married. She gave up her teaching job, left her rented flat, and moved into Nick's cottage on the Marlborough Downs. He had chickens and a vegetable garden. Janice was very happy for a while, though looking back, the signs had always been there, even the first time they met.

It had seemed a dream come true.

Until it was not.

It was September when Janice found the ruin for the second time. She went back to the wood often, but the ruin had eluded her. She trailed up and down the holloway looking for the animal track that had invited her into the wood, but spring and summer brought an exuberance of growth, hiding the way. Soon after that first discovery, bluebells poured through the wood, and perfumed stripes of wild garlic. The wood was about an hour's walk from home now she knew the best way, so Janice walked there every week, sometimes more. In early May she heard a cuckoo. Sometimes she spotted roe deer bounding away. On one side of one track through the wood was a fallen tree stump, as tall as she was and twice as wide, rotting and enveloped in soil. Fancifully she called this the old moss woman, for her shawl of velvet moss and emerald crown of grass.

Janice trailed back and forth through the wood looking for the ruin. She searched her paper Ordinance Survey map and studied older maps online, but none gave any hint about the possibly-gamekeeper's cottage. She pored over satellite images on Google Earth, but the photographs had been taken in summer and leaves obscured the woodland floor. It seemed odd she could not find the place in a wood that covered maybe ten acres but those ten acres covered a peculiarly wrinkled edge of the downs, a twisted fold of the chalk with plunging slopes and old dry valleys, parts of which were inaccessible unless approached in precisely the right way and from a particular direction. And the wood was nominally private – so several imperious, if slightly listing, signs declared – except for bridleways along two sides. The mooted privacy made Janice cautious of too much exploring, though she did risk it from time to time, usually during the week when the dog walkers and ramblers were few and far between.

She had moved to Wiltshire a month before the wedding. Only Emma knew much about the blossoming romance. She came down from Leicester for the marriage. Janice's father and his wife travelled over from France, meeting Nick for the first time. She invited three remote cousins, who did not attend. It was a winter wedding in the village church: frost on the ground, white roses and ivy in her bouquet. Inside the church, sunlight beamed through stained glass windows depicting lurid fourteenth century images of demons and monsters, cavorting in blue and blood-red in the palaces of hell. But in the window over the altar, Jesus hung meek and benign on his cross, celebrated by angels, surrounded by lilies and roses. The congregation sang 'All Things Bright and Beautiful', breath clouding in the chilly air, and it seemed to Janice that the moment was so entirely perfect it could not be real. Nick's hot hand warmed hers as they walked back down the aisle, past his silent parents, his lively crowd of friends, past Emma and her boyfriend, her father and his wife, and out, into the sparkling graveyard and their new married life.

When she resigned from her job to move to Wiltshire, Nick suggested that she take a year out to concentrate on her ambition to be an illustrator. He could afford to keep them both for a while, he said. When she demurred, reluctant to be a burden or to lose her independence, he reminded her how exhausting she found her job, and how frustrated she felt not to have the time or energy to pursue her dream.

'Just for a year,' he said. 'Give yourself permission. Why don't you? If you don't like it, if it doesn't work out, apply for another teaching post.'

So she agreed – gratefully. He was right of course. Just twelve months to see if she could do it, a chance to spread her creative wings. Every month he deposited what he called an allowance into her bank account. It wasn't much, but what did she need money for, here? And she did all the housework and gardening, administered the home, which was only fair if Nick was supporting her, and he worked long, long hours as a management consultant for companies with contracts in the National Health Service, a role that took him right across the country.

It was hard to start with, making a routine of work from home. Nick gave her a little room on the ground floor at the back of the cottage to be her studio. He had the cottage set up when she moved in and was not keen to let her change anything, but this tiny studio was the one space she had free rein to adorn as she pleased. She put her books in the little bookcase, and strung wires under the ceiling from which hung images and prints that inspired. She was a talented draughtswoman, with an eye for detail. Her illustrations tended to the miniature and the surreal – intricate drawings of tiny scenes. She was inspired by Beatrix Potter and Sean Tan. Nick had taken a deep interest: he helped her draw up a plan for her year in art, with goals and targets. He had ideas for her success. He was proud of her talent.

Still, it was hard to start with. The initial excitement faded. The cottage was silent for ten hours a day, sometimes more. The novelty of her isolation soon wore off. Nick had welcomed her into his delightful circle of rambunctious friends, a whole readymade social scene of warm, interesting people, but they all had jobs to go to during the day and, too, she was a little shy of them, these good-looking, glossily well off, confident folk, of a different social tribe to hers.

A routine took shape. Janice worked in the morning from seven, when Nick left, till one, when she had lunch. Then she went for a walk. At first these were half-hour strolls, along the length of the village and back. After a couple of weeks she bought the OS map and slowly discovered and explored the network of green lanes and bridleways, footpaths and byways, that spread from the village in the river valley up and over the Marlborough Downs.

What a falling in love it was, this discovery of a landscape, and the changes it underwent week by week, as spring overcame the winter, as the lanes and hedgerows unfurled their coats of green, as the daylight stretched into the evening. Her walks grew longer. The landscape became known, step by step, piece by piece.

She researched the landscape and made notes and maps and drawings in a special sketch book she carried with her: *an expansive rolling plateau of cretaceous chalk, sparsely populated, sweeping views. Isolated deposits of clay and areas of field flint. Numerous dry valleys. Sarsen stones, which are the post-glacial remains of silicified sandstone, lie in the valleys of Piggledene and Fyfield. Ancient drove roads, chalk-cut white horses, precious chalk stream, prehistoric monuments.*

Since early March, when she first saw the ruin in the wood, Janice had collected flint nodules. They were scattered all over the downland fields and lanes, so she chose carefully. Some were shaped like fingers or bones. She found a round one the size of a dumpling that seemed to be hollow inside. She could hear a faint rattling when she shook it. Mostly, she picked up the ones that looked little people. They stood on the long shelf above her drawing desk, regarding her as she worked. She drew them again and again, trying to catch something of their unique shapes, their personalities. Sometimes she caught herself and laughed: my friends are stones. Stones and lanes. Her Oadby life seemed far away. Emma – who had seemed almost put out by how handsome Nick was, how picturesque the wedding – had not maintained contact.

My friends are stones, she wrote, under a sketch in her notebook.

But as spring progressed, things began to change. When Janice started her walks of discovery, Nick insisted she texted him her route and then sent another text when she was safely home. He was worried for her safety, a young woman walking alone. This seemed sensible.

He usually rang her once during the day and at first this seemed a warming sign of his devotion but when she realised how upset he got when she missed his call for any reason, this feeling cooled. She had lived so much alone, and so independently, that his management chafed. When she protested, arguments started for the first time. In fact, it would be wrong to describe them as arguments because Janice did not argue: Nick argued. Whatever measured assertion she made, he responded with forceful persuasion. She didn't understand, he only wanted her to be safe, he was looking out for her, he understood her, didn't she realise how hard it was for him, with his cold parents who effectively abandoned him, he had trust issues, and he needed her to be consistent.

Any conflict with Nick made her feel physically ill. Eventually she would surrender and apologise, and then he would apologise too and tell her how much he loved and needed her. There would be cuddles, and sex.

Relationships were hard work, Janice told herself. They still didn't know each other that well. This was still a breaking-in period; conflicts should be expected. When Janice complied, Nick calmed down.

The months passed. In summer they travelled to Berlin for a week, and the strife of the spring seemed to melt away. Combine harvesters worked on the golden fields covering the downs, and the nights drew in. One of Nick's friends organised a dinner party on the night of the autumn equinox. It was unseasonably warm so they ate at a table under the old apple trees in the orchard at the back of their house, two villages away. Solar powered lights, hanging from the trees, came on as the light faded. A tawny owl hooted from the other side of the stream, which ran through the long garden. Eight of them in attendance: an excellent meal of Wiltshire beef, and afterwards measures of sloe gin, from a distillery near Swindon.

Janice was quiet in the gathering, even after a few drinks. But she enjoyed it – the food was good and Nick was boasting about the progress of her portfolio of illustrations. They had a collective moan about Brexit (someone's Polish cleaner had returned home), and then began talking about plans for a new housing development on the edge of Marlborough, which divided opinion. Nick slipped his hand under the table to take hers. He was deep into the debate but glanced at her every now and then, so she knew she had not slipped from his thoughts.

Later, the gathering split up. Janice joined the women inside the kitchen, where they made hot chocolate. The men continued the discussion outside. Janice was nervous to be alone with them – the other three women had all known each other for a long time. They had high level jobs in corporate communications and software consultancy, drove hybrid four by fours and possessed a kind of confident glamour, like a varnish. But they were friendly to Janice, and curious. They kept telling her what a great catch Nick was, how lucky she was, *how good-looking* he was, which they said so often (it seemed) that Janice was convinced the subtext of the repetition was *compared to you Janice.*

But maybe she was paranoid. Something had changed since she had taken up these long walks. She had not lost weight but her shape had altered: she was fitter and stronger. The exercise and fresh air had brightened her skin too, banished the waxy look. In fact one of the women, Suzanne, made a joke about her being pregnant, having that glow.

They all looked at her closely then but Janice laughed it off.

'Oh no, no,' she said, blushing.

When the other two went outside with hot drinks for the men, Janice was left alone with Suzanne. She smiled kindly at Janice, with a close look, and said:

'I think Nick would love to have children. He always said so. I hope it happens for you. He's a great guy. You're very lucky. And him keeping you financially too!'

Janice blushed again, tongue-tied. She had detected a sharp edge to that final comment. But she had to ask:

'Suzanne – I wonder – you know Nick well?'

'Oh yes. I've known him for years and years.' She was almost proprietorial.

'Well, it's just. He can be controlling sometimes. I mean, quite controlling, I wondered ...'

'Controlling? What do you mean?' She shook her head, with its curtains of expensively dyed blonde hair, and glanced away from Janice. 'Nick, oh no, he's terrific,' she continued. 'He's been such a good friend to me, to all of us.' She looked back at Janice with a peculiarly icy stare which Janice read as *he's my friend, friends don't say bad things about each other, I'm a good person, I am not talking about Nick with you.*

And Janice realised that Suzanne was solely Nick's friend, not hers, and could never be turned to, for help.

'Sure he is,' Janice said weakly. 'Of course you're right. I know it's just that he cares. He worries, you see, when I go out walking on my own.'

'I'm not surprised,' Suzanne said. 'I wouldn't go walking on my own. It's not safe!'

Dispirited, Janice made an excuse and scooted to the downstairs toilet. She stayed where she was, sitting on the toilet for several more minutes, pressing her face into her hands. The conversation with Suzanne had her all tightly wound. But why? What was she afraid of? It was not as though Nick had done anything dreadful. He cared about her and he was a bit bossy. She pulled the flush and slowly washed her hands.

The kitchen was empty but one cup of hot chocolate waited for her on the table. As Janice picked it up, she could hear the voices of Suzanne and the others outside the back door.

'Can you imagine?' Suzanne's voice. 'All those glamorous girlfriends and then he marries that plain little virgin!'

Laughter followed, a peculiar sound like glass breaking into sharp pieces.

'Oh come on Suze, don't be mean. She's a sweetheart. A surprising choice for Nick, sure. Aren't you just a teensy bit jealous?'

'Oh no. I got over Nick a long time ago. I'm very happy with James, thank you very much!' More laughter.

Janice's hand trembled. She took two, three deep breaths then she scraped a chair on the tiled floor to make a noise so they should know she was on her way. The laughter stopped and when Janice stepped out the back door, Suzanne met her with an almost convincing smile.

It was midnight when Janice and Nick got home. By then, Janice had worked up a head of fury and frustration. On the outside, she was polite and calm but inside, anger burned. During the ten-minute drive, he continued the discussion about the housing development, using Janice as a silent audience while he thought aloud. He was not in a good mood either. Janice wanted to speak, had to speak, but she did not know how and where to start. The bottled up rage made her feel nauseous. She could not even look at him.

Eventually, as they stepped into the cottage, he noticed.

'What's up?' He sounded irritated.

Janice took a deep breath. She wanted to tell him, but to do so required a huge effort – breaking down a peculiar internal barrier.

'What? Tell me.'

She took another tense breath then forced herself to say it.

'What did you tell them about me? Did you tell Suzanne I was a virgin?'

A succession of emotions seemed to ripple swiftly over Nick's face, one after another.

'What are you talking about?'

'I heard her Nick. She and the others – having a laugh about me being a *plain little virgin*.'

'Of course I didn't. And if I did, so what? I can remember telling James you were innocent. I mean, that was a compliment. I was,' he gave a theatrical smile, 'showing you off.'

'And you telling James means they have all talked about it. Something so personal and private! Oh Nick, how could you?' The anger was melting into tears now, an overwhelming sense of shame at the violation of her most private self. But Nick's tone switched to attack.

'For crying out loud, it's no big deal. Why are you making such a fuss?' The volume of his voice had risen. 'Take no notice of Suzanne, she's a complete slut. She's jealous of you, that's all. You don't make her look good.'

'Nick, did you used to go out with her?'

'A long time ago. Years ago. What of it? She's with someone else now. It's ancient history.'

'I wish you hadn't told them. It wasn't right.'

'How dare you tell me what to do, and what I can and can't say to my own friends? You're trying to control me! What's wrong with you?' The volume went up again. He was actually shouting now. His eyes narrowed, his face went red. His head seemed to drop into his shoulders and he jabbed his finger at Janice. 'You were an embarrassment tonight, anyway. I don't know why you are having a go at me. You hardly said a word all evening. Why can't you speak up? Why didn't you join in? Haven't you got any ideas in your head? Didn't you ever learn any social skills, like normal people?'

The rant went on. Janice did not move, or respond. He had never spoken to her like this before. It took all the strength she had to stand up straight and hold onto herself. After a while, she could make no sense of the tirade, only weathered the onslaught of the voice, a voice like a bludgeon that hit her again and again. Why couldn't she say, 'I don't want to be with a man who would call a woman a slut'? Why didn't she defend herself against these damaging accusations? Why couldn't she fight back?

Because he was right of course. Because he was not saying anything she had not thought about herself, because the nasty, weak voice in her head told her yes, yes, you know this is true, all of it, you deserve it. She stood there, mute, accepting the onslaught.

In the end he stopped and Janice burst into tears, her body shaking. Then he put his arms around her and gave a sort of apology, in a voice thick with victory, and said he still loved her, he alone, and he took her to bed. She lay down and curled up, knees to chest, her back to him, unable to sleep, tense and stricken, tears still leaking from her eyes. After a time, she drifted into shallow dreams in which Nick was shouting at her still and she was begging him to stop. Then she sat up, still mostly asleep, and reached out to him, but it seemed his head on the pillow was a pile of ash.

In the morning, Nick was cheerful, behaving as if nothing had happened. It was Saturday but he had work to do. He brought her coffee in bed, kissed her on the forehead, and said goodbye. He had gone by eight.

When she had tidied the kitchen, made the bed and fed the chickens, Janice picked up her notebook and map, her sandwiches and flask, and headed outside.

For the first hour of walking, her head ached, mind thick with the porridge of insults and invective. As she moved into the second hour, striding up the white path, it gradually ebbed away. The voice was still present, but at a distance, easier to ignore. Up on the high downs, vast fields spread away, and it seemed she was on the roof of the world. The sky, almost purely blue, arched over her head. The hedgerow along one side of the lane glistened with red rosehips and glossy hawthorn berries. With no particular route in mind, her feet carried her along the scarp face overlooking the Pewsey Vale, down, and up, and then along the holloway to the wood: the beloved wood.

On the day of the equinox, the leaves were still green. A recent spell of rain had given the foliage a lustre that it had lost in the dry, overcast August weeks. Berries everywhere. Brambles springing over the lane, jewelled with blackberries in various stages of ripeness: pale green, soft pink, red, ink black. To the left, over the low wood bank, she glimpsed movement through the low trees -- a deer perhaps --then the gaping holes and heaps of chalky soil dug out of a complex badgers' sett. Janice's mood lifted further. From the badgers' refuse pile she picked up a flint, shaped a little like a turtle's shell, with a singular knobble, like a head.

Janice headed deeper into the wood and saluted the moss woman, whose green-grass hair had faded to a dry bleached-yellow, and there, impossibly, off to the right through a gap in the trees, hazy with distance, was the clearing, the mound, and the old ruin.

How could that be?

Had the vegetation died back just enough to make it visible again? How could she have missed it, again and again?

Janice moved forward and back, on the spot, altering her line of sight. It *was* hard to see. The slightest change of perspective made the old walls invisible and the ruin merge into the wood. The colours blended and faded into their surroundings unless you were looking along this specific line. Pleasingly odd, this magical subterfuge.

She strode towards it, leaving the bridleway, trotting between clumps of bramble and bracken. The ruin was further away than she had first thought, and she was out of breath, sweating but elated, when she reached it.

The ruin? Not quite as she had remembered though that had been six long months ago. Not so much a gamekeeper's cottage as … a tiny chapel? A hermitage perhaps, one of those eighteenth century follies, chalk block chequered with squares of field flint, and a single band of red brick near the middle. The thatched roof was whole and complete and in the doorway was a stout wooden door with black iron hinges. This was not the same place, evidently. And yet.

Impossibly, it was the same place. She knew it.

Janice got her breath back as she stared and stared at the shrine. The light had changed. A cloud covered the sun creating an overcast kind of twilight, as though a thunderstorm was approaching. She felt uneasy, sensing a presence here. Was someone else inside the building? She wanted to look, but was nervous. That first time, the place had been deserted, open to the sky and the moving air, utterly without presence. Something had changed.

She glanced over her shoulder, sensing movement behind her, in the trees. The wind rose and fell. The grass murmured around her feet.

In her hand, the turtle shaped flint was warm. Janice had forgotten she was carrying it. She lifted it up. What's going on, she thought, directing her enquiry to the flint nodule. Are you with me, or against me? The flint's patchy chalk-white patina glimmered in the low light. Go inside, it seemed to say. What have you got to lose?

'Okay,' she said out loud. Her voice echoed off the trees.

The oak door yielded easily, revealing a small, shadowed interior. The single window was filled with green stained glass so thick she could hardly see outside. The wide fireplace had been cleared of twigs. A light hung on a chair from the centre of the roof, a candle in a prism of glass. Above the fireplace, the flint, and the niche she had placed it in, were five times the size they had been. The flint's rudimentary stumps had grown and extended, making a more obvious humanoid shape, though one with an unsettling kind of monstrosity about it.

Staring at the little flint god, feeling its smaller brother in her hand seem to wriggle, Janice's heart skipped a beat. The candle above her head flickered.

She backed away till her back pressed against the opposite wall, then lowered herself to the ground. Shadows danced over the walls. Janice stared at the little god and emptied her mind, trying to hear what it was saying, what it wanted heard.

Hard to say how long this lasted, the listening. Her head filled with darkness. The shadows left the walls and swarmed towards her, suggestive smoky shapes: badgers and foxes, creeping animals prickled like hedgehogs with odd human faces, then older beasts, grey wolves, bristled pigs with tusks, and a tall human figure with cleft hooves for hands and the upright horns of a roe deer on its head. They emanated, all of them, from the flint god, were aspects of it – this much she understood. They roamed the forests of her mind, the tunnels and caverns of her thoughts.

And then, in a moment, they were gone.

It was all over. She got back to her feet, stiff and cold, and left the shrine, gripping the turtle-shaped flint in her hand.

Back on the path, her phone jumped. It was seven o'clock, twilight filling the wood. Messages and texts. Dozens and dozens – a river of anger that flowed down and down the screen as she scrolled. Where was she? Where was she? Where was she?

Janice did not go out walking on her own after that. Nick had nearly called the police this time, he told her, sure she had been abducted. He was worried sick. His worry – that she had been murdered – or perhaps, Janice privately wondered, that she had left him after their row the previous day – relieved itself in a second epic verbal assault.

It was not safe. She could have been killed. He had no way of finding her. Finally, when he had undermined her enough to break her resolve and reduce her to tears, he said they would walk together at the weekends when he was not working. He put his arms around her: sorry, soothing, comforting. It was because he loved her, because he was afraid, because she didn't understand the dangers.

Once Janice had surrendered the solo walks, equilibrium was restored. She did not raise the issue of his long working hours and threw herself instead into creations for her illustration portfolio. When he was at work, at least, she could relax.

Alongside the illustrations, which she shared with Nick, she added to her second, secret book more research and drawings to the field notes she had written during her solo walking days.

Flint, she wrote, *there appears to be some uncertainty about exactly how it forms in chalk. Flint is a form of quartz, made of silica. One theory is that holes bored by undersea crustaceans and molluscs filled with a gelatinous material from once living things that became silicified in the chalk over millions of years ... Flint is so hard it made the blades and scrapers and arrowheads used in the Stone Age.*

The year tipped into the dark. Janice continued to draw, inspired by the late autumn plants, the thorny figures she spied in the naked hedges. She did sketches of the summer's flowers and herbs. In November, strings of berries, blood-red witch's beads, hung the hedge at the back of the garden. She scribbled in her book:

Black bryony – tamus communis – also known as black-eye root, only native member of the yam family, twisting climber with heart-shaped leaves and shiny red berries. All parts of the plant are toxic. Berries irritant, emetic.

Beyond the window, a cold wind blew over the hill rising to the downs. The chalk stream flooded and spilled over the garden. Just before Christmas, Nick and Janice attended another dinner party with his friends where Nick announced to them all that Janice was pregnant. A toast was raised and they all seemed so pleased for them. On icy mornings before dawn, Janice hunched over the toilet, throwing up, her knees pressing on the achingly cold stone floor.

On Christmas Eve, alone in the house, she called her father over the internet and told him the news about the pregnancy.

He was so far away. He looked strange and familiar at the same time, making her stomach clench with longing. When he congratulated her, it was all Janice could do to stop herself bursting into tears.

'Are you okay love? You look, I don't know. You don't look very happy.'

'I'm fine Dad. Fine, all things considered. Just nausea, you know? And it's winter. And I'm a bit lonely. It's so dark, and Nick's working so hard.'

'Haven't you made any new friends? You must know some people there by now.'

He looked nonplussed.

'Oh. No. Not really. I've been busy too.' She did not want to tell him how resistant Nick was to her making friends. It was hard to explain how he did it, really. He never told her she could not have friends but working from home, she did not meet anyone. If she tried to go out in the evening – to a yoga class or a college course – Nick talked her round, explaining how much he needed her to be with him when he was home, he had not seen her all day, and so on. It was always easier to submit.

'You could come here,' her dad said. 'Come and stay.'

'Maybe after Christmas,' she said. The effort it would take seemed insurmountable. When the call cut off, it was as though a thread had snapped in the air and then the silence in the house seemed more intense than ever.

She was not stupid. In her more lucid moments, she knew what was going on, that Nick's behaviour was unacceptable, that she should leave. But something held her, like an enchantment. He was the first man to have aroused in her such intense physical passion and it held her like a drug, feverish and compelling. Even during those times when he was telling her how useless she was, or when she was an irritation to him, she could not escape this terrible, craven longing, as though she would crawl over the ground to him and lie at his feet, if only he would touch her, put his hands and mouth on her face, her neck, her body. Something essentially animal about it, this oppressive addiction and her horrible surrender.

And often he would be sweet, and funny and kind and vulnerable; making her breakfast in bed, plumping her pillows, wanting to take care of her, the mother of his future child, the love of his life, and the memory of his shouting faded, and she would tell herself yes, this is the real Nick, the one I love. He would promise to be better. She would hope and hope that True Nick would remain and life would be good and the relationship would be all the wonderful things it had been and could be and sometimes was: she, Nick and their little one in the country cottage on the downs.

They had a quiet Christmas together. Nick was in good spirits and had a couple of days off work. They even went to the pub in the afternoon, and on Boxing Day went for a long walk. Then January set in, and dreary weeks of rain. The nausea passed but Janice was often too tired to get out of bed. She wondered if this was even related to the pregnancy or was something else, a decline of the spirit, an exhaustion of the mind. She would force herself to get up and dressed. It was too cold to work in the little studio so she sat at the kitchen table near the stove, a blanket over her shoulders, dreaming about her midsummer-due baby, about this being evolving inside her. Time stretched: centuries filled a single day, eons extended over a week.

The first flush of green returned to the hawthorns. Spikes of wild garlic emerged from the soil under the bare ash tree in the garden. One morning, when Nick had left for work and Janice was still in her pyjamas, she heard the crunch of the gravel on the drive. Looking out the window, she saw Suzanne stepping down from the silver Lexus. She glanced around then headed for the front door.

Janice felt a flood of panic. She was not dressed. What did Suzanne want?

'Nick's not here. He's at work.' Janice kept the door mostly closed, showing only her face.

'I know. That's why I ... I mean, I wanted to see you.'

'Me?' Nothing about this encounter made sense. Suzanne waited, her golden tresses extending on the wind, a modern-day Botticelli painting come to life.

'Can I come in?'

'Yes. Sure. Come in. I'm sorry, I haven't dressed yet.' Aware of herself, bare-faced, un-showered, un-brushed, Janice backed away from the door and gestured to the kitchen. 'Sit down. I'll be right with you.'

Janice hurriedly dressed. Her feelings about Suzanne were complex: hostility, resentment, and yes, jealousy too, towards this ex of Nick's, this ex who had described her as the 'plain virgin' with that broken glass laugh. Painful images of Nick and Suzanne having sex rose unbidden in Janice's imagination. Ridiculous of course, she scolded herself. Of course he has a past.

Suzanne had taken off her coat and hung it on the back of a chair. She had put the kettle on, and was walking around the kitchen picking things up and putting them down again. She used to come here, with Nick, before he met me, Janice thought.

'So, how can I help?' Janice said. She took over the coffee making and the two women faced each other, sitting either side of the table. They made awkward small talk at first – about the pregnancy, about Suzanne's work. Then an almost imperceptible tremor crossed Suzanne's face.

'I've been wanting to talk to you for a while,' she said. 'But I couldn't bring myself to. But I have to.'

'I see.' Janice heard the iciness in her own voice, though inside she was boiling over with emotion, a peculiar combination of heat and fear.

Suzanne gulped:

'I've been seeing Nick. Seeing – I mean sleeping with Nick of course.' Now she had begun, the words poured out. 'And I've found out, he's been cheating on me. I mean, not with you, I knew about you, but with other women. When he's away working, well he says he's working, and sometimes he is. He's been picking women up in bars and hotels when he's away. You know what he's like, how he makes you feel, like you're the only person in the world. He seems to listen, but he isn't really. He is looking for weaknesses he can use. It's what he does. So I knew about you but I didn't know about the others, he's been lying to me this whole time, and I'm worried James has found out, he never trusted Nick very much, he'd got some real stories to tell about him, but I loved Nick, I didn't believe him, didn't want to believe him, but I know it's all true now.'

The monologue went on a long time, mostly repeating the same things again and again. Janice did not speak or move. It was as though she were turning to stone, rigid and cold, and Suzanne was far away, talking talking talking, though her tears were spilling, over those perfect mascara-ed eyelashes and the porcelain curves of her cheekbones.

Finally the speech wound down and stopped. Suzanne glanced up at Janice, as though she were surprised she was there at all.

'How do you know about these other women?' Janice said.

'His phone. He left it in my car. I learnt his password years ago, and he's never changed it. Careless really, for a man like him. Messages, pictures, the lot. I took screenshots. Look.'

Suzanne handed her mobile over. Janice glanced at the contents then handed it back. She did not say anything. The two of them were silent for a while. Suzanne took out a tissue and wiped her face. Finally Janice said, with steel in her voice:

'I have one question, Suzanne. Why was it cheating when he was with those other women, but not cheating when he was with me?'

Suzanne blinked rapidly. 'I ... I don't know. I mean, because I knew about you. It was different.'

'Different? How?'

'I thought I was special.'

'You thought I was the plain wife and you were the beloved courtesan. But you've discovered instead you were just one of a long list of extra-marital lays.'

Suzanne flinched and a fresh flood of tears filled her eyes.

'I deserve that, obviously,' she said. 'But yes, you're right. That's it.'

'Why exactly are you telling me?' Janice said. 'To get back at Nick presumably. Not for my benefit. I mean, you evidently don't care about me. You don't care about me being cheated on.'

Suzanne rallied a little. She wiped her eyes again. 'Yes. What are you going to do?'

Janice paused.

'I don't know yet. I need to think. I have one thing to ask you, and you owe me that much. Keep all this to yourself, for now. Don't go to Nick about it. Let me work this out.'

Suzanne, whose face was now all red and melting, looked intently at Janice. 'You're a cool customer,' she said. 'I don't know how I expected you to react, but it wasn't this.'

As soon as Suzanne had gone, Janice dropped to the ground as though her bones had turned to water.

The world capsized.

It seemed that a huge glass sphere inside her body had imploded into a multitude of tiny fragments. She had felt it happen, that breakage, in the moment she saw the images on the mobile phone. A cataclysm; a falling apart.

Despite everything – Nick's irritation and bullying and rages – she had never doubted his faithfulness. That had bound her to him on some essential level.

It did not seem possible. She had an instinctive belief in her own body – that its singular and overwhelming desire for Nick had been reciprocated. This was not an intellectual idea, nor a romantic fancy, but a kind of fixed signature written on her bones and flesh, in the way every cell in her body seemed to turn to him, like a compass to the north.

And she had been wrong – wrong to the root of her – wrong to have felt that this was the same for him too.

It was agony, her body seeming to rip apart, to be pulled to pieces. She could not survive this pain. Nothing could ever be the same again.

At last, Janice picked herself up from the ground. She put her boots on and headed out into the cold air, out along the lanes and over the fields. She walked for hours and miles, crunching over frosted mud and silver fields, until on a roundabout route, exhausted and distraught, she found herself at the wood.

Cold blows the wind tonight true love, and gently drops the rain.
I never had but one sweet heart, in greenwood he is lain.

Her old walking song kept repeating itself over and over in her mind. She climbed the hill in time to the rhythm.

In greenwood he is lain ...

The old moss woman stepped out from the side of the lane and stood in front of her. Still in threadbare wintery apparel, she was all rotten wood bones beneath the lush moss cloak. Her hair was long and white, bedraggled strands of last year's grass around a face of dark, yawning gaps and hollows, which might once have frightened Janice. The moss woman moved slowly, shoulders hunched, her feet the broken, knotted roots of trees, her hand, reaching out, a warped barky mass of twig. When she opened her mouth to speak, wet earth fell from her lips. The sound was rough, like a rook's call, but words were hidden in the sounds.

'Come with me,' the moss woman said. 'Back into the old wood.'

Janice took the offered hand and the knotty fingers closed over her own. The moss woman shuffled forward, leading her into away from the path and through the trees.

It seemed a long walk to the shrine – through sunshine and bluebells, then into deep snow, where trees glittered with ice. Soon Janice saw yellow leaves on birch trees, the gold of autumnal oaks. The moss woman stopped, untied a string of crimson berries from a bush and twined them into a crown on her own grassy head. Then they walked on into the heart of summer, and sunlight, among tall foxgloves, which were like sentinels carrying silken banners of white and purple. The moss woman sprouted curls of perfumed honeysuckle.

Through the journey, growing louder, Janice heard a peculiar singing, a single penetrating note, a sound like a thread of light, usually imperceptible, being the resonance of the supernatural.

Bright days, starry nights, tempests and heat; the wheel of the seasons, turning over and over.

Cold blows the wind tonight true love …

The shrine had vanished. The mound itself had opened, revealing the stone lintels of a large barrow, a mouth in the Earth with a fire burning inside. The moss woman gestured her to enter.

Janice was afraid. It is hard to measure the extent of the Underland. She could not see walls or ceiling, only a fire burning in the middle of the dark. Anything could be hiding here, watching, waiting. She remembered childhood fears, walking across the landing at the top of the stairs in the night, not knowing what might be behind her, the prickle on her neck and back, the urge to look over her shoulder, which must always be resisted. She stepped towards the fire.

At first the shadows were there, the small prickled creatures with human faces, the smoky wolves, the man with the roe deer horns and hooves for hands.

When they melted away, something rattled over the ground. Looking down, she saw the turtle flint and the other flint creatures she had collected. They were lively now, jumping up and down, trying to get her attention. They joined in a circle around her and around the fire, and began a curious dance, peculiar and playful, unnerving, and strange to witness. But not alarming, no. She knew they did not mean any harm or malice. They were celebrating her, cheering her on. Janice had imbued them with life through her attention. She was queen of the flint people.

She crouched down to meet them, listening to the clamour of their tiny voices and accepting their joyful homage as they touched her feet and legs and patted the palms of her hands. Then the fire leapt and roared, and they all backed away, leaving her alone in the dark again. Sparks of blue and green jumped from the flames.

On the other side of the fire squatted the god. Its huge head was made of flint, dark and pale greys in patches, moist and shining, edged with the rough white of a flint's exterior skin. The two dark hollows of its eyes glittered with grains of crystal. Its long teeth and pointed nails were slices of black quartz. Its body was flint and sarsen stone, bound together with belts of iron and copper, studded with shining yellow orpiment. Dapples of lichen, silver-grey and ochre, mottled its chest.

The god inclined its head and seemed to smile. Its teeth shone in the firelight.

'I was almost gone,' it said. 'I'd become so small. So much diminished.'

Whether the voice was aloud or only heard in her mind she could not be sure but it rang like a giant bell, a sound that echoed through the caverns of her brain. She understood that, as with the flint creatures, she had heard the whisper of the mineral god and that by listening, through her attention, she had given it scope and nourishment. She had enlarged it.

The god's long arm unfolded, and in the shining palm of its hand she saw a red fruit, cut in half. A fat bead of juice, like blood, was poised on the glistening surface of the fruit's lush flesh.

'Would you stay with me?' it asked. 'I could take you in my arms and tell you stories of the long ages of the Earth, and the songs of my beginning, of the monsters of the oceans, and the beasts that climbed out of the waters.

'I could tell of the peoples who found me and gave me a voice, who gave me names, who told me their stories, and spoke to me and listened to me.'

Janice thought of the shadow creatures, the flint people, sensing them in the darkness beyond the light of the fire.

The bead of juice quivered and spilled over the edge of the fruit's cut edge. For the first time, Janice felt the child inside her move: a subtle, unmissable quickening. But she was torn, longing to escape the pain outside, wanting the surrender to the dark, to leave it behind, the hurt and loss without end.

'No,' she said. 'No I can't.'

The god's face expressed something like pain, head tipping forward. It closed its hand, squeezing the fruit to a pulp. Juice leaked between its fingers. Then it looked up again.

The flint god revealed its dark teeth.

Then it stood up and stamped its foot. The ground fell away

and Janice fell down, and down into the dark, through the chalk and under the chalk: gone to ground, buried under the Earth. The imprisonment was like death, trapped where there was no light or air, no escape, only the slow alchemical process of change.

How long does it take to turn flesh to stone?

Millions of years: the infinitesimal transformation, as the once-living tissue of sea sponges and siliceous plankton slowly accumulates in hollow spaces, hardens into a mineral as hard and sharp as flint, a mineral that sparks fire.

Rain was falling on her face. Janice lay on her back in the mud. She was filthy, clothes sodden, boots and clothes full of dirt and last year's leaves. Dirt was pressed beneath her fingernails and in her hair. When she opened her mouth, dirt fell from her lips.

When she looked at her mobile, she saw it was six o'clock.

I never had but one sweetheart ...

When she saw the list of messages and voicemails from Nick, she threw the mobile away, far into the trees.

When she got home and Nick started shouting, she ignored him and walked into the bathroom. She locked the door behind her so she could have a shower. When she looked in the mirror, she saw the grey mineral glitter in her eyes, a mercurial glint in her hair.

After she had dressed, Janice went into the kitchen and started cooking dinner. Nick started ranting again but she was impervious.

'I won't talk to you until you can speak calmly,' she said. 'And if you keep shouting at me, I shall leave.'

'If you try to leave me I'll come after you,' he took a deep breath and kicked up the volume another notch, to somewhere new, 'and I'll kick your teeth in.'

The shouted words hung on the air. Janice stopped what she was doing and turned around.

'If you threaten me again, I'll call the police.'

She waited a moment, then coolly continued preparing the food.

Nick had never threatened violence before. She was not entirely certain if he would follow through with his threat or not, but she was no longer afraid.

'Don't turn your back on me!'

Janice put the saucepan down and slowly turned to face him again.

He had his fist clenched, raised high. His whole body was poised, full of fury. This was it. He was going to beat her. He could kill her. Still, Janice stared at him, flinty and unflinching. She was not the person she had been. Some tender, irreplaceable part of herself had been transformed.

If he hits me, she thought, it will break his hand.

Nick hesitated. The moment stretched. His fist began to tremble. Then slowly he lowered his arm and all at once he seemed to crumble, melting down, slumping into a chair by the table. He burst into tears.

'What's happened to you?' he said. 'What's going on? I was so afraid. I thought you had left me.'

She turned back to the saucepan and did not answer. He cried and pleaded. He literally grovelled at her feet and begged her to speak to him. Finally, exhausted, he did as she said, and sat at the table. They ate dinner in silence. They went to bed without speaking.

Four weeks later, Nick's friends came round for dinner: it was their turn to host. Now she no longer cared, and knew he would not actually assault her, Janice managed Nick easily enough. He was hangdog and penitent all the time, desperate to please, terrified she would leave him. He came home from work on time and talked constantly about the baby and the life the three of them would have together, a fantasy of adventures and holidays and good times.

Janice was in no hurry -- she had plans to make. She sorted out her finances and, after swearing him to secrecy, told her father she would come to stay with him in France, just for a short time, while she decided what to do with her life. Her dad was delighted. Stay as long as you like, he told her. Plenty of room, grandchild, opportunities and so on.

On the day of the dinner, Nick prepared a wild mushroom risotto with hen-of-the-woods and chanterelle mushrooms he had bought online. He cooked them in butter, white wine and fresh cream, with the chopped whites of leeks and plump Arborio rice. For her part, Janice prepared a beautiful fruit flan, a sumptuous, glistening dish of richly coloured berries: blueberries, Morello cherries, red currents and strawberries. In their sweet glaze, the fruits shone wickedly, darkly crimson, a tempting witch's dish.

The meal was a great success. Janice, no longer caring, allowed herself to be sharp and snarky, making the others flinch and laugh at the same time. Her pregnancy was starting to show. The oddly metallic strands in her hair seemed to shine and her skin glowed. She was fierce and lambent.

Black bryony, tamus communis ... berries irritant, emetic.

When you grow a little harder, you lose a part of who you are but it is often the only way to survive.

She had found two berries from the moss woman's crown in her coat pocket. They were rather withered and dry, perhaps not potent. When she served the flan, Janice was careful the slices she served to Suzanne and to Nick contained one of the berries each. She hoped the acidity of the red currents would cover the potential irritation of the juice in their mouths. One dry berry was hardly likely to kill them, but it would hurt. They would be sick and miserable all night. They would blame the mushrooms.

The following morning, as Nick lay sweating and groaning in bed, Janice quietly packed her last few possessions, including the notebook of chalk and flint, of gods and berries. She would write about them and recreate them, in chalk and pastel and paint.

The taxi drove through Marlborough and then north along the old Roman road, which rose and fell over the curves of the downs. Flints lay scattered over chalky fields. Rooks circled overhead. Janice absorbed the view. In the Underland, the flint god was waiting.

She would be back again before long, with her child, to set up her own home. This was her place: where she belonged.

WHEN EVIL WALKED AMONG THEM

Severe winters can occur in England, but generally they are restricted to the North and the Midlands. Hard winters are far less common in the South, and extremely rare in the West Country, which all-year-round receives the full brunt of the Gulf Stream. It's perhaps no surprise then that one particular year, when the West Country was stricken by one of the most extreme winters in British history, gave rise to an event so eerie that it would be celebrated for decades to come as the day when Satan himself walked across Devon.

On the morning of February 9 1855, the inhabitants of Totnes in south Devon rose, as they had for weeks, to Arctic air temperatures, bitter frost and thick snow. This morning though, there was a difference. In an age when there was no mechanised traffic and when there was no farm-work to be done because of the time of year, very few folk were out and about, and thus an almost unbroken blanket of white covered the town.

Almost unbroken.

Because a single set of footprints was visible along the main street. Measured and found to be between ten and 20 inches apart, they were clearly the marks of a biped, ie a being that walked on two legs. And yet they were not footprints in the conventional sense, but hoofprints, and large ones at that, measuring ten inches in length and eight across, meaning that whoever this hoofed, two-legged being was, he possessed immense physical stature. Even more chilling than this, the prints appeared to have been made by hooves that were heated. The snow lay over a sheet of ice frozen so hard that it was impenetrable to ordinary footfalls and even passing wagon wheels. But not impenetrable to these hooves, it seemed, which had melted their way clear through to the ground underneath.

However, the strangest part of the discovery was yet to be made. Because when townsfolk in Totnes began to follow the trail, increasingly frightened about what they were going to find at the end of it, some of them arming themselves with guns and pitchforks first, it led on and on and on, away from the town and across the countryside, never once breaking, passing through Exmouth and over the Exe Estuary to Dawlish, before cutting north, finally ending at Littleham on the opposite coast, a distance of well over a hundred miles. And all the way along that meandering course, remarkable things were seen, to which literally dozens of witnesses, more and more folk who took up the pursuit, would later attest.

The hoofprints ascending the sheer walls of buildings and then going over the roofs, the people inside swearing they'd heard nothing.

The hoofprints crossing enclosed gardens or yards to which all access was barred.

The hoofprints crossing frozen rivers, the hoof-shaped holes melted into ice so thick that ducks and other waterfowl were encased in it.

The hoofprints going up tree-trunks, and through pipes and culverts that were too narrow for all but the smallest animal (one under-road storm drain was reputedly only eight inches wide!).

Most frightening of all though was the moment when the hoofprints approached a certain church in Woodbury. Here, the hooves appeared to have superheated themselves, not just melting their way through the snow and ice but actually burning hoof-shaped marks on the road underneath, and then on the door and the wall of the actual church as if its mere presence was a source of annoyance.

But maybe this preponderance of demonic detail should give modern observers pause for thought, West Country tradition being filled with stories about the visits of devils and demons, said entities then finding themselves repelled at the doors of chapels to local saints or by the prayers of particularly devout ministers.

So, is this just another tall story from the annals of religious-minded Devonshire folk?

Well, needless to say, no devil of any sort was sighted. The trail ended on Devon's north coast, with no visible trace of the person who'd made it. And when the snow melted in the next few days, the bulk of the physical evidence went with it. That the West Country was a more God-fearing place than many around this time is proved by an incident from 15 years earlier, when a similar case of unexplained hoofprints travelling a tremendous distance was reported from Glenorchy in Scotland, though the local assumption there was that the culprit was an unidentified animal.

Crude sketches were made of the Devonshire tracks, but no photographs were taken, and in fact no witnesses were spoken to by outsiders for many years, the case only finally coming to the attention of the rest of the world in 1950, when a bundle of paperwork, the property of a certain Reverend H T Ellacombe, vicar of Clyst St George in the 1850s, was uncovered, which made numerous references to the incident.

Modern theories vary widely as to what might have caused the curious trail.

There are hoofed animals aplenty in that part of the world, everything from cattle to donkeys to goats, and it's an obvious deduction that one of these might have made the prints. When a counter-argument was put that no farm animal, in fact no animal of any sort found in Britain, was so large or could seriously have travelled over a hundred miles of its own volition without at some point stopping to rest and being spotted by those in pursuit, the answer was equally obvious: it wasn't the trail of one animal, but of several, different trails crossing each other and becoming confused, those following now so terrified that they failed to understand what they were seeing.

Alternative explanations were even offered at the time, a couple of them rather outlandish. For example, in the Rev Ellacombe's paperwork, there's evidence that an associate of his, another Devonshire clergyman, the Rev G M Musgrove, claimed that two kangaroos, having escaped a local menagerie, were responsible, though Musgrove later retracted this explanation, saying that he'd invented it to assuage the fears of parishioners who were becoming too frightened for their own good.

More plausible theories have since been offered, namely that beyond the boundaries of Totnes itself other folk began to fake the prints so to draw attention to their own towns and villages. It was certainly deemed highly possible that the hoofmarks apparently burned into the walls of Woodbury church were the work of fakers with a branding iron.

Of course, all of this is guesswork. The lack of any real evidence has confounded both sides of the argument. No one can say with certainty what happened in Devon on the eve of February 9 1855, but many of those who live there even now are quite certain.

It was the Devil. And he walked among them.

EPIPHYTE
Thana Niveau

'All I'm saying is that geology isn't a proper science.'

Kari continued walking for a couple of paces before stopping and turning to look at James, her eyebrows nearly reaching her hairline. 'What?'

James shrugged. 'Just saying.'

'*Proper* science?' she repeated, sounding incredulous. 'Guess what? Without geology we wouldn't know that the Chicxulub asteroid impact was what killed the dinosaurs.'

'Shai-Hulud?'

Kari tried to look annoyed. 'No, not sandworms, you colossal nerd. Rocks. Rocks from space. And are you *really* insulting my triple-great grandmother? On our third date?'

James grinned. 'I'm just winding you up.'

It wasn't a real argument. Just a continuation of the banter that had begun two days before, when they had first met in the ruins of Okehampton Castle. Their flirtatious chat had turned into lunch, then dinner, then finally the realisation that there was no need for separate rooms in separate B&Bs. The pretext was that it was simple practicality. Joining forces meant more money to spend on food and wine and tourist tat, as well as the added safety of having a buddy once they set out across the open moorland.

Their second 'date' had been a tour of picturesque villages and market towns throughout Dartmoor, and another night together in a B&B. They would be combining their itineraries from there. Kari had seemed genuinely excited by the prospect of wild camping on the moors, something she admitted she'd never have felt comfortable doing alone.

Her own plan was to explore specific places in a battered old book she had inherited – *An Elementary Treatise on the Cornubian Batholith, and Associated Intrusive Bodies on Dartmoor*. James thought it looked like a memoir with delusions of academia. It was barely thirty pages long, but professionally produced. Most importantly, it had been written and illustrated by Kari's great-great-great grandmother, Esther Villaverde, who James imagined must have been something of a rebel in her day. He pictured a plucky suffragette weathering a storm of male outrage. *A LADY scientist??? Why, they'll want the vote next!*

They spent the morning in Wistman's Wood, an ancient and eerily beautiful forest of stunted oaks and boulders shrouded in vibrant green moss and lichen. On the ground it grew like thick carpet, spongy to the touch, while on the trees it appeared more delicate, lacy and curled at the edges. Contorted branches clawed at the sky as if to escape the sea of smothering green and gold.

'It's like a fairyland,' Kari breathed, gazing in wonder at their surroundings. 'I've never seen anything like it.'

'Me neither,' James said.

What he kept to himself was how uneasy the wood made him feel. It was beautiful, certainly, but also somehow … off. He couldn't put his finger on what was bothering him, but the place just felt *wrong*. Like somewhere people weren't ever meant to be. Slivers of the bright summer sunshine found its way through the tangled branches, but the air was still icy against his skin. James rubbed the gooseflesh on his arms as he followed Kari deeper into the trees and boulders.

On the map Wistman's Wood was tiny, a thin strip of jagged green isolated in the pale yellow and brown expanse of the moors. It didn't seem like a place where anyone could go missing. And yet people did. There was even a legend about a lost dog whose ghostly yipping could occasionally be heard. But there was nothing to hear now. No dogs, spectral or otherwise. No people either. The silence was absolute.

All around him crouched gnarled trees, hunched and misshapen by their burden of age. Some looked as though they'd grown weary of holding their arms up. Huge boughs hung down from the trunks in many places, looping and dragging along the ground among the rocks and bracken, all of it coated with moss. In places it was hard to tell where the grass ended and the moss began.

Kari, however, still seemed enchanted. 'Look at these flowers,' she exclaimed, peering closely at a cluster of drooping oak branches.

Despite his discomfort, James drew closer to see. Sprouting from the carpet of green were sprays of little yellow flowers. The blossoms were only as thick as a finger, and oddly twisted, each like a tiny coiling tornado. Some arched upward, gaping like mouths, while others hung suspended from aerial roots that looked too thin to support them. They were the ugliest flowers he'd ever seen.

'I'm no expert,' he said, 'but those don't look like they belong here.'

'I know, right?' Kari's eyes sparkled with excitement. Whatever weird effect the area was having on him, she was clearly not susceptible to it. She waved her hand in front of the flowers and they shivered with a papery rustling.

It must have been the movement that released their fragrance. If you could call it that. James winced. It was a bitter, astringent odour, like green tea that had been brewed too long.

Kari dug in her backpack for Esther's book, paging through to a section on Wistman's Wood. There were some quite competent nature sketches of the trees and rocks. Below that was a detailed inset drawing of the ugly flowers.

'I guess they do belong here after all,' Kari said, 'if they were here when Esther was.'

The sketch showed an almost pornographic level of detail, accentuating every unpleasant feature. The flower consisted of either a single curled petal, or many that had fused into a funnel shape. James imagined it was a one-way trip for pollinating insects.

Above the sketch in old-fashioned handwriting was the phrase: *VESPERTINE-FLOWERING EPIPHYTE*

'Is that its name?' James asked.

Kari shook her head. 'That just means it flowers at night.'

'So why's it flowering now?'

She shrugged. 'I don't know. I guess it is pretty shady in here.'

'And "epiphyte"?'

'Means it grows on another plant. See the roots?'

He looked at the thin twining tendrils anchoring the little flowers to the branches. They were even living on the boulders, their roots splayed across the lichen like a network of veins. 'So it's a parasite.'

'Actually, no, epiphytes are symbiotic. They don't harm the host. Like all the moss and lichen here – they're epiphytic too.' She read from the book: '"The flower looks like a cross between an orchid and a thornapple." Yeah, I can see that.'

James was feeling out of his depth, and very relieved he hadn't mocked botany as well as geology. 'Thornapple?' he asked helplessly.

Kari smiled kindly and touched his shoulder, as if to reassure him he wasn't being thick. 'Deadly nightshade family. Don't worry, I'm not really a witch.' She winked.

'Was Esther?'

The idea seemed to appeal to Kari. Her smile widened. 'Wouldn't that be something!'

A breeze set the awful flowers waving and the sound was too much like whispering for comfort. James suddenly felt very cold and he looked at his watch to disguise a shudder. 'We'd better get moving if you want to reach Grimspound.'

The abandoned prehistoric settlement had been Kari's primary destination. There was something in Esther's book she especially wanted to see there, something carved into one of the stones. Hopefully not the triple-grandmother's initials. James had just wanted to camp on the moors and he was happy to do that anywhere. You were supposed to stay away from tourist spots so as not to spoil the vista for sightseers. No one wanted their panoramic photos contaminated by splashes of primary-coloured nylon. But he didn't think anyone would notice if they waited until nightfall to pitch the tent.

118

'It's still early,' Kari said. She was kneeling beside a boulder to take photos of the flowers that had colonised its surface.

'Yeah, but it'll take us about three hours to hike there.'

Branches rattled and clacked overhead as another frigid gust swept through the trees. This time Kari felt it too. James watched as her expression changed from fascination with her photographic subject to surprise and discomfort. She had taken off her hoodie and tied it round her waist, but now she tore it free and put it on again. She looked tiny and vulnerable, huddled on the ground among the scattering of boulders.

'It'll be warmer once we're on the move again,' James said. His own jacket was buried in his backpack and he didn't want to waste time digging it out. 'I'm cold too. Let's go.'

He held out his hand to help her up from the ground. She took it and let him pull her to her feet. The knees of her jeans were stained bright green.

James hurriedly checked his own clothes, not keen on the idea of anything from the sinister wood forming a symbiotic relationship with him.

Fortunately, Kari was still oblivious to his discomfort with the area. 'Is Hound Tor on the way? I want to see the stones there.'

James checked the map on his phone. 'That's a little further east. We can go there tomorrow from Grimspound.'

As they emerged from the shadows Kari cast a final look over her shoulder at the wood. James did not look back.

It was early evening by the time they finally reached Hookney Tor. They had stopped for lunch in Postbridge, and once they were back on the moors, they'd been distracted by a visit from some friendly Dartmoor ponies. The shaggy little ponies were clearly used to being fed by tourists, and Kari happily surrendered the apples she had in her bag. Once the treats were gone, the ponies wandered off, lazily grazing their way across the moorland.

The hilltop of Hookney Tor was strewn with granite

outcrops. Kari posed for a selfie with Esther's book. 'For my mum,' she said. 'Me and the intrusive bodies.'

James smiled. 'I think *we're* the intrusive bodies.'

The book's introduction explained that the rock formations resulted from the crystallisation of magma that had not erupted as lava but instead slowly cooled beneath the surface of the earth. The movement of the molten rock was preserved by the horizontal striations in the solidified granite. It was easy to see where the magma had swelled and subsided again and again. Countless years of erosion had eventually exposed the bedrock, revealing weird and wonderful shapes that had inspired imaginations for centuries.

James' more modern guidebook featured photos of such famous formations as Bowerman's Nose, Black Tor and Great Staple Tor. Hookney Tor was dramatic, a granite tower rising like a castle on the hilltop, affording spectacular views across the landscape. Below it the ancient settlement of Grimspound was laid out like a floor plan.

A huge stone perimeter wall enclosed the remains of several roundhouses. The wall was oddly eye-shaped, with a distinct and imposing entrance flanked by much larger stones.

'Incredible,' Kari breathed, gazing down at the site.

James nodded, trying to picture what life must have been like for the inhabitants of this harsh, primitive setting. The wall was impressive enough as a ruin, so it must have been truly something before the passage of time had worn it down. Why had these Bronze Age settlers needed such a massive barrier between them and the rest of the moorland? Surely a fence was all that was required to keep livestock from wandering off. And in the case of ponies, the promise of apples might have been enough.

Kari was paging through her book again and she held it up to show him a sketch Esther had done from a different vantage point. An arrow pointed to one of the wall stones, with a cryptic notation in the margin: *CROATOAN.*

The word came from the lost colony of Roanoke in late sixteenth century America. The people had vanished from the settlement without trace, leaving behind only the single word *Croatoan*, carved into a post. To this day, their fate was still unknown.

James gazed down at their own lost colony in wonder. 'Is she suggesting the same thing happened here? That they just vanished into thin air one day?'

'I don't know. But she certainly seems to think they left a similar message.' She peered at the drawing and then turned the book to orient it to their perspective. 'It should be there,' she said, pointing. 'Three o'clock from the entrance.'

A long winding path led from the tor down to Grimspound, paved with ancient cobblestones that jutted up at odd angles.

'It doesn't look all that different,' Kari said, 'even a hundred years later.'

'Just a handful of seconds in geological time, I guess.'

She smiled. 'Making peace with geology now. Esther's ghost approves.'

James returned her smile, but the idea of ghosts prompted an unwelcome flashback of Wistman's Wood and those hideous flowers. That papery rustling. That smell. He suppressed a shudder and gestured towards their destination. 'Shall we?'

Together they picked their way down the hill. Avoiding the rocks was tricky. They stuck out everywhere, and they weren't always visible. More than once James placed his foot on a tuft of heather only to meet uneven stone beneath. He was in proper hiking boots, which helped him keep his footing. But Kari had only worn trainers and she stumbled more than once on the way down. He caught her the first time, loving the way her body felt in his arms.

She laughed brightly and kissed him. 'My hero!'

The idea gave him a childish little thrill, and by the time they reached the ruins he was beaming. The weather was glorious, sunny and warm, and to his delight there was no one else about. It seemed like they had all of Dartmoor to themselves. He had completely forgotten the disquiet he'd felt earlier. It was as though nothing else existed in the world except him and Kari.

Although they could have clambered over the wall with little effort, they decided to walk the entire way around to enter through the gateway. The huge stones dwarfed them as they passed through. It was like stepping back in time. James gazed around at the enclosure, imagining the people who had called it home.

You could be forgiven for mistaking it for a field of rubble until you noticed the symmetry of some of the clusters of stones. It was easy enough to see where roundhouses had been, and his imagination filled in the gaps by adding thatched roofs and rough-hewn doors. He crossed the threshold of an obvious doorway, bookended by two tall stones, like a smaller version of the main gate. Inside, the floor was hard-packed dirt. Any windows would have offered only a bleak view of the moors – an endless expanse of ochre grass, bracken and jagged upthrust granite.

But maybe it had looked different back then. Maybe there had been more trees. Wistman's Wood could have occupied most of Dartmoor for all he knew. And people in the past would have done exactly what people in the present did: harvested the resources until there was nothing left. Maybe that was why these little settlements were nothing but ghost towns now.

There was movement way up on Hookney Tor, but it wasn't tourists. Four white ponies were grazing at the base of the granite fortress. The animals must have followed them, hoping for more treats.

'Hey Kari, look –'

He turned, but she was no longer beside him. He felt a brief and inexplicable flash of panic before spotting her on the opposite side of the enclosure. She was on her knees by the perimeter wall, digging at something near the bottom with a trowel.

'What are you doing?' he called.

'Digging!'

He grinned. Well, yes, he could see that. He jogged across the field to join her.

'This is it,' Kari said excitedly. She chopped at the grass where she had been digging, exposing part of a buried rock.

'Pretty sure you're not supposed to ...' But James didn't finish his sentence. He was too curious.

It took some time for her to dig down far enough to fully reveal what she was looking for. The hole was more than a foot deep when she finally sat back and dusted soil from her hands. 'There.'

Intrigued, James crouched down beside her to see what she had uncovered. Etched into the stone was some kind of symbol. Many of the rocks all across Dartmoor had been defaced by people wanting to leave their mark. EMMA WUZ HERE. R+J 1998. The usual sort of crap stupid humans felt compelled to do when confronted by something ancient and permanent. This just looked like a shapeless scrawl, weathered by time.

'OK,' Kari said, 'we found it but what is it?'

'Bronze Age graffiti?' James offered.

They both peered closely at the carving and Kari used her finger like an archaeologist's brush, sweeping soil from the indentation. James took a picture with his phone and enlarged it, then used different filters to enhance it. Finally a combination of greyscale and high contrast made the image take on recognisable form. It was stylised, but clearly a flower. Specifically one of the ugly, coiling flowers they had seen in Wistman's Wood. He felt a twinge of uneasiness.

'Whoa,' Kari breathed. 'That's weird, right?'

James nodded. There was no way any modern tourist had carved that there. The symbol had been buried too deep. But why? Erosion should have exposed it, not hidden it. And how had Esther even known about it? Unless it had been exposed a century ago and then hidden again. How? By the natural ebb and flow of the land? Or deliberately? He didn't like the idea of it being concealed on purpose. That thought led to another. Something he'd read about once.

'I can see the gears turning,' Kari said, watching him.

'Yeah. I was just thinking about how people used to hide objects inside the walls of a house. For luck or to ward off evil spirits. I guess a symbol could serve the same function.'

But why this hideous, evil-smelling flower?

Kari looked doubtful. 'I don't know. There's nothing else in the book. Just the location and the sketch. And "Croatoan".'

'Well, that mystery was never solved. Maybe this one won't be either.'

He didn't share his actual theory, which was that Esther had likely been more than a little eccentric, if not mad. Sprinkled in amongst dry, dusty facts about the Cornubian batholith were cryptic drawings and personal observations that would invalidate the whole book if she'd written it today.

James looked up at the sky. The sun was setting and the moors were still deserted. Even the ponies had gone. 'It's getting dark,' he said.

'Can we camp here? In Grimspound?'

'I don't see why not. There's no one to report us. We can pitch the tent inside one of the houses. Bronze Age Airbnb!'

It was shortly after midnight when the knocking started. James and Kari both bolted upright, woken by the noise of something repeatedly hitting the walls of the tent. To James it sounded like a shower of acorns, but they were far from any trees. And besides, the thumps of impact weren't coming from above.

'There's someone outside!' Kari hissed.

James' heart was pounding, but he tried to act calmer than he felt. 'Probably just people trying to scare us off for camping here,' he whispered.

'They're doing a good job!'

'They'll get bored and go away.'

They stayed quiet and listened. There were no voices outside, no laughter or footsteps, none of the sounds you'd expect to hear if you were surrounded by people.

When the thumping showed no sign of abating, curiosity got the best of James. 'I'm going outside.'

Kari grabbed his arm. 'Are you crazy? What if —'

'We can't just cower in fear until dawn. I'll be all right.' He hoped.

He grabbed his torch and pressed it against his thigh to hide the light. Then he slowly unzipped the tent flap and poked his head outside. The noises hadn't stopped. And now he heard a different sound, a soft buzzing. He aimed the torch to the left, illuminating one exterior wall of the tent. And laughed with relief when he saw what it was.

'What?' Kari called. 'What is it?'

Fluttering clumsily around the tent – and battering it – were huge moths. He shone the torch out into the night and immediately drew even more attention as they clustered around the light, fighting to get closer.

'Moths,' he said. 'Really big ones.'

Kari immediately appeared beside him to look. She gasped. 'My God, I've never seen so many in one place. They're like a flock of bats!' She waved her hands gently to deflect them from hitting her in the face. Several had already landed on James. Each was the size of a hand, with long scalloped wings.

'I guess they were drawn to the light inside the tent,' James said. 'I didn't think it was bright enough to attract attention.' They had left a small LED lantern on as a night light, covering it with a shirt to dim it. But the moths had still seen it. Kari switched it off. Now the moths were only swarming around the torch.

'Turn that off too,' Kari said, her voice full of wonder.

James obliged and they stood for a moment in darkness. The moon was almost full, its brightness illuminating the jagged edges of the stones around them. The unearthly glow transformed the once-familiar landscape into something eerie and strange.

As his eyes adjusted James could make out a curious gleaming along the perimeter wall of Grimspound. It was more than moonlight. It looked like the phosphorescence you saw in caves. And all around it he could see the darting shapes of moths.

'What is that?' he asked.

'I don't know but it's everywhere. Look at the houses.'

It wasn't just on the boundary wall. The rest of the ruins shared the same unnatural glow, shining across the stones in uneven areas. There was an especially bright patch a few yards away, on the nearest house.

'Let's go and see,' Kari said.

James wasn't as keen but he followed her anyway. Her hair shone with cold blue moonlight and she was little more than a silhouette. He caught up and took her arm to reassure himself that she wasn't just a shadow.

When they reached the crumbling wall of the house they stopped, staring. All across the stones were the ugly yellow flowers. And all around *them* were the moths. They hovered like bumblebees, extending long tubes to drink whatever was inside the coiling blossom.

'Night-blooming,' Kari said, something like reverence in her voice.

It was only then that James noticed the smell. The same chilly green smell from Wistman's Wood. And with it came the unnerving sense that they were being watched. Something was very wrong here.

'Kari,' he whispered, 'these weren't here before.'

'Are you sure? They were all over the trees and rocks in the forest.'

He swallowed. 'I'm sure.'

The flowers quivered with the movement of the attendant moths, adding their whispers to the flutter of wings.

'Come on, let's get back to the tent,' he said.

'Wait a minute. I want to see something.'

Before he could stop her, she took the torch from him and sprinted across the enclosure. James watched the beam of light bouncing across the ground and knew where she was going. He was about to call to her when she cried out and the light disappeared.

'Kari!'

He froze, listening. After a moment he heard her groan with pain.

'I'm OK,' she said, sounding much too far away.

He thought he heard her say 'my ankle' and he cursed under his breath. 'Stay there. Don't move. I'm coming!'

The moonlight was enough to guide him to the tent, where he stopped short. The nylon was glowing. Just like the wall and the stone houses. And growing from the fabric in several places were the yellow flowers. Their tiny roots were stitched across the surface of the tent, glistening like luminescent slug slime. Gritting his teeth against a surge of nausea, he pushed open the flaps and ducked inside to grab the LED lantern.

Carefully watching where he placed his feet, he made his way to Kari, who was by the wall where she had been digging earlier. She was sitting on the ground cradling her right foot. Darkness streaked the grass around her, shadows that proved wet and immoveable when James shone the lantern there. A jagged shard of granite protruded from the ground beside Kari, also stained with her blood.

'Guess I should have slept in my shoes like you did after all,' she said with a sheepish little laugh.

But the last thing James cared about was scoring 'I told you so' points. There wasn't just blood on the rock that had injured her; there were also flowers. And the symbol she had unearthed on the wall was now surrounded by the real things. The thought rose in his mind that the flowers had been summoned, and he pushed it down.

'We have to get you back to the tent,' he said, trying to keep his voice steady. 'Can you walk?'

She laughed again, but it sounded forced. 'I'm fine,' she said. 'Don't make a fuss!'

He looked around for the torch but couldn't find it. The lantern would have to do. He helped Kari to her feet, shuddering at the sight of her bare skin touching the ground. There were moths there, resting with their wings outstretched, having drunk their fill from those parasitic blossoms. No, he reminded himself. Epiphytes. Symbiotic.

Kari stood on one foot but when she tried to put weight on the other she cried out and crumpled to the ground. James had been too distracted by the moths to catch her in time.

'Jesus Kari, I'm sorry! Come on, hold on to me.'

There was no false bravado this time. She hissed with pain as she got shakily to her one good foot. 'I don't think I can walk,' she whimpered.

'It's OK, I'll carry you. It's not far. We can call an ambulance.'

'Out here?'

'I'll carry you up Hookney Tor if I have to.' But even though she was small and slender, he was no superhero. He'd be able to get her to the tent but no further.

Kari held the lantern while he carried her, trying to ignore the crunch of insect bodies beneath his boots. The green smell was all around them, making him lightheaded.

There were even more flowers on the tent now, and the moths had renewed their frenzy, dancing around the blossoms, spreading them like a disease.

'Hey, look,' Kari said, 'the flowers.' She gave a strange little giggle. James didn't like the sound of it.

He sat her down on the sleeping bag and zipped the tent, shooing a few fluttery trespassers out as he did.

'Ooh, that doesn't look good,' Kari murmured, prodding her leg. Her words were slurred, as if she were drunk.

James stared at her injured foot. The ankle was bent at an unnatural angle that looked agonising. But Kari only giggled. Whatever was out here must be having some kind of narcotic effect on her. Christ, had those poisonous flowers got into her bloodstream? There were slimy smears of yellow and green all over her hands and clothes.

He gently turned her leg to see how bad it was. A ragged gash ran from her ankle halfway up her shin. Blood was oozing from it, coating her foot in gore. But what horrified him was not the wound itself but what – there was no other word – *adorned* it. The broken skin had a lacy silver edge, just like they had been seeing all day on all the surfaces where it could grow. Lichen. Fungus. Whatever it was that the tiny white tendrils needed to take hold. And there they were, threading through the curled edges of both vegetation and torn human skin.

Kari's socks were by her trainers and he grabbed one, wadding it into a ball. 'Sorry,' James said, 'this might hurt.' Then he scrubbed at the wound, trying to scrape away the plant life colonising it.

Kari screamed and struggled, but James kept her leg pinned.

'I'm sorry, I'm sorry, I'm sorry,' he babbled. 'But I've got to get them off you.'

He tried several times to clear the wound of invaders but Kari wouldn't hold still. He was out of his depth. He grabbed his phone and stabbed frantically at the nine button. Nothing happened. He looked at the screen.

EMERGENCY CALLS ONLY

He cursed. 'What the hell do you think this is?' He cast about for Kari's phone, but she'd been using it to take pictures all day and it was dead.

They'd had a signal up on the tor. He was sure of it. It would only take him ten minutes or so to get back up there, then ten minutes back. Could he leave Kari that long? What choice did he have? She was back to her drunken giggling again, waving her hands at several moths that fluttered right in front of her eyes. He shuddered as one landed on her face, heavily enough that he actually heard the soft thump. The insect just sat there on her cheek, its wings fanned out across her skin, completely covering her left eye. As James watched, it unfurled its proboscis, reaching for a patch of yellow goo on her skin. With a cry of disgust he brushed the creature away. He had to go. Now.

'Kari, I have to leave you for just a few minutes. I'll be back soon, I promise. Please stay here. Don't leave the tent. Don't …' He didn't know what else to say, and she didn't even seem to be hearing him anyway. 'I'm getting help. I'll see you soon.'

It took all his willpower to turn away and leave her there, alone in the dark. Except she wasn't alone, was she? And it wasn't exactly dark. Not now.

James gritted his teeth, blocking out the insidious whispers as he zipped the tent closed. It felt like zipping up a body bag. He shoved his phone down into his pocket and held up the lantern. Resisting the urge to run, he forced himself to walk briskly but carefully out of the enclosure and up the long winding hill.

The air was thick and heavy, clouded with moths. Occasionally he felt the soft thud as one landed on him. Their numbers were so great that he could actually feel the breeze of their wings as they fluttered close to him. And at times they clustered so densely around the light source that they almost blotted it out entirely. But the moonlight was enough to see by, and the ghostly glow of the stones was lighting his way to the top of the hill.

Grimspound seemed miles away, and now it resembled an eye more than ever, bulging from the ground, glaring up at him with baleful intent. James snatched his phone out and was relieved to see three bars. This time the call went through and a woman answered.

'We need an ambulance on Dartmoor. In the Grimspound settlement. My friend is hurt. I think she's broken her leg and she's acting really weird, like she's poisoned.'

A moth dropped heavily onto the glowing screen and he shook the phone to get rid of it.

'Yes, we're *in* Grimspound. We were camping. Please come as soon as possible!' He could hear his voice rising in panic even as he tried to slow down and provide the relevant details. The woman wanted him to stay on the line but he cut her off. 'I can't stay here. I have to get back to her. Please hurry. Ambulance! Grimspound!'

He rung off and again had to stop himself pelting down the hill. Every second he was away from Kari felt like an hour.

He tried to keep his eyes focused on the ground in front of him but the glow seemed to beckon him to look up. When he finally did he froze in astonishment. All across the moors, as far as he could see, were tiny trails of gleaming yellow. It was on his clothes, his skin. A moth knocked into his temple and he felt a dewy wetness there. He could see the yellow streak in his peripheral vision.

Something tickled the back of his neck and the sensation travelled down his spine. He could feel the tiny feet of a moth making its way along his skin, painting him with pollen. Or whatever it was that came out of those awful flowers.

Ignore it, he told himself. *Nearly there, nearly there.*

After what seemed like years he finally reached the settlement. It would be easy enough to clamber over a low part of the wall, but the idea of crushing those flowers beneath his bare hands made his insides lurch. He hurried around the perimeter to the towering gatepost stones and raced inside.

There was no need for the lantern at all now. The tent shone with an unearthly, alien vibrance. The hum of flying moths filled the air, dispersing the foul perfume of the flowers.

James ran the last few yards and tore open the zip. 'Kari! I'm back, I—'

But she wasn't there.

He swore and dashed back out again, scanning the glowing landscape, searching for her. He returned to the stone with the carved symbol but she wasn't there. He called and called, but there was no answer.

Swallowing his terror, he forced himself to scour the entire enclosure, going step by step, examining each of the ruined houses. He knelt in the grass, looking for footprints. But how could she have gone anywhere? She'd have to have crawled, and even with his twenty-minute absence, she couldn't have gone far.

He cried her name until he was hoarse, only vaguely aware that the light was fading. The cloud of moths had thinned as well. It was getting harder to see. The moonlight still illuminated the stones but the yellow gleam was gone. So were the flowers. Now he couldn't see them anywhere. Had the moths eaten them?

At last, blinded by tears and despair, he collapsed outside the tent.

The sky was tinged pink with the first rays of sunlight by the time the ambulance arrived. There was the sound of hurried footsteps. Voices. Someone was shaking him.

James stared around, wild-eyed. 'Kari,' he said, his voice barely a whisper.

'We're looking for her,' said a male voice to his left.

James looked up to see a man in a fluorescent yellow paramedic uniform. 'We'll find her.'

'Yellow,' James murmured, clutching at the man's sleeve. 'Flowers.'

The paramedic smiled pityingly and patted James on the shoulder. 'You can send her flowers in hospital. Just take it easy now. Can you walk?'

As the man helped him to his feet, James looked back towards the tent. Two people had dismantled it and as they carried it away from the ruins of the house he noticed something odd. There had been two stones forming a doorway. He was sure of it. But now there was a third. It was smaller than the others, paler. But even from a distance, James could see the fibrous roots criss-crossing its surface.

THE HANGMAN'S PLEASURE

For such a pleasingly pastoral landscape, the West Country has generated some violent passions over the centuries. Despite its rolling farmland and bucolic villages, it is this part of England where two of the bloodiest ever revolts against the English Crown took root, the atrocities that resulted spawning a plethora of hauntings.

To start with, the Prayerbook Rebellion occurred in 1549, at the height of the Reformation, and was a bona fide *war between the region's Protestants and Catholics. It stood out even at a time when it was commonplace to witness extreme sectarian violence. Caused by the imposition of an English language prayerbook, which was widely seen as one Protestant liberty too many, it provoked a Catholic uprising all across Devon, which saw an armed force marching under the banner 'Kill all the Gentlemen', Exeter besieged, and a number of pitched battles fought in which hundreds were slaughtered. There was also the near-unbelievable Clyst Heath Massacre, where government forces under the Earl of Bedford cut the throats of 900 bound and helpless Catholic prisoners in less than ten minutes.*

As is so often the case when gruesome crimes occur in English history, ghostly remnants are still said to linger. In Sampford Courtney, where the rising began with the slashing to death by billhook of a farmer called Hellyons, who had rebuked the rebels, gasps and chokes are still said to be heard on the spot where he fell, the eerie atmosphere in the village inspiring M R James to write his famous ghost story, 'Martin's Close'. Likewise, phantom shapes have been reported on Clyst Heath, even though it's now a populated suburb, while a spectral figure seen dragging a headless corpse through the streets of Exwick (an apparition that led to the police being called) is thought to be connected to the violent retribution taken across Devon by government forces once the revolt had been crushed.

But in terms of grisly horror, stories like these pale to insignificance when you roll forward 136 years to the Pitchfork Rebellion of 1685.

It was still an age of religious strife, but this was more like a political power-grab, or an attempt at such. It centred around James Scott, the Duke of Monmouth, the illegitimate son of Charles II, who on his father's death in the February of that year became convinced that he should be crowned the next King, and was furious when the throne passed to his father's younger brother, James.

A notorious drinker and gambler, Monmouth was clearly in with the wrong crowd. Already a long-term malcontent, it wasn't difficult for those around him with ambitions of their own to fill his head with nonsensical fantasies that the new James II could easily be dethroned. It was certainly true that James, as a Catholic and something of a misanthrope, was not exactly beloved of his people, but he was always capable of swift, decisive action and determined to hold onto power.

The rebellion began in the West Country, where Monmouth, who'd been popular there in the past, arrived that May from self-imposed exile in Holland. A brief time of premature celebration called the 'Duking Days' followed, during which he was proclaimed King in Taunton market place. On hearing about this, James wasted no time, sending significant forces west under the command of his most competent soldier, the French-born Earl of Feversham. In response, Monmouth, who was accompanied by a few hundred professional troops and Protestant diehards, was able to raise an extra 4,000 men, though the majority were uneducated farmworkers and their equipment mostly the tools they worked with every day (hence the name later given to their movement). After a series of skirmishes, all of which Monmouth lost, his army was finally confronted by the King's red-coated regulars in the Somerset Levels, at a place called Sedgemoor, on July 6. What followed was one of the most one-sided battles ever fought on English soil, the rebels charging bravely with their forks and hoes against rank after rank of musket-wielding infantry, and then facing squadrons of mounted cavalry, who made bloody hay as they galloped among them.

The King's army didn't have it all its own way. They suffered around 200 fatalities of their own, but considerably more of the rebels were killed on the field, around 1,300, while near-enough all the rest were taken captive, and it was these who were to suffer the most. King James, who'd felt threatened since his coronation, not just because of his Catholicism but because of his questionable accession, was bent on making an example of the miscreants. Thus, the five judges he sent down to the West Country to deal with them were instructed to be harsh, though one of them was infamous for this already.

No one needed to tell Lord Chief Justice George Jeffreys, the Hanging Judge, to be tough on law-breakers. It was his natural instinct. So, he made no complaint on hearing that immediately after the battle, dozens of rebels who'd surrendered had been summarily shot by Feversham's firing squads, while others were lynched along the roadside by their captors, who'd thought it a shame not to make use of a row of empty gibbets.

Of course, those who did stand trial didn't fare much better.

Jeffreys held court in Winchester, Exeter, Taunton and Wells, passing judgement on an estimated 1,300 prisoners in a session that would later become known as the Bloody Assize. Straight away, some 200 were convicted of high treason and sentenced to be hanged, drawn and quartered, which was exactly as gruesome as it sounded, the victims hanged until they were almost dead, then cut down, castrated, torn open with red hot implements, disembowelled while still alive and hacked into quarters, said chunks of flesh and bone to be displayed on city gates in all rebel enclaves.

Monmouth himself, captured shortly after the battle, met an equally brutal fate. Only nine days after Sedgemoor, he was beheaded on Tower Hill, Jack Ketch, the notoriously incompetent headsman, failing to finish the job in seven strokes, his assistant having to complete it by sawing with a serrated knife through much of the duke's remaining tissue. (As an even more macabre aside, it wasn't long after this when it was discovered that the Royal Family didn't possess a portrait painting of Monmouth, and so his head was stitched back on and his corpse propped up for a posthumous sitting).

Of the remaining rebels, about 500 more were sentenced to straightforward hanging and gibbeting. One Benjamin Hewling met his fate among this group, his sister having paid Jeffreys £1,000 to spare him the gutting and quartering. The remainder, about 800 in total, were then transported for life as indentured slaves to the sugar plantations in the Caribbean, many dying from typhus in the rat-infested slave ships long before they arrived, the rest, if one believes the 1922 Rafael Sabatini novel (and the 1935 Errol Flynn movie) **Captain Blood,** *chained, whipped and mistreated in sundry other ways until none save those who* *escaped and became pirates were left.*

It didn't even end there, as Jeffreys then ordered a round-up of the many prostitutes who had entertained the rebel army and had them all flogged.

Yet again, the reverberations from the Bloody Assize appear to have been severe in the spirit realm. By night it is said, the tramping of many booted feet can still be heard heading away from Taunton Castle, along with frantic pleas for mercy, the shades of the triumphant loyalists leading the ghosts of their prisoners to execution again and again. Inside the castle meanwhile, sounds of a riotous feast often disturb the nighttime quiet, local gossips describing it as Monmouth and his men endlessly toasting an anticipated victory that would never be theirs. Sedgemoor itself, a dreary place in the autumn mist, is notoriously haunted; phantom lights and the ragged figures of wounded men have been reported, cries and screams and even gunfire heard. A running ghost is attributed to the soul of a young rebel who was famous for his speed, and who was told that he'd be spared if he could outrun a galloping horse; he tried but of course failed, and so was run through with a sword as he lay exhausted.

The Hanging Judge himself is also said to haunt a number of locations, usually those inns where he stayed, the great buildings where he held court and the prisons where his victims awaited execution. His presence is often said to be revealed by cruel, disembodied laughter.

As a footnote, Judge Jeffreys has continued to be of interest to the horror fiction world ever since. In 1971, he made an uncredited appearance in Piers Haggard's ground-breaking folk horror movie, Blood on Satan's Claw, *which concerns an outbreak of evil in a 17th century West Country village and the emergence among the local possessed children of an actual physical devil. Students of the genre will be quick to point out that the character, played with memorable iciness by Patrick Wymark, is referred to simply as 'the Judge', but it's clear who the blueprint for the unnamed personality was, as at one point in the film he toasts 'Our Catholic Majesty, the King over the Water', which is a direct reference to James II after he was deposed in 1688.*

But I reiterate that this part of the tale is fiction. In truth, Judge Jeffreys didn't survive his master's downfall, not even to live quietly in a peaceful West Country village.

He was thrown into the Tower of London, and left there to die.

IN THE LAND OF THUNDER
Adrian Cole

Deep beneath the earth it slept the deep sleep of eons, a power beyond human imagining, detached from the world above, impervious to change, immutable. Unknown and unknowable, outside time, dreaming in other dimensions, waiting.

Somewhere on the highest uplands of the Moor, set at the heart of a wide, flat expanse where only the short grass and heather grew, a single tall stone rose up, a long, gnarled finger, pointing at the heavens. Several meters high, the menhir had been slotted into the ground by men of another age, its rugged stone tapping into the earth. From its vantage point at the apex of the long valley it looked out on the world, a solitary observer, alone and untouched for millennia. Around it the clouds formed and shifted, and the elements sighed or roared, season by endless season. The beating heart of the Moor pulsed through it in the Land of Thunder.

Delve studied the ragged facade of the old building. Ragged, because it looked battered and blown by decades of strong winds off the distant moorlands to its north, and salt-whipped blasts from winter seas to the south. Being hidden in the heart of the city hadn't spared it the kind of weathering that had brought most of the other buildings around it to ruin, clearance and replacement. A red-brick Victorian fortress, the library held on to its existence defiantly, like an old warrior on one knee, stoically resisting change, though Delve surmised its days were numbered.

The archives it contained, the priceless old records, had kept it going through the voracious progress of the computer age, but even these historical treasures would either be relocated or transformed and pumped along the electronic information highway before long. The library's defenders were mostly old men and women now, the best of them long gone, and in most cases forgotten. They graced a local cemetery, and even that had a number on it, due for change. The city planners were hungry for what they called brownfield land.

Delve had left his car parked down a narrow side street, where there was plenty of room. It was a rough area, but there was nothing to indicate the vehicle would be attacked by kids with little better to do on a wintry Wednesday morning than climb all over it or rip open its tyres. There were other areas in the city where such barbarism was par for the course.

Delve decided the library must have been converted from something else at some point in its hundred year history. Not a church, but a chapel, maybe, or a chantry. It was the long, tall windows that suggested it, with their stained glass, rainbow colours of blurred images. Certainly it had a distinct air of refuge about it.

He glanced around him, a little nervously. He'd almost convinced himself the bad old days were behind him, the reliance on alcohol, beer and chasers, which had wrecked his family life. He'd been free of booze's grip for a year, and the things he'd seen, the nightmares conjured by the heaviest, uncontrolled bouts, had not returned. Nor had the shakes. Stay sober and they won't, his doctor had told him, and he'd been right so far. Even so, Delve remained apprehensive, mistrusting every shadow.

As he went through the library's arched wooden doors into the lobby, the feeling of sanctuary was reinforced, as if he'd left some kind of threat behind him. Others may have taken comfort from its quaint mustiness.

A number of modern strip lights hung incongruously from the high beams inside the main chamber, their bright glare shafting down into the tunnels lined with row upon row of books and manuscripts. The gaps in these suggested that the withdrawal and relocation programme was already well under way. Delve stood by a counter and waited. In a moment an elderly man emerged from an office that had been squeezed into a corner, almost as an afterthought.

He was unprepossessing, wore bland jacket and trousers and looked directly, almost challenging at Delve. Maybe he didn't really want anyone else in here, poking through the collection, violating its pages. 'Mr John Delve?' The man made it sound oddly formal.

Delve nodded, deciding that he was probably doing the guy a disservice. 'Yes, I rang yesterday. I'm visiting the city. Looking up some old family records.'

'Oh, yes, you're a journalist.' The man spoke with sudden enthusiasm rather than the unease with which a lot of people greeted members of the profession. Lawyers, estate agents, journalists, all monsters in the modern world.

'Well, I did a bit of looking through what we have, Mr Delve, and I did find a few things that might interest you. You said you were writing an article?'

'That's right. You're probably not familiar with my column. I like to dig into almost forgotten historical mysteries. As often as not they're dead ends, but they provide a bit of entertainment for the readers over their Sunday coffee.'

'Yes, I've read some of your pieces. *Dig and Delve*. That's your byline, isn't it?' The man smiled neutrally.

Delve nodded. It wasn't brilliantly original, but people remembered it.

'I found them quite good fun. You do your research thoroughly.'

'I'm particularly keen to write this new piece, as there's a family connection. My ancestors were from the South West. As far as I can tell, originally farmers who moved into the city to make a bit more of themselves. One branch took to the military life.'

There was a table and a few archaic chairs between two bulging presses, and the librarian had set out various books, maps and pamphlets there, evidently having been busy on Delve's behalf. 'Let me know if you need anything else,' he said. 'Otherwise I'll leave you to it.'

Delve took out his tablet with a private grin. Heresy, probably. He should be jotting down his notes in a paper notepad with a biro, which as a junior he'd done for years. He sat at the table and pulled the first of the books across to him. Light fell on it from one of the windows, an odd mixture of colours, blended by the stained glass. He glanced up at the window's impressive twenty foot height, trying to pick out its details. If they were meant to be biblical representations, he couldn't identify them. They seemed to be more abstract, as if the glazier had set them into their lead casings randomly, colourful mosaics celebrating the imagination rather than anything specifically religious. The power of God, or the light of angels, maybe that was the idea.

It wasn't long before he found his initial family references. The historical incident that had first attracted his attention had been a notorious one in this part of the world. It concerned a Captain Thomas Shortland, the Governor of Dartmoor Prison two hundred years in the past. There was an entire chapter on him in the first book Delve opened.

The notorious prison, built in one of the most remote and inhospitable parts of the country at Princetown, in the heart of bleakest Dartmoor, was completed in 1809, using the labour of several thousand French prisoners from the Napoleonic War. They endured atrocious conditions, savage winters and the incessant mists as they cut granite from the local quarry and erected a nightmare in its stone, their own living purgatory.

Delve tried to picture the scene in his mind. He'd not yet been up on to the higher lands of the Moor and the grim, grey village there, but even from the city where he now sat, sixteen miles away, the tors and high ridges of the Moor cast a long shadow in the north, bleak and forbidding. He glanced at the high window, and for a brief moment it seemed to ripple, as if his dark thoughts were reflected back from its numerous glass fragments. Somewhere beyond them, a wind rose across the cityscape, a mournful backdrop to the history he was trawling.

Another war, the Anglo-American War that ended in 1814, brought fresh prisoners to Dartmoor, for the most part replacing the French, who had been released after Napoleon's initial defeat and imprisonment on Elba. Six thousand Americans were incarcerated in the living hell of Dartmoor Prison long after their war ended, as their governments argued callously about who should ship them back to America. Their sojourn became unbearable, as the Governor, a man wedded to strong drink, cursed and cajoled them, determined to make examples of them, unforgiving and brutal.

Delve wiped sweat from his neck as he read the unsavoury account. If this man had been his ancestor, he was an embarrassment to the family, a cold-blooded sot whose horrific treatment of the prisoners was conducted so far from the rest of his world that his superiors took little or no interest in the way he managed things.

Outside, the wind had strengthened as if gathering force with every damning sentence Delve read, and it began to churn the air around the old library, almost in protest at the evils perpetrated so long ago. The tall window creaked, like an old galleon straining at its moorings, its timbers stretched. Delve watched the glass. The whole structure belled inward slightly like a wind-filled sail, which was impossible, of course. It couldn't do it without shattering. Nevertheless Delve shifted in his seat, turning his back on the multi-hued glass and the gathering gusts outside.

He returned to his reading. Events in the prison came to a terrible head one April night, when Shortland was shown a hole in the prison wall which the Governor convinced himself was an attempt by some of the prisoners to dig a tunnel to freedom. Enraged, his fury fueled by a prolonged drinking session down in the city earlier, he lost his temper and called in men from a regiment stationed in the village. The prisoners, thinking a fire alarm had been raised, broke out into the main yard, forcing the main gates. Shortland ordered a bayonet charge, and then insisted his troops open fire. Seven prisoners died, seven more needed amputations and fifty were severely injured. Only the disgust of the soldiers, most of whom refused to kill the prisoners and fired over their heads, stopped wholesale slaughter.

Behind him, Delve heard the outrage of the wind, as though it gave voice to its own disgust at the events of the past. Again the creaking came and he turned. The glass window panels bulged in a score of places, like plastic sheets bent inward as if human faces were pressed up against them outside, eyeless, but with open mouths, screaming in protest. Screaming at him? Delve shrank back in sudden terror. If that glass cracked and whatever was out there entered, he'd be engulfed.

This is insane. I haven't touched alcohol for a year. I can't be suffering DTs again, not sober. It's just not possible.

He tore his eyes from the glass and the things that gaped.

'It's a pretty ghastly story, isn't it?' said a voice behind him, jerking him back to reason. The librarian stood over him, and Delve gasped. He was dazed for a moment, flushed with sudden sweat, but dragged himself away from the threat from the tall window.

'Yes,' he said. 'Bloody awful.'

'Of course,' said the librarian blandly, 'he got away with it. They always do, don't they? There was a formal inquiry, and he was exonerated. The military looked after their own. Like the Church. And politicians.'

'What happened to him?' Delve wasn't sure if he had any great desire to read more, not today at any rate.

'Usual thing. The Army moved him on. Nice promotion, out into the sun. He became Commissioner of Port Royal Dockyard in Jamaica. Nice work if you can get it. He had ten years or so, then died of yellow fever. Unpleasant, but he got off lightly, wouldn't you say?'

Delve risked another glance at the stained glass window. The librarian hadn't seen what he'd seen. It must have been illusion. Now the window was motionless, the terrifying faces behind its glass gone. But the wind continued to claw at it.

'I'm making some tea. Like a cup?'

'Uh, no, that's very kind, but I need to press on. I'll come back if I may. I need to go up to Princetown this afternoon. I'd like to see the prison.'

'This storm has settled in for the rest of the day, so it'll be pretty wild up on the moors.'

'That's okay. I need some fresh air.'

'Don't say I didn't warn you.'

Delve drove through the gathering winds of the gale, slowly rising up along the lower skirts of Dartmoor, the road winding through the great shoulders of its granite tors, becoming more exposed as the early afternoon wore on. Clouds raced in bloated packs overhead, already lowered on to the upper crags, blotting them out, bringing a greyness to the terrain, a premature evening that threatened to worsen with every mile driven. He'd booked himself into a small hotel in Princetown a few days previously and was determined to reach its cover, do his research on the prison, and bed down for no more than one night.

The wind was strengthened by horizontal shafts of rain that slapped up against the side of the car in a disturbingly effective attempt to roll it over, and twice Delve had to grit his teeth against sudden swerves that could have had him veering into the ditches at either side of the road. He passed Merrivale, where the old quarry that had supplied not only Princetown but all parts of the world with granite in its heyday, had become a grey scar on the side of a huge tor's flank. Now closed, the quarry's buildings and rusting machinery were only vaguely visible, a bizarre, gaping tomb in the Moor's wilderness.

Further on, rounding another sweep of road, Delve was confronted by a further spectacular construct. Rising out of the murk, high overhead for nearly six hundred and fifty feet, was the Princetown aerial, the metal mast that was the television transmitter for the lands surrounding it for miles. Delve knew the village must be close by.

He turned a curving bend and again almost swerved. A

company of men, some fifty or more of them, was trudging up the hill. As Delve drew alongside them, he was appalled by their condition. What in God's name had they been doing? They wore rags, ill-fitting and tattered, and didn't seem to have a pair of shoes or boots between them. They were filthy, coated in dust and muck, as if they had just emerged from a mine or pit, and their bare arms and faces were uniquely pale, their haunted eyes sunken, staring ahead of them like men plodding to the gallows.

As Delve passed each couple, he realised with a fresh start that they were chained together in pairs, each pair linked on to a longer chain. Prisoners! But they were wretched beyond belief. Like something from the past. He gasped. The past? *Two hundred years* in the past? Merrivale Quarry, which he'd not long passed, had been closed in 1997, so they couldn't have come from there. And the current authorities could not possibly have meted out this sort of treatment to modern prisoners. Was there a festival on?

The men's faces began to turn, almost in unison, so that those dreadful eyes gazed at Delve, accusing and hateful. Something in him had animated them. They were like ghastly dolls, jerked to life, their bare hands, blistered and bloodied, lifting as though they would grab at the passing vehicle and worse, its occupant. Delve felt their fury like an embellishment of the storm. He saw an out-flung arm, its claw of a hand pointing directly at him, the wild face behind it animated by a kind of madness. The men carried tools, picks, stonework axes and long, spatulate chisels. Suddenly another arm rose and one of these came spinning through the air and struck the right hand window. Immediately it turned to a spider's web of cracks, but mercifully the glass held. Delve swerved across to the other side of the road, putting his foot down so the car leapt forward, beyond the row of prisoners. There seemed to be no guards, no one in charge of these men.

Delve glanced into his mirror. Mist was swirling around him now, mingled with the low clouds, and in minutes he was into a new region, another world. Driving was dangerous in this murk, and he was thankful nothing was coming the other way. Behind him the chain gang had been swallowed by the gloom, with no chance of catching up with him. He could have believed he'd imagined them, but for the mass of cracks in the door's window. By the time he reached Princetown and found the hotel where he'd booked in, he had just about calmed down. If the receptionist thought his nervousness and slightly unkempt appearance was odd, he didn't comment.

An hour later, showered and refreshed, Delve was surprised to look out of his bedroom window and see that the clouds had gone and the afternoon was bright with sunlight. The sky overhead was blue.

'You get used to quick changes here,' said the receptionist, when Delve commented on it. 'This can be the prettiest place in the country, or the gloomiest,' he laughed, 'all in a matter of an hour or two.'

Delve got back into his car, but not before glancing all around him at the streets and the woods on the hill rising up beyond the houses, where deep green pine trees rustled in a breeze. There were a few people going about their daily business, but no one suspicious and certainly no hint of the grim chain gang he'd seen. He ran his fingers over the cracked glass. It was real enough. He wondered about reporting the incident, but thought better of it.

Instead he drove the short distance to the prison and parked close to the main gates. The amount of granite that had been used to construct the prison was almost total, the grey stone giving an impression of depth and strength, resistance to any force. If anything could withstand the batterings of the local weather extremes, granite could do that easily. It gave an impression of timelessness, and the prison looked as if it could stand for all time. Delve walked along some of the narrow roads around it, taking pictures with his mobile phone. Even in this bright daylight the high walls and such buildings as he could see beyond them had a sombre, forbidding quality to them, as though every massive stone of their construction carried its own tale of pain and misery, a cyclopean memorial to whatever lives had been lost erecting it.

The huge blocks were topped with immense, fat chimneys that had the appearance of something from a Victorian factory, looming threateningly over the whole construction. There was no smoke emerging from them now as Delve studied them, but he could picture voluminous clouds of it spewing forth as if from the furnaces of some satanic cavern. Tiny windows looked out over the Moor, dull eyes on a terrain that was mostly duller, as though the prison had been set here at the very edge of hell itself, with brief glimpses of a miserable afterlife. It was, Delve realised, the perfect deterrent to any prisoners thinking about escaping. He'd read that those who had made it out of the granite fastness had either died on the Moor, or been sucked in by its bogs, easily recaptured, glad to return to the lesser hell of incarceration. Delve wondered about the days of the French and American prisoners. Their lives inside had been far worse than anything in recent years. Maybe attempted flight across the terrors of the moorland would have been preferable to the atrocities of the Governor's reign.

Delve had to steel himself to visit the Museum, and once inside it, studying some of its records and seeing some of its exhibits, he began to get a sharpened view of what the prison had been like. Particularly unnerving were the examples of convict restraints, which would have been used in the time of Thomas Shortland. The manacles were a bad enough example of man's potential for cruelty, but the straitjackets and the flogging equipment came as a shock. Reading about them would always be disturbing, but to see them really brought Delve's horror home. Somehow it seemed to him that these frightful objects retained the blood and sweat of the men who'd been tormented by them. His mind flipped back to the chain gang he'd seen on the road. Those men would have been subjected to these instruments of agony. Delve looked into the men's eyes again, understanding the pain that flooded them.

Outside in the late afternoon, he was relieved to get some air. He'd recorded as much information as he needed for his article. Maybe a meal and a good night's sleep would set him on his way. Another day of reading up on reference material at the old library, and he could go home.

The hotel evening meal had been pleasantly enjoyable. As he sat back and sipped at his mineral water, his host began taking away the plates and cutlery.

'Everything okay?'

'Very nice. Ideal after a day like this. That's a nasty wind out there. Spring seems a long way off.'

The man laughed softly. 'Yeah, we're usually a bit behind the rest of the world. May Day in a few weeks is usually when we think about spring.'

'Do you have any festivals happening? Before May Day?'

'No, bit early for all that. Things are quiet right now.'

Delve was thinking about the strange procession he'd seen. 'Nothing to do with the old quarry?'

The man frowned in concentration. 'No. Merrivale closed nigh on twenty years ago. Not been any activity there since, although the village is still going.'

'When it was working, did the prisoners work the quarry?'

'Yeah, they were the first to dig it out. Built the prison. Labour didn't come any cheaper! Merrivale did well in its heyday.'

They exchanged a few more pleasantries. Back in his room, Delve prepared to read through some of his notes, scribble down the bones of his article, shower and go to bed. Looking through his stuff, he realised he must have left a couple of pamphlets he'd picked up in the Prison Museum in his car. It was parked in the hotel car park, so it wasn't too much of a fag to go and retrieve them.

Outside it was a cold night, cloudless with bright pin-pricks of stars peppering the heavens. He got the pamphlets and re-locked the car, turning to head back to the hotel. As he did so, something moved in the shadows alongside the hotel. The light there was poor, the way to the front of the hotel unlit, a blind spot. But there were other movements in it. Several shapes were lurking there, a group of men, little more than blurs. Delve would have walked past them, but the cold hand of irrational fear had gripped the back of his neck. He looked around him for another way into the hotel. There was a door at the back, light somewhere inside.

He went to it quickly, and heard the shuffling of footsteps as the group of men also moved. Something else chilled him. The sound of chains clinking. This was ridiculous, he told himself. He must be superimposing something of the day's shock when he'd seen the convicts.

Thickening shadows came around the side of the hotel as he reached the door and tried the handle. The door was locked. He could try knocking, but the chances of being answered before the shapes reached him were small. Instead, he turned and started to run back towards the car. He saw with a new flush of horror there were other men there, bone white faces picked out by the curved moon above the Moor. Faces that glared, eyes that burned. One of the men pointed to him. They were trying to say something, but their voices were no more than deep croaks, the sounds confused.

He veered away, across the almost empty car park. There was a small wall surrounding it, a metre high drystone wall, typical of this area, stones laid by skilled men without the use of any mortar, fitted together precisely, an ancient barrier against the wildest weather. A single gate broke the line of the wall and Delve rushed for it. Behind him he heard men shuffling after him from several directions. The gate wasn't locked, set on a latch and he fumbled it open and went through. Blind instinct drove him now.

They were after him like a pack of dogs. He ran up into a clump of pines. Mercifully the ground underfoot was solid, a bed of packed needles where no undergrowth had been generated. His breathing quickly became laboured, the meal he'd eaten heavy in his gut. *Ten years ago I'd have been twice as fit and with more stamina*, he told himself. It was a lie, though. Ten years ago he'd been a slave to the poison, a boozed-up wreck heading for a train crash.

He allowed himself a brief backward glance. Dozens of shapes were clambering up the slope, men that looked in this half-light more like apes groping their way forward on all fours. It hampered their speed and he realised if he could muster the strength to do it, he could put some distance between himself and them quickly. He reached a ridge, still well below the upper crest of the tor, and ran along it, an easier task than climbing. Below him he made out the shapes and angles of the upper village houses, most of them in darkness. Somewhere a dog howled, and others joined in.

Once clear of the houses, he was almost smothered in darkness. He felt certain there was a road not far below him. If he could reach it, he could move more quickly away from the pursuit and get back into the village. There must be somewhere he could evade those men. Another pub. People would think he was off his head, but to hell with what they thought. He just wanted to get free. He scrambled down the slope and saw the road like a thick, dark river. Once he got to it, he turned to look back up the way he'd come. His pursuers weren't in sight, but he was certain they would still be after him.

He jogged along the road as a sudden gust of wind hit him like a punch and he had to duck down to save himself being knocked off his feet. What had been still air suddenly twisted about him, a living vortex that seemed to have conspired with the men chasing him to bring him to his knees. Something white flapped in the air above him, like a huge, distorted gull. He ducked again but the shapeless horror found him and wrapped itself around his head and shoulders. He wanted to scream, but his nose and mouth were clogged up by the damp mass and as he clawed at it, ripping sections from it like rotted flesh, he thought he would suffocate.

He got it free of his face and pulled most of the remainder off with one desperate heave, realising with a sob of relief what it was -- a sodden newspaper, windblown and aimless, not a spirit of the moors. As he tore it angrily apart and let its pages dash away in another gust, he caught sight of part of it, a photo and the date. It was today's, April 6, 2015. He had no time to dwell on it: the pursuers were closing again, their hunched shadows bobbing, their silence unnerving.

For a moment he was confused about direction. He had partly stumbled into one of the low ditches that ran along the roadsides. There were confused sounds along the road, muffled by the wind, which increased by the minute. A fat bank of cloud pushed down from the slopes of the tors on all sides, its appearance abrupt and threatening. Delve jumped on to the soft heather and started climbing. If he stayed on the road now, he'd be an easy prey. Better to make his way around the lower tor and back to the village.

The nature of the terrain, with its small collapsed banks and jagged rocks, forced him upwards. The cloud hadn't reached him yet, burgeoning into the valley below and starting to blot out the road. As it shut out the view, he saw the first lights of the village. He was climbing the wrong side of the valley! In the confusion below with the newspaper he'd somehow turned and was going northward. Before he could start the downward climb back to the road, the clouds rolled over it. The pursuers came out of it. Scores of them broke from the road and on to the lower tor like a sluggish but inexorable tide. He would have to go on climbing, his only hope that the clouds would wrap him and conceal him.

Fortunately the heather was low and tightly packed here, a carpet that afforded him a good grip, and he was able to force himself to go on, even though his breathing was becoming more laboured, the ache in his chest more pronounced. Fear gave him energy. Time had already started to warp. He had no idea what time he'd come on to the Moor, or how long he'd been labouring across it – he'd taken his watch off in the hotel. His sense of direction was also becoming vague, though he assumed by climbing he was heading north. Princetown must surely be somewhere to his right, so he angled his climb, hoping to come back to it in an arc.

Now and then, through a brief break in the swirling cloud, he heard the sounds of the laborious chase: the clink of chains, the crunch of heather underfoot. No voices, though, which made the hunt more terrifying. *Why the hell are they after me?* he repeatedly asked himself.

After that, his journey became a dogged trudge through thickening cloud as the wind whipped up strongly while he rose to the higher slopes of the tor. Its dull roar blotted out everything else until he heard a deep, far-off rumble, thunder in the distance, up in the heart of the Moor. He'd become disorientated. Princetown was somewhere to his right, as he thought, but he was in danger of by-passing it. Where was the road? It would guide him. Maybe if he got as high up as he could and then waited for a break in the cloud, which could dissolve as abruptly as it had materialised, he could get his bearings.

Brief sounds to his right and below him forced him to veer away and upwards once more. He was on more level ground now and the shifting cloud revealed another slope rising in the near distance. Its offer of a better view spurred him and he forced himself to keep climbing. The clouds were thinning, encouraging him, and the wind was dropping as he picked his way through small outcrops of granite. Behind him the wall of cloud pulsed with its own energies like a restless sea, and though he could no longer hear anything within it, something told him it hid the pursuers, who were still coming for him, a mob of them. He imagined their garish, white faces, their accusing eyes.

Below him on the right, the tor slid away into a deep valley, carved an age ago by the fiercely flowing brook that cut down from even higher tors north of him. There were a few scrubby, stunted trees in the valley, and a low, wire fence. Princetown was nowhere to be seen, and the tall mast that would have pin-pointed it was invisible. If the clouds had cleared behind him, he knew he'd see it and be able to use it to guide him. Something else moved down in the valley, a shape, too vague to identify, but it was something alive, loping parallel to him. He had no choice but to go forward.

The valley's details became easier to see in the starlight. There was a small wood on the opposite side to him, a long, dark ribbon, its trees almost flattened by the prevailing wind up here, somehow grasping enough soil through the boulders to enable its existence. If it were Wistman's Wood, the ancient oak grove so popular with tourists, it meant he was heading in the opposite direction to Princetown. Not only that, but he was going right up into the heart of the Moor. He had to cross the valley and find the path from the wood back southwards to the road.

As he prepared to clamber downward, he saw and heard his pursuers, dozens of whom were in the valley. They'd followed him along the lower slopes of this tor and there was no way he could avoid them if he tried to get across the fence. All that mattered was that he escape them, that much he was sure of. The one thing that kept him going was the fact they had not closed the gap on him: if anything he was widening it. Again he found himself climbing up the face of yet another steep tor. As long as he knew he was heading north, he could swing round at some point and head back. He had to cling desperately to that belief.

The threat of exhaustion was the problem now. He wasn't properly kitted out for trekking the moors, his jacket and trousers too thin, his shoes not sturdy enough. He was damp and getting colder. So many people got caught out on the Moor and succumbed to exposure. It was bad enough by day, but this cold, wind-blasted night was wearing him down, more and more. And out here there would be no shelter. Even the sparse stacks at the crest of some of the tors, with their clusters of boulders, offered minimal safety. As if to underline his grim thoughts, another bank of cloud rolled in from the west, a fast-flowing tide which caught him up in a moment, the wind mocking him, followed by grumbling thunder, much closer now. Hell, if he went into a thunderstorm, it would mean rain, and up on these merciless heights he would be finished.

Time and distance had again become so distorted he had no idea how far on to the high moorland he had come. He paused briefly, trying to penetrate the cloud, but it held, the wind incessant. *They're here*, his mind shouted above the roar. *I'm surrounded. No way out.* And another even more terrifying thought hit him like a fist. *I need a drink. God, how I need a drink.*

He'd almost succumbed to the blasts of air, his legs aching so much he wanted to drop to his knees, when he saw a narrow tunnel through the cloud banks. It led across the flat plateau of the tor's summit for a hundred yards or more. At its end there was a solitary shape, a black finger, pointing directly upwards, a stone, an ancient relic of a people from another time. A menhir. Its uniqueness, its solitary appearance in an otherwise barren, inhospitable landscape, frightened him, and yet it was like a magnet. He felt a bizarre flow of energy in his lower limbs and a sense of being *tugged*.

As he started towards the stone, he realised the prisoners hadn't herded him at all. The stone had drawn him, like some ancient occult priest, pulling him to the sacrifice. He fought the drag in vain, his legs refusing to obey his brain, as though he were caught in a whirlpool, being sucked towards its heart. The cloud rolled in, blotting the vision, then broke again, and did this several times, until Delve stood under the shadow of the rock, panting like a spent hound and helpless to resist.

It was some twelve feet tall, probably four feet wide, and was deceptively thin. He had a vague recollection of it from the various books and records he'd been reading about the Moor around Princetown. The Beardown Man. Yes, this must be it, a prehistoric remnant of a culture that had erected and revered such monuments. As he stood before it, a bemused supplicant at the foot of an elder god, the world became suddenly extraordinarily silent.

The clouds dissolved and the night sky opened up once more, its stars somehow more dazzling, their light brighter than any starlight Delve had known previously. As the cloud fell away, the wind dropped to nothing, not even a breeze, and an almost supernatural stillness gripped the wide plateau. One last boom of thunder muttered somewhere to the north. Delve turned, and what he saw made him drop to his knees, the last of his resistance seeping away like the clouds.

They were all around him, encircling him some thirty yards

away on all sides. The prisoners, the frightful beings who'd toiled at the stone quarry and been crammed into the prison. Not today's residents. These were from another time. Two hundred years ago. Today's date, of which he had been so unpleasantly reminded by the flapping newspaper, was the anniversary of the killings, the Americans massacred by the soldiers.

Each of the figures raised an arm, pointing at Delve. To his utter horror he heard again the low rasp of their combined voices, like another gust of fetid wind. This time those voices merged to form a single word, rolled out gutturally, like a curse.

'Shortland.'

His name. He gaped at them as they repeated it. He tried to shout his denial, but his voice was a low croak. 'David Shortland. I'm *David* Shortland, not Thomas.' Two hundred years separated him from his ancestor, but as he'd already sensed, time here was distorted, changed, blurred. 'I'm not the Governor.'

Nothing registered on their faces to suggest they had heard him, nor cared what he was trying to tell them. Instead they started to close in, their hands like weapons, readying to take their revenge, weighed in flesh and blood. He rose unsteadily and was powerless to resist the pull of the stone, crushed back against it. It was warm to touch, even through his damp clothes. He felt the ground vibrate as the prisoners shambled forward, their numbers swelled to a hundred or more.

Behind him the stone reverberated to the trembling of the ground. Its heat grew in intensity, as if it had been ignited from within like a huge battery. Delve shuddered as he felt the thing hum into life. It had pulled him to its flat surface like a magnet, trapping him like a fly, spreading him on its vertical altar for the horrors to come. Light flared high overhead, the return of the thunderstorm, spearing downwards, striking the stone, the lone conductor. Delve was rocked, but not harmed, though his bones grated.

The prisoners were closing in for their bloody vengeance, but an abrupt explosion of light from the stone bathed them all in brilliant white. Its power was so intense that Delve had to close his eyes, still unable to break free of the stone. Thunder rocked the entire plateau as though a dozen heavy artillery guns had fired simultaneously, shaking the ground as if a huge beast had awoken.

Delve dropped like an empty sack. He groped about blindly and found the base of the stone, pressing both hands to it as though it were a door that would open and let him into a safe place. Silence came down abruptly. Silence and darkness. The vivid light had gone as if it had never been. A wave of emotions swirled around Delve, sweeping up all the anger and hatred that seethed beyond him, calming it, sucking it down into the earth, the amalgamated misery of those lost years buried at last. *Rest*, the air seemed to breathe, speaking not to him but the horde of prisoners.

It was a long time before Delve could open his eyes. The crowding prisoners had not reached him. Instead they were crumbling like sand, dissipating like the clouds. Across the flat top of the tor, starlight gleamed from the bare rocks. There were more of them now, one for each of the prisoners, a small tombstone.

Delve got to his feet. The shivering cold had left him and whatever power burned in the Beardown Man had reinvigorated his aching muscles. The irresistible grip of the stone relinquished him, as though he had imagined it. Freed, he'd lost that damning desire for a drink that had welled up so terribly. The stone had brought him here not to sacrifice him, but to heal him – he felt as though something dark and insidious, coiled up inside him for years, had been burned away.

In the distant south, the television aerial at Princetown rose as a bank of lights, beckoning him back, a promise of release from this nightmare. Threading carefully through the scattered stones, he felt a sense of relief, as if a circle had been closed, a deep wound healed. Behind him he thought the tall stone menhir hummed softly like a generator. Perhaps that's what it was. Then again, it may just have been another gust of wind, closing time's portal.

THE THING IN THE WATER

Few Britons of a certain age will be able to forget Lonely Water, *a public information film produced by Illustra Films for the Central Office of Information in 1973. It was written by Christine Hermon and directed by Jeff Grant, and narrated by horror movie veteran, Donald Pleasence, who assumed the guise of a mysterious cowled and hooded entity that haunted the banks of lonely lakes, rivers, streams and other waterways, watching dispassionately as young children, sometimes alone, sometimes in small groups, got themselves into trouble while ill-advisedly swimming.*

It was part of a large-scale televised campaign of that era, produced on behalf of the British Government, to advise and caution members of the public about a variety of potential dangers they might encounter in everyday life. But Lonely Water *was perhaps the most memorable of all, not least because it was given such prominence on television due to rising concerns about accidental drowning deaths, particularly among the young. Partly, this alarming trend was the result of much abandoned industrial land, including millponds, flooded quarries, canals and underwater mine-workings, being left unfenced. But it was also the case that significant numbers of the British population still could not swim. It's no coincidence that it was around this time, the late 1960s and early 1970s, when the British Government began to promote widescale organised swimming tuition.*

All these measures were successful. In the UK in the 21st century, inland drowning statistics have improved dramatically since 1973. However, Lonely Water *still has the power to chill and enthrall. Partly because it was so unashamedly done in the style of a full-on horror movie, but also because it drew, maybe unintentionally, on age-old, deep-rooted suspicions that dark water was often the abode of evil spirits, and that people drowned in it had either been lured in, or quite literally dragged in.*

Of course, this sinister myth was not unique to the West Country. In the distant past, it was a commonly held belief all over Britain

156

('Jenny Greenteeth' in England's Northwest, 'Peg Powler' in the Northeast, the 'mere-wives' of East Anglia), and probably the world over (the Russian 'Vodyanoi', the German 'Nixie', the Japanese 'Kappa'), but in Britain, in Devon in fact, the River Dart certainly seemed to claim more than its fair share of innocent lives. So much so that it soon was the subject of a popular if macabre rhyming couplet:

> *River of Dart, Oh River of Dart!*
> *Every year thou claimest a heart.*

It should be no surprise that the River Dart lies in the middle of so much Devonshire folklore. It's one of the most spectacular rivers in England, flowing from two main sources, the East Dart rising at the great Northern Fen, the West Dart at Flat Tor, the waters converging at Dartmeet and continuing south across Dartmoor, the vast sweep of undulating wild country already so evocative in English mystery and tradition, finally emptying into the sea at Dartmouth, where it passes between the twin medieval fortresses of Kingswear and Dartmouth Castle.

If more than an average number of lives have been lost in the Dart over the years, it shouldn't be unexpected. The river is deep and runs very fast over numerous sections of rapids and waterfalls. When it's in full spate due to snow-melt or heavy rain on the high moors, it's a ferocious sight. On top of that, people often make the mistake of attempting to ride it in kayaks, to cross it by wading and even to go swimming there. However, it isn't just the death statistics that have tagged the River Dart with its menacing reputation. Belief that a malign intelligence lurks within the water is a very ancient one, as we've seen, but there is recent evidence for it too.

Sometime in the 1880s, Jan Coo, a farmworker who was based at Rowbrook Farm, very close to Dartmeet, was toiling on the land with various colleagues when he heard a strange and alluring voice, a woman's by the sound of it, calling his name in singsong fashion from somewhere down by the river. Though his friends urged him not to respond, and he initially tried to resist, he soon became captivated and hurried down to the riverbank alone. Needless to say, he was never seen again.

In itself, this supposedly true story is proof of nothing. But take it in tandem with another snippet of folklore concerning the River Dart and it becomes much more frightening.

Because the river, they say, 'cries'.

What they mean by this is that several times a year, usually during the winter, it calls the names of those it intends to drown, and if these unfortunates hear it, they seemingly have no option but to go down there and meet whatever fate is in store for them.

As far as my own researches can tell, this makes the devil of the River Dart almost unique in British mysticism. The Grindy Lows and Wet Jennies elsewhere in the UK supposedly lurk beneath the surface and pull you in if you stray too near. I've never heard it said anywhere else that they summon you by name and you throw yourself in.

Perhaps unexpectedly though, there is a possible explanation even for this eeriest of fables. Naturalists out on the loneliest parts of the moor have also reported hearing the River Dart 'cry', describing it as a spooky sound that is very reminiscent of a female voice wailing or singing. Subsequent investigations have supposedly discovered natural causes, the waters droning uncannily when travelling at a particular speed and depth over a series of curiously-shaped granite outcrops known as the Broad Stones.

That may be a mundane explanation for the mysterious and dangerous entity that supposedly inhabits the River Dart, but if you prefer the darker, scarier version, don't worry, you aren't alone. Many people still vanish into that foaming torrent. Far too many, local folk will say, for it to be anything like a normal occurrence.

UNRECOVERED
Stephen Volk

I could tell on sight exactly what they made of me. Bare arms covered in tats. Doc Martens. Short hair. No make up. *Lesbian.* On my part, a bunch of hefty blokes getting off an army truck, my presumptions were just as stereotypical. Plainly they'd be knuckle-draggers, illiterate, sexist, right wing, interested mostly in larking around and necking pints, brimful of macho bullshit.

Turns out, we were both off the mark. Bigtime.

Hand on heart, I fully expected thumpers and breakers, used to cracking heads and blowing up things, but it soon became apparent the technical side of the trades they had learned in the forces were exactly the skills we needed in the field. Precision, the ability to absorb information and follow a brief, but also knowing when to refer upwards in the chain of command. Which in this case – ha ha – meant me.

I was prepared for the usual unimaginative nicknames – Taffy, Smithy, Chalky. In fact, to my surprise, apart from the notably talkative Harpo, Poshie (who really wasn't, to my ears), and 'Donuts' (first name Duncan, geddit?), they mostly went by the common or garden names they were christened with: Andy, Wayne, Chris, Simon, Jamie, Luke. One thing I thought they would bring was the ability to fit in a team. And I was right.

Inwardly, my eyes rolled as Tony Burford welcomed them on day one. Tony always thought that floppy safari hat gave him the air of Indiana Jones, but in fact it made him look like the emaciated brother of one of the *Hairy Bikers*. I knew right away the boys found him comical – as did I, to be honest – but they never disrespected him in any way, not within my earshot, anyhow. From the off, it put me on the back foot to see that they inherently accepted his expertise, even though, to them, he was a bit of an alien life form.

Me, they were more wary of.

I was an unknown. I was a woman, for a start.

It was called Project Orinoco. What it had to do with a South American river, fuck knows, unless someone high up in the military was a secret Enya fan. Funded by the Heritage Lottery Fund, the idea behind it was to give ex-soldiers a taste of new disciplines into which they could transfer their skillsets, as some way of rekindling some sense of self belief, or self-worth, now they were in Civvy Street. The strap line on the reading material was: *Helping veterans' recovery through archaeology.* Meaning physical and psychological recovery. For people who'd seen more in their young lives than I ever wanted to see in some late night horror film.

How archaeology was meant to do that, I wasn't sure, but was keen to find out. Particularly if they could give us extra manpower to help one of our most interesting excavations in years. If that makes me sound a bit of an opportunist going in, yeah. Maybe. And why not? If it worked for us and worked for them, it was win-win. I had no objection to hanging out with some fit-looking young men who occasionally took their shirts off.

But these weren't Rambo types who wore their kills on their sleeves, or talked disparagingly about 'towel-heads'. As Captain Dominic Hussey (Bosnia, Basra, Kabul), the creator of the scheme, was keen to point out when he briefed us, these were people who had seen combat in Iraq and Afghanistan, and might have had physical injuries that were life changing, might suffer from PTSD, battle with suicidal thoughts, or all of the above.

Their pasts were damaged: A devastated, bombed-out landscape, every building a husk. A place you wouldn't want to visit, let alone live there. If they were doling out acts of aggression in a former life, for Queen and country, they were victims of violence now. They'd paid a hell of a price, and deserved a fair crack at a future. I was more than happy to facilitate their passage back to normal life, or help them in that direction, if we could. Just as long as they were happy to get their hands dirty.

All this happened at a bit of a strange point in my life, which was about to get significantly stranger.

Just before the Orinoco briefing, I was having a drink with one of the girls working on the Roman mosaic at Wilcot Verecunda. I happened to say I had a nagging pain in my right breast that wouldn't go away. I thought it was a pulled muscle, but maybe subconsciously I knew something was wrong. I didn't know she'd had a mastectomy but she was immediately in my face to get it checked out. Thank God I did, and caught it early. Fragments showed up like flakes in a snow globe on the X-ray; shards of an exploded dum-dum bullet, hanging in space. The doctor said I was lucky. They were pre-cancer cells and there was a good chance chemotherapy would wipe them out. She was confident, she said. But she wasn't the patient. I was.

You hear talk of endless vomiting, of constant rushes to the toilet. It wasn't a bed of roses but I wasn't like that for me at all. You hear what people say, how dreadful they feel, and you feel guilty. I wasn't flattened, but I did pee a lot, several oceans, probably. But I was busy, which helped me put it out of my mind, or try to.

My first treatment was the day after the squaddies' big black size twelves hit the mud. I didn't tell any of them. Why would I? It was none of their business. They had a job to do, and so did I.

The site of the dig was a protected scheduled monument called Conigre Hump, not a million miles from Roundway, where evidence had been revealed of a Neolithic settlement, a Bronze Age burial mound, and an Anglo Saxon cemetery – triple whammy. The catch being, it was at risk. Burrowing badgers had caused a lot of damage. Artefacts had been found by metal detectorists, but there was a time limit the DIO gave us to work on MOD-owned land, it being a designated Training Area. Devizes Museum was alerted, and sent in professionals from

Wiltshire Archaeology, such as myself, a couple of interested parties from academic institutions, and a flotilla of volunteers. But we required more boots on the ground, and boots on the ground is what we got. The previous November, volunteers had disclosed human bones outside the barrow, indicating the burial site was vulnerable to heavy farm vehicles and machinery. Consequently, we didn't have time to mess about.

As luck would have it, within the first few days Corporal Stu Duggan unearthed what he called a 'bucket' in one grave that turned out to be a yew and copper drinking vessel, much jollity ensuing about the thought of some bearded Saxon quaffing ale from it.

The boys played it down, but the success lifted their spirits, I could tell. Usually they met in the pub of an evening for cards, banter and a few drinks, but that night they got hammered, as testified by the hangovers they brought to work the next day, making it (to me) a result, in more ways than one. The celebration meant they cared about what they were doing, and that was great.

It was also a relief. We knew going in, it would be a disaster for these guys if we found nothing, the project a dispiriting and futile experiment which might contribute to a backslide in the soldiers' mental health. Luckily, that wasn't the case, and we all quickly noticed the pleasure they got from the smallest discoveries. They showed impressive focus on the task in hand, be it a large job or small, I suppose being used to serving as a small cog in the machine, the big picture only seen by officers many miles, or a continent, away. To them, this was instant gratification.

Plus, what was healthy, as I saw it, was that they had to lay aside sense of competition or winning. There was no us and them. No territory was to be gained or lost. Field archaeology required persistence and patience. Concentration of a different kind than military activity demanded. No stress, no anxiety, no lethal weapons were involved. No sniper with your head in their cross hairs. Gradually it dawned on me that the very *absence* of adrenaline coursing through their veins might make the situation at the dig very scary for them. One of the many things I learned to take into account.

Largely, I admired the way in which they just 'got stuck in' even though it was way outside their comfort zone. Si Littlefield said it was 'like digging a grave with a fork and spoon'. Except they weren't digging one. It was the opposite.

Chris Brinscombe, the one with the prosthetic hook and thumb instead of a hand, joked that he intended to get a new one fitted with a trowel and a brush. One wag said it would have to wait, since he was already waiting for one to replace his pleasuring finger. 'Am I, though?' Chris said with a shit-eating grin, brandishing his *left* hand with the middle digit extended and aquiver. The others howled with mirth.

But from the off, one guy stood out.

Not because he was bigger than the others or more commanding in appearance, or even unusual in any way. Even perhaps because he wasn't.

He didn't erupt into noisy laughter quite as easily as the others, and when a grin came, it seemed more in the nature of a purposeful disguise than something that came naturally. I noticed the rim of his pint glass often went up to cover the fact he wasn't smiling at all.

He was twenty-seven, I found out, but looked to me more like seventeen. Not a gym bod like a lot of the others. Slim and wiry. More fat on a chip.

Close to, you could see a constellation of pits all over his face which I first took to be the aftermath of teenage acne, and a bigger scar on his temple, next to a small but unsightly lump where it looked like something was lodged under the skin. By contrast, a beautiful tattoo of a flying hawk was inked on the side of his neck. When he stripped to his T-shirt on a hot day I saw an M16 rifle along the taut muscle of his inside right forearm, and on the corresponding left something in Latin, which turned out to be the motto of his brigade:

Parce mihi Domine nihil enim sunt dies mei
(Spare me, Lord, for my days are nothing)

I often think about those words. What they meant in the context of a soldier's call to arms, and what they meant in view of what happened to him, and to me.

Don't get me wrong. Luke Stubbings was still one of the lads, still buying his round, and I remember the night he joined me outside for a sly cigarette – my last, but he didn't know that – happy to accept a roll-up and light mine from his battalion-crested Zippo. Happy, also, to accept a little you-know-what in the tobacco mix too. Looking up at the stars as he exhaled those distinctive sweet, pungent fumes.

'Medicinal,' I said.

He didn't reply. Shy, but not stand-offish. Still waters run deep, as my mum would say. And with him, as it turned out, they very much did.

On site, I'd see him with earphones on, cutting the world out. As well he might, but I didn't think mental isolation was a good thing, for him, or for anybody. One day I went over and tugged them off. He looked startled, like an admonished schoolboy. I put one bud to my own ear. Iron Maiden.

'At least it's not James fucking Blunt,' I said.

He smiled, but that was as much of a reply that I got.

I asked why he didn't leave the headphones off for a bit. I said a friend of mine rode a bicycle with them on all the time. She didn't hear a car coming at a junction, was in hospital for six months. Hit by an Ocado driver.

'No Ocado drivers round here.'

'I know. But you're missing all this.'

'All what?'

'Life,' I meant the trees, the ploughed fields, the rolling Wessex hills with their patchwork patterns straight out of a Ravilious painting. 'Listen. You never know what you might hear.'

Luke paused, taking in what I'd said.

'Crows.'

I said I thought they were more likely rooks – the nests in the trees were fairly conspicuous, and rooks made a racket when their territory was threatened. But if he focused on that other sound in the gaps amongst the cawing, there was a woodpecker, I reckoned.

He concentrated. A moment later his face opened, hesitantly, in childlike joy. I honestly thought for a second I could see the five- or six-year-old he once was, the little boy who had been open to wonder. What had happened to that little boy that was gone now?

I said we could take a walk in that copse after lunch and see what we came across, if he liked.

He didn't answer. I could see he was worried what it would look like if he traipsed off into the trees with thunder thighs. The ribbing from his pals would be horrendous, and I instantly regretted I'd suggested it.

Before his lack of eye contact became embarrassing for both of us – and before our one-to-one was noticed by his peers – I told him he could download the app for identifying bird song, if he was interested. 'You just hold up your phone, record it, and the app will tell you what species it is.'

'For real?'

'For real.'

I helped him find it on his mobile and he downloaded it in seconds. I noticed a tremor in his hand, no doubt a side effect of his whatever medication he was on.

'Go for a wander. Play with it.'

'Sweet. Thanks.'

'No problem.'

I got up, dusted the dirt off my knees and got back to work.

'You're doing great, by the way. Well done.'

Our first major find was a skeleton we archaeologists named 'The Queen' but the squaddies dubbed 'Boudicea' (said the old-fashioned way). Nowadays we call the Queen of the Iceni, her of the spiky chariot wheels, 'Boudicca', but I think the guys had a problem conferring the syllable 'dick' to a woman without smirking.

'Got to respect the Bode,' one of them said as we salvaged a duo of bronze and gold leaf brooches of the 'fibula' (or 'safety pin') type, implying that this well-off Saxon woman wore jewellery from an earlier era, showing off her status by sporting a Roman antique. We subsequently unearthed numerous glass beads and copper rings, giving the impression to the military side of the team that she was 'Proper blinged up'. But the importance of the discovery wasn't lost on them. Wayne Fajardo had said with genuine feeling as he held an inch-long horse and rider that he felt privileged to be the first person in over a thousand years to look at these things, while another added that it almost did your head in. I'd also seen the delicacy with which they worked around the pin in order to get it out of the ground intact. Full marks to them.

I'd gone from scepticism to being impressed, and wasn't sufficient of an arsehole to keep that opinion to myself.

It was an up for the veterans, too. A win they took to The Bear with them, which had become their watering hole of choice. I have to say, if many of them were on meds for anxiety or depression, or taking antipsychotics, they certainly didn't worry about mixing those substances with alcohol. In fact, I got the strong impression that for some, alcohol was their self-medication of choice.

I could talk. Morphine dolly.

At one point an old boy came up to them and laboriously went around shaking each of them by the hand, then giving a limp salute before returning to the bar. To my surprise, it put a damper on the proceedings. The lads went quiet for a while. I broke the silence with some quip or other, I forget what. 'Sometimes you get people talking about heroism and all that bullshit,' said Leon Barrass, staring into his beer. 'There's nothing heroic in war. It's cruel.' Another spelled it out for me: 'You come home to the nationalism. All you want is a guitar, a bench in the park, and a bottle of booze.' The mood needed lightening but I wasn't the one to lighten it.

Harpo made a solemn toast. 'To absent friends.'

Luke Stubbings looked pale. While the others had talked falteringly about heroism, but shared freely, knowing they had the emotional support of the group, he hadn't said a dickie bird.

As the work at Conigre Hump progressed, I got used to seeing the green sweatshirts decorated with the Project Orinoco logo – a rifle crossed with a spade, topped with the three feathers of the Prince of Wales, who supported the initiative.

If 'Boudicea' was a bolt from the blue, our next find truly knocked it out of the park. We knew it was something spectacular, because we found evidence of chalk deposits all around the pit, indicating there was once a kind of coffin, which was incredibly off-brand for the period.

There was a boss from the front of a sixth century shield lying near the surprisingly intact skeleton, given it was Early Saxon. The boss itself was iron, while we also dusted off the grip from the back of the shield, and quite soon afterwards in quick succession, two spear heads and a 'scramasax' – basically a single-edged sword – with a blood groove making it easier to extract after usage. With a maplewood scabbard and hilt of antler, it unmistakably denoted the importance of the grave's occupant.

'Nice bone structure.'

'Cheek bones to die for.'

As professionals, we tried to avoid such remarks, but couldn't come down like a ton of bricks on the squaddies for the odd insensitive observation. The atmosphere changed, however, as I explained that the shield would have been placed over the face of the dead man as a mark of respect shown to this person, who was clearly a warrior, since he'd been buried with his shield and weapons at his side.

I was surprised – and perhaps shouldn't have been – at the depth with which they felt a bond of kinship to the deceased.

'One of us,' they immediately said.

'He knew what war was like, not only for himself but for his family back home. Just like we do.'

'He knew about the loss of friends in battle.'

For sure. With the painstaking uncovering of the skeleton, the orbits of the eyes slowly cleared, the mouth, lower jaw, teeth, there emerged a feeling in the ranks – *ranks?* – that a ceremony of some kind might be in order.

'Was he a Christian? What was he?'

'Anyone know any Anglo Saxon prayers?'

Nobody laughed. Nobody knew if it was a serious question.

There was an unnatural – or at least *rare* – stillness in the air as we stood around the newly-exposed bones, and a stillness settled on our activity too, as if we were all suddenly reminded that we were working in the midst of a graveyard; a place of death. That these weren't mere artefacts, beads, pottery, 'stuff' – they were the ruins of a life. Probably one that had been cut short before his time. Whatever thoughts that fact had rekindled in the soldiers' minds remained there, but Tony read the situation deftly enough to call an early lunch.

Luke Stubbings loitered behind as the others drifted off to the portkabin for their sandwiches, cake and soft drinks.

'What will happen to the bones?'

'They'll be examined by specialists,' I said. 'Afterwards, maybe brought back to Devizes museum. The skeleton will be put on display with all the relevant information. A historical find. Educational.' I could tell that this didn't satisfy him. He still looked inexplicably worried, so I added: 'They might be old bones, but everyone is aware these are still human remains. They will be treated properly.'

He looked at me suddenly.

'I know,' he said, almost defensively, before walking off briskly to join the others.

I wasn't hungry, so hopped back into the hole, crouched down and continued brushing dust off the dome of the left of the skull. The sun had baked the soil to a fine powder, so that you could chip it and flick it off – much easier than scraping at mud. I had to fight being OCD about it, but I couldn't resist going at it for another five minutes.

Soon I noticed that the rooks were silent. At first I thought a pang of post-chemo sickness had blocked my ears, but no.

I looked up in the direction of their nests, and saw what looked like a large piece of cloth up in a tree, as if caught there, flapping in the wind. Except there was no wind. None that I could feel. Inexplicably, a nausea I hadn't experienced before caused my stomach to clench. The shape, changing like a stain in water, was green-brown, dappled. Frenetic. But it must have dislodged itself from the branches, because I looked down at the skeleton of the warrior for only a second, and when I looked back, it was gone.

The next day a TV crew arrived to film a local news item. I recognised the girl doing the interviewing. Puffer jacket and white trainers that weren't going to be white much longer. Dom Hussey with his Eton/Sandhurst good looks was there to provide a talking head and I watched her nodding empathetically as a couple of the lads did their bits to camera. It was PR, but I found it queasily intrusive. They weren't soap stars, this was their lives.

Wisely, Luke alone stood far back from the proceedings, as if he was an innocent bystander rather than an active participant. I knew the feeling. I had no intention of my ugly mug being teatime viewing either.

For additional visual interest they'd roped in a local history buff to dress up as a Saxon chieftain and, God, did he love it. Sutton Hoo type helmet, wolf skin round his shoulders, flowing ginger beard tossed by the wind, the lot. I imagined him sitting in full Dark Ages regalia at home, pegging out his washing or having his Crunchy Nut Cornflakes.

'You'll take our land but you'll never take our freedom,' Jamie said under his breath, brandishing his coffee spoon to the skies.

Sniggers all round.

I sipped my own beverage from my THIS IS WHAT AN AWESOME ARCHAEOLOGIST LOOKS LIKE mug, peering beyond the camera to where the history buff was talking about the fabric of his green-brown cloak. How it would have been dyed, and how that dye denoted whether you were wealthy or not.

'Today I will mostly be wearing ... shite.'

We were glad when they had their footage – the soldiers' tales of trauma and recovery probably edited down to four minutes of soundbites – and had cleared off in the pristine white off-roader they arrived in. I didn't honestly give a shit, except that my head was throbbing like a bastard and it had cost us valuable working time.

As a dusky redness bled from the west, the team went to wash up and bugger off. I was about to bugger off too, when I saw across the expanse of oil seed rape to the left of the raven-populated wood – maybe four, five hundred yards away – the backlit shape of a man, the setting sun burning an aura around the outline of his head, eating into it, making it not look like a complete head at all. Cloth fluttering like a torn flag from his shoulders.

'I thought Gandalf got a lift back into town when the film crew left,' I said when I'd entered the portakabin.

'Far as I know, he did.'

'I heard him say he wanted to be back home in time for *Countdown*.'

A general shaking of heads. *For fuck's sake.*

I looked back out through the window of the portakabin, semi-opaque due to the mud on the outside, but there was no sign of the silhouette in the rape field.

'I bet he sleeps in that bloody costume,' I said as the sun shone directly into my eyes from the horizon.

'Probably fucks in it.'

'Too much information,' I said.

The dig was always preferable to a hospital day – all disinfectant smells and mawkish, life enhancing quotations on the walls – personally, I was happiest digging in the dirt 24/7, but a break from routine was always welcome for the lads, so as a treat I arranged for them to see the osteo-archaelogist working on the remains. I thought they'd find it interesting, and they did.

Their attention was that of rapt schoolboys as Epona Phillips showed them, wielding male and female leg bones, that the ancient skeleton was definitely male. She furthermore explained she could tell the age at which the person died from the X-ray evidence of wisdom teeth, which typically happen in late teens, early twenties.

'Meaning the warrior was the roughly same age as many of you guys.'

Then came the high point. The computer-aided reconstruction of the face, based on the shape of the skull and estimates for the thickness of skin, et cetera. This was the part they'd all been waiting for. Put it like this, they were a lot more interested than when I tried to explain the joy of the Munsell soil chart or the importance of a pH meter.

'Looks like Thanos on an off day,' said one.

Laughter, of the nervously-inappropriate kind.

Then followed a minute of awed silence as the visualisation turned three hundred and sixty degrees, swivelling to the left and right on a horizontal plane until it made eye contact with us.

'It's like we've brought him back to life,' said Stu.

'Yeah. It's definitely his round,' said Poshie. 'He's had his hands in his pockets for twelve hundred years. Tight bastard.'

'Speaking of which,' said Luke Stubbings. 'Who wants a pint?'

Naturally, they all did.

'My mouth is as dry as a Saxon's jockstrap.'

'Is that dry, though?'

'Or is it just really, really soggy? The Prof can tell us over a customary libation.'

I declined, this time. Yesterday's chemo had taken its toll and there were enough ferocious chemicals coursing through my body without adding to the carnivalesque cocktail. Epona took my place and I wondered if I should warn her, or her liver, what she'd let herself in for.

'A few dozen lengths to clear my head, get the heart rate going,' I said to Luke a few days later as we were scraping around a few feet from each other in the Conigre cemetery and he'd remarked that I always arrived at camp with wet hair. 'I know if I don't do it I'll feel sluggish all morning.' Swimming had become a daily habit, and I liked the discipline, even if lately I felt wrecked doing half the lengths I used to take in my stride. 'You should try it. It's a good thing to do.'

'Not if you get stared at,' he said.

I immediately felt guilty. Some of these guys had marks on their bodies. Of course they did. Battle scars. And if they didn't, I suspected they weren't that comfortable in their skin at the best of times. Not enough to show it off to all and sundry, anyway.

'You don't have to go to a public pool. You can go wild swimming, in the outdoors. There's a brilliant place by the river at Stowford Manor Farm, near Trowbridge. Never anyone there. Not the time of day I go, there isn't.' I told him what time, and he laughed.

'I need my sleeps.'

'No you don't. You need this.'

To my amazement he agreed to give it a go. The following Tuesday I parked next to the artists' studios, we walked down with our towels as the sun came up, and plunged in. His first reaction to the water was that of a scalded cat. Fitting, then, that I called him a pussy.

When he clambered out, shivering, and sat side by side on the bank with the place to ourselves, it struck me again how young he looked, with the lanky limbs and big feet of a fast-growing teenager rather than a full-grown man. I was pushing forty, and some of them were touching thirty, or older, but they all seemed like little boys to me.

I donated him my rainbow tin of goodies, saying I'd given

up, which he didn't question, and he smoked a roll-up as the sun edged up through the mesh of the branches, splintering light at us as we listened to the babbling of the stream, hypnotised by the way the water made patterns over the rocks in the shallows. A Friesian cow nosed down from the field opposite and lapped up a drink with an enormous tongue. He took two cans of Stella from his rucksack. I said it was a little early for me. He said it was too late for him.

The ring pull clicked and fizzed. Beer shone on his lips. He seemed in no hurry to return to the car or the dig. We were still there at 7.30 when a buxom mother – real milkmaid type with red cheeks, I presume she lived on the farm – arrived with a couple of toddlers in tow, divesting herself of her flowery dress and submerging.

The sheer pleasure all three expressed made me grin, but as Luke watched the kids playing, laughing shrilly, his own features tightened.

'Gatesy had two kids. Never stopped talking about them.'

I didn't know what to say, so I said nothing.

'They don't tell you it'll look like the Bible. You know, the way stories from the Bible look in the films, with the deserts and the rocks, that colour, the brightness, and the men in robes and head scarves and beards. It hadn't changed for thousands and thousands of years. People hadn't changed. They were still fucking each other up, and there we were with all our twentieth century bollocks trying to stop them. It was mad.'

He finished making another rollie, put it in his mouth and lit it. The smoke made him blink and he plucked strands of tobacco from his lips before taking a second drag.

'We were two weeks out of Kandahar. The insurgents were on the far side of a gulley, or so we thought. Lima Delta were already on the other side. We were waiting for air support as our guide dogs to help them. All of a sudden they were all around us. Taliban. Our radios were shot up, none of us knew we were going to be rescued. They were picking us off. Snipers. There was only one thing for it. Get through that fucking gulley or die like sitting ducks. We sent through an LSV and a

Foxhound. The vehicles could act as shields, we thought.'

He dug in his bundled trousers and extracted his wallet, producing a small, tattered photograph of a group of soldiers, stripped to the waist, knotted hankies on their heads, with Majorca sun tans. Except this wasn't Majorca. It wasn't some 18-24 holiday. He pressed his thumb just beneath the grinning face of a Black guy, shaved head, with the same hawk in flight tattoo on his neck that Luke had.

'Gatesy was first up. That was Gatesy. Leader of the charge. Mr Invincible. Total muppet. He made you …' I don't know what the rest of the sentence might have been because he didn't complete it.

'Trod on an anti-tank warhead. Nine hundred grams of RDX and TNT mix. Have you got any idea what that does to a body?'

I shook my head.

'No, well, put it like this. It's not much of a body after.' He gazed at the small photograph without blinking. It trembled in his fingers. 'The sound of it going off … it just robs the air. Then the second sound kicks you in the ears. *Bam!* He was singing about Major Tom. And there he was, floating in a most peculiar way … and the stars did look different … On that day they did. And even when he lay there howling – the half of him that was left – the bullets kept hitting him. Both his arms were blown off, one leg six feet away, half his face. *Fuck …* And he kept trying to get up, using that one arm. And I'm like, *No, keep down, don't do it, mate, you're done, you're fucked.* But his guts were spilling out, his jaw hanging off. He was calling for me and he was ribbons. That was all that was left of him and he was screaming. And I was crawling away, away from him, on my elbows.' He bent both arms up, fists against his chin, showing me the white crescent-shaped scars where pins had been put in. 'I couldn't fucking wait to be anywhere but there.'

He folded the photograph and inserted it firmly in his wallet, putting it back in his camouflage trouser pocket.

'The AH64s must've come. I don't remember. I blacked out. Woke up in Camp Bastion. How the fuck I got there I have no idea. The RAMC checked me out for spinal injuries because I couldn't move my back and legs, but in the end they put it down to shock. I had four weeks in hospital. Physio got my legs working.'

Now I understood the small, pitted scars all over his face. His cheeks had been peppered by shrapnel from the explosion that killed his best friend.

'Gatesy's body was unrecovered. I got out. He didn't.'

'I'm so sorry.'

He approximated a shrug, like what difference did sorry make? It was what it was. But that was a coping mechanism, like everything else. He was built not to show it. Pain. Distress. Anger. Loss. *Shove it in the fuck it bucket.* That's what the army had taught him to do, so efficiently. And here he was.

'I dream about him. All the time. I dream I'm there, in the gulley, with all them Terry rifles pointing down at us, bricking it. It's always the same. In the dream the gunfire stops, I crawl over to him on my elbows and try to put him together again, fix his arm back on, push his insides back in, but I can't. And he's trying to say something to me and he can't, because his lower jaw doesn't exist anymore.'

'I'm so, so sorry,' I said again. It sounded even more trite and pathetic the second time, but I had no other words.

'He was a good soldier. It should have been me instead of him.'

'No, it shouldn't.' I could see he was in hell.

'You're there for your brothers. That's all you are. If you don't do that, you're nothing.'

I told him it wasn't his fault. The enemy was to blame for his friend's death, for all those deaths, nobody else. But I could see he wasn't listening.

'You sound like that shrink. She didn't know what it's like either. You can't know what it's like. Not unless you were there.'

That's what they shared, these lads. This awful, vicious, punishing bond of suffering in a way that nobody could ever understand but each other.

'In the dream, sometimes he puts his arms around me and

holds me and I can't escape. And I wake up and I can't breathe. I've got to dreading going to bed because I know I'll have to go to sleep and it's the same thing every night and it'll happen all over again.'

He leaned back and stretched across to his jacket and liberated a pack of Benson & Hedges. Took one out, then, as an afterthought, offered one to me. I shook my head. He remembered I'd said I'd given up. I said it was okay. The Zippo clicked three times before working.

'Is there a part of you, d'you think, that feels you deserve that punishment?'

He grunted.

'I want it to stop, I know that.' A long drag found its way to his lungs. The children laughed and threw pebbles at each other. 'If it doesn't stop, I'll lose my shit. I mean, literally, I'll lose my mind.'

He stood up, threw away the barely-smoked cigarette into the river, pulled on his T-shirt, then the rest of his clothes, and walked back to where 'the gherkin' – my lime green VW – was parked. I picked the cigarette stub from the water, wrapped it in tissue, put it in my pocket, and followed.

Alcohol and stupid games have always been a reliable way for men to avoid discussing their emotions, and, unsurprisingly, young testosterone-filled army types were no exception. They played Shithead for matchsticks, chasers lined up in military fashion, and if you didn't want to get the piss ripped out of you, better not turn up. On this particular evening, how I got my snow white hair (from the age of twenty-three, thanks very much) was the cause of much speculation. I didn't tell them it had happened almost overnight when my father died.

'From shock, when she saw her first penis,' said Leon.

'Absolutely,' I agreed, without missing a beat. 'It was when I first met you. I expected it to be a lot bigger.'

They laughed like drains. A sound I'd become fond of.

Luke was there, that night, drinking heavily, but his eyes

were sour and grey. Knocking them back in that robotic way that meant he was searching for oblivion, not enjoyment.

'Perhaps it would have been bigger, if you were better looking.' His smile wasn't a nice one, and didn't suit him.

The rest of the boys immediately clocked it was a bit near the knuckle. In fact, his jibe had gone down like a lead balloon.

'Nice one, Luke,' murmured Jamie.

'What?' Luke hated that his pals had sided with me in not finding his repartee amusing. 'Fuck off.' But I was his real target. 'And you can fuck off too.'

'All right, I will.' Bemused rather than hurt, I pushed my chair back, slugged back the last half inch of my lager and headed for the door.

'Zoe? Mate?' Chris Brinscombe called after me. Too late. I was out of there.

Pissed off now. Not so much because of the insult – *sod* that – as a sense of, what? Rejection? No – *ingratitude.* If, in the cold light of day, having brooded on it, Luke felt so terribly fucking uncomfortable offloading to me about his dead friend or his dreams, or felt embarrassed at spending time with me – and this was his way of pushing back at that, shoving me away from him, whatever, frankly, that was his problem.

Bollocks to it.

I was glad to get home to my mother's house, crashing and walloping in the kitchen to cook her a meal, trying not to snap at her. It wasn't her fault. And it wasn't her fault my head was muggy.

I'd moved back since I broke up with my boyfriend – for my good, and his. It wasn't ideal. He was twenty years older than me and an alcoholic. Been in rehab twice and both times told if he carried on drinking the way he was, he'd die. But both times he carried on, regardless. Regardless of those who cared about him.

I phoned him, mainly to calm down after The Bear, now mum was settled with her cottage pie. He was all right. He sounded out of breath. I asked if he'd been out of the house. I could tell in a second he was sozzled. Just knew and didn't ask because I couldn't deal with the lies all over again. *Pete, just shut up.* I asked curtly if he wanted anything. He rattled off a few essentials and said a supermarket shop wouldn't go amiss. I could have told him yet again he could set it all up online and it would get delivered, but I couldn't be arsed. I said I'd pop into Sainsbury's the following day. He could pay me back at the end of the month.

'Bless you, you're an angel, Zo.'

'Yeah,' I said, but wanted to say: *I've got cancer, babe. Thanks for asking.* But couldn't do that to him. Couldn't do it to mum, either. She couldn't have handled it.

Ever since dad died, she's been lonely. Makes no secret of it. That's why I'm there. My bedroom is the same. All the childhood toys gone. Same wallpaper.

We get on all right. She has her health problems.

As long as I can remember, on my birthday she'd always give me a ten pound note from her purse. 'Get yourself something you like,' as she presses it into my palm. Nowadays the tenner goes towards the bills. Where else would it go? Oh yes, that sparkly Gucci frock I needed to go to the Oscars. I was forgetting.

She likes watching telly, but I try to get her out. The Salisbury Playhouse is her favourite. We saw that comedian from the telly playing Shakespeare. Was he good? No, he was terrible, but she had a whale of a time.

I thought about getting an early night, then thought about Luke Stubbings again, to whom sleep did not come easily, and felt guilty about my own self-absorbed feelings, when I should be sparing a thought for his. What had I been through, after all, compared to him? It produced a churning in my stomach and I called out to mum over the sound of the TV set as I pulled on my coat, telling her I'm going out for a bit, I won't be long, there's somebody I need to see.

The squaddies hadn't moved from the same chairs, a cityscape of empty glasses in front of them. Except Luke's chair was empty. Someone said he'd gone for a slash. Someone else said to Donuts, go and help him look for it. Harpo was up, commandeering the next round, giving me a pint tip gesture.

'How was he?' I asked.

'Stubbings is Stubbings.'

They quickly dropped the subject and clearly weren't concerned, so why was I? Did I really think he might do something stupid? I was afraid to put such a fear into words – partly in case it made it a real and tangible possibility, and partly because it might make me sound like a knob. Did they talk about that kind of thing – *suicide* – between themselves? If they did, it didn't mean they'd appreciate me barging in with my two-penneth. I could really tread on some toes and offend them badly, which I didn't want to risk. So, on the pretext of checking on my mum, I stepped outside and rang him.

No answer.

I returned as the bell clanged last orders. I gave in to a Jack Daniels, no Coke. It nearly burnt my mouth to cinders.

'Hey, you're hair's turned black again.'

'Down my trousers, maybe.'

I left as Harpo was attempting to coerce the landlord in the direction of a lockdown. Obviously they were up for an all-nighter. I wasn't.

When the cold night air hit me, it both slapped me awake and informed me I was a lot more inebriated than I'd imagined. Or it was Chemical Me too weak and wobbly to stay the course. The JD had made the inside of my mouth sticky, but I was positive it was anxiety making me uptight, not the booze.

Ignoring Chemo Brain, I called Luke's number again as I crossed the Market Place car park. While it rang, I espied some local tearaways in The Brittox karate-kicking a cardboard cut-out figure outside the Polish deli. I thought, if they liked knocking hell out of things, they could join up. Find out what violence was really like. *Dickheads.*

No answer. Again.

I stepped around a puddle in front of me, reflective and oily. Under the street lighting it looked black. I wondered what had broken for it to ooze out of. What had smashed. What had been punctured or ripped.

At the corner of Snuff Street lay a misshapen black bag left out for refuse collection. No tag or label on it, as the council decreed. More sizeable than the usual bag of rubbish, and bent over in the middle, with lines across its midriff like wrinkles in a garment.

Behind me, the street yobs were effing and jeffing more loudly, and I heard broken glass, which made me quicken my pace, distancing me from them.

The black plastic bag shifted awkwardly as I passed. I could tell now, to my alarm, it was a person, some drunk trying to pick himself up off the pavement. Without staring, I tried to analyse what I still held on my retina. I hadn't made out a face and I hadn't made out hands. Just something trying to lift itself up on one struggling arm. Like some obscene, futile press-up.

In my head, I told it, or him, to *fuck off.*

Bags were bags.

I didn't look back at them.

I didn't look back at anything.

Snuff Street cut through to New Park Street, which is busy by day but dead by night. I hurried across into Couch Lane, passing under the archway proclaiming THE WHARF CENTRE, which I knew to be a café and gift shop next to the locks and narrow boats, and a small theatre. The narrow alley was lined with redbrick terraced houses and unprepossessing shop windows for organisations like the Wiltshire Centre for Independent Living (WiltCil) and the WI. Never thronging with people at the best of times, tonight was no exception.

Except I sensed someone close. As a woman you get that sense, even though you don't hear anything, sometimes. You just feel it. I do, anyway. Maybe as women we are hypervigilant. Maybe we have to be.

My first thought was a rational one – ha ha – that it was one of the lads and I'd forgotten my rucksack, or my credit card, or my jacket, but I was wearing my jacket, my rucksack was on my back – and wouldn't they speak? Wouldn't they call out my name?

And if it wasn't one of them, who was it? One of the piss artists I heard smashing a shop window? If it was, I didn't want to confront them. And if it was just a *man* ... what man?

Feeling a tightening in my chest, I resisted the temptation to up my speed, in case it gave the wrong signal. What the right signal was I had no fucking idea. But I couldn't look back. Because though my brain told me nobody was there, my instinct told me –

Fuck.

There *was* somebody ... or something ... still there, still behind me.

I could hear its breath now as if it was playing to me over headphones – constricted, muffled and claggy. Something to which breathing did not come easily ... if it came at all.

My bladder loosened. My control loosened. I could feel everything in me threatening to come apart.

Fuck you, Chemo Brain.

Eyes fixed on the road ahead, I broke into a run, almost without realising, as I crossed the canal bridge, the entrance to the community hospital on my right, to cut along Dyehouse Lane – NO THROUGH ROAD – to my mum's house in Rotherstone. Except out of my peripheral vision, without moving my head, I could see a shadow cast below on the water of the canal. Hardly a shadow, hardly a lump, not even a head, not even shoulders. Hauling itself, limbless. Dry. Brittle.

Ruined.

Flying through the door, I slammed it after me as my bladder finally gave out. In the same moment I heard the shrill, hollow *BLAM!* of a bullet hitting its target, making me jump and let out a bleat. The sound had come from the lounge.

Almost afraid to look, I crept along the wall, felt around the corner of the door jamb and switched on the light, dropping to my knees as I found a framed photograph had fallen from the mantelpiece to the floor.

My mum was calling my name but I was unable to speak. The last three or four minutes a blank, as black as the night that had threatened me. How had I got there? Is that what fear does? Was it death I got a taste of?

I turned the photograph face up. It showed my parents in radiant smiles on their wedding day, a crack in the glass bisecting the picture, separating them. It shook in my hands.

I had wet myself. Upset and humiliated, I hurried to tear off my jeans and put them straight in the washing machine, hands shuddering as I filled the tray with washing powder and Comfort, pulling on a pair of leggings from the laundry basket. I felt like a child again. A naughty, frightened, dirty child and I wondered if this was what dying felt like, and I cried, alone.

In the cold light of morning, I began thinking the force of my slamming the door had dislodged the picture. That was the only logical explanation. I'd been stupid. Idiotic. The bullet was just the sound of the glass cracking as it hit the side of the grate. It was obvious now. So obvious. What a fool.

Over breakfast I told mum her wedding photograph had fallen and broken, but not to worry, I'd get a new frame when I next went into town. She didn't seem upset at first, but her lower lip quivered and she dabbed her eyes with a tissue, bless her. I said I was sorry, I didn't know how it happened. 'It means something,' she said. I rubbed the back of her hand and said I knew it did.

It worried me that there was no sign of Luke at the dig. As hours ticked by I became more agitated, with good reason, I think. Turning up was a big thing to them. Letting down the rest of the team broke the most basic code of the military. The one thing they lived by.

I phoned him again, seething by now. I left messages, concerned at first but increasingly more abrupt. Finally he picked up. Claimed he had a bad guts, had been throwing up all night. I knew it was a lie. 'I'll be right in,' he said. 'Please yourself,' I said, and hung up. Unable to let it rest, I rang him back: 'Meet me at Caffè Nero in half an hour.'

He didn't stand out in his army fatigues. You got used to

seeing lads in battledress when you lived in a garrison town.

'I'll get you a coffee.'

'No you won't.' I got my own. 'What are you playing at?' I asked when I sat opposite him. No foreplay. No pleasantries. I was angry.

He didn't offer any apology for what he'd said to me the night before. That was fine.

I've met men all my life who thought it diminished their ego to say sorry when they were in the wrong. I just behaved as though it hadn't happened and waited for the truth to come out.

'I tanked up on caffeine to stay awake. Couldn't face another night of …'

'Of Gatesy in your dreams.'

He didn't need to nod. 'I fell asleep at 7 am. Didn't wake till ten.'

My first phone call.

'I'm fucked.'

'No, you're not.'

I didn't want to tell him what happened to me on the canal bridge. I wasn't ready to hear out loud what I thought about that myself yet.

'Did you go to the funeral?'

He shook his head, finding it hard to meet my eyes. 'Couldn't. I was all over the place.'

'His wife. She must've been devastated.'

His face became ugly with self loathing. 'If you want me to feel bad, stick it in a bit deeper, and twist it.'

'Sorry.' I backed off, stirred sweetener into my Americano and sipped it. I thought of the broken photograph of my parents, how it had fallen inexplicably. Husband and wife shattered apart.

'Did you contact her when you came back?'

Luke didn't lift his gaze from the table.

'Maybe you should. I think you should. Write to her.'

'Why would she want to hear from me?'

'You were her husband's best mate. Why shouldn't she?' I

watched him staring at his beverage, which was becoming darker and more sludgy, the square, puffy tea bag floating on its surface. Like he was waiting for someone more experienced to scoop it out. 'There's an old saying ... Be afraid, and do it anyway.'

'Now you sound like that shrink again.'

'Let's get back to the site and get those womanly hands dirty. Come on.' I rose and dumped my coffee in the nearby bin. He hadn't moved.

'What'll I tell her?'

'Tell her what you feel. Tell her about her husband. Tell her everything.' I hesitated, knowing I was asking a lot. 'What have you got to lose?'

'She'll hate me.'

'You've got to risk that possibility. What other road do you go down? What else is going to break this cycle in your head? It may be tougher than anything you've done in combat, but it could finally put your demons to rest. I think so, anyway.' He looked small, childlike. 'Do it.'

A week later, he told me he'd written to Sabian Gates's widow. While Si Littlefield was over chatting to the university people at the specimens table (discussing a votive we'd found in the shape of an eye; sadly the iris, probably made of glass or onyx intaglio, was missing), Luke took the opportunity to confide in me that he'd received a reply to his letter. I think he was afraid to tell me about it until he had.

'She said some nice things. Said Gatesy always talked about me. Said she'd like to meet me.' He'd taken out the reply from his back pocket. Pale blue paper, folded, and I could see the ghost of careful handwriting through on the other side, but he didn't read it aloud and I didn't ask him to. It fluttered in the breeze but he held it tightly.

'Got her phone number?'

He nodded.

'Phone her.' I scraped at the collar bone protruding from the earth near my right knee. 'Go and see her. Go and see those kids.' I blew residual grit into a cloud of dust. 'For your peace of mind.' I stood, hands on hips, wiping sweat from my brow with my wrist. 'Talk to her about Gatesy. Tell her what he meant to you. More importantly, tell her what his wife and family meant to him. They need to know, and you're the person to do it. It's what he would have wanted, isn't it?'

'I think it is.'

'Right.'

I was going to ask, did he think that was what Gatesy was trying to tell him in the dreams? Not to put *him* together, because he never could. That was the past. The person Luke had to piece together was himself.

I felt peculiarly restless that night, the conversation preying on my mind. Why it should *prey* I had no idea, but I was in no mood to depart for a session at The Bear. Strangely, Stubbings was. He was really up for it. I actually think I saw a spring in his step. Talk about a weight being lifted. The marvels of two folded sheets of cheap writing paper.

I returned to the dig about nine o'clock, after it had become dark. My headlights threw the excavations into stark relief; red and white tape fluttering between stakes, the metric sticks, a stray soil bucket. I don't know why I wanted to be there, alone with my thoughts, amongst the treasures and the dead.

At the end of my conversation with Luke, he'd opened a packet of Benson's and handed me one, automatically, without thinking, then paused. I'd smiled and taken it, dropping it in the breast pocket of my lumberjack shirt.

A man was crossing the field of rapeseed under the mid-grey pool of the sky. His head was slumped forward. The residue of the dusk on pollen or insects in the air created a pink mist around him. His clothes were baggy. He walked away until he became tiny. Then just became a part of the darkness, blending into everything around him.

In the glow of my headlamps, I dug a hole in the ground

with the heel of my DMs, big enough to drop the cigarette into. I filled it in and flattened the surface with the palm of my hand.

Luke Stubbings did go and see Gatesy's widow. He never came back.

A couple of weeks later I got a call on my mobile, awkward at first, worried I thought he'd deserted. 'Don't be silly. We don't have AWOL in archaeology. Besides, you were a volunteer. But you should let Dom know. Where are you?' He said he was going to stay in Warminster. He'd got a job. Nothing great. Tyre and exhaust centre. MOTs, that kind of thing. 'I know my way around a Mastiff, I sure as hell know my way around a Ford Transit.' The children were fantastic. 'They said I was a soldier, just like Daddy.'

'His wife doesn't hate me.' He sounded astonished at the fact. Perhaps reluctant to say it in case he jinxed it. 'She was all right, Tansy.'

I felt honoured he'd divulged her name.

'Good,' I said, looking across the figures of his Project Orinoco mates, bent in toil. I was astonished in my own way he hadn't rung them. He'd rung me.

'I think she forgives me. I wish I knew that he did.'

'Maybe he does.'

I thought the line was dead because he went silent for a minute, probably more.

'She said, "It could have been you, you could be dead." I said, "I am." She said, "No, You're not."'

The quiet air hung between us again and as I heard kids playing in the background – on a garden swing, or in a playground, hard to tell – I thought of the children splashing in the river at Stowford Manor Farm.

I wished him well. I asked him to stay in touch, but fully expected he wouldn't. And that was okay.

Three weeks later I received something in the post, c/o Archaeology Dept, Devizes Museum. A photograph of Luke in jeans and a white T-shirt, gripping the wheel of a rollercoaster car, face contorted in mock terror. The woman beside him, pretty, with shoulder-length blonde hair, giving a *What a wuss!* expression. The two children behind, two mixed race girls, looked about eight and ten. The elder was giving a catwalk madam pose. The younger tugging her mouth to twice its natural width.

I turned it over.

Be afraid. Do it anyway – Luke x

I have no doubt now – nor did I then – that because of what Luke did in contacting his widow, of being there to protect her and look after her, as I sensed he now would, Gatesy's uneasy spirit was at rest. I also knew with just as much certainty that soon, if not already, Luke Stubbings would sleep soundly once more.

There was always a sadness when a project came to its natural end. When the JCBs turned up to backfill, allowing the badgers to return to their habitat. I like to think the squaddies of Project Orinoco came through it with a sense of accomplishment. That it gave them something in dark times. One said on his departure that they learnt from the best. I don't know about that. But they did learn the beauty of stillness, and the special kick derived from tiny, seemingly insignificant discoveries that were actually keyholes into eternity. I hope, for some, it kindled an interest in the past which hadn't been there before. When you've looked into the eyes of a skull from over a thousand years ago, it puts a perspective on the present. I've experienced that. I hope they did too.

I don't know if a maudlin aspect descended as our days drew to a close, but for some reason there was no inclination from Harpo and Co. to give the last skeleton a name, jokey or otherwise. Perhaps they'd matured. *As if.* Whatever the reason, when we dusted off the skull, broken jaw bone, and scattered rib cage of the twenty-sixth and final skeleton in the Anglo-Saxon cemetery, they dubbed it simply '26'.

We uncovered it bit by bit, revealing piece after secret piece, lost in time like the whisper of a sphinx. We did not know who the occupant was, there were no belongings to light our path or accord him status. Both its arms were missing. So was one of its legs.

Some of the Historic England team chatted about dismemberment as part of an ancient ritual. I wasn't listening by then. It was only important that we had found him and disinterred the remains.

'Are you religious?'

'Not really,' I said.

'Christian?'

'Not really. No. Not at all.'

When the experts had gone, it was clear to me the soldiers craved some kind of prayer for the dead. I couldn't provide one, but suggested we all took a moment for our thoughts. They all bowed their heads.

'Rest in peace,' I said when I opened my eyes. The lads pointed imaginary rifles at the sky, and pulled imaginary triggers.

Presently, as with all the discovered bodies, '26' was taken to the osteo-archaeologist. My colleagues in the WFA were wetting themselves with excitement the day we arrived for the result of the facial reconstruction to be revealed, but I had to slink away because I knew whose face I would be looking at.

Entirely my imagination, of course. What else could it be?

The skeleton of a thirty-year-old man, lost in a horrific fire fight in Afghanistan, found lying deep in an Anglo Saxon grave that hadn't been touched for centuries … impossible.

Nevertheless I had the feeling that someone who was lost was found. Some wrong had been put right in the universe – whatever the laws of physics, or reality, said.

There was just one thing left I wanted to do. I knew someone who worked at Devizes Museum. She thought I was mad, but she was a mate. I persuaded her to surreptitiously put the rollercoaster photograph that Luke Stubbings had sent me in the case with the bones of '26'. No visitor will ever see it under the baize, of course, but the important thing is, I will know it's there, and that's all that matters to me. Perhaps I'm crazy, but I hope it helps the soldier rest easy.

Parce mihi Domine nihil enim sunt dies mei

As the cotton wool wiped off the blood off the new tattoo on my inner forearm, I felt like a wound had been disinfected. Not my wound, but Luke's. It's not healed, but the poison has been sucked out. I don't know what made it happen, but I think it was all the dead man wanted in the end. The Baggy Man. Gatesy … Not revenge, not even comfort for his own soul, but continuity for his loved ones.

You can look down at the skeletal remains of '26' lying under glass in the museum (10 am–5 pm, 11 am– 4 pm Sundays), but there's not much of him. We never did find the missing leg, the two missing arms, the half a missing jaw.

I know it's impossible, but I believe in the impossible now.

I had my final chemotherapy last month.

To celebrate getting the all-clear, I took my mum to see some dance by Ballet Rambert at Salisbury Playhouse. Just human bodies moving in air, is all it was. But I found I couldn't control the tears rolling down my cheeks.

The cloud of pre-cancer cells, the fragments, no longer show on the scan. The oncologist tells me it's gone away. But it never goes away, does it? Death is ever present. Not just for soldiers. The battle is never won. We carry it, all of us.

The best we can do is live with it, till we don't.

PRIESTS OF GOOD AND EVIL

Like many predominantly rural areas, England's West Country is riddled with local ghost stories, the antagonists of which are little-known outside their home parishes, primarily because there are no famous names attached.

It's often been commented on by ghost-hunting enthusiasts that the two most frequently sighted spectres in Britain are those of Anne Boleyn and Mary, Queen of Scots, who are said to walk in halls, castles and country houses the length and breadth of the realm. Other celebrity ghosts linked to a wide range of locations include Sir Walter Raleigh, Lady Jane Grey and Charles I. But the vast majority of English ghost stories concern the wandering souls of unknowns, everyday folk who passed away in sad or distressful circumstances, and who have attempted ever since to reconnect with the living to impart some vital memory or message. One exception though, are the hauntings at Lapford in central Devon. Because while these tales are not known widely outside the bounds of the village, the troubled spirits are said to be those of two men who during their lifetimes were fairly well known.

The first of the Lapford ghosts, the 'good one' for want of a better term, is said to be that of Saint Thomas Becket. Becket, you may recall, was the Archbishop of Canterbury savagely butchered in his cathedral in 1170 by four knights acting on the indirect orders of King Henry II, who at the time was engaged in a power struggle with the English Church. Becket was a Londoner who had no obvious connections to Devon, let alone Lapford, but his ghost is said to haunt this area because it is associated with one of his murderers, William de Tracy, Baron of Bradninch, which is only 25 miles away. De Tracy, as part of his penance for killing the archbishop, restored the local church, now dedicated to Thomas Becket, and founded another one in nearby Nymet. This might explain why, early every Midsummer Night (St

John's Eve), Becket, wearing his full bishop's regalia yet dabbled all over with blood, is seen galloping through the village towards Nymet. Some say this is to arrive there in time for Vespers, which was the service he was about to celebrate on the night of his murder.

However, a far more sinister apparition is that of a local man, John Radford, who became famous for entirely different reasons.

It's ironic that Radford was also a clergyman because his wickedness seemed to know no bounds. Despite being vicar of Lapford for many years in the mid 19th century, Radford was widely hated but also feared. A physically brutish individual, he behaved more like a gangster than a village vicar. A self-appointed money-lender (or loanshark), he charged exorbitant interest and was known to beat and even horsewhip those who defaulted on debts. One fellow was said to have been forced to eat a foul sandwich prepared for him by Radford: two slices of dried bread, with his bill inserted in between. He might have objected, but the vicar had a pistol trained on his head at the time. He was also a terror to women, particularly young village girls, many of whom he ravished and impregnated (one of these committing suicide afterwards).

However, his most serious offence, at least the most serious one ever put on legal paper, was murder. The victim was his own curate, who finally objected to his heinous deeds. Radford is said to have flown into a rage. He beat the curate, looped a rope around his neck, threw it over a beam in the rectory, and hoisted him upward, literally hanging him until death. Radford was arrested and brought to trial for this crime, though his defence, namely that the curate had committed suicide, was, to the utter disbelief of the judge, accepted by the jury. Noting that the jury was comprised of Radford's parishioners, the judge reprimanded them, demanding to know why they had done it when there was clearly so much evidence against the offender.

The jury foreman replied: 'Us haven't hanged a parson, and us wasn't going to.'

Radford finally died in 1861, though from his deathbed continued to terrorise folk, threatening the mourners that if he wasn't laid to rest in the chancel at St Thomas's, like a good rector, he would haunt the entire village for evermore. Unable to obtain permission to bury him inside the church, the villagers found the next closest option, just outside its north door, though folklorists have noted with interest the old rural tradition that if the Devil ever approached a church, it would be from the north side.

Anyway, Radford was as good as his word. To this day, he is said to wander the village at night, his horrible dead face peering in through cottage windows, his bony fingers tapping the glass, particularly if there is a lone female at home. His cross is now the only one in the churchyard to stand upright, as it fell over so often after first being placed there that it eventually was fixed in concrete.

There is much debate as to what ghosts are. If one takes the purely spiritual explanation, they are the souls of the departed seeking to make amends for wrongs done in life. Except that this clearly isn't the case with John Radford, who appears to be enjoying his fiendish reputation even from the afterlife (and if there is such a place as Hell, it hasn't managed to contain him yet). Meanwhile, the presence of Thomas Becket, a martyr, who in the eyes of the medieval Church, did no wrong, would seem to suggest that even those sanctified after death may still have business on this mortal coil.

GWEN
S L Howe

It was tourist season and Ed had just returned from guiding a small group of middle-aged women along the South West Coast Path. As always, he wanted a drink, but his liver was shot and he wasn't allowed alcohol anymore. Even so, he went to his usual bar. A place that generally catered for locals, including fishermen and tour guides.

Ed ordered a Beck's Blue. It was the closest thing to real beer he could get now, and he didn't mind the fact it was zero alcohol. It was more about the taste.

As he took his usual place at the bar, he noticed the woman sitting a few stools away from him. She was petite and pretty with long red hair that fell in fashionable waves over her shoulders. She wore a long taupe trench coat and red stilettos – clothing you'd expect to see a decade ago but somehow appeared right on her. She was not the sort that usually ended up in this dump. No, he'd expect her to be in the wine bar down the road, or the cocktail bar where all the young trippers ended up partying until the small hours. Not here, waiting to be fodder for the locals.

He glanced around, noting that everyone but him was ignoring her presence as she stared down into her almost empty glass. It was odd really, as some of the younger men were more than likely to hit on her, trying their luck. But it was as though she was invisible.

Ed shrugged. Perhaps she'd already turned some down before he arrived?

He took a swig from his cold beer and let his mind drift. He could almost feel the alcohol buzz, but he knew it was just his taste buds tricking him. Even so, he went with the feeling because the memory of the boozy rush had to be enough.

'My name's Gwen,' said a voice close to his ear.

Ed came out of his reverie and looked to his left. The woman was now sitting next to him and she was watching him with intense, green eyes.

'You asked my name …' she said.

'Oh. Right. Yeah,' Ed replied.

He didn't remember asking her anything. He'd been thinking back to his younger days, though he wasn't exactly over the hill at forty-two. Even so, it wasn't like him to drift off like that. Not since his drunken days. He glanced at the beer bottle. Had he been given the wrong one? No, the label said it was 'alcohol free'.

'I hate drinking alone,' she said.

Ed looked around the bar again. The moment was surreal. Why was she talking to *him*?

Another beer appeared before him and the woman's glass was now full. Though Ed didn't know what it was she was drinking.

'You're a local, aren't you?' she asked.

'Yes. Lived in Devon all my life,' Ed said. 'Where are you from?'

'Here,' she said. 'Though I haven't been back in a while.'

'You don't sound local,' Ed said.

She smiled. 'It's been many years since I visited.'

Ed studied her face. She was young: early twenties at the most. He knew then that the woman was having a laugh at his expense.

'Where did you live then?' he asked, playing along.

'Underwater, near Ilfracombe,' Gwen said.

Ed laughed. 'Right! Just been there today, have you?'

Gwen smiled. 'I emerged from there.'

Ed shook his head, she was either trying to mess with him or completely crazy, he wasn't sure there was much distinction.

'And how was the old place?' he asked.

'Wet,' she laughed.

'You're a funny girl,' Ed said, but he was starting to feel

awkward about the conversation.

'I prefer mermaid or siren to "girl",' Gwen said.

'I bet you do!' Ed forced a chuckle.

His head was ringing a little and he felt tipsy, which was impossible. Maybe Gwen's company was making him giddy. He hadn't chatted to a woman like her for a long time. He wasn't the sort they usually went for and he'd given up trying years ago.

He glanced at them both in the mirror behind the bar. Him, with his weather-beaten skin, and Gwen with her beautiful fresh young face. Now, as he saw them both together, they didn't make such an odd couple. She smiled back at his image.

'You look nice to me,' she said.

'I don't have a wife,' he said even though she hadn't asked him. 'I almost married, but she went away to university and got big ideas. She never came back here. I mean, why would she?'

'You were left behind, forgotten about because of your love of this place?' Gwen asked.

Ed nodded. Gwen was easy to confide in. Why was that?

'The water drug ...' Gwen said. '*Alcohol* ... You used it too much after that?'

Ed hung his head, as though he'd just admitted his deepest shame. He barely noticed her peculiar description of beer.

'It made you ill?' Gwen pushed.

'Yes. Sclerosis of the liver. It wasn't just beer. It was the hard stuff too.'

Gwen frowned as though she didn't understand what that meant.

Ed pointed at the bottles lining the back of the bar. 'Vodka. Whiskey. I'd drink a bottle a day. Beer was just the stuff I had in between. Like water.'

'And that was bad,' she said.

'It nearly killed me,' Ed said and he wondered why he was making this confession to a complete stranger.

'We've met before,' Gwen said. 'A few years ago.'

Ed shook his head. 'I'm sure I'd recall *you*.'

He squinted at her, trying to shape the memory of a younger

version of her in his mind. He couldn't imagine her any other way than she was right at this moment.

'You've got me confused with someone else,' he said and now it made sense why she was talking to him.

'No. It was you, Ed. Though you were called Eddie in those days.'

Ed swigged his beer and frowned. 'No one has called me that for years,' he said.

He looked around the bar. Someone was setting him up. It was obvious now. Gwen was a plant. A joke at his expense. He tried to catch the eye of Seth playing pool with his brother Eric.

'I get it,' Ed said. 'Those two? Right?'

Gwen looked at Seth and Eric. They continued playing as though they were the only people in the bar.

'What about them?' she asked.

'They put you up to this.'

'Up to what?'

'Pretending you know me. The mermaid stuff. All that.'

'I don't understand,' Gwen said.

'Back in the day, on one of those really bad days, I apparently claimed I saw one,' Ed explained. 'But you know that already. It's why you're here, talking to me.'

Gwen shook her head. 'No one put me up to talking to you. We have met before Ed. Down on the beach. It was night. I was singing and you came to me.'

Enough is enough!

Ed looked at the face of the woman in front of him. Her eyes were wide and guileless, but he really didn't like being taken for a fool.

He put down the bottle of beer, climbed off the stool and walked out of the bar without saying another word.

He marched down the street, angry. *Those tossers!* They were still taking the piss, even after all these years. What did a man have to do to leave his drunken past behind him? He wasn't that person anymore. Why didn't they just leave him alone?

He reached his street and turned into it. He saw his car half way up the road in front of his house. He never drove when leaving the pub, a habit he'd retained even though he'd been sober for years. Besides, the walk kept him fit. Helped clear his head after a long day of dealing with tourists. He had reached his front door before he realised the exercise hadn't worked for him this time. He felt confused. Messed with. It wasn't funny.

Those bastards!

He opened his front door and went inside, slamming it hard behind him to relieve some of the fury. The loud crash didn't help much though.

He paused in his small hallway. The two-up two-down house had been left to him by his mother. He'd lived in the house all his life with her, until cancer had taken her from him. His Mum had been one of the reasons he was able to get a grip, that and the fear that just one drink might see him off. But Mum was gone, and the house was his now. He'd been lonely before, but it was lonelier than ever since her death.

Ed kicked off his shoes. Mum never let him wear them in the house and the habit was deep seeded. He went into the small living room and dropped down onto his sofa. He switched the television on after picking up the remote from a small coffee table near the couch. The six o'clock news was on, reminding Ed how early it was. The evening would drag before him as it always did.

After a while, he found he wasn't listening to the TV and switched it off. His mind was elsewhere. Thinking back to that gorgeous vision even though he knew he had hallucinated the whole thing. Ed had been in his thirties at the time. He wasn't sure now how long ago it was, except it was right before his illness and at a time when he was rarely sober. All the days, weeks, months, blurred into one during those years. He closed his eyes, and imagined he could hear the waves, crashing against the cliffs as if trying to force their way onto the land …

Drunk on vodka, stoned on weed, Eddie stumbled down to the beach. He swayed for a moment, enjoying the salty breeze that wafted across the water. The air grew hot despite the wind, heat rushed up into his face. Eddie experienced a moment of panic believing in that second his blood was boiling in his veins. He waded into the sea fully clothed: a man on fire trying to quench the flames. He submerged himself, feeling the cold, black water soaking through his clothing to his skin before a void in his mind opened up and Eddie blacked out.

He woke on the beach, the fire inside him had cooled and Eddie lay shivering in the sand. He couldn't recall why he was there, or how he was so wet until her saw her.

She was in the water. Singing. Or calling. It didn't matter which. Eddie was mesmerised anyway. She sang a song that Eddie knew well, it was the story of his misery, and the tale unfolded beautiful and painful as it tore at him lyric by lyric.

Eddie climbed to his feet. He swayed with the sound: a cobra victim being hypnotised before the reptile moved to strike.

'You're going to die,' she said. 'You're full of poison.'

'Don't be stupid,' he said.

'I can smell it on you. A wave of rot. Death will come unless you change your ways.'

'Death comes to us all. Who are you anyway? You think you're some kind of …' He wanted to say 'angel' but even in his drunken state he knew that line was corny.

'No. I'm a mermaid or a siren, whichever you prefer,' she said.

'You're not,' Eddie said feeling a surge of anger as she teased him. 'You have legs, see? Mermaids have tails.'

'That's silly,' she explained. 'How would I come on land to seduce unsuspecting victims, if I had a tail?'

The girl was mocking him but Eddie didn't have the strength to walk away and so he sank back down onto the sand and looked at her.

'I come back every few years,' she said.

'Holiday?' he asked. 'That's all this place is good for.'

She smiled and he watched the dark red hair lighten as it dried and became a red red, like pillar box or something. His mind jumbled it with the red of a bus. He knew then she was definitely making up what she was. Mermaids couldn't have hair dye that colour, could they? That was a very human thing. His mind told him, Mermaids would be blonde probably, although he had no clue why he thought that.

She watched him with an expression he didn't understand at first because it changed the shape of her eyes, narrowed the line of her jaw.

Predatory. He thought she reminded him of a wolf hunting its quarry in a cold bleak landscape. Hungry to the point of starvation and loss of rational thought. A creature relying on instinct, rather than any moral code and it occurred to him he was that prey: the nourishment for something higher up the food chain than himself.

She moved closer and sniffed him. Her pink tongue emerged from her lips and, with a prehensile twitch, she tasted his skin.

'Go away,' she said. 'You aren't ready.'

With her words, the strength returned to his limbs. Eddie stood up and half turned but he wanted to stay.

'It's a pity,' she said. 'As you answered my song. So few do these days. Go.'

Eddie stumbled back and along the shore but didn't leave the beach. Instead, he turned around and watched her drifting back into the water like a ghostly wraith rather than a creature of the ocean. He waited a while, thinking she would come out again. When she didn't, Eddie began to worry. What if the girl had drowned? He would be in trouble because he didn't do anything.

Acting on instinct, Eddie pulled out his mobile phone and called the lifeguard. Within a short time, the beach was teaming with people, the lifeguard boat was out on the water and Eddie was in the thick of it all with the local bobbies questioning why he was out there ...

Eddie opened his eyes, bringing his mind back to the present. Of course, they'd searched for the mystery girl but never found her. There had been questions about what he'd 'taken'. He was known in the area for his substance abuse, and the consensus was that he'd imagined the whole thing. Tripping on magic mushrooms perhaps. Either way, his encounter with a mermaid made the news and became a local yarn that was often brought up to make fun of him.

A week later, he'd collapsed and ended up in hospital. That was when he'd learnt he had to stop drinking. He was slowly killing himself with alcohol and drug misuse. It had to stop if he wanted to live. And Ed, in the end, had chosen life, even though for a time it felt that all pleasure had been leeched from it.

As time went on his sober mind had filled in the blanks.

There probably had been a girl swimming. He'd more than likely scared her off in his drunken state. But a friend who worked at the local police station had told him there were no missing persons fitting her description and so, as the years went on, he'd begun to believe he had imagined her after all.

After a few years, the local lads had stopped referring to him as 'mermaid man' and he'd built a little respect for his continued sobriety. Ed would never drink again and he hadn't substituted his addiction with worse ones. In the back of his mind, he'd always thought of the mermaid vision as his own mind sending him a warning. That message had been received and understood and as his Mum had deteriorated before his eyes, Ed was glad he'd been the son she needed him to be in her final days. Ed was proud of that.

Now though, he felt like a failure again. Seth and Eric were dicks, and he knew he shouldn't let them get to him, but the girl … using her like that! A girl that fitted the description of the one he'd imagined! That was just too cruel, wasn't it? He wondered what he'd ever done to them to deserve such punishment. The locals never forget his past, even when they were quiet about it for a year or two. It always came back. Those two made sure of it.

Not for the first time he toyed with the idea of selling up and moving away, but he had no idea where he would go when his entire life had been in Devon. What would he do somewhere else? He knew this place like the back of his hand and he would never have that kind of local knowledge of anywhere else.

Feeling restless, Ed stood up. He didn't want to watch mundane TV programmes, or the depressing news. He had to get out, take a walk, maybe along the coastline above Ilfracombe beach. Making up his mind, he pulled on a light jacket, picked up his keys and went out.

Ed reached the cliff top and looked down at the beach. In the summer, when the evening remained light, the sand below would be full of people until nine or ten o'clock every night.

Beyond that time, teenagers would gather around small portable barbeques or cobbled together fires, drinking beer, laughing, singing and dancing until the early hours. During May though, the beach was always deserted in the evening because it wasn't warm enough and the tide would come in early.

Ed sat down on the grass and looked out to sea. Back in the old days, he would smoke something on this spot, and let his mind wander into some abstract territory. Now, down below he saw a couple walking with their dog on a leash, adhering to the rules enforced at this time of year. Ed followed their slow progress across the sand until they vanished from view around the rocks. He stood up, and made his way down to the beach, followed the footprints across the deserted went sand.

In the distance, probably from the town, he could hear a haunting melody that was familiar, but he couldn't place. The music flowed around him as though it were coming from the sea. Ed made his way along the shore as though an invisible cord was wrapped around him, pulling him towards his fate.

The damp sand squelched around his trainers but Ed didn't notice: he walked on the beach in all weathers and knew the areas where there might be possible quicksand and, even on a subconscious level, he avoided them. He padded over to the water's edge. The tide was coming in, but Ed knew it wouldn't be high for another hour.

The music grew louder. There was a mist forming over the water about half a mile out. Ed squinted as he watched the vapour float closer. The melody increased in volume and intensity. To Ed it was like the screeching of gulls mixed with the crashing of waves: a discordant cacophony of sound that few musicians could recreate. His head hurt but he couldn't walk away. Even as the sea lapped around his feet, an invisible force kept him rooted to the spot.

He peered into the haze, expecting – hoping – to see the mermaid again. If she existed in his sober state, it would be proof that life could be unexpected, and new. That other creatures existed than those subjected to the human condition. Evidence that his life was not so pointless after all.

The mist cleared and Ed became aware of the sea around his ankles. He glanced at his watch. Half an hour had passed in the blink of an eye, and the tide was pouring onto the land, snatching at the sand like phantom fingers with every ebb and flow.

Released from the water's hypnotic presence, Ed stumbled back, mimicking his movements from years ago. But this time he turned, pulling himself away from the ocean as he headed back the way he came.

Walking along the cliff tops, Ed glanced down once more. The tide was high, the beach was covered and the water flowed against the rocks below the cliff. For a moment Ed thought he saw someone in the water, a shadowy figure swimming toward the beach, but by then the light was so murky he wasn't sure what he was seeing. With an effort, Ed walked away. He was unaware of his soaked trainers and the wet jeans that clung to his legs below the knees.

Ed's dreams were full of strange images. His brain was fevered and confused. The features of his imagined siren took on the face of Gwen, the woman from the bar. His dream self was back on the beach, watching her emerge naked from the sea. She walked towards him and the dream conversation followed the line of the one he originally imagined all those years before. Only this time Gwen's hand reached out and began to pull him into the water.

When he could no longer walk along the sand bed, Ed tried to return to the beach, but the long red tendrils of Gwen's hair wrapped around him, preventing him from swimming away. She held him above the water as though she were trying to save him, and then her mouth opened.

Ed screamed as she pulled him towards rows of vicious serrated teeth.

Ed woke. Soaked with sweat, he pushed away the bedclothes until the cold night air hit his damp flesh. The air was a shock.

He shivered, pulling the duvet back over his cooling body. It was as though he had just crawled from the freezing cold water straight into his bed. As he mopped his face with the sheets, his lips tasted a salty tang.

After that, Ed couldn't go back to sleep. His mind replayed the dream with terrifying clarity. It was only when he saw the dawn peeking around his ill-fitting bedroom curtains that he was able to close his eyes once more. Even then, his mind was tortured with the memory of the monstrous mermaid's teeth and the absolute certainty that one day she would devour his soul along with his flesh.

Ed cancelled the tour he'd been booked for that morning because he had caught a chill the night before. He was sick and weak and the fever-fuelled dream had left him with anxiety. A dark depression pulled at him. Ed wasn't used to feeling down – he tried not to feel at all most of the time – but the four walls of his home crowded in around him, until, sick or not, he had to go outside.

Though he decided fresh air would be a good thing, he avoided the cliffs and the beach, taking a stroll down Ilfracombe High Street instead. The streets were quieter than usual but the walk did him good and he felt the anxiety that had followed him since his dream slipping away to the back of his mind. He was, after all, very practised at pushing down his emotions until he could deny their existence.

By the time he got home, Ed was more grounded and by the afternoon he was more like himself. Especially as the cold that he thought he was brewing dissipated along with the depressive mood.

Since he had embarked on his sober journey, Ed wasn't given to flights of fantasy, nor did he believe that Gwen was really a mermaid and that she wanted to kill him. Throughout the day, his rational mind told him how insane the idea was. He reminded himself that Seth and Eric had set that whole meeting up and they had brought back the paranoia of his drink and drug fuelled past.

Real life is not reflected in those insane days, he thought and then recited it in his mind like a mantra until he began to believe it.

He thought about going to the pub to satisfy a sadomasochistic urge to torture himself again with his former addiction. But as he reached the front door the impulse went away and he changed his mind. After that he made himself a microwave dinner and sat watching something banal on the TV until it was a reasonable time to go to bed.

A few days later, Ed met a group of tourists and began the walk along the coastal path, telling them all of the local history. By this time, he had almost forgotten about the dream and the girl from the bar, but that day he had the urge to throw in some mythology and so he made up a convincing but terrifying story about sailors being lured onto the rocks.

'They say the siren feeds on human despair,' he said, ending the story.

'Why would it do that?' asked a female voice from the back of the group.

'Because it stops them thinking about their own loneliness,' Ed said.

The group parted as the woman came forward. Ed frowned as he found himself faced with Gwen once more.

'That's an interesting view,' she said.

Ed recovered his composure and finished the tour in his usual professional manner. Afterwards, as the group dispersed, Gwen held back.

'I don't know what happened the other night, but I'm sorry if I upset you,' she said.

'I don't enjoy being laughed at,' Ed said.

'The tour and walk were very good, though my legs are tired. I'm not used to walking quite that much,' Gwen said.

'I suppose that's because you swim the distance usually?' Ed snapped.

'Can I make it up to you?' she said.

Ed frowned again. 'What? Another chat at the pub for your friends to see?'

'I don't have any friends here. But I thought maybe you could invite me to your place.'

Ed took a step back. 'Why would I do that?' he asked.

Gwen smiled. 'I'll see you around seven.'

She walked away before Ed could respond. But he watched her walk away, before, shaking his head. Her behaviour somehow confirmed that she was a very strange woman regardless of who put her up to pestering him.

When the doorbell rang, Ed was confused. No one ever called at his home, certainly not in the evening and then he remembered Gwen's words. He hadn't taken her seriously because he didn't think she knew his address, but then he realised that Seth and Eric had probably told her where he lived. He ignored the door for a few minutes, waiting, hoping she would leave, but when the bell rang again, he just couldn't leave her standing there.

Gwen was wearing the same taupe trench coat when he opened the door: Ed noted that it had seen better days.

'Are you going to invite me in?' she asked

'I didn't think I'd see you again,' Ed said but he stepped back and indicated for her to enter because he didn't know what else to do.

Once she was inside the house, Ed felt awkward. She took her coat off, revealing a knee-length black dress. She kicked off her sensible black court shoes in the hallway and walked straight into the sitting room as though she'd been there before. Sitting on the sofa in the space next to where Ed usually sat, Gwen crossed her legs and it was then Ed noticed that they were bare.

He floundered in the doorway until Gwen turned her green eyes to him and patted the seat beside her. Embarrassed, Ed came into the room and sat down.

'Relax,' Gwen said. 'Anyone would think you haven't had a female in your house before.'

Ed didn't admit that he hadn't. It was uncomfortable, no longer being alone. He'd often craved companionship, but now that he had a visitor, he didn't know what to say, or how to make small talk.

'Would you like a drink?' he asked. 'I don't have any alcohol ...'

'Water,' she said.

Ed hurried away to fetch a glass, giving himself a minor respite from the intrusion.

Every second of the next hour was torture for Ed, though Gwen appeared to be unaware of the fact as she chatted about the walk, and expressed her pleasure at his local knowledge. Even though he placed the glass of water down on the coffee table before her, she didn't take a sip from it. Ed wondered if all women were as strange in private as Gwen was.

When she stood and announced she needed to leave, Ed was relieved. He followed her to the front door and opened it without saying a word.

Gwen slipped outside, disappearing into the night as though she had never been there at all.

After locking the front door, Ed made his way up to his bedroom. Now that he had spent more time with Gwen, he was less anxious. It was disturbing having someone like her in his home but it had reinforced to him that she was just a normal woman and not, as his dreams had suggested, a carnivorous mermaid.

He went into the bathroom and brushed his teeth, using the routine to bring his world normality back into focus. He swilled his mouth, then patted his lips with a towel, before turning off the light.

By the time he reached his bedroom, Ed was chuckling at his own nervousness. He must have appeared like Steve Carell in *The 40-Year-Old Virgin*. In fact, the thought of it made him feel like laughing out loud.

He turned the landing light off and opened his bedroom door and that was when he found Gwen waiting for him.

Her hair flowed around her as though it had a life of its own. Ed felt the chill of cold water lapping around his legs as he was pulled deeper into the ocean. He didn't recall walking there, or even if Gwen had actually ever been in his home, but now he knew for certain that his dreams had been a warning that he should have heeded.

Gwen pulled Ed to her. Her mouth was wide and smiling but she knew he couldn't see her for what she really was.

Ed looked down at the place where his hand had once been. He felt no pain, just a passing relief that without his fingers, he could never give into the urge to drink vodka again.

Gwen sucked and chewed. The taste of Ed's blood made her light-headed with pleasure. His thoughts slipped over her, sweet and delightful as human sugar must be. It was moreish, addictive.

He was floating now, a torso in the water. The cold didn't touch him as the numbness in his skin seeped deeper into his soul. Ed could feel a distant tug and pull of sharp serrated teeth, nibbling on his face, chest and stomach. His damaged lips forced a smile as he gave himself over to it. On a primal level, Ed understood that he was not the addict now: he was the drug.

Gwen licked her lips as the last of Ed disappeared into her huge gullet. She had first caught him with her song twelve years ago. Back then his misery was just over a simple human female. Not enough for her to feel the full radiance of his pain. It had been a long wait until Ed was ready to be consumed and his addictions had to be vanquished first: no siren in the sea could stomach alcohol, or even normal unsalted water as it was poison to them. Of course, it wasn't just loneliness and despair that attracted her to Ed. There was a whole range of emotions needed. There had to be some doubt, some uncertainty of his own feelings, followed by a moment of euphoria. Only then had Gwen savoured him. Only then could she get the true fix she needed.

Gwen had no wish to consume a diseased liver. For that reason, it was the only part left and she threw its poison from the ocean, out onto the rocks, where the gulls swooped down to finish what she'd left.

Full for many a season, Gwen dived down into the water, and swam away from the English coastline. There were warmer climes to enjoy until her urge to return and her terrible hunger and addiction would rear its head again. She could only satisfy it here, and that was fine with Gwen, because there were so many lost souls on these shores just waiting for her call and when the time was right, another one would reveal itself to her.

THE PIXIE'S CURSE

For all kinds of reasons, it makes no sense to get on the wrong side of the faeries. The folklore of the entire United Kingdom, in fact probably the entire planet, is filled with examples of unwise mortals who tried to dabble in or simply got curious about the mysterious magical beings who in myth and legend have long lived next door to humanity and yet have remained almost completely concealed from it.

In Scotland for example, the Gan Ceanach was a male faerie who when a village lass requested a love charm from him so that she could lure one of the local lads, responded by using it on the lass herself. She thus fell hopelessly in love with the Gan Ceanach, while he vanished, leaving her lovelorn for the rest of her days. In a story dated to 1745, a lad was hunting on the moors over Elsdon in Northumberland, when he allegedly encountered the Brown Man of the Moors, a dwarf-like faerie who was angry to see the hunter's bag full of game, as he took it on himself to defend such creatures. The lad fled home, very frightened, the Brown Man's threats to take action if he ever hunted again ringing in his ears. A few days later, he went out shooting again, but promptly fell ill, ailing rapidly and dying before the year was out.

Of course, we've come a long way since the days of Victorian nursery books and writers like Enid Blyton, who depicted these entities in mostly benign terms, creating images in the average child's mind of diminutive ballerinas with butterfly wings or jovial gnome-like characters who wouldn't be out of place with Noddy in Toyland. But it's possible that even now we underestimate how sinister their reputation was in days of yore, and it's in the West Country where we find one of the best ever examples. In truth, this should surprise no one given how rich the region is in fae lore, but there are few tales as unnerving as that concerning the Blackdown Pixie Fair.

For the uninitiated, Pixies (or Piskies, if you come from Cornwall) are a brand of faeries almost unique to the English West Country, though it would take a folklorist of exceptional courage to chance his or her arm at defining them. Some have asserted that pixies were generally friendlier to mankind than other types of faerie (though they could be dangerous if antagonised, as this story seems to suggest).

The annual Pixie Fair was said to be a regular event on the Blackdown Hills in south Somerset during the 17th century. Mortals, of course, were never welcome, but that didn't stop certain courageous folk from attempting to spy on it. The odd events that supposedly happened on these occasions are many and varied, but not all bad.

One fellow, for example, saw hundreds of miniature pavilions with small people, very much in the guise of those described in later children's books, brightly clad, some with diaphanous wings, others with preposterous noses and ears, some with grasshopper legs etc, all buying and selling wondrous goods, and mingling in a state of good cheer. So captivated was he that he broke from his cover, walked down into the fair, and bought a pewter mug, accepting his change in the form of pebbles, though the following morning the mug had become a toadstool and the pebbles were gold coins.

However, on other occasions, there were problems.

One story tells how another man entered the fair and stole a gold trinket before riding quickly away on his horse. The next day, the gold had turned to tin and his horse had become permanently lame.

Then there was the particularly grim business of the man from Combe St Nicholas, who one day in or around 1630 was found on the Blackdown Hills in a state of mumbling semi-paralysis. Removed to his home, a local physician could do nothing for him, though the man recovered sufficiently to explain that he had been spying on the Pixie Fair, and having heard stories that others who had risked going into it had made good, finally plucked up the courage to go in himself. The moment he entered, there was no sign of anything. No people, no tents, nothing. However, when he returned to his former position, he heard noises behind him. He looked back and the fair was in full swing again. He attempted to enter it a second time, with the same unsuccessful outcome, but the third time, he strode about aggressively, demanding the right to buy goods. Several times then he thought he was pushed by invisible hands, and becoming frightened, he tried to leave, only to find that he no longer had full control of his legs. His other symptoms set in quickly afterwards, and within a few days of getting home all four of his limbs were paralysed, a condition he remained in for the rest of his life.

So, what do we think happened?

A modern explanation is that the intruder suffered a severe stroke. Could his story that the pixies inflicted this punishment be nothing more than a nightmarish fantasy, which broke over him as he became ill, perhaps partly due to the infamous location into which he had strayed? Or alternatively, could it just have been a lie? Was he angry that he'd found nothing on the Blackdown Hills and had not come away with gold in his pocket, and when he was so stricken was it a natural thing to blame it on the Little People who'd disappointed him?

The Pixie Fair is no longer held on the Blackdown Hills, or at least no one has reported it in recent times. Perhaps unwilling to attract further attention, the pixies have taken it elsewhere. Though alternatively, since the man from Combe St Martin, it may just be that no one has dared go up there to check.

WATCHER OF THE SKIES
Mike Chinn

Judging from the photographs Adil had downloaded, Werechurch hadn't changed much in over half a century. It was the sort of small, chocolate-boxy English market town he'd always thought never actually existed. There was a central main road – remarkably free of parked cars, which in itself was a minor bloody miracle – lined by shops, banks, and a couple of pubs, all in a bewildering number of styles. Like they'd been added one by one, over the years, by builders totally indifferent to what had gone before. There were Tudor half-timbers, small Georgian cottages, plenty of indeterminant age and period – not a few of which had been somewhat half-heartedly modernised. A few pedestrians walked along the narrow pavements, dressed for the warm summer weather. Adil couldn't tell if they were locals or tourists.

He spotted the pub where he was staying, the St Aldhelm's Well, opposite some sort of memorial sprouting in the middle of the road – the street widened slightly to accommodate it – and parked his Citroen C3 right outside. The pub looked old enough to have been around since before Werechurch existed: brick, plaster, black wood frames, and not a right angle anywhere. Adil was surprised the place was still standing.

Opening his window he leaned out, checking up and down the half-deserted street. He couldn't see any parking notices, and none of the people walking by so much as glanced at him. Couldn't shake the feeling they were giving him the once over, though, behind his back. Judging him. It was probably okay to leave the car here, though. He'd ask when he checked in.

He opened the Citroen's tailgate and pulled out his suitcase. As he did so his eyes were caught by a display in the small bookshop next to the pub, behind what he thought of as a Dickensian bay window. A small selection of cheap, gaudy paperbacks, all on one subject. The Werechurch Shape. Well, obviously.

Adil swung down the tailgate, locked the car, and wheeled his case into the pub. It was cheerfully dark inside, smelling of polish and beer. There were no customers. Too early, maybe? He hoped it wasn't an indication of a lousy place to stay.

He rolled up to the bar, looking and listening for any indication of bar staff. After a moment a young man appeared, frowning at Adil momentarily before a professional smile spread across his face.

'What can I get you?'

'Adil Kumar. I reserved a room.'

'Ah yes. Mr Kumar.' He rummaged underneath the bar, producing a thick, rather tatty A4 sized notebook. He flipped through it, running his finger down a scratchy list of names. 'Here we are. If you'd like to follow me.' He stepped from behind the bar and headed towards the greater darkness at the back of the room. Adil started to follow. The young man opened a doorway, and cracks of sunlight cut through the gloom. 'I'm John, by the way. Shall I take your case?'

Adil shook his head. 'That's okay.'

John shrugged and swung the door fully open. Adil followed him into a sunlit courtyard, surrounded on all sides by timber-framed brick walls. Probably used to be a coaching inn, thought Adil, glancing around to see if he could spot an entrance to the courtyard. There was a narrow arch to his left, although it looked too low to squeeze any kind of horse and carriage through. Maybe there'd been some restructuring since those days – although that rather went against Werechurch's Olde Worlde, if slightly chaotic, charm.

They went through another door, almost directly

opposite, and into a corridor that could have been in any budget hotel. John stopped by the first room they came to, opened the door, and stepped through. Adil followed.

It was a small room, with a single bed and tiny wardrobe. It would have been roomier once, but a modern en suite bathroom now took up half the floor space.

John handed Adil an old-fashioned mortice key. 'Is this suitable?'

'It's fine.' Adil had known worse – and it was only for a couple of days. A thought came to him. 'Do you validate parking?'

The other man looked puzzled.

'My car's parked on the road. Does it need validating? Or is there a car park?'

John shook his head, expression clearing. 'Ah. Yes, there's a private car park behind the pub, Mr Kumar. Take the first right. We don't tend to park on the road in Werechurch. Like to keep the place tidy.' He pronounced it *Werry*church, Adil noticed.

'So you're not expecting hordes to turn up?'

'I'm sorry?' John looked genuinely baffled.

'The sixtieth anniversary? The Werechurch Shape?' Adil remembered to pronounce it properly. 'It's only a couple of weeks away.'

There was a blank pause, then John laughed. 'That's old news, Mr Kumar. No one bothers about it now. Apart from the occasional flyer saucer nutter —' He broke off, looking embarrassed.

'Relax, I'm not one,' said Adil. 'At worst I'm agnostic, at best a total sceptic. I'm a reporter, and you know how cynical we are.' He grinned to show he was sort of joking. It didn't seem to put the other man any more at ease. 'Still, the place next door's selling books about it ...'

'Trying to, you mean. Have a look at how faded those covers are. If Martin sells one a year, I'd be surprised. Would there be anything else?'

Adil shook his head, mildly disappointed. He'd hoped the

locals would have been only too eager to bang on about their history.

John left him to unpack.

In his dream his phone was vibrating on the night stand, loud and angry. Adil half woke, a hand groping for his phone in the dark. It took a couple of seconds before his brain caught up: it wasn't his phone. From above him came a sharp, rumbling clatter, like bricks or something sliding down the roof. Except it didn't stop. Whatever it was kept on, rubbing at his nerves as much as the roof tiles.

Adil sat up, swinging himself out of bed, half angry, half alarmed. He was expecting the ceiling to collapse at any moment. He opened his room door; the rumble grew louder. The corridor was just as dark as his room. It made the constant jagged rumble worse somehow. Adil made his way towards the courtyard door, his still fogged brain latching onto some vague idea of evacuation. Fire drills. The moment he swung the outer door open, the rumbling stopped. Silence was pretty much absolute, except for the faintest of hums somewhere inside his head: an audio after-image.

Adil stepped into the courtyard, half expecting to see fragments of chimney or shards of roof scattered across the cobblestones. There was nothing. Except for a woman in pyjamas, gazing up at the sky, a distracted frown on her face. She was around thirty, Adil guessed, with long dark hair that might have been brown.

'Woke you too, huh?' he muttered.

She looked his way, for a moment confused. 'Who could sleep through that?' she said eventually. She sounded Scottish.

Adil glanced round the courtyard, at the archway and the dark street beyond. The place remained quiet, as though the woman and he were the only people in the pub. Or Werechurch, for that matter. 'Everyone else seems to be managing okay.'

She laughed softly. 'Selective deafness. And sixty years of

practise.'

Adil shook his head, turning to go back to his room.

'Are you staying here?' she called after him.

He paused and faced her, nodding again.

'You must be the reporter, then. Adil – something …'

'Kumar,' he added. Then, because he figured it was expected of him, 'You?'

'Roberta Richards. Bobbie.' Her smile widened into a cheeky grin. Adil was too tired to wonder what she found so funny.

'Yeah, fine. Night …'

'For a reporter you're very lacking in curiosity.'

'I'm a half-asleep reporter.'

She stepped a little closer. 'If you want to know anything about the Shape, I'm your girl. Lord knows the locals are no help.'

Adil muttered something he hoped sounded appreciative and returned to his room. For some reason he half expected that awful noise to start up the moment he lay down.

Wide awake after a pile of scrambled egg, toast and two coffees, Adil leaned back in his window seat. Last night had taken on the fuzziness of a dream, and he was just on the verge of convincing himself that's all it was, when Bobbie Richards walked into the room. She spotted him, waved briefly, and headed in his direction. In the sunlight streaming through the window at Adil's back he saw that her hair – now pinned up – was, in fact, chestnut brown. Her eyes were also brown, almost black. She sat, facing him.

'Are you one of them?' he said, keeping his tone neutral. 'A flying saucer nut?'

'Most people simply say good morning.' She sounded amused. 'And only people like John –' she nodded towards the bar ' – talk about flying saucers.'

'UFOs, then.'

She tutted. 'If you're going to write about such things, you'd better get your terminology right. These days it's UAPs.'

'What?'

'Unidentified Aerial Phenomena.' She raised her voice. 'John! Double espresso, please!'

Adil wondered how she knew the man was even in hearing. 'Which means?'

She turned back and winked. 'There's something funny in the sky but we don't know what it is.'

'Like last night.'

She shrugged. 'Was it? I don't know. Last night was an instance of unexplained sound phenomena – the latest of many over the past sixty years. Nobody knows what it is, and the locals don't talk about it.'

'Really?' Adil leaned back. 'Doesn't sound likely. Don't they want the tourism? Look at that place in the States: Rose something or other –'

' – Roswell.'

'That's the place. Got a whole tourist industry built up around it.'

'Ah, that's because the Roswell Incident – *whatever* it was – was a one-off. A big mystery to hang your business on. Here the fun never stopped – *viz.* last night. Isn't that right, John?'

The barman was approaching, carrying a pale mug that gently steamed coffee fumes. He set it down and gave the woman a patient smile.

'No idea what you mean, Miss Richards. Can I get you anything else, Mr Kumar?'

Adil glanced at the mug Bobbie was presently sipping from. It smelled inviting. 'Yeah, another coffee would be great, thanks.'

John headed back towards the bar.

'I still don't buy it,' Adil said to Bobbie. 'The Loch Ness monster's an ongoing thing, and the Scottish tourist people are perfectly happy.'

'Nessie doesn't wake you up, or create a mysterious hum that goes on for days, or appear as a bright formation of lights in the night sky. All at random.' She put down her mug. 'Imagine the whole town is haunted by a poltergeist – you know what one of those is, I hope – noisy, mischievous, unpredictable, maybe even a touch malicious. It's enough to make anyone jittery.'

'So why isn't Werechurch in the news more.'

She gave him a frank look. 'I would have thought you'd know that better than anyone. Old news, Mr Kumar. The media lost interest in the fabled Shape years ago.'

Old news. That's what John had called it too. 'I'm here,' Adil said, glancing up as John brought his coffee. The barman backed off quickly, making it plain he really didn't want to know what they were talking about. Much.

'Yes, and I'm quite surprised, to be honest. Why?'

'Next year will be the sixtieth anniversary –'

'– Nine years ago was the fiftieth – a much rounder figure for a centre spread.'

Adil sighed. 'Okay, I'm doing it on spec. I heard about the … Shape last year and thought I'd write a retrospective. Hawk it around the tabloids. One of them is sure to bite.'

'I admire your optimism, Mr Kumar –'

'– Adil.'

'Thank you. You say you heard about it, but how much do you actually know?'

'Some. The highlights. I was hoping the locals would fill me in.'

'And now you know better.' She settled back in her chair. 'In 1965, odd things began to happen in Werechurch. Noises like you heard last night – people thought their roofs were being torn off – sometimes accompanied by a sense of tremendous pressure, as though an invisible force was pressing down. Strange lights, daylight discs –'

'What?'

'Apparently solid, metallic objects observed during the day. Classic flying saucers – it was the '60s, after all. Then there was the famous photograph. No one ever agreed on what it was – the picture we all know was blown up from a small corner of the negative and could be anything, frankly. Up to and including a hoax, of course. No one's ever proved it one way or the other.'

Adil pictured that image – he'd downloaded it along with the old snaps of Werechurch. An irregular oval, so enlarged the film grain was visible. It definitely could be almost anything – from a genuine old-style flying saucer to a hole on the ground. Or something quickly scribbled using a marker pen. Whatever the viewer wanted to see.

'Werechurch basked in its fame,' Bobbie continued. 'For a while, anyway. Visitors on their way to Longleat or the New Forest took a diversion to look around the town, see if they couldn't spot the Shape for themselves. No one ever did, of course. No credible sightings, and most importantly, no more photographs. By 1966 the world had moved on, leaving Werechurch and its strange phenomena behind.'

Adil laughed. 'Funny you should say that. When I arrived yesterday I thought the place looked … I don't know. Quaint. A mash-up of old-fashioned styles.'

She looked at him sharply. 'We're quite proud of that.'

'And you say the odd things – the phenomena – continue to this day?'

'Everything: sounds, sightings. And not a shred of proof. No more pictures, no audio, no movies.' She tapped her mug with a bright red fingernail. 'It's become something of a cliché that at the moment something like Nessie or a UAP comes right up to you and poses, your camera stops working for some reason. Or your phone. These days just about everyone's carrying a camera in their pocket, yet …' She spread her hands.

'Frustrating.'

'That's one word for it. You're quite honoured, by the way. First night, and you get a demonstration.'

'Funny, I don't feel honoured.'

She pushed her mug away. 'Anyway, after a while the curious stopped coming, leaving Werechurch's only claims to fame being en route to Salisbury Plain or the Lions of Longleat. Tourists stay, for a night or so, but they're always on their way to somewhere else. Of course, if they're really lucky they get a taste of what you heard last night, but that usually persuades them to move on the next day, if they hadn't planned to already. Which just leaves people like me —'

'Flying saucer nuts.'

'— As you say. Werechurch's biggest crowd are investigators of the strange and bizarre - not that there's many of them, these days.' She stood. 'But, since you're here, would you like me to show you where the photo of the Shape was allegedly taken?'

Adil couldn't see much from the roads: every one seemed to be lined by tall hedgerows, which blocked the view. From what he understood, Werechurch was on the same chalk uplands as Salisbury Plain; which as far as he could tell meant generally flat with only the gentlest of undulations. The only way to see anything other than leaves and trees was find a break in a hedgerow and go through. And so far he hadn't spotted anything like a gate wide enough to get his Citroen through.

'So where's this hill?' he asked. He was finding it hard to imagine anything higher than a two-storey building. In this landscape it'd be pretty obvious.

'Not far now,' Bobbie said. She leaned forward, peering through the windscreen. 'Nearly there I think - Yes. Pull in on the left.'

Adil saw a gap between two gnarled trees and slowed the car. He pulled off the road onto a dry track running through an open gate. Five yards on the track narrowed to a stony footpath. The grass all around was crushed and dry. Another car was parked on the right: a metallic grey SUV.

'Pull up anywhere,' said Bobbie, somewhat redundantly. It didn't look as though there'd be a fight over parking spaces.

Adil turned right, parking alongside the SUV, leaving a six-foot gap. 'So this is where all the best UFO watchers come?'

'Not really. This is for the fort.'

'The what?' He had images of a stone castle straight out of an old Hollywood movie.

'Prehistoric hill fort. Or what's left of it.' She opened her door and slid out. Adil did the same. Bobbie pointed up a shallow slope. 'The highest point for miles around. Where else are you going to put it?'

'Where else.' Adil grabbed his shoulder bag off the back seat and locked the car. Bobbie was already heading up the incline – such as it was. Adil slung his bag and fell in behind her.

Down in the town it had been a sunny, still day. As Adil climbed he felt the breeze freshening. Definitely a high point. He was surprised there wasn't at least one wind turbine in sight.

After five minutes or so Bobbie halted. Adil reached her and looked around. They were definitely at the top of a hill, albeit a pretty low one. Maybe a hundred feet, if that. Even so he could see for miles in every direction: flat agricultural land stretching out like a yellow-green sea.

Bobbie was standing next to a waist-high concrete plinth. She patted it, like it was an old friend. 'Nods Hill. Just around here was the hill fort.' She included the hilltop with a wave of her hand. 'You can't really see where it was – unless you're an expert – so you'll just have to take my word for it. Aerial photographs show it best – the imprint it's left on the land.'

Adil knew what she meant: the way even the oldest signs of man were revealed from up high through aerial photography. A sort of ancient map permanently drawn onto the landscape.

'Over that way –' Bobbie was pointing ' – is Somerset. Which means this hill is right by the border. A liminal spot.' She turned to face him. 'Except, of course, the border between counties is a man-made construct rather than a natural one, like a river.' She shrugged. 'Still, the border is in people's minds, so that may be enough.'

Adil stood on the other side of the plinth. It had a metal plaque screwed into the top, the paint dirty and chipped. It said something about Nods Hill Fort, but he didn't have the patience to waste his time decoding it. 'And what's "liminal"?'

'It means belonging to or being between two different places or states. Like waking and sleeping. Traditionally lakes and rivers have been considered borders between different states of being, or worlds.'

'So that photo was taken up here?' He scanned the clear blue sky. Nothing but a few soaring birds. What else did he expect?

'That was the claim, although there were no reference points, even on the complete negative. It could have been anywhere.'

'You believe it was a hoax?'

'Until it can be proven one way or the other, I have no firm opinion.'

Adil unzipped his shoulder bag and took out his phone. He turned on the camera and took a couple of snaps of the view from the hill. He turned slowly, recording images every few seconds. On impulse he also snapped a couple of the concrete plinth and the uncared-for plaque screwed to it. He switched the camera app off and dropped the phone back in his bag.

'Hoping for something juicy to turn up in one of those?' smiled Bobbie.

Adil laughed. 'If one does, at least I have reference shots – and a time stamp.' He leaned a hip against the plinth, for the moment just enjoying the scenery —

The sky tilted. There was a roaring in his ears – just like the sound that had woken him last night, but right behind him. It towered over him, watching, judging. He jerked upright, spinning around —

Everything was quiet, except for his racing heart. It pounded in his chest, his throat. He sucked in an unsteady breath.

'Are you okay?' Bobbie was staring at him.

Adil shook his head. 'Just went lightheaded for a second …' Maybe he shouldn't have had that third coffee. 'I'm fine.' He tried out a laugh that didn't sound all that convincing. 'Country air. Too strong for townies like me.'

Bobbie stared at him a moment longer, then nodded. 'You

seen enough?' She shivered. 'Don't know about you but it's chillier up here than I remember.'

'Yep.' He settled his bag more firmly on his shoulder. 'Back to the St Aldhelm's, eh? I need to make some notes anyway.'

'Fab.'

They returned to his car. Adil noticed the grey SUV had gone. He hadn't seen anyone else around, though.

He woke up in the dark, half expecting to hear that tearing noise again. Instead, everything was still. He couldn't hear a sound from the corridor or the courtyard. Had he been dreaming? He couldn't remember anything – certainly nothing that would have woken him up in the wee small hours, that was for sure.

What was the time anyway? he wondered. He went to turn over and look at his phone on the nightstand, but he couldn't move. His entire body was rigid, unresponsive. The only parts which seemed to be working were his heart and lungs, and they were rattling away too fast and too shallow. Was he having some kind of panic attack? That would be a first – Adil never got rattled. Nothing had ever fazed him, even in his schooldays. He rode out every storm on a tide of calm some people had seen as indifference. It was a positive trait in a journalist: he could stay placid and unmoved in the face of the most aggressive and rude interviewee.

He didn't feel so placid now.

He tried to turn just his head, but it remained locked in place. Totally frozen.

Worse, he had the feeling someone else was in his room, just out of vision, watching him. Adil couldn't tell if it was just him projecting his unease, but he had the feeling whoever it was had positioned themselves deliberately, knowing Adil was immobilised, not able to twitch so much as an eyeball. Had they drugged him somehow? There was no way Adil could check if the room's small window was shut.

He was definitely beginning to panic. That single, unusual

response just made it worse. Fed on itself in a cycle of fear, ramping up the anxiety until he felt like he wanted to scream – if only he could move the appropriate muscles.

The presence came nearer. He thought. How he could tell since he couldn't see a fucking thing, but … It was standing right over him. He sensed rather than saw it. There was nothing to see, even though the room wasn't that dark. He should see something. Someone …

It was pressing down on him now, crushing his chest, trying to stop what little movement there was left in his lungs. And still he couldn't see anything. Only feel the crushing weight, the sense of malignancy, or anger. Whoever was in the room with him didn't like Adil. They wanted him gone. Out of the way. Any way they could. And if that meant suffocating him --

The crushing weight abruptly vanished. He could move.

Adil flipped over, looking around the dim room. There was no one. The only sound was the hammering of blood in his ears, his shaky breathing.

He grabbed his phone and checked the time. It was seven minutes past three. Another first: Adil never woke up in the early morning. Not since he'd left puberty behind, anyway.

He got out of bed and went into the bathroom, pouring half a glass of water from the tap. He gulped it down and returned to bed, certain he'd never get back to sleep. He was too wired now.

The next thing he knew it was half-seven, and his phone alarm was beeping loudly.

'Sleep paralysis,' said Bobbie between sips of her morning coffee. They were in the bar, Adil's barely-touched breakfast congealing on a plate in front of him. 'It's a well-known phenomenon. Never had it before?'

'If I had do you think I'd be this shook up?' he snapped.

'Fair point.' She placed her mug on the table. 'At certain times during the sleep cycle your body enters a state of partial paralysis – during dreams, for instance. It doesn't want you thrashing about during a bad nightmare and hurting yourself. That's the stuff of films and telly. If you awake during this period – or partly awake, I suppose – it's quite unnerving. You feel like you're being crushed or choked, something nasty's sitting on your chest. And of course it's dark, so that just makes things worse. Wears off once your brain kicks into gear.'

Adil picked up a slice of toast, looked at it, then put it down again. 'Well, it frightened the crap out of me!'

'Always does, first time. You'll know better next time.'

He stared at her amused expression, wondering if she was joking.

'What is interesting though,' she continued, 'is the sensation of being crushed puts me in mind of the phenomenon reported by people during the height of the Shape's fame. Only that was usually during the day, and the victims were wide awake. Or so they thought.'

'Victims?'

'I'm pretty sure that's how the people of Werechurch thought of themselves back then. Not now, of course. Although people like you tend to remind them.'

'People like us, you mean.'

Bobbie chuckled. Another private joke. She picked up her coffee and took a deep swallow. 'So what are your plans for today?'

He hadn't really thought about it. He still felt tired, as though he'd actually been up all night. 'Dunno. Maybe talk to a few more people.' Although he'd tried that yesterday afternoon, with barman John and a couple of people in a coffee shop. They'd been polite, not quite shutting him out, but it was pretty clear no one in the town wanted to talk about anything that might involve the Shape. As though it was a private thing. Nothing that concerned anyone else – especially reporters. Adil had the feeling even bringing up Father Christmas might be treated as suspect. After all he flies through the air, covering the whole planet in a night. And Rudolf's nose glows.

Bobbie was standing. 'Well, I have my own notes to make. Try to have fun – although I think that's unlikely.' She quirked an eyebrow, turned and left.

Adil fell back in his seat, sighing loudly. He was starting to wish he'd never come here.

Bloody Werechurch Shape!

In the end he found himself driving back to Nods Hill. He stood by the concrete plinth and looked around, not at all sure what he thought he was going to see. Then he took out his phone, went online, and searched for anything on Werechurch, or the Shape, that he hadn't already found out.

As he'd suspected, there was precious little new about the place. Just about every article he found was pretty much what Bobbie had told him. There was a brief Wikipedia entry, but everything else seemed to be just a copy and paste of that text. No original research. A spiral of non-news, circling the plughole, one day to vanish down there forever.

Adil had the feeling the people of Werechurch would be perfectly happy with that.

He continued scrolling, recognising repeated words or phrases. Even searching for anything on Bobbie brought up a big fat blank. She'd published nothing that he could find. How long had she been visiting Werechurch? He didn't think she'd said. He wondered why she bothered to keep coming back. Habit? A few days holiday? If anyone wanted to get away from it all this was definitely the place.

He glanced over his shoulder. For a moment he'd been certain someone was standing immediately behind him, checking out his phone screen. The hill was deserted. No people, no insects that he could hear, no birds in the clear sky. He had the place to himself.

Except he couldn't shake the sensation of being watched.

He looked all around again, slowly, carefully. If there was anyone they had to be hiding behind the hedgerows down by the road and watching through binoculars. He smiled at the idea. The locals hadn't struck him as the kind who skulked behind twitching curtains. Quite the opposite.

He glanced back at his phone screen. A link caught his eye: something to do with a magazine called *Discus*. He'd almost scrolled straight past it. He opened the link and scanned the text. *Discus* was – or had been – one of those cheaply printed magazines of just a few pages which was all about flying saucers, abductions, and little green men. Someone had scanned every issue as PDFs and put them online. One in particular – the link that had come up with regard to Bobbie's name – was dated July 1967 and covered a weekend meeting at Werechurch that was, naturally, all about the Shape of two years earlier. There had been twenty-three attendees, all staying at the St Aldhelm's Well, where they'd also held a series of talks. The article was quite earnest, treating the events at Werechurch with deadly seriousness. In fact it sounded as though the whole weekend was pretty po-faced, everyone taking the Shape and attendant phenomena at face value. The aliens were here, and they were watching us closely. A real barrel of laughs, Adil thought.

There were two images accompanying the article. One, naturally, was the ubiquitous blur of the Shape; the second was a group photo of all the attendees, standing outside the pub entrance, looking suitably serious. All except one: just visible in the back, grinning at the camera as though she was the only one in on the joke.

Adil expanded the image. The larger it grew the more pixelated it became, even so he was pretty sure it was Bobbie. And even from the poor quality image, she didn't seem to have aged one bit.

'Have you got a painting in the attic or something?'

Bobbie glanced up from the corner in the bar where she was bent over a notebook, scribbling away. For a moment she frowned at Adil, then her resting face smile came back. 'Sorry?'

He placed his phone on the table, already open at the *Discus* article, zoomed in on the group photo. 'That is you, isn't it?'

Bobbie picked up his phone, squinted at it, turned it around a little, then put it back down. 'God, don't we all look serious? In which corner of the Dark Web did you find that?'

'You haven't changed one bit.'

She puckered her lips. 'Well, thank you.'

'Seriously, Bobbie. That photo's almost sixty years old, yet you don't look any different.'

Some of the playfulness faded from her expression. 'Didn't your mother ever tell you there are some things you never discuss with a woman?'

Adil knew he shouldn't push it, but he couldn't stop. 'I looked you up. It took some doing, since even in this age of information technology there's bugger all to find. You were born in 1940. That makes you eighty-two ... eighty-three ... Yet you don't look any older than someone in their very early thirties.'

'Well, I admit I dye my hair ...' She wasn't smiling now. She was staring hard at him, in disappointment, or disapproval. The scrutiny made Adil nervous. He turned around, not to take his eyes away, but because he thought there was someone else in the bar watching them. The place was empty. It was always empty.

He faced Bobbie again. 'How many years have you been coming to Werechurch?'

'I thought I said. Ten —'

'Not fifty? More? Did you even leave in 1967?'

'You're being ridiculous.'

He was. And rude. He couldn't help it. He was staying in a town that didn't seem to have changed for decades, talking to a woman who – impossibly – hadn't grown any older.

'After that weekend in '67 you more or less disappeared from UFO investigative circles.'

'I've been researching —'

'What, exactly?' Moving quickly, before he could think what he was doing and his common sense stopped him, he grabbed her notepad and flipped through it. It was filled with crude sketches, rough ovals of every size. Some in pencil, some in ballpoint. The Shape? No notes, no text. Just endless repetitions of the same image.

Adil closed the book and dropped it on the table. Bobbie stared at him, her eyes hard and unreadable. Adil backed away, embarrassed by his own actions, nervous for some reason. He glanced fitfully over his shoulder again. The bar was still empty, but he couldn't shake the feeling of being studied.

Mumbling something that might have been an apology, he fled the bar, returning to the street where he'd left his Citroen. A young couple opposite, standing outside a florist that didn't seem to have any flowers, was staring at the car with curiosity. Their eyes shifted to Adil, and they turned, walking away along the deserted pavement. Unhurried. Indifferent.

He got into his car and drove, paying no attention to his route. Hedges rose up on either side, blocking his view. All he could make out was the road ahead, and the road behind in his mirror.

Adil wasn't surprised when he pulled up at Nods Hill, but he wouldn't get out. He stayed in the car, eyes fixed on the gentle rise before him, and the plinth in the distance. He wanted to get out. He wanted to stay put.

He pulled out his phone and opened up the image viewer. The photographs he'd taken earlier swiped past as he looked at each one. Then he went back and looked at them all again, more slowly, taking his time, absorbing what he saw.

Even though the plinth showed up as just an indistinct blur, on each image the Shape hung above the hill. Sometimes nothing more than a distant smudge, sometimes a colossal oval filling the sky. Glistening. Sharper than the original newspaper image, it was --

Adil rammed his phone back into a pocket. He shook his head in denial. No, he was wrong. He had to be. He was going as crazy as Bobbie. As crazy as everyone in Werechurch - after all, madness would explain their odd behaviour, wouldn't it? Some sort of mass psychosis.

He opened his window and leaned out, slowly raising his head to peer at the sky. It was still clear, still empty of anything other than the sun.

He sat back in his seat. His breath catching, heart racing.

Some sort of local phenomena, he thought. Something that affect cameras – both film and digital. Radiation, perhaps? Hadn't he read somewhere that the South West had unusually high amounts of radon gas?

He could feel eyes on him. His neck prickled. He turned in his seat, searching. He saw no one. He hadn't before.

He stepped out of his car, shielding his eyes, squinting. The car park remained deserted. Nods Hill's slope was empty.

Adil got back into his car, starting the engine, fumbling as he tried to get it into reverse. Engine screaming, the Citroen backed straight into a gatepost. Adil tried to get it into forward gear, but the ground seemed to be trembling and his hands couldn't grab the gear lever.

The sky roared. Everything shuddered. Adil was surprised the hill didn't shake itself to pieces. A moment later, the engine died. Adil tried to move, to get out of his seat, but he couldn't move. He was pinned like a butterfly on display. Crushed down by a sky quake.

The clear blue sky blinked slowly and stared down on him. Amused. Indifferent. Inimical to change.

Adil wanted to run. He was terrified. Yet he wanted to stay, to be comforted.

If he fled – if he *could* flee – he'd always be terrified. Panicked. He never panicked. If he stayed, if he surrendered, there would be peace, and quiet; a continuation of the calm life he had always known. No questions, no concerns. No ...

Adil sat in his dead car, wondering. He felt the Shape waiting patiently, knowing he would make the right decision. They always did.

VIXIANA

Dartmoor is famous for its mires, which are often as deadly as they are beautiful. Vast accumulations of organic material filling deep depressions in the topography and becoming waterlogged mainly through rainfall, they present to the inexperienced eye an unbroken, flat terrain, a level, emerald vista that just invites the unwary to stray across it, but are basically immense peat bogs, which have sucked down every type of unfortunate, from innocent moorland ponies to disoriented hikers and walkers.

The old myth that the mires of Dartmoor are bottomless is of course nonsense, but seeing that the floor to many of them is the bedrock of the landscape itself, they can be many hundreds of feet deep, which means that the reclamation of bodies is almost impossible, if they can even be located.

But perhaps the most notorious of all Dartmoor's mires is that running alongside the old Tavistock-to-Chagford track. Not so much because a commonly used footway passes close by, which has certainly caused an unusually high number of casualties, but because of its association with the nearby and very sinister Vixen Tor, a huge and unusually shaped granite outcrop.

Vixen Tor, also referred to as the 'Sphinx of Dartmoor', is a distinctive feature on the western part of the moor, which can be seen for many miles around, but unearthly tales are connected to its formation. It was named, or so the stories tell (and they were widely believed) after a medieval sorceress called Vixiana, who first created it by enslaving a tribe of moorland gnomes and forcing them to build it, and who then lived there alone, a baleful force at the very heart of the West Country's most desolate region. No fixed dates are attached to this story, but one must assume that because the mysterious hag, whom everyone in the county was terrified of, inhabited a cave in the tor for many years from where she worked malicious spells, without anyone making any attempt to arrest her, it must predate the witch-hunting era. So, we are looking at Devonshire prior to the 1600s.

By all accounts, Vixiana was the archetypical beldame: tall and wizened, with long ratty hair and hideous facial deformities, who, because of her curious gait and crooked posture, could be seen coming across the moor a long way in advance. Devon folklore insists that she never had a good word for anyone, and despite her great age, was capable of physically attacking those she disliked, raking the flesh from their bones with her long, dirt-black fingernails.

Even in these small details, the story is already starting to sound like the type of propaganda that circulated about those social outcasts who in later times would be tried for witchcraft on spurious evidence, and sometimes hanged.

But it gets worse.

Vixiana supposedly had the power to summon mist. Her favourite game was to sit atop the tor and watch as lonely travellers made their way along the Tavistock-to-Chagford track. As soon as they reached the region of the mire, she'd weave a mist to blot out their vision and throw her voice back and forth, calling to the wayfarers to be careful, telling them to mind their footing, to go to the left or the right. Helpless and blinded, they would ultimately blunder into the mire. The last thing they usually heard as the peaty sludge closed over their heads was a ghastly cackling from the top of Vixiana's stronghold.

In due course though, as with all evil characters in these stories, her comeuppance came about. A robust farm-lad was making the journey, but having been given a magical ring that would turn him invisible (now, there's a 'fairy tale' type artefact that we haven't seen before!), he was able to turn the tables on Vixiana. Just before she summoned her mist, he vanished, and knowing the district well, picked his way to solid ground, where he lay in wait, cloaked from his tormentor's gaze. Frustrated, the witch came down from her perch, hobbled to the edge of the mire, dispelled the fog and strained her eyes across the moor to find him, unaware that he was right behind her. With a single push, he pitched her into the mire and then stood watching as she sank screaming from view.

We can only surmise about the origins of this folk-tale.

Was a shunned personality forced to live in the isolation of Vixen Tor in real life, and did she become a figure of fear and ridicule to those who passed by? Did she eventually die there alone, or was she, as the tale suggests, lured or even thrown into the bog?

In an age of rudimentary education, it would be easy to believe that, if someone you already didn't like or feared was living close to a place where, through sheer misfortune, more people died by accident than was normal, then this person might be responsible. It isn't much of a leap either to think that, in an age before witch-trials were held, an individual who was reviled and claimed to be one of the 'cunning folk' as a form of self-defence, might be disposed of illegally, the story then embellished to make it look as though she were the villain and her murderer the hero.

But this is often the way with age-old tales.

There are countless ways to interpret them, and just because we in the 21st century don't like to think there was something malevolent about Vixiana, that doesn't mean there wasn't.

Vixen Tor is no longer accessible to the public. All kinds of reasons have been offered. Curious visitors were causing damage to the ecosystem around the mire, or it was an insurance risk for the owners as people had been injured while climbing the tor. Protest groups and walkers' associations have confronted the land-owners many times since barbed wire was erected in 2003, but to no avail.

The mysterious rock-form that was supposedly built by gnomes and became the castle of a witch still stands, silent and aloof, unapproachable by man.

BULLBEGGAR WALK
Paul Finch

'But it's rich folk coming in from London and the like who are making house prices round here what they are,' Ned protested.

'And at the end of the day, is it really our business if people want to come and live here?' came the angry response, delivered through a swirling cloud of pipe-smoke. 'Should local folk be the only ones to enjoy this part of the world?'

Ned put his pint pot down at that. 'Well, you've changed your tune ...'

'That's because someone's gone and disappeared, isn't it? Because suddenly it isn't just talk any more, Ned Pasco.'

'I didn't tell him to go down there, did I!'

'No, but you dared him right enough. And after all that grief you heaped on him last Saturday, is it such a wonder he took you up on it?'

Ned was left bewildered. The mumbles of agreement he'd elicited from the various ruddy faces surrounding him in the snug of The Barleycorn inn last Saturday evening, when he'd been haranguing the latest moneyed outsider to move to Luxcomb Bay, were notable by their absence this following Wednesday, when he'd popped into his local again for a midweek pint and suddenly found himself being upbraided by, of all people, Doctor Melbury.

The burly medical man, a familiar enough presence in The Barleycorn, but one who usually kept his gruff opinions to himself as he smoked and sipped his ale and generally pored over his newspapers in the corner, had straightened up at the bar-counter the moment Ned had gone in there, puffing on his pipe in surly and disgruntled fashion.

'But it's all rubbish, isn't it?' Ned finally said. 'I mean, the

Bullbeggar ...'

'Rubbish, eh?' the doctor retorted. 'And you claim you're a true-born Devonshire man?'

'I *am* a true born Devonshire man!'

There was no dispute on that score. Ned had finally got defensive and not a little angry, his integrity being so unexpectedly called into question. But Doctor Melbury didn't back off from the confrontation. He leaned even closer, his face reddening between his lush, white side-whiskers. What was more, other regulars appeared to be backing him up. There were grunts of approval with every cross word he muttered. Several of them glared at Ned over the GP's broad, tweed-coated shoulder.

'A true-born Devonshire man, yet you call it rubbish.' The doctor shook his shaggy head. 'Or are you just getting some practise in for when the police come round asking all sorts of damn fool questions?'

Ned was *really* startled by that. The police? He'd never thought ...

'If you're not, you best had,' Doctor Melbury warned him. 'Because all the rest of us are doing it.'

As he set off towards the golf course the following day, Ned couldn't help but feel a little guilty about the situation regarding the young London chap. Things had gone wrong between them as soon as he'd heard that the newcomer had just moved to the area, though, in retrospect, Ned didn't suppose the new man had been all *that* offensive a sort. It was undeniable, however ... there was something inherently irritating about the London wealthy.

It had always bemused Ned, who was now retired but still lived in his father's old fisherman's cottage, and who all his working life had been a farm labourer, and as a result had never had more than a few ha'pennies to rub together, that the vast bulk of England's affluence seemed to be condensed in the capital city and the leafy stockbroker belt encircling it. He was sure that London had its own fair share of social ills. He'd only ever been to its plush West End, but look at Exeter. That was a big city and at least half of that was a squalid mess, so it seemed reasonable to assume that the greater part of London would be the same. But there was something about London richies, as opposed to other kinds, that was particularly galling to Ned. Perhaps it was their pretentiousness; so many of them affected a left-wing, socialist-themed agenda, yet nearly every one of them had university and public school backgrounds, or lived in sprawling mansion houses in Hampstead or Kensington, and spoke in what Ned regarded as a 'BBC accent,' an articulate and perfectly modulated form of English with no trace of region or class. By their very manner and attitude, you could tell that they saw themselves as an intellectual elite, as the natural-born rulers of their world, and that no other situation was within their comprehension.

Even more aggravating was the fact that this latest specimen – Hendon-Cooke, Ned thought his name had been – had sought to slum it in order to fit in here. Though he'd doubtless be more comfortable in the slick suit and tie of the City, where he was apparently 'something in conglomerates', he'd turned up that first night at The Barleycorn in a tatty sweater, faded corduroy pants and a pair of big, scuffed work-boots, which he'd probably picked up from a flea market, and which wouldn't have seen a real day's work since their previous owner had expired, almost certainly after a lifetime of back-breaking drudgery.

Despite his holding these views, Ned didn't regard himself as a working class hero. That dubious concept had never been part of Devonshire life. Devon was essentially a rural corner of England, famous for its high, sweeping moors and wooded, Arthurian coastlines. But like so much of the modern countryside, it only stayed that way through the conservationist efforts of its own people, who had not just striven hard for their keep, but who had always gone out of their way to preserve the ancient land in its wild and serene state. And now it was being invaded by money-minded men like this Hendon-Cooke. They came down here in their Jags and Bentleys, buying up the old barns and farmhouses, and transforming them into swish pads full of mod cons, which even then they would only use as weekend retreats from which they could noisily tour the area, or complain long and loud about the smell of manure on the fields or the ringing of the parish church bells on Sunday mornings.

But the real upshot of this had been the astronomical rise in property values. All at once, now that the nobs were looking to buy, even the lowliest woodland hovels were on the market at figures that were more like telephone numbers than realistic prices. On one hand it had meant that people like Ned Pasco were suddenly sitting on goldmines, though if they never intended to leave this part of the world, which Ned didn't, those were goldmines they could never mine; but at the same time it was driving families and young 'uns out of the district altogether. However you put it, and that bloke Hendon-Cooke had sought to argue his corner at first civilly, but later on, as he got more of the local beer down, heatedly and soon with a contemptuous sneer on his face, that sort of thing could never be right.

Ned strolled across the village centre, walking-stick in hand, as he pondered. He passed The Barleycorn without a glance – fickle sods, the blokes in there – and turned eastward up Hardbottle Lane. This was quite steep as local roads went; eventually it overlooked the harbour from a considerable height. Many was the time when holidaymakers, who Ned had no beef with at all as they poured their cash into the area's coffers and thankfully departed again, would park up en masse at the top just to take in the view.

It was a pleasant scene and no mistake, especially now, at mid-day, with the fishing fleet (what remained of it!) back in, the various barques and trawlers jostling together along the stone quays. Nets were suspended between them, and tackle spilled in heaps over the jetties. Gulls and guillemots wheeled back and forth, making a racket fit to wake the dead. A lot of the lads were still standing about in their boots and oilskin overalls, chatting, though doubtless a few had now found their way into the waterside pubs for lunch. Tourists were also present, peeking through the mullioned windows of the harbour's many quaint shops. Most of the buildings down there, shops and cottages alike, had been constructed from boulders found on the surrounding beaches, and though a local ordinance held that all had to be whitewashed, there was little if any uniformity in their height and shape. Some of their roofs were thatched, some slated, one or two even tiled. Architecturally, it was a jumble, but it was a harbourside jumble, a *Devonshire* harbourside jumble, and somehow that made it permissible.

Ned continued up the hill, enjoying the warmth of the June sun, and the fresh, brine-scented breeze. The only cloud on his horizon was this business with the London chap, Hendon-Cooke. Ned didn't really know what the circumstances were surrounding his so-called disappearance, but it seemed he'd been gone for a couple of days now, and his girlfriend, a bleached blonde, leather-jacketed piece of totty, who'd come roaring down from the Home Counties in a brand-new Porsche, had been the one to raise the alarm.

Ned thought about the bloke again and tried to convince himself that, even if something bad *had* happened to him, it had only been what he'd deserved. Despite the Londoner's initial attempts to be friendly that night in the pub, his true personality had finally seeped through. First off, reasonable phrases like 'freeing up the economy' and 'the area needs a cash injection' had sprung to his lips, but later, as the discussion had transformed into an argument, they'd started to hear things from him like 'the world's moved on', 'no-one has a God-given right to live here anymore,' and at last, 'what makes you lot special?', 'idiotic lack of understanding', 'bumpkins!', 'local yokels!'

'Go on, you keep calling us names,' Ned had finally said. 'That's one sure way to win friends round here, isn't it?'

'I'm clearly not going to win friends, whatever I say,' Hendon-Cooke had replied, hemmed in at his corner of the bar.

He was quite a short man, but young and with neatly combed reddish hair. By this time, he'd also turned red in the face, and despite being seated on a high stool, was looking small and vulnerable. 'Why should I carry on being polite to you all when you've already decided you can't stand me?'

'You think we're just a bunch of dozy country folk who are below you, yeah?' Ned had said, sensing that the unwanted guest was close to vacating the pub, and hopefully the village.

'I think you're a bunch of hicks. But that owes more to your attitude than who you are.'

'Presumably you reckon you're superior to our country ways?'

'Did I ever say that?'

'If you're so superior do you think you could take the Bullbeggar Walk?'

'The what?'

There'd been an immediate silence in the pub. A silence so melodramatic, so like something from a bad movie that it was almost comical. Young Hendon-Cooke, had he not been half-cut, might've guffawed and declared that they were having him on. Instead, he'd simply looked baffled. 'What on Earth's the Bullbeggar Walk?'

'Just a tradition of ours,' Ned had replied. 'Something you and your swanky London friends would have a good laugh at in some wine bar, no doubt.'

'I've never even heard of it.'

'Because you're an outsider. But if you want to be accepted here, you've got to go and do it.'

'All right, Ned,' a warning voice had interjected. 'Enough's enough, eh?'

That had been Ernie, the genial landlord, who, in truth, had probably been discomforted by his locals' verbal attacks on the London chap, but who hadn't wanted to offend them, they being his bread and butter and all.

'But what the hell is it?' Hendon-Cooke had demanded.

Ned had greeted this with a simple shake of his head. 'You've paid five-hundred grand to live in our village. That's an awful lot of money if you're going to spend the rest of your time here being treated like an intruder.'

'Well that's down to you, isn't it, Mr. Pasco. I didn't feel like one 'til I met you.'

'No ... it's not down to me, young fella. It's down to the bullbeggar.'

'What *is* the bloody bullbeggar?'

Good question, Ned thought, as he continued his stroll. He was now halfway around the golf course, the entrance gates to which were located at the top end of Hardbottle Lane. He wasn't a member, so he'd accessed it by a gap in one of its hedges, and had now reached the rough on its western edge, terrain that was already proving difficult. Its thick summer growth had risen almost to knee-height, and Ned – at sixty-six, and a martyr to his legs – was having an awkward time of it. It was a good job he'd brought his stick, he thought, as he beat his way through.

But that question again, that nagging question. The bullbeggar? What exactly was it?

The truth was that Ned didn't really know. He was no student of mythology. If anything, it was nothing more to him than a phrase, though he *did* remember what he'd learned from old school stories; namely that the bullbeggar, a supernatural entity, came into being when two irreconcilable enemies were buried together in the same grave. As far as Ned knew, this bullbeggar thing, which was constructed by the *faerie* as a sort of mockery of humanity, would spring to life at the very place where the enemies' grave was located, and would adopt various of their features, including their hostile and conflicting personalities. It would then go raging about the district, causing as much anguish and misery as it could. According to tradition, this particular bullbeggar had come into existence over a thousand years ago, sometime in the late 1060s. Around this period, it was said, with the Norman invaders in the ascendant, the remnants of the old Saxon nobility were fleeing westward, seeking sanctuary on the western fringes of Britain. On the way, they were constantly harried by the forces of William the

Conqueror, and many additional skirmishes and minor battles were fought. One morning, close to the hamlet of Luxcomb, a Saxon housecarl and a Norman knight came face-to-face on a lonely coastal path. They joined battle, but both men were so skilled in arms and so fevered with loathing for each other that the fight lasted the better part of a day until they both collapsed, each one suffering mortal wounds. Time passed, and with no-one to help, the two combatants died. The following morning, they were discovered by local peasants, who being descended from the ancient tribes of the British, the people of Dumnonia and Corn Waleas, had love neither for Saxon nor Norman. The corpses were thus flung together into a pit, and soil was shovelled over them.

From this moment, the folklorists would later write, the bullbeggar began to roam.

It haunted this tiny corner of Exmoor for decades, terrorising lone travellers, emptying whole villages, until at last drastic action was taken. It was now the twelfth century, and Bishop Osric of Taunton, who would later be canonised as Saint Osric, took it upon himself to exorcise the spectre. He arranged for the mingled bones to be dug up and disposed of by being cast into the sea. He then said a Mass upon the site, and a small church was built there, so to sanctify it. However, the desired effect was never achieved. The bullbeggar was laid for a brief time, but once the venerable old cleric had died, rumours began circulating that it had returned, though now it had a greater territory to dominate; in fact, it extended its activities down the path to the shoreline itself.

Belatedly, it was realised that once the bones had been thrown into the sea, a new conjoined grave had been unwittingly formed, only now beyond the reach of men, so the bullbeggar would rove and wail and torment the local population for evermore.

Ned still didn't accept that he'd actually dared the silly sod to come this way.

All he'd really done was mention it. Okay, it would be fairer to say that he'd taunted the bloke with it, but at the end of the day what the heck was the Bullbeggar Walk? Nothing more than a path down to the sea. A little-known path admittedly, but still just a path. It wasn't even officially called 'Bullbeggar Walk'. It was only known as that in Luxcomb village.

Ned continued alongside the golf course. He waved his stick in greeting to a small clutch of golfers about fifty yards away. They acknowledged him with nods and smiles. Those men would be outsiders too, but at least they were only visitors, enriching the district rather than making it uninhabitable. Not, Ned had to admit, that it would be easy to make such a place as Luxcomb Bay uninhabitable. It really had to be one of the most scenic spots on either of Devon's coasts. Luxcomb Golf Course – 'an exquisite and testing georama for the serious sportsman,' according to *Golf World* – was the usual expanse of manicured sward, dotted here and there with stands of pine, ornamental fishponds and the ubiquitous white sand bunkers. But beyond it, and beyond the line of trees that fringed its northern edge, the sea created a majestic backdrop, particularly on a day like today, with the noon sun riding high and the coastal waters glinting and sapphire-blue. At first glance, it was like something from the Med or even the Caribbean.

No, for all his grumblings, Ned knew that it would be many decades, if not longer, before the incoming tide of metropolitan wealthy could really spoil the atmosphere of this place.

He spotted the church.

And his spirits soured a little.

Saint Osric's, the church of the legend, occupied the northwest corner of the course; in fact, it was encompassed by it, though, being tucked out of the way, no-one could ever claim that it was obtrusive. Even if they did, tough luck on them; the church was officially an ancient monument, and well protected by rules and regulations. Ned gazed at it as he approached. It was a squat, granite structure, not especially large and with a single arch over its front, where a bell had once hung. Sorely weathered, its aged brickwork was covered all over by thick tendrils of lichen. Even then, its simple grey exterior stood out sharply against the sumptuous greens.

Its front door, a heavy slab of oak, studded with brass nail-heads, stood wide open as though in anticipation of Ned's arrival, and once again he found it hard to believe that this structure was truly the original building, though archaeologists assured people that it was. Of course, Ned was fairly certain that it was now unused, at least in the way that churches were normally used. So thinking, and assuming he wouldn't disturb anyone at their devotions, he stepped casually inside. A simple stone font sat within the porch, alongside an 'honesty box' and beyond that, accessible through a wide archway, was the main body of the building. It was about sixty feet long by thirty feet wide, smoothly flagged and entirely bare of furnishing; there were no pews or chairs, not even a pulpit. The altar was little more than a raised granite platform, lacking both table and tabernacle.

Ned strode forward, his footfalls clicking in the dusty stillness. This sort of spiritual abandonment wasn't unique down here in the West Country; many of these ancient monuments now existed solely for the purposes of tourism. Doubtless this one would be regularly maintained – probably by some trust or other, if not English Heritage themselves – which explained why the place was so clean and in such generally good condition, but Ned doubted that services were ever held here.

He halted in the middle of the nave. A row of pillars ran down either side, forming alleyways between themselves and the outer walls. They were smooth, entirely free of the traditional designs and religious iconography that one grew so used to. Even the Stations of the Cross were absent. Ned had heard that the first Normans were a pious and ascetic people, who had introduced a very austere style of architecture to England, and that most of its early medieval churches still reflected this.

Of course, in that respect, Saint Osric's, with its famous stained-glass windows, stood out like a sore thumb. He strolled on. Apparently these particular windows had been installed in Victorian times. Some deluded but no doubt well-intentioned philanthropist had decided the shrine needed that little bit extra to ensure that the visitors came here. Hence the glazed images now on view, all beautifully made and of the usual Christian significance: apostles and angels, scenes from the Bible, pilgrims *en route* to Canterbury.

With one exception.

The one in the far right-hand corner.

Ned, who had never actually visited Saint Osric's before, had heard much about this particular window, and had often wondered what it looked like. It seemed that the Victorian artisan who had fitted out the new casements had in this one instance been allowed to call upon the old legend surrounding the origins of the church.

Ned stared up at it. It was certainly impressive in its colour and its detail. And not a little sinister. In its foreground, a churchman, probably Bishop Osric himself, an archetypically penitential figure in the sandals and dark robes of a Benedictine monk, his head shaven in a tonsure, his bearded face suitably solemn, leaned with one hand on a wooden staff and with the other passed blessings on a tangled patch of briars near his feet. More mysteriously though, in the background, a woodland trail rose to the ridge of a hill, and atop it, a gibbous moon sat against a sky of purple clouds. Framed on this moon was what at first glance appeared to be a silhouetted group of misshapen individuals all clustered together, though no fine detail of them was visible. The mysterious grouping was entirely black and featureless, its presence in the scene unexplained.

Unexplained, that was, to those who didn't know the story.

Because if one looked again at the oddity on the hill, one might suddenly conclude, however nonsensical it may seem, that one was actually looking at a single figure. An outlandish figure admittedly, a ludicrous figure, a grotesque parody of a figure, but a single figure nonetheless, despite the four sturdy legs on which it was balanced, despite its immensely broad shoulders, and despite, on top of those shoulders, the distinct outlines of two separate heads.

Five minutes past the church, Ned came off the golf course entirely.

The rough gave way to ragwort, knapweed and deep, interwoven brambles, which might ordinarily provide him with an impassable barrier, though forty yards to his right a beaten trail was visible through it, affording easier access to the shadowy thickets beyond. Ned held back for a moment. Aside from the distant *wishing* of the sea and the cheerful laughter of some golfer far behind him, there was scarcely a sound. Odd, given that it was the height of a summer's day on the edge of woodland; for once there was no crying of seabirds, not even the twitter of sparrows.

As he was proud of saying, Ned was a local man born and bred. Despite this, he was another who had never made the Bullbeggar Walk, though in his case it was more through circumstance than superstition. Now, however, having been challenged on this in the pub last night, he'd opted to put it right, whether the woods were unusually quiet or not. Not that he thought the London chap would actually have bothered with the Walk either. Why should someone like Hendon-Cooke, a self-proclaimed modernist, a sophisticated type who spent most of his time in the breakneck but very real world of international money markets, attach any credence to so daft an old wife's tale?

Unless he'd felt he had to prove something.

And that was an ugly thought, Ned decided, as he set off along the trail. Suppose Hendon-Cooke had tried to come down here and had lost his footing? Suppose he was lying hurt somewhere? There was no point pretending otherwise; if that was the case, Ned was at fault, and he knew he couldn't let that happen, though he was already getting tired himself, which didn't bode well. Both his knees were aching, and that was after a straightforward half-mile march across the flattish contours of the golf course. The path, which consisted mainly of loose soil and pebbles, was also proving precarious. It steepened quickly as the hillside plunged downward through the trees towards Bullbeggar Cove. Again, Ned had never been down there; by all accounts, it was a nice spot, sheltered, very peaceful. But few holidaymakers ever found their way to it. Those from outside the area didn't know it existed, while those from inside tended to give it wide berth. It seemed ridiculous now that he thought about it. How could any fabled creature as preposterous as the bullbeggar actually be taken seriously in the twenty-first century?

But ironically, the environment now matched the mood of the old story. The underbrush to either side of the path grew swiftly into a profusion of matted greenery. Overhead, low, leafy boughs became an opaque canopy, blotting out the sunlight. The trail, which dropped at an ever more fearsome gradient, continually bent out of sight just ahead. Dense groves of hawthorn flanked it, their twisted branches reaching into the path, snagging and scratching, and suggesting, rather disconcertingly, that it was even less well used than Ned had imagined. Eventually, the path had darkened until it was like a tunnel; it had become closed-in, claustrophobic, and only now did it occur to Ned that if something *had* happened to Hendon-Cooke, it might also happen to him.

He'd proceeded down here on the assumption that a city man could easily come to grief on a woodland walk, whereas a country man never would. However, the path became progressively looser and more broken, all stones and rolling bits of twigs, and he was constantly slipping and sliding on it, and it suddenly seemed obvious to Ned that *he* was far more likely to have an accident than someone in his late-twenties like Hendon-Cooke. And furthermore, if he did have a fall, and ended up injured, would anyone come down here and find him? People didn't routinely visit this place, as he'd already seen.

Of course, all of these were quite reasonable fears, and Ned, being a bold, hardy sort, didn't allow them to prevent what he considered to be his mission of mercy. So, he continued resolutely downhill, though his feet repeatedly threatened to skid from beneath him, and his hands were scored and slashed where he'd grabbed at branches.

But something else was nagging at him too.

Everything around him was familiar: larches, elms, maples, not to mention the gorse, the bracken, the hawthorn, the hair-grass emerging in thick, waist-high clumps, yet the way every branch and twig seemed to mesh together almost frenziedly, forming impenetrable walls of vegetation on both sides, it was almost unnatural. English flora rarely grew this way, in thick jungle-like masses so knotted together it could physically prevent you from thrusting through it. And wasn't that briar he could now see woven in there as well? Long, ropy straggles of briar snaking in and out of everything else, just waiting to snarl him should he accidentally go blundering into it. And yet, in addition to all this, which again posed a reasonable fear, as no-one wanted to get torn and entwined in rank tangles of undergrowth, there was still something else, some other, darker feeling of menace down here that he found it difficult to put a name to. The rational man inside told him that this was fear by association. He already knew the legends of this place, and so it struck him as eerie whereas to some stranger it might appear perfectly pleasant and normal. (Ned had once been to Loch Ness, and remembered being daunted by the darkness of the water; other Highland lochs he had visited during the same holiday had looked exactly the same but had felt far less sinister.)

In any case, whether he liked it or not, his continued descent was becoming a matter of gravity rather than obstinate will. The slope had steepened to such an extent that Ned knew he could tumble twenty or thirty feet if he fell, stopping only when he came up against some boulder or tree trunk. To counter this, the path was starting to zigzag; a reassuring sign, he supposed, as it meant that at least some time in the past human beings had come this way and had consciously responded to the danger.

That was when he heard a loud *crackle* in the undergrowth.

Ned stopped abruptly, though it wasn't easy. The soles of his absurdly ill-chosen lace-up shoes tried to run ahead again on the crumbly surface. He managed to anchor himself by grabbing hold of a hawthorn bough, in the process embedding his palm with thorns. For a moment he ignored the searing pain and stopped to listen and survey the surrounding foliage. Though he strained his eyes to penetrate the greenish gloom, he saw nothing. A moment passed, and cursing himself for a fool, he continued down.

He didn't think he could be too far from the bottom now. A strong sea breeze chilled the sweat on his neck and forehead. This gave him new vigour, and Ned began to hurry, almost recklessly so. A few seconds later he saw daylight ahead and at last found himself descending into Bullbeggar Cove itself.

The first thing that struck him was the sunshine; it was still bright and warm.

Pleased that he'd made it without mishap, Ned ambled forward over a gently sloping rubble of shingle and driftwood, before strolling out onto firm level sand, where he finally stopped and drew a satisfied breath. The job was half done. Excellent. This would teach those bastards in The Barleycorn.

He assessed his surroundings.

At this time of day the tide was low, but only a hundred or so square-metres of beach was visible. To the east and west, jumbled banks of weedy, barnacled rocks gave out to sheer cliff-walls. This meant that the cove was actually more of a canyon. Overhead, Ned saw a narrow strip of azure sky. He imagined that on a stormy day, the sea, which often arrived on this shore in colossal breakers, when funnelled through such a tight crevice would explode across the entire beach. When you considered that, it was no wonder this secluded place was deemed unfit for holidaymakers. And again, that was a reassuring thought; it gave an alternative explanation for Bullbeggar Cove's evil reputation.

It might also explain, he thought, what had happened to Hendon-Cooke.

Not that the sea was rough now. As Ned strode forward, he didn't think he'd ever seen it so placid. Calm wavelets lapped the toes of his shoes. The surface was millpond-smooth. Further out, framed between the lowering cliff walls, it rolled a gentle blue rather than heaved in iron-grey swells. But he still scanned the waterline as though expecting to find a grisly relic of the unwary visitor bobbing about, though doubtless if what he feared had actually come to pass, said evidence would now be several miles along the coast, washed in at Ilfracombe, or sucked up the River Taw towards Barnstaple.

At which point, Ned thought he heard voices.

Distant voices, but heated, as though two men, somewhere close by, were engaged in an angry confrontation.

He looked around and then up, anticipating figures on the high parapets; walkers possibly, bird-watchers, even park rangers. But nobody was visible. And now the voices had faded again, as though carried off on the wind.

Ned listened hard, but heard nothing else.

In fact he'd heard so little the first time that it was difficult to make out what they'd been saying, and the 'echo chamber' effect of the cove hadn't helped. One of them had muttered something like *praelic antecrist* … whatever that meant. While the other? Well that was even more confusing. Hadn't he heard the other say *merde de cochon*? *Merde de cochon* …? Didn't that mean 'pig … or pig-shit?' Something like that, at least.

And wasn't it French?

Ned decided that he didn't want to stay down here any longer. The sun seemed to have gone. Was it already so late in the afternoon? A dimness had fallen, and an increasingly stiff breeze blew. Even the water had started to ruffle, small spurts of froth arcing up off it. And then it struck him how problematic the return journey would be. He eyed the slope that he'd so struggled to keep his footing on as he'd scrambled down. It towered over him. It was densely treed, but from this low angle seemed almost as perilous as the two perpendicular cliff-walls that hemmed the cove from east and west.

There was no other way back of course, but he still hesitated.

He wasn't a hundred per cent certain he'd be able to make it, though he'd never know if he didn't at least try. Resolving that anything was better than staying down here, because it had also now occurred to him that if it *was* later in the afternoon than he'd thought, the tide would rise, and by the looks of the heaped shingle and driftwood at the head of the beach, it would rise considerably, even on a calm day like this, he commenced the ascent.

He felt that if he could keep a slow but steady pace, he would re-emerge onto the golf course within a half-hour or so. It was vital not to overdo it. If he pushed his arthritic joints too hard, they'd give out, while not three years ago he'd been hospitalised for two nights after Doctor Melbury had detected what he thought might be a heart murmur.

So, Ned went uphill cautiously, starting the ascent in an easy, relaxed manner. But it didn't take long for him to feel shocked at how swiftly and steeply the path rose in front of him. Soon he had to lean forward to make any progress at all. Momentarily, it seemed like an idea to discard his stick and scrabble up like a dog. But pains were already shooting through his limbs, while his spine curved at an agonising angle. His breath came in ragged heaves, his lungs straining inside him. Sweat overflowed from his brow into his blinking, stinging eyes; he repeatedly had to take off his cap to mop it away.

And yet the ordeal had only just begun. Even when the trail began zigzagging, levelling out for brief periods, it tilted sideways, its dry surface shifting and breaking beneath Ned's feet, giving him acute problems of balance. He took progressively longer, more regular rests. Ridiculously, though it was probably due to the gathering dusk, the vegetation seemed to close in around him. Swarms of midges had appeared, pestering him relentlessly, often adhering to his sweat, wriggling and itching on the side of his face. The heat grew intense, so that Ned had to loosen the collar button of his shirt. He thought to unfasten the waistcoat under his jacket, but no.

One had to maintain decorum. That Hendon-Cooke, and his ragged sweater, and his worn-out pants, and his ludicrous designer work-boots … thinking that was how country folk were supposed to appear, looking as though the wind had brought him in.

Ned's blood boiled. He wasn't giving in to that nonsense.

And then he heard something again. Just as he had before.

At first he thought his own breathing was grating in his ears. But no. It wasn't that.

He stopped and listened, and noted that there *was* a faint shuffling out there, somewhere to his right. He stared into the matted vegetation, but still saw nothing.

Twigs snapped, however. Leaves rustled as they were thrust aside.

Which direction it was moving in, he couldn't really tell.

And what exactly could it be?

Ned was puzzled, but also frightened.

The rational person inside him wrestled to overcome this. Likely it was some ram or sheep that had blundered down from the pastures above. Or maybe a deer. There were red deer all over Exmoor, not to mention straggling herds of wild ponies. Any one of those innocent creatures could have wandered off the beaten track and got lost along the coast. Yet somehow, none of these thoughts gave Ned comfort.

He renewed his climb, driving himself harder than he'd originally intended, and subsequently tripping over broken branches or strands of creeper, and again staggering and slipping on the countless loose, rolling stones. The tempo of his heart again began to rise, to hammer inside him. His breathing came in raw, gulping gasps.

And now he fancied that that other being – whatever it was – was also moving uphill. Alongside him even. Surely that couldn't be right? But the more he listened the more he realised that, actually, it *was* right. It was indeed moving alongside him, almost parallel. What the devil … was he being stalked or something? This was ridiculous. There were no predatory animals in this part of England.

It occurred to him that the mysterious Beast of Bodmin reputedly prowled only fifty miles to the south. Once a mythical creature, modern science now held that it might be a breed of large cat, possibly a leopard or panther, several specimens of which had escaped from captivity a few decades earlier. The theory was that they had adapted to the British climate and were now creating a breeding population that was slowly spreading out over England's southwest. But even then, there'd never been any reports of a human being attacked by these beasts. And if it *was* a panther or a leopard, Ned certainly couldn't imagine it making the racket that he was listening to. Because, it could have been his mind playing tricks on him again, but this thing was now causing a disturbance in the undergrowth that could only be described as *thunderous*. It must be huge, ungainly, and it was progressing uphill with even greater awkwardness than he was, albeit more robustly. He fancied he could hear grunts of exertion, and a repeated *swish-chop* as though it was hacking its way through. What was more, its advance seemed to be getting louder, as if, as well as clambering uphill, it was inclining *towards* the path?

Did it intend to overtake him? To head him off?

Ned gave a wheezing whimper as he drove himself on and up. He was racked with pain and fatigue. Sweat streamed down the inside of his ill-suited clothes. His hands were dirty and cut to ribbons from his frantic grasping at roots and branches. It occurred to him to call for help, maybe even to scream, but he didn't have the wind for it.

Surely it couldn't be much farther, though?

And just as he thought this, the sun appeared in the west; at least, the upper rim of it did, and this was enough to send spears of light down through the previously impenetrable woodland. He must be almost there. He nearly shouted with relief, though in truth the thrashing in the underbrush had become horribly close. He imagined that if he turned his head left, he'd see whatever was causing it lurching through the final few feet of foliage.

In fact, from the corner of his eye, he *did* see something.

Something broad like a bull, yet upright. Something greenish and black, as though covered all over with dirt and leaf-mould, something twisted, misshapen, and moving with a hideous, jerking gait. Despite his breathlessness, a shrill screech tore from Ned's chest. He gathered what remained of his strength to make one final dash. Discarding his stick, he now *was* scrambling on all fours. His flayed hands clawed at the gritty, stony soil; the knees of his trousers tore as he dragged them through it.

But at last, at long last, the gradient started to ease.

Suddenly he was on two feet again, pumping his aged legs as they carried him upward. Around him, the undergrowth thinned, and directly ahead, he spied that wild tangle of matted grasses on the edge of the golf course. That would hinder him too, but he would get through it. He could get through anything now. And he *did*, finally breaking from the cover of the trees, plunging to his knees through untamed flora, but all the way encouraged because at last he'd sighted the smooth green shoulder of the golf course, and over the top of that, the empty bell-tower of the small church. Ned's breath cut like razors in his throat and chest. Hot spittle flowed from the corners of his mouth. His legs had virtually rubberised, but he kept going, not caring what damage he might be doing to himself.

The next thing, he was tottering across the lush, cropped turf at the fifteenth hole. On all sides, fairways rolled regally away. No golfers were visible, but that didn't matter because the church was just ahead – thirty yards, twenty yards, ten – but now, once again, Ned fancied he detected pursuit: a rumble of galloping feet, like the fast approach from behind of a horse or some other four-legged beast.

Gasping in agony, he stumbled the remaining five yards. The church door was still open, and a split-second later he'd entered the cool mustiness of its interior, the air *whooshing* in and out of his tortured lungs. He slammed the door closed and thrust his aching back against it. There was no lock to turn, no bar to bring across, but surely that wouldn't matter. That thing … that vile *thing*, could not enter here, for this was a holy place, a sanctuary.

But then a hideous doubt crept into Ned's mind.

Suppose ... just suppose ...

He whirled around, the perspiration sopping his clothes turning abruptly to ice. He backed away, retreating unsteadily through the arch into the main body of the church, where it was cooler still, and thanks to the lack of sunlight shafting through the tall, stained-glass windows, dark, like a sepulchre.

Suppose ... just suppose ... as he had suspected before ... but it wasn't possible ...

Rubbish! Of course it was possible!

No services were held here these days. Saint Osric's was a monument, a tourist attraction, an old and empty shell.

In which case ... good God, had they deconsecrated it?

Had the diocese decided that because there was no congregation to be catered for here, they could no longer afford to maintain it as God's house?

Even as these chilling thoughts raced through Ned's tormented mind, he backtracked across the nave, not seeing what he was walking towards. It was only instinct that halted him with his heels on the very edge of a pit that had not been there before. He pivoted slowly around and gazed down at it.

And at what was inside it.

And was stunned. And horrified. And appalled.

Someone had pried up one of the heavy granite paving-stones. It now lay aside, and beneath it a trench had been dug in the rich, black soil. And inside that trench ...

Ned was transfixed. So much that he scarcely heard the *creak-click* as the front door of the once sacred building was opened and closed again.

Hendon-Cooke ... poor Hendon-Cooke ...

Nausea flooded through Ned.

That great gash in the Londoner's forehead, the one dividing him between the eyes, through the centre of his nose, almost to his teeth. Could that be a cloven skull? The sort of damage a Saxon battle-axe might inflict? And that grotesque, gaping wound in the middle of his blood-soaked chest, which surely could only have been delivered by some cruel-tipped weapon driven with unimaginable force. Was that the work of a Norman longsword?

Ned tried to scream, but the bile and saliva coagulated in his gagging throat.

So much so that it choked him where he stood. So much so that he barely even heard the *clomp* of multiple malformed feet as they entered the nave behind him.

Stories still circle about the Bullbeggar Walk.

People, mostly golfers looking for lost balls, claim to hear things down there from time to time: a clumsy crashing about in the undergrowth, two voices endlessly bickering on the high coastal wind. However, it isn't the same as before. All things change, and local legends owe much to fanciful embellishment, and that might explain a lot. But if one had believed this tale in olden times one might have expected to visit that lonesome spot and hear snatches of sentences and argumentative words spoken in French or ancient English. More likely now, or so the folklorists say, you'll hear different.

One of the voices, for instance, is said to be quite modern, almost 'BBC-like'.

The other, they'll tell you, has the unmistakable tone of a true-born Devonshire man.

THE TEDWORTH DRUMMER

The publication of the book, Saducismus Triumphatus, *in 1681, was not in itself a seminal event. The work of Joseph Glanvill, a celebrated 17th century thinker and intellectual, it was something of an atavistic tome, clearly inspired by the Puritan views of his early life. Among other things, it attempted to roll back the increasingly rational response to the problem of witchcraft.*

The immediate years after the Civil War saw a huge transformation in England. At the encouragement of the newly restored Charles II, there was a huge outpouring of art, scholarship and philosophy, and the witch-hunting craze, brought properly to England by James I in 1603, suddenly seemed like ridiculous superstition. For example, Matthew Hopkins, the infamous Witchfinder General, had died in 1647 from tuberculosis, which he'd allegedly contracted when angry villagers swam him as a witch himself in their local pond, and was regarded by this time as a war profiteer and 'fingerman' (ie a professional false witness). Capital punishment for witchcraft wouldn't be abolished in England until 1735, but witch trials were now fewer and fewer, and acquittals happened more and more.

Convinced that witches were real and that the powers of devils and demons could be harnessed, Glanvill used Saducismus Triumphatus *to try and reverse this new thinking, dedicating a whole section of his book to showcasing the compelling mystery of the Tedworth Drummer.*

For a brief time, the haunting at Tedworth (now Tidworth) in Wiltshire was as famous in its day as the hauntings at Amityville and Enfield in the 1970s. Even such luminaries as Samuel Pepys and John Wesley wrote about it, expressing fascination for the bizarre series of events. It all began in March 1661, when a veteran of Oliver Cromwell's army, a drummer called Drury, who had now attached himself to a group of travelling beggars, was arrested by the bailiffs of Tedworth for seeking to obtain monies by deception. The magistrate, John Mompesson, was unsure about his guilt, but had the suspect's drum confiscated while he looked into the matter further, taking the instrument to his own home and hanging it in an upstairs bedroom. Not long after this, strange and frightening things began to happen.

The sound of a beating drum was heard both inside and outside the house late at night, and then during the daytime, and then continuously. No source was ever detected, but Mompesson quickly came to believe that it was loudest in the room where the confiscated drum was being kept, even though no one was ever in there. After this, the drumming sound amplified because now, it seemed, there was more than one drummer and they regularly beat out tattoos on furniture, on doors, even on the roof of the house. The drumming apparently ceased briefly during a three-week period when Mrs Mompesson was in labour and then afterwards when she needed rest. But after that, the drumming recommenced with ferocity, so loud that even neighbouring households heard it, and now there were other manifestations.

Items of furniture and clothing were thrown around, as witnessed by many individuals. The children of the house were particularly tormented, all developing the conviction there was something under their bed at night, something that panted and scratched on the floorboards like an animal, and indeed, servants also attested to this.

A certain Reverend Cragg was summoned, and on his arrival to say prayers was greeted by a veritable maelstrom of activity, all types of items flying back and forth. He himself was struck by a walking-stick.

Clearly observable all through this period was the entity's gradual increase in strength and rage. By the January of 1662, it was able to vocalise, supposedly speaking to members of the household from the chimney, then commencing an unearthly singing, declaring itself over and over to be a witch. At night, when it wasn't drumming, occupants of the building were terrified to hear the sound of a large animal roaming the passageways, snuffling, grunting and snarling. On one occasion, when Mompesson scattered fine ash on the floor to see if it left impressions, the footprints revealed were horrific: neither animal's nor man's. In the darkest hours of the night, the doors to the servants' quarters would be flung open and something unseen would yank their bedclothes away. A particularly doughty male servant was manhandled aggressively, repeatedly pulled from his bed.

It was around this time that Joseph Glanvill himself was invited to attend the premises, later reporting in Saducismus Triumphatus that he was startled by the things he experienced. A figure made of matchwood dancing as though of its own accord, and when shot by Mompesson, bleeding what appeared to be real blood. A conversation he had one night with an invisible being, and on asking what it wanted, being told by a harsh, disembodied voice: 'Nothing from you!'

Again, we must draw analogies with the so-called hauntings at Amityville in New York State and Enfield in London, in 1975 and 1976 respectively, because remarkably similar events went on to occur at Tedworth. Sulphurous fumes were allegedly detected, and a female servant was terrified out of her wits by an actual apparition, which she described as indistinct but glaring at her with blood-red eyes (shades of Amityville?). After that, the children themselves were physically attacked, thrown around their bedroom with increasing violence (Enfield?), their chamber pots poured into their beds.

Belatedly it seems, John Mompesson demanded an audience with the itinerant drummer, Drury, who was now in prison for theft. Drury openly admitted that he had bewitched the Tedworth house, sending a demon to harass the family. Mompesson demanded that he be tried for witchcraft, which he duly was at Sarum, but the death penalty for witchcraft could only be sought in England if it could be shown that someone had died as a result, and nobody here had, and the malefactor was thus spared the ultimate punishment (which he had always been likely to in this slightly more enlightened era). Sentenced to be transported for life, Drury supposedly persuaded the ship's captain to release him before they set sail, threatening to invoke cataclysmic storms otherwise, at which point he seems to vanish from history, though before this, he'd supposedly told fellow convicts that he drew his power from a grimoire given to him by an aged magician.

The haunting had now caused such a sensation that a Royal Commission arrived at Tedworth to assess it. However, the commissioners were unimpressed, seeing and hearing nothing they felt was supernatural, deciding that it was either a hoax or that credulous men had been duped by natural phenomena. Joseph Glanvill berates them for this in Saducismus Triumphatus, arguing that the new *skepticism was going too far and that evil as a sentient power should not just be dismissed out of hand because the investigators had seen no evidence of it themselves.*

Unfortunately for Glanvill, other investigators since then have also come down on the side of the rational. In 1841, both the American Methodist, Amos Norton Craft, and the Scottish writer and psychologist, Charles Mackay, re-examined the case and concluded that it was a web of trickery perpetrated by Drury's fellow travellers, who were angered by what befell him. Later on, in 1908, the journalist Addington Bruce also dismissed the episode as a fraud, blaming the Mompesson children, whom he said were either deliberately or unconsciously the cause of the disturbances.

THE PALE MAN
Andy Briggs

Reflection. There are moments in your life that allow you pause and contemplate. Such moments arrive unasked for, just in time for the critical junctures when decisions must be made.

Decisions that can make the difference between life and death. It is such a narrow margin that it is all too easy to miss such opportunities, in which case all you can do is observe.

But I'm getting ahead of myself. The road trip was a spur-of-the-moment decision. A bolt from the north to the West Country. A razor-sharp transition between the urban concrete life I've endured to wide open spaces. Change. The opportunity to start again.

It wasn't my idea. Sarah had made the suggestion. Keep off the motorways. Take the A-roads and laze along the beaches until we run out of land. But the first stop was Somerset, that part of the land known for loud festivals, rolling hills that bring to mind Hobbits, cheese, and warm beer.

That was the plan. But plans are made to be broken. Promises mere pledges to break.

Now I can only watch as events unfold.

But that's getting ahead of myself again. Only this afternoon the rolling hills had been consigned to imagination. Sarah had Googled the route on her phone, picking out the most obscure locations she could find in between releasing her seat belt so she could lean over the seat and readjust the pile of bags filling the backseat. Such was my haste to leave they'd been haphazardly thrown in like a Jenga tower, and every time I graced the brakes one of the bags would make a bolt for freedom and slam against the windscreen.

Not that I couldn't see much through the windscreen. It was

allegedly the start of the summer, but the earth rebelled against the very notion and a cool mist smothered the undulating land in a veil of ashen grey. It gave no hint of abating as the digital clock on the dash ticked over to four in the afternoon. It would soon be dark at this rate. And it had rendered Sarah to almost monosyllabic responses as she spent more time refreshing the apps on her phone and harrumphing because nobody had updated their social media feeds in the last ten seconds. The phone network was there, the GPS was working, but even though she had communication to the world in her palm, she felt as if she'd fallen off the face of the earth. At least it had stemmed the constant stream of questions, which had thankfully faded as we left the M6 and headed southwest. It seemed as if my personal life was as tiresome to her as it was to me. I'd left behind an abusive relationship. We both knew I should have done it long ago, just as we were both aware the last thing that I wanted to discuss was real life.

'I'm hungry.' It was nothing more than a plaintive comment, but one occurring with increasing regularity.

'Check if there is anything coming up. A KFC. Little Chef. There's got to be something off the motorway.'

Sarah stabbed her phone's screen with theatrical force. I could hear her nail clacking the glass. 'Nope. Nothing. There's no internet connection.'

'I heard your email ping a minute ago.'

'That was a minute ago. And that was spam. Spam can get through any apocalypse.'

My gaze strayed to the GPS map on my phone, perched against the dashboard's audio entertainment screen. Music had been killed long ago in favour of silent contemplation. The map was animated, showing our steady pace along a gentle, meandering road. No turn offs. No side lanes to venture down and, outside the windows, nothing more than a hint of shapes in the fog. Blemishes of black on grey. It felt as if nothing had changed for hours. Perhaps the GPS was stuck in a loop. I tapped the screen to refresh the display, just in case.

The machine replied in a curt male voice. '*Turn around when possible.'*

Sarah sniggered. 'See? Even he doesn't know where we are.'

'What the hell …?' The exasperated sigh hissed through my lips. We'd diligently been following the thin red line on the display all day without a hint of trouble. It still pointed the way ahead. Even if the road was relatively straight, I was nervous about taking my eyes away from the void, yet my frustration was building. I tried to zoom out of the map twice, expecting it to expand so we could see the nearest towns and cities encircling us, but the display showed nothing but blank, un-downloaded space.

'It's crashed —' I began as the soulless voice piped up.

'Continue for ten miles.'

'There you go,' I said with barely disguised relief. 'We're doing fine. There'll be a signpost or something at the next junction.'

Sarah suddenly gesticulated ahead. 'STOP! STOP!'

I automatically moved my right foot over the brake and applied too much pressure. I jolted forward in my seat. The belt bit into my right shoulder. With a wet slap of flesh, Sarah, who was already craning forward, gurgled as her seatbelt whipped across her throat, choking the words from her. She dropped her phone – both hands thudding against the dash to secure her in place. A loose satchel on the rear seat hurled between our headrests and snapped the rear-view mirror from its bracket. The bag firmly thumped against the glass before toppling onto the gearstick and handbrake.

The car skidded several yards across the asphalt and stalled before my left foot could find the clutch. With a gruff cough, Sarah slumped back in her seat and rubbed her throat.

'Christ! What're you doing?'

'You moron! I thought I was about to hit something!' I snapped. 'Why did you scream like that?'

She glowered, still rubbing her throat, then stabbing a finger toward her side window.

'There's a tearoom! I didn't know the choice was starve to death or die in a tragic car accident.'

The leather on the steering wheel creaked as my grip increased, but it served to absorb my anger. In the murk outside stood a two-storey building, crafted from centuries old Cotswold stone, its rosy complexion tarnished and aged over time. Over the years, the gnarled hand of subsidence had gently tugged at the centre of the building, so now the façade gave the appearance of a disapproving frown. The old uneven windowpanes were opaque cataracts laced with lead. It was all cropped by bushy thatch that was matted with moss and debris. A black wooden shingle sign was carved with white letters: THE PALE MAN. The crude image underneath was a white outline of a man on a flaking green background. It looked as though a child had drawn it.

Perhaps once it had been a farmhouse. It was difficult to tell as the entire building was framed by thick fog, as if the hands of time had plucked it from the surrounding world. The timeless illusion was spoilt by a modern metal A-frame sign next to the open porch door, advertising afternoon tea and scones. There was something unsettling about this place. A sense of being observed, although the dense mist proved that such an undertaking would be impossible.

Sarah's hand was already on the door handle. 'Park up. Let's eat.'

While it was true that I was hungry, I doubted a sweet afternoon snack would be enough. If it wasn't for my need to pee, I think I would've put up a little more resistance. Instead, I sighed and tossed the errant satchel onto the back seat, further dislodging others. The engine restarted on the second attempt, growling to life with the overpowering smell of petrol. Michael would've blamed me for flooding the engine. The mere reminder of him brought back that voice ...

I shook away the thought and pulled onto the gravel sideroad that served as a parking area. Wordlessly, we climbed from the car. The doors closed in rapid succession; the firm thumps swallowed by the mist. Even our own footsteps on the gravel seemed unnatural and displaced, as if they were not our own. I shivered as the sudden temperature drop tickled my neck and sent tingles down my spine. Sweat beaded on my forehead. It was the most unusual weather

Sarah flashed a thin, almost apologetic smile, which spoke volumes about her unease. After what she'd just helped me through, that was saying something.

The green paint on the door was flaking in fingernail sized chunks and it was so stiff to open that I thought it was locked. Inside, wooden floorboards had been polished and smoothed over dozens of decades. They creaked as they bore our weight. I'm five-foot six, yet the timbre ceiling still seemed oddly low, making me stoop even though there was no need. Half a dozen heavy oak tables and chairs were neatly arranged and dressed in chintzy table clothes and elaborate doilies. Horseshoes and abstract farming tools from a bygone age decorated the walls.

'Maybe it isn't open?' Sarah ventured in a tone that suggested she was having second thoughts. I wouldn't stand for that. I didn't want to be here, but I was damned if I'd now admit it, especially when it had been her idea. I sucked in a deep breath. So far, the day had been manic. I couldn't afford to lose it now.

'Hello?' I called out. 'Are you open?'

The room suffocated the words.

What little light there was came in through three huge bay windows on the far wall. The design hinted at a magnificent countryside vista beyond, but right now they offered an opaque view of nothing.

'We should go. Maybe there's a Maccies or something close,' Sarah said, turning on her heels – then she gave a short shriek that sent a jolt down my spine.

Behind us, an old woman had silently appeared. In a tweed dress that reached just below her knees, and a threadbare green cardigan, she stood with both hands clasped in front of her naval. Her shoulder-length hair was snow white, but bounced with the vigour of a long-forgotten youth. Her round wrinkled face was set in a pleasant smile, but it was the eyes that made me shudder. Milky white. Whether blind from birth or cursed by cataracts, there was no escaping her disability.

'You'll be wanting somethin' to eat?' she said in a soft voice, dripping with a diehard Somerset accent.

'If you're not open —' I began.

'We're always open, me dear. Rain or shine.' She gestured to the tables set before the window. 'Please, follow me.'

Allowing a blind woman to escort us to our seats felt wrong. Yet quibbling with her was the sort of thing that would get us cancelled in the current reaction culture. Sarah and I exchanged a look as the woman gingerly felt her way along the backs of the chairs. She was surefooted, but the gentle scratch of her fingertips along the polished wood made the situation uncomfortable. She led us to a table in the middle of the bay windows and gently pulled a chair out for one of us to sit. The heavy wood screeched as she did so, like nails down slate.

'Take a seat, me dears.' She gestured to the window. 'The best view in the house.'

Sarah took the offered seat. I pulled out the chair opposite and glanced at the monochrome fog outside. Neither of us had the heart to correct her.

'Very nice,' muttered Sarah.

Sitting, I noticed there wasn't a menu on the table, or any table. There were no boards offering the dish of the day, which further made me think the tearoom wasn't fully open.

'Do you have a menu?'

'I'm afraid our range is a little limited today. Truth be told, I was startin' to think nobody was comin' in today. It's all been a tad quiet. Quiet for some time ...' the last was said with an air of sorrow and her smile faded. She gazed, or at least faced, the direction of the mysterious view and seemed to freeze in position. As I was about to speak, the old woman became suddenly animated again. 'I could rustle you up a ploughman's?'

'That would be great,' I said, more out of relief than desire. 'And may I have a coffee too?'

'I'll have the same with a Coke,' said Sarah.

'I'll see what there is.'

The old woman slowly turned and felt her way towards a

dark oak-panelled door I hadn't noticed in the side wall. Sarah raised her eyebrows in amusement, but didn't speak until the woman had left the room. Then she leaned across the table, barely raising her voice above a whisper.

'Do you think she's making the food herself?'

'God, I hope not.'

Sarah chuckled and leaned back in her seat, shaking her head in disbelief. For the first time since she'd helped me leave this morning, I saw a genuine smile. The slight surrealness of the encounter was just what we both needed to detach us from what had happened.

'When the food comes, check she still has all her fingers,' I hissed, already laughing.

Sarah grinned. 'You're sick.' She peered out of the window with wide eyes. 'Still, that's a hell of a view.' She spluttered with laughter at the absurdity of it all. I followed her gaze. The fog seemed coarser this side of the building, layered with shaded textures that constantly flowed. Darker tendrils stretched and eddied against the glass as if probing how to get inside. I was turning away when a shadow crossed outside. It was so quick, so startling, that I snapped my head up for a proper look, but it had gone.

'What's the matter?' The levity had disappeared from Sarah's voice, perhaps driven away by my expression.

'I thought I saw ... something.'

'What?'

I slowly shook my head, trying to recall details. 'Somebody. Walking past.'

Sarah shrugged. 'So?'

Perhaps it was the sense of isolation foisted upon us by the fog. It wasn't as if we were hundreds of miles from civilisation. We'd been driving down a major road, albeit a quiet one, because of the weather. With each passing moment, the notion that nobody else was around became sillier. Like most of the county, the area around us was undoubtedly farmland, and as far as I knew there was a bustling farm just yards away.

I forced a smile. 'I'm tired. The last few days have taken it out of me.'

That was half-true. It had been months of falling in and out of an abusive relationship. It was unhealthy, but I couldn't help it. Physical blows weren't traded, at least not until the end. I could still feel the bruise on my ribs every time I took a deep breath. No, these were psychological wounds designed to strip away confidence and wear down self-worth. Sarah was aware of a part of this. We'd been friends since uni and could read the subtext between each other's lines, doing away with the need to explain. Her eyes scanned my face with mild concern about my state of mind.

I closed my eyes for a moment to compose myself. It wasn't actually the thought of something passing the window; it was the way it moved. Swiftly, and with an awkward, disjointed motion. In the haze of my fatigued memory, it reminded me of bad stop-motion animation. And that meant I was more tired than I thought.

I rubbed my eyes with the heels of my palms. 'I need that coffee.' The liquid squelch from my eyeballs made my stomach turn. Perhaps it was an unconscious association with the old woman's blindness.

'Do you want me to ask her for a double shot?'

The idea that the coffee would be any more than a spoon of a cheap instant blend from a jar amused me, but the growing sense of fatigue crawling through my limbs made the suggestion appealing. The last twenty-four hours in particular had been a toll, both physically and emotionally. I may have snatched thirty minutes sleep in the interim, and now sitting here it was catching up with me, aided by the warm air inside; somniferous like a heavy blanket kneading my shoulders. The room was so silent that I could hear the blood throb in my ears, as if my head was encased in a soundproof booth ...

'Hey?' Sarah had been talking, and I'd zoned out. She was looking at me through half-closed eyes. 'Where did you go?'

I drummed my fingers on the table and stared into the void outside. 'I'm exhausted.'

'Not the greatest idea to be driving across the country in the fog, then.'

'A necessity. Not a want.'

'I know, I know.' She wanted to say more, but bit her tongue. We'd argued about Michael many times before and now the die was cast it was pointless discussing it further. She gently rapped her knuckles on the table, currying favour from the gods of luck. 'And it's the right plan. We stick with it, which means you need to keep it together.' She must've been aware of her harsh tone because her freckled face softened, and she combed a strand of red hair over her ear in that endearing way men found cute, and I found manipulative. 'I've always said you had to get out of that situation. Just keep that in mind. It's over. Time to turn a new leaf.'

I cast a look around the room, paranoid that the unseen were eavesdropping on our private moment.

Sarah continued. 'You're not running. You're starting again. You're *leading*.' She reached across the table and squeezed my hand.

It was the psychological cheerleading I needed right now. I nodded and forced a smile, but before I could speak, the shuffling of feet caught our attention. The old woman had entered through the side door. She was carrying a tray. A pair of cups and saucers jangled with each step, and even seated I could see the liquid sway precariously to the edge of the cups. She didn't lift her feet, instead scuffed her way through the maze of tables without once faltering. She reached us and set the tray down with an overly loud clatter. There were two plates filled with cheese, a dollop of chutney, bread, a chunk of butter next to a green garnish of curly lettuce, all bookended by a large pork pie sliced down the middle to reveal glistening pink flesh.

'There we go, me darlin's,' she said with a smile. Her fingers gingerly traced the edge of the plates before she picked them up and set them before us. Before she could reach for the saucers and spill the coffee over us, Sarah and I scooped them from the tray and set them on the safety of the table.

'Thank you,' I said.

Sarah frowned at her coffee and mouthed the word 'Coke?' I firmly shook my head; it wasn't worth quibbling over with a blind woman.

'Looks wonderful.' I smiled at the woman before realising the futility of the gesture. The plate was too neatly arranged for her to have created the meal, so I assumed there was a cook out the back. Still, it was odd they'd send an old blind woman to serve.

'It's all we had left,' she reiterated. 'No supplies for weeks now.'

'Weeks?' Sarah couldn't keep the surprise from her voice.

'Time ... it's muddled.'

'Surely you, or your ... business partner, have been to town since then?'

'No.'

'Or to the village.'

The woman smiled and shook her head. 'I don't get out much these days, and it's been oh so quiet recently.' She hooked her hands together and stood, unmoving, gazing out of the featureless window.

'What about deliveries? Surely, they've come?' I ventured.

'Not a soul.'

'No customers, or --?'

'Not recently. They miss out on that view,' she said wistfully. 'Although I'm told that will change.'

I glanced out of the window as an automatic impulse to please her – but was caught by what lay outside. The mist had parted, forming a tunnel that bleached the sky and the surrounding countryside, but revealed a set of nearby hills. Etched on the flank of one directly opposite, was a huge chalk figure of a stooped man wielding a cudgel.

'Wow,' Sarah muttered as she noticed it. 'I'd heard they had those carvings around here, but I've never actually seen one before.'

'Ah, you see it?' The woman's smile pulled back the thin skin on her cheeks in an alarming fashion, revealing crooked yellow teeth. I forced my gaze back to the hill.

'Is that the …' my memory groped to recall Sarah's internet research while on the road. 'Cerne Abbas …'

'That's not here, darlin'. Around here are mostly horses. *This* is our secret.'

'The Pale Man …' Sarah said knowingly as she recalled the name of the tearoom.

'How big is it?' With no other landmarks, it was impossible to judge.

'Depends …'

'Must be old,' said Sarah with a laugh. 'Looks like an infant drew it. Those ancient druids were pretty crappy when it came to art.'

'Perfection is in the beholder's eye.' The woman's smile had morphed into a tight-lipped snarl. Her tone contained slivers of ice. Sarah opened her mouth to fire back a knee-jerk quip. Knowing her, it would be something wholly inappropriate and accidentally offensive. I quickly interjected.

'Who created it?'

The woman inhaled several raspy breaths before answering. 'Pagans, long ago. Before the Romans. Before most things. It was a time when we needed a guardian. An earth spirit to look after the land. And us.' When I looked again, the fog had returned, blotting the view. 'He's always watching,' she added in a whisper. Then she broke from her reverie and gestured to the food. 'Enjoy your meal.' She turned and shuffled from the room once again.

I looked at the ploughman's on my plate and was surprised to find my appetite had vanished along with my need to pee. Sarah's knife and fork raked across the porcelain as she set about deconstructing her food. For whatever reason, the conversation with the old woman had me feeling queasy. Or was it the image of the figure on the hillside? The giant chalk effigy carved in an odd stoop as if the weight of its weapon was pulling it down. Or was it the fact the image was a simulacrum of the figure crossing the window that I'd seen minutes earlier?

The truth was probably closer to the fact I was on the verge of a breakdown. I probably caught a fleeting image of the carving as the mist swirled and my imagination filled in the rest. I needed sleep. I needed food.

The ploughman's on my plate now looked unappetising. Up close, the crisp lettuce was limp, its edges brown. The cheese was glistening and rubbery, with black veins running through the yellowing skin. It produced an acrid aroma that stung my nostrils. Even the chutney looked more like an unidentifiable, congealed heap of black. How I'd ever thought it looked delicious, I couldn't say.

Sarah made appreciative noises as she shovelled a forkful into her mouth. I used the tip of my knife to angle the pork pie half around. A knife, I couldn't help but notice, that was tarnished with small brown stains.

The meat in the pie glistened with a raw red texture. Surely it had been cooked. The jelly encasing it slowly oozed from the crust, running into the chutney. In an instant, I felt bile in my throat and snatched the coffee. I took a big gulp. It was lukewarm and bitter, triggering a further gag reflex.

'This is something else,' Sarah said, cramming a quarter of the pie into her mouth while already chewing the last mouthful. I could see the half-masticated food coating her teeth in an entirely unattractive way. I looked away.

The mist had parted once again to reveal the figure on the hill. I had been wrong. It wasn't stooped, but stood erect, with the cudgel angled over its shoulder in an almost jaunty manner.

'Does that look different to you?' I murmured. By the time Sarah turned, the mist rolled in, blocking the view. She gave a quizzical *mmm?* But didn't stop inserting another mouthful of cheese. 'I just saw the hill again. The carving. It looked … different.'

She shrugged and sipped her drink, eyes widening. 'That's good coffee!'

I circled a finger towards the window. 'It was standing …'

'Maybe there's more than one? There's supposed to be horses and that guy with the big schlong.' She giggled like a teenager and jerked her fork towards the window. 'That guy certainly wasn't packing.'

The smell from my plate was becoming increasingly unpleasant. I pushed it away, eyes fixed through the window. This time I saw the fog part, as if a cleaver had hewn it in two. Both rolling banks coiled aside, exposing a straight view to the hill.

A hill devoid of any figure.

'It's gone!' I hissed in shock. I glanced at Sarah with wide eyes, and she quickly followed my gaze outside. The fog smothered everything.

'Are you sure you're okay?' she asked. 'You're starting to freak me out. And you know it takes *a lot* to do that.' Her words were loaded, but I was certain about what I saw.

'The carving has *gone*,' I said, raising from my seat and moving closer to the glass. 'I swear to God it was there one minute and then the hill was a bald as Mike's head.' I moved so close to the glass that my forehead touched the uneven material. It was cool, thick, and yellowing, filled with imperfections from the moment it was poured centuries ago. I cupped my fingers around my eyes in case I was the victim of an optical joke. I could see nothing but intently swirling mist. 'I can't see it …'

'There's nothing to see.'

'That's my point!'

With a sharp huff, Sarah dropped her fork on the plate and shoved it aside. 'Jesus! I don't need this right now! How many times a day do you need to wind me up? This is getting to be a record, even for you.'

I stepped back from the window. Maybe she was right.

Then the fog thinned, revealing the hill as a vague shadow in the distance and concealing details from the curious. There was no figure on the hill … From the small escape of air from between her lips, Sarah had noticed it too.

'See?'

She leaned across the table and squinted. 'It's difficult to see *anything*. Especially a few lines on the ground.'

I didn't know if she was trying to convince me or herself, but I didn't need detail to tell me there were no ancient white lines etched on the surface.

'I'm telling you ...'

I trailed off as several faint thuds sounded in rapid succession before being swallowed by the dense atmosphere. We exchanged a look.

'What was that?' I whispered.

Sarah glanced towards the kitchen, concerned the old woman had fallen – but the sound had definitely come from outside. Then it came again. Distant, yet heavy. My eyes darted to my foul cup of coffee on the table. The liquid danced across the surface. Sarah had seen it, too.

'Thunder ...' she said.

'Let's go.' My hand dipped into my pocket and felt for my purse. It wasn't there. I had a vague recollection of slipping it into the glovebox when we'd filled up at the last service station. 'Do you have any cash on you?'

Sarah produced a small purse from her pocket, which was already open. She slid out a worn Visa card. 'Who uses cash anymore?'

'Only places like this. I'd be shocked if she'd heard of credit cards. I need to get my purse from the car.'

I motioned for the door. Sarah stood and flashed a look of alarm towards the kitchen door.

'Don't leave me here alone,' she snapped.

'I won't be a second.'

Another tremor vibrated through the floorboards.

'I'm coming with you,' she said sharply.

'If we both walk out, the old dear might think we're doing a runner.'

'So?'

'So it strikes me that this is the sort of place farmer's shotguns are ready primed behind the counter.'

Another tremble. The room grew darker.

'The power must be out,' Sarah said, looking around in alarm.

'There are no lights in here,' I pointed out, and nodded towards the window as the shadow vanished and the light intensified once again. Something had definitely passed the window, blotting the sun.

Sarah forced a chuckle devoid of humour. 'This is ridiculous.' I reached out to squeeze her arm, but she was already moving to the side door. 'Excuse me! Hello?' She called out. We both remained stock still, waiting for a response. 'Hello? We'd like the bill, please?' Nothing. She looked at me and tilted her head towards the exit. 'Well, we tried to pay.'

That was good enough for me. I managed three long strides towards the door, the floorboards wearily creaking beneath my grubby Nike trainers. My hand slipped into my jacket for the car keys.

They weren't there.

'I could've sworn ...' Glancing around, I spotted them on our table. I don't recall taking them out, but I'd be the first to admit that my memory wasn't in the best condition at the moment. I doubled back and scooped them in my fist. The diversion lasted only seconds, yet when I turned, I started – the old woman was standing in front of the exit with her usual placid smile and an eight-inch carving knife hanging from her right hand. Sarah saw I was staring and whipped around in alarm, her eyes falling onto the rusty blade.

'You called, me dears?' The woman said with her unfocused smile. She was looking in my direction, but her gaze lingered on some infinite spot behind me.

I coughed to find my voice. 'Yes. The bill, please. We need to go. I'm meeting my boyfriend,' I added the detail to telegraph that *people know where we are.*

The tip of the knife danced in the air like a conductor's baton.

'Most certainly. Did you enjoy it? Your meal I mean?'

'It hit the spot,' Sarah forced a smile. 'And excellent coffee.'

I pointed towards the door behind her – then felt immediately foolish. 'I've left my purse in the car. I was just going to get it.'

'Outside?' The woman was piqued.

'Yes ...'

The point of the knife drifted earthward and inscribed a

small circle as she thought about what I'd said.

'Are you sure?'

This was ridiculous. After recent events, I was obviously working myself up. Looking for suspicion and blame wherever I could. Michael had that effect on me. That's why I ended it. My shoulders tensed as I drew to my full height in an automatic, if futile, gesture to threaten a blind old woman.

'Unless you take credit cards, I need to get my purse.'

After a few seconds of indecision, she waved the knife towards the door, causing Sarah to take several nervous steps backward.

'Cash only, I'm afraid.' She tilted her head to the exit. 'We have dessert if you're wantin' to stay.'

'No.' I was perhaps a little too firm as she pointed the blade towards the door.

'If you're needin' to venture to your car ...'

The way she said it sent waves of doubt through me. Sarah sensed my indecision and extended her hand to me.

'No offence, but I don't want to stay here. I'll get it.'

So much for sticking together. I scowled at her and tossed the keys over. She deftly plucked them from the air. 'It's in the glove compartment.'

With a nod, Sarah darted out, leaving me alone with the old woman. The squeak of the hinges, followed by the gentle click of the closing door, was all that broke the silence, which swiftly returned at full volume.

'Not the best time to be venturin',' the woman said quietly.

'You mean the fog?'

Her brow knitted. The weather was seemingly news to her. 'I mean midsummer.'

'I'm afraid I'm not superstitious.'

'You don't have to believe in somethin' to make it so.'

I rubbed my dry eyelids with a simple pinch between my thumb and middle finger of one hand. I wasn't in the mood for riddles.

'Just like I don't believe you're dashin' for a meetup with your young fella,' the woman said after a long pause.

'Like you said, you don't have to believe in something to make it so.' I couldn't help noticing that the woman hadn't moved from between me and the exit, nor made any attempt to put the knife down. What kind of threat did she think I presented?

The room trembled again. This time the metal farming implements on the wall shook in their mounts.

'What is that?'

'That is absolution, dear.'

Her vague comment didn't register immediately. There was another sound hidden by the shudder. I would have sworn it was metallic and laced with broken glass. The old woman must have heard it too as she half turned to the exit and in doing so took a step to the side, leaving a clear path to the way out. Without hesitation, I bolted forward. My hand was on the door handle, putting my weight into opening it, before the woman sensed my movement.

'Wait!'

Her warning went unheeded, and, in an instant, I was outside and hurrying towards my car. The fog was thicker than it had been. The road was less than six yards away, yet was nothing more than a dark stripe in the murk. What was in focus was my car.

Or what was left of it.

The bonnet and front seats had been mashed into the ground so hard that the front wheels had split apart and now lay like a dissected metal insect. Broken glass lay around the wreckage. The roof had crushed in at an angle; the bonnet crushed around the engine block. The back of the vehicle was relatively unscathed, save shattered windows and crumpled fenders. It was as if it had been trampled by some giant foot.

'Sarah!?'

My scream was consumed by the fog. The ice-cold air plucked my skin, yet beads of sweat formed on my brow. Each breath felt laboured as the air became as thick as soup. It may have been the onset of a panic attack, or the realisation that what I was seeing couldn't be happening. It was impossible.

Perhaps the woman had laced my drink with a hallucinogenic? Perhaps the stress of the last day was taking its toll on my fragile metal state?

There was no sign of Sarah. There was no blood.

There was not a single sound.

I took an involuntary step towards the vehicle. 'Sarah!?' I cried out again.

A soft creak of metal made me stop in my tracks. It had come from the car. Was she trapped inside the crumpled mess? I strained to listen …

And my gaze was pulled upwards as a shadow loomed in the fog beyond the vehicle. A distinctly human shape some forty-feet tall resolved itself in the mist. It was stooped, pulled to one side as it dragged something behind it.

Impossible. Yet there it was.

And behind, the hints of something I hadn't seen when we arrived. More vehicles. Several cars and a minibus, all smashed, rusted, and abandoned, stacked to the side of the tearoom.

My guts churned with ice-cold needles, and the muscles in my legs trembled, refusing to cooperate. The giant lurched forward at the same time the noises from the car increased. If Sarah was taking refuge in it, there was nothing I could do. Ashamed of my cowardice, I fled back to the sanctity of the building – faintly aware of a maelstrom of air passing close behind my head. The downdraft propelled me through the tearoom door with such force I dropped painfully to my knees on the floorboards beyond. My imagination screamed that I had just missed being bludgeoned by a giant's club.

'What the hell is going on?' I screamed into an empty room. The blind woman had gone. Before I could even contemplate looking for her, the sound of grating metal came from outside. It was my car. I could swear it was the sound of the mangled boot opening.

And that's when the full chill of dread struck me.

Without thinking, I rolled onto my back and viciously kicked out at the door. My trainer caught the edge of the wood, and I followed through, slamming it closed. Just in time, too.

The distinct sound of approaching movement across gravel rose with a slow inevitability.

Something was coming this way.

'No, no, no …' I couldn't stop uttering the words like a mantra as I scuttled backwards on all fours, my eyes fixed on the door. I moved with such haste that I powered into the table behind me and toppled a chair onto its side. The edge of the thick oak struck the back of my skull with such force that my vision was suddenly marred by blinding white flashes. Each pulse stabbed a needle of pain into my eye sockets. If it wasn't for the sheer terror surging through me, I might've passed out.

When the volley of fireworks ceased scarring my retina, the room came back into focus, but much darker than before. Perhaps there was some monstrous shadow blotting the windows as it peered inside, searching for prey, or were my eyes still compensating for the light show they'd just endured. Whatever the cause, I couldn't shift my gaze away from the door.

It was open.

In my brief miasma, something had stepped inside, but from my position low on the floor, I couldn't see what it was. I held my breath, but the impact with the table had set off a faint tinnitus ringing that set my teeth on edge and masked any sound of movement.

The past twenty-four hours raced through my mind, unwanted and unprovoked. Michael scowling as his fist struck my ribs. My wild uncoordinated punches and kicks. My frantic call to Sarah as I babbled inconsolably. A swirl of images as we packed the car with everything I could shove into bags. The both of us weighing the boot down to close it. Sarah's comforting smile and reassuring words that everything would be okay. The race out of the city towards the far-off West Country and the promise of freedom. I could still recall the adrenaline rush – and subsequent crash as we drove into the fog.

A table near the door moved. The wooden legs scraped across the floorboards as its heavy weight was inexorably pushed aside. A chair toppled noisily over. My view was blocked by another table between us, but there was clearly nobody standing there. Which meant they were crouched low.

I could just hear the gentle shuffle of limbs brushing the floor and the creak of wood as the boards took the weight. Had Sarah been injured? Unable to call out for help?

Fear replaced logic, and I scrambled further backwards, this time ducking my head under the table and nudging aside a chair that was hemming me in. I didn't have far to go before I found myself pressed against the wall.

The room was still swimming in darkness. I rapidly blinked, hoping to regain my full vision, but every time my eyes closed, it felt as if I was wiping my lenses with grit. Each blink became painful until I was forced to keep my eyes open.

I became aware of somebody standing to my left, just behind me. My head snapped up to see the blind old woman had emerged from the kitchen. She was so close I could smell the mustiness of her clothes. Her pleasant smile was in place, and those white eyes peered at me. *She saw me.* She saw the terror on my face and in my heart. I opened my mouth, but she placed a wrinkled finger over her lips in a signal to remain silent.

Another clatter of toppling chairs forced me to turn my attention back to the room. Wood ground against wood as another heavy table was pushed aside ... then I saw the approaching figure and my heart caught in my throat, choking the scream I so desperately wanted to unleash.

It was Michael. His white shirt and crumpled blue jeans stained with dried blood. A rip in the collar and down to his heart exposed the now-congealed slash of flesh I'd inflicted upon him in our apartment. His neck was swollen and twisted from when it had broken as I kicked him down the stairs. One eye socket was crumpled from the impact, his bald skull caved-in on one side. His leering mouth bloodied; top lip severed in two by broken teeth. He looked just as pathetic in death as he had in life. A meek man. A waste of life and my time. I should've left him numerous times, but his pitiful whining always drew me back. He wouldn't let me go, no matter how viciously I beat him. The pain in my ribs twinged as I sucked in a deep breath. Only recently had he begun fighting back. Showing a little backbone for a change. But it wasn't something I could encourage, although I hadn't meant to kill him. That had been an accident. If it wasn't for Sarah's suggestion to dump him some bog out in the West Country, then I would've left him in the apartment. Of course, it would only be a matter of time before the putrid smell of rotten flesh would've alerted the neighbours, and then my life would have been over.

It was over anyway. His rotten corpse had clawed its way from the boot and come to claim revenge. It was a hideous sight, but my mind had crossed a mental event horizon and was now wallowing in the realm of insanity.

I started to laugh.

I was laughing so hard that I didn't feel the first two plunges of the knife into my shoulder blade as the old woman thrust the blade down. It was the savage third blow that severed my arteries and vocal cords. And still the blows kept coming in a rain of agony. Watched on by the destroyed face of my ex-boyfriend, hunched on all-fours. A pale man who was silently judging me.

A sense of detachment came over me as I slumped to the ground. A vague memory of half-digested facts. Something about the eyes still seeing for six minutes after death. Evidently my brain was still functioning too, even if I was, for all intents and purposes, dead.

It was long enough for the old woman to drag me into the kitchen. The wooden floor turning to thick grey flagstones. Just the right surface to dismember me. I was beyond pain as the cleaver took my right leg off from the kneecap. It took four powerful blows to hack through the sinewy flesh and bone.

I'd lost all sense of time, but surely the void would swallow me soon. My eyes were fixed open. I had no way of unseeing the sacrilege she was inflicting on my body. Had I really become some offering for an otherworldly pagan, or had I succumbed to a drug fuelled stupor?

I couldn't tell.

I couldn't even cry out a warning as Sarah entered the room. It took a moment for the grisly sight to register with her as she locked eyes with me. I watched her face contort with disgust – then horror. The old woman turned towards her with the cleaver raised. But it wasn't needed. It was a mere distraction from the movement *behind* Sarah. Michael pounced, forcing Sarah down. Her face struck the stone flags with force.

Then a grey cloak of fog swept into the room, obscuring everything, and robbing me of reason, sanity, and life. Every fibre of my being stretched as the mist absorbed me. If this was death, then it was a strange one. I suddenly felt surrounded by thousands of other restless souls, crammed together as if in a chicken coop. I couldn't speak to them, or reach out, but I was all too aware of their shared pain ...

... And the view.

A shared view. Thousands of eyes peering out from the same vantage point high on the hill, overlooking a quaint tearoom, the garden of which was filled with decaying vehicles like a macabre scrapyard. Each vehicle a tombstone for their victims. The gentle mist caressed the landscape like a protective cape, searching ... sensing ...

Waiting for the next vehicle to pull up outside. Like this one. The arguing occupants ignorant of the figure on the hill watching.

They'd be aware soon enough.

The Pale Man was always watching. Always judging.

BY THE AXE, HE LIVED

For many years, the occupants of Appledore on the North Devon coast would report hearing strange and disturbing sounds at night on a stretch of shoreline road that had been known for a long time as Bloody Corner.

The noises were said to be varied, though all of a distinctly barbarous tone.

On some occasions, for example, nighttime travellers would be persuaded to head the other way when they heard what sounded like the aggressive chanting of multiple male voices, the chant itself described as pagan and dark-hearted. On other occasions, a single harsh voice, again male, made itself known, calling out a curious piece of foreign doggerel, which an Icelandic speaker wrote down as: Við öxina lifði ég. Við öxina dó ég. *It is believed to be Old Norse, and translates into English as: 'By the axe, I lived. By the axe, I died.' However, passers-by have been most distressed by the shrieks of what sounds like an invisible battle, along with the clashing of innumerable blades.*

'It was like one of those modern reconstructions, where there are thousands of people involved,' a visitor to the area told the press. 'But it was the middle of the night, and it was really savage ... it scared me to death.'

There was also the account given by a lone coastal hiker who was travelling towards Bloody Corner one night, when he heard voices and just ahead, spotted what looked like a camp built across the road, complete with large bonfires, the light of the flames playing upon a huge banner, which billowed in a wind the hiker couldn't feel. Emblazoned on the front of it was the outline of a great black raven.

In local tradition, all of these tales are connected to the long-held belief that a Viking warlord called Ubba was once slain here along with his entire war-band. Locally, for example, there is Hubbastone, where a Dark Age cairn is said to contain Ubba's bones.

For a long time this story was little more than a myth, though

282

recent scholarship has now linked the area to the death of an infamous character from real-life history.

Ubba Ragnarsson was one of the leaders of the 'Great Heathen Army' that invaded mainland Britain in 865 AD. This was a massive military operation even by Viking standards, and in due course led to the collapse of several Saxon kingdoms, including Northumbria, Mercia and East Anglia. It was also notorious for the many atrocities committed against the native populations and their rulers. The army's overarching commander was Ivar the Boneless, who in legend, if not established historical fact, first came to Britain to avenge his illustrious father, Ragnar Lodbrok, a Viking raider of earlier days executed by King Aelle of Northumbria when he was flung into a pit full of vipers. Historians differ as to how many brothers Ivar had, though all seem to agree that most of them came across the sea with him, and the other one most frequently mentioned in the annals is Ubba. What's more, Ubba appears to have been second only to Ivar in terms of the cruelty he enjoyed inflicting.

While Ivar is credited with sacrificing King Aelle to Odin via the gruesome ceremony of the Blood-Eagle, both brothers are said to have flayed and burned certain victims, turned others into heimnars (captives left alive but with all four limbs lopped off and the stumps seared so they'd forever be a burden on their families), and for marching particularly brave opponents around oak trees carved with runes, their intestines first having been nailed to the wood so that they'd slowly disembowel themselves. But it is Ubba alone who reportedly ordered the brutal death of King Edmund of East Anglia.

Again, the records are vague, some claiming that Ubba cut Edmund down in battle, though most say that Edmund was captured, tied to a tree and instructed to renounce his Christianity, and that when he refused Ubba had his men shoot the king full of arrows.

As already mentioned, there is much uncertainty here.

From 793 onwards, Britain and Ireland were subjected to repeated Viking attacks, all kinds of Scandinavian potentates, minor and major, seeking to claim land, booty and slaves, or simply to make themselves famous back home. Many had similar names, so it is not uncommon for even the most diligent of historians to confuse them. However, it is held as increasingly certain that the Ubba who sailed to Britain as Ivar the Boneless's lieutenant was the same Ubba who invaded the West

Country, namely the Devon coast at Appledore, with a significant force in the year 878.

Even though 13 years had passed since the original invasion, the Great Army was still active in the British Isles. Ivar had taken his own war-band to Ireland and Ubba was busy ravaging Wales, but the bulk of the force was still in England. The only English kingdom holding out was Wessex under its young ruler, Alfred (the future Alfred the Great), and it was here where the two most senior Viking leaders remaining, Halfdan and Guthrum, were concentrating their efforts. Over the Christmas of 877, the heathen force launched another massed attack on this last outpost. While Halfdan and Guthrum struck Wessex from the east, subsequently defeating Alfred at a place called Chippenham, and driving him into the Somerset marshes, Ubba crossed the Bristol Channel from Wales, and attacked it from the West.

It was a well-planned pincer movement, but Ubba's part in it was less successful.

Though the novelist, Bernard Cornwell, would award the glory for Ubba's bloody defeat at the battle of Cynwit to his fictional hero, Uhtred, in actual fact it was a Devonshire thegn called Odda, who, though he had less warriors than the Vikings, lured them into a false sense of security by feigning a retreat into the hillfort of Kenwith, now Countisbury, and that night, as the Vikings made camp and celebrated what they assumed would be an easy victory the next day, attacked them under cover of darkness.

Recent research can now therefore assert that a great Viking war-chief called Ubba, almost certainly Ubba Ragnarsson, died with nearly all of his men during this action, historians pinpointing the site of the fatal battle at the place now known as Bloody Corner.

We can try to persuade ourselves, if we wish, that the eerie sounds reportedly heard in that place for as long as anyone can remember – violent war cries, or a lone, angry voice announcing his presence over a thousand years after his death – are simple folk-tales. But if so, the coincidence, one must admit, is remarkable.

LITTLE DOWN BARTON
Lizzie Fry

The sun set over the North Devon link road. Up ahead behemoth wind turbines stretched their blades into the pink and purple skies, the fields beyond them lost in the gloom. Evan couldn't see the animals in the fields, even though he knew they were there. The cat's eyes on the three lanes of the carriageway glinted like malevolent demons.

For the umpteenth time that evening, Evan instructed his phone on the dashboard to make a call. The line was engaged. There was a part of him that knew the outcome; that his mad dash from London, up the M5 and into the heart of his home county would be pointless. He was compelled to do it anyway.

Evan had been built that way.

'I'm leaving,' Jenny had told him that afternoon.

Evan didn't reply. There was nothing to say.

He watched his wife move around the room. The shape of her limbs was jagged as she threw belongings into bags with savage abandon. Like so many women she'd fallen in love with Evan for *his potential*. She'd never seen him for who he really was; she'd filled in the blanks herself with beliefs about a man he'd never been. He'd been amazed and then appalled such a vibrant and headstrong young woman would want him. She could have had her pick of the bunch, yet she'd chosen *him*?

As time went on, Evan had begun to pity her.

Twenty minutes later, Jenny's elder sister arrived. Her own mouth twisted in contempt, she muscled past Evan without a word when he answered the front door. He retired to the kitchen, leaving them to it. He heard them trotting up and down stairs, the two women muttering in pointed whispers.

Half an hour after that, they finally left. Neither said

285

goodbye to him. The front door slammed, reverberating through the terraced house he and Jenny had shared for so long. Evan had felt alone all of his thirty-nine years, but now he really was.

He was only surprised it had taken so long.

Evan flicked the indicator at the roundabout near the Little Chef, leaving the link road for the A339. He peered over the steering wheel and saw the signs for the quarry, no longer blasting for the day; he ignored the village of Bray Ford nestled in the valley to his right.

His little car wound its way around the bends, passing fields and the cold chimneys of second homes. When Evan had been a boy, families had lived all around here, but even twenty years ago the North Devon economy was in its last gasp. Calamity after calamity had been visited upon farmers. The children of locals had given up the ghost and moved upcountry in search of jobs and lives that did not depend on the land.

Evan had done the same. He'd studied hard in the local comprehensive, his goals clear in his mind. His mother had cried when Evan had received top marks for his exams. He'd had his pick of universities, the first real choice he'd ever been given.

Yet it wasn't pride that fuelled his mother's tears, but the knowledge Evan would be leaving. She understood from the steely look in his eye and the firm set of his mouth that he would not be returning, even before he told his parents his plans.

Evan had been true to his word. He'd asked for nothing, filling in paperwork himself and forging signatures. He took only a small case of clothes, plus the money he'd saved up working weekends and school holidays at an ice cream parlour in Combe Martin. He ignored the sting of his conscience on special occasions such as Christmas, birthdays, Mother's or Father's Day.

Later on, he'd told Jenny his parents were dead. She'd had no cause to disbelieve this. His parents never contacted him and there had been virtually no one on his side of the church at their wedding. Even his best man had been Jenny's family: her younger brother, Simon.

Evan shut down that avenue of thought. None of it mattered any more. That part of his life was over. Even before he'd slid behind the wheel of his car, Evan knew he would never see his wife again. There was something inevitable about his actions that day; like he'd always known he would return to his roots. Everything had led to that moment of being called back to the farm.

Literally.

The phone call had come in the late afternoon or early evening, about three hours after Jenny had gone. Evan knew who it was before he'd even lifted the handset to his ear. He hadn't needed to check the number on the screen.

He didn't say anything, but the caller did not speak either. Even so, the connection transcended the years. It reached its phantom fingers down the phone line, grabbing at Evan's guts and twisting them.

'Mum,' Evan said at last.

His mother sighed in that way of hers. He didn't wonder how she'd known Jenny had left him. His mother had always had a sixth sense, like she'd been able to see through to his soul. That had always made him abandon any attempt at lying, even by omission. There was no point. Evan would roll over and submit, every single time. His father would too.

On the phone, Evan's mother didn't seem sad; more exasperated. *Whatever will I do with you?* she'd say to Evan as a child, tutting and shaking her head. She looked the archetypal farmer's wife: ruddy cheeks and round as an apple. She'd blot her hands on her apron and then open her arms to him. If he didn't trot over to her and lay his head on her huge bosom, there would be hell to pay.

Anything to keep her happy.

'I'm coming home.' Evan said, replacing the handset.

The wheels of Evan's car left the tarmac and the road well-travelled. He slowed down, an instinct preserved after so many years away. He could not see the farmhouse. There was no light pollution bar his own vehicle headlights. The wheels crunched over the dirt track, stones and grit spraying as he made his way towards the childhood home he had spent so long on the run from.

Out of the darkness, huge gates loomed under the twin spotlights of his car. Evan blinked in surprise as he took in the huge chains that were looped around the gate and its fence posts, along with liberal twists of barbed wire.

The old sign proclaimed *LITTLE DOWN BARTON*, but it was peeled and almost illegible. Next to it were various hand-painted signs reading *KEEP OUT* and *NO TRESPASSING*.

The gate looked as if it had not been opened in years. Evan tried ringing the farmhouse again, but once more there was no answer. Just the engaged tone.

He should have guessed his mother would pull a stunt like this. She could have sent his father out to open the gates, but only she would require Evan's presence back home, yet make it as difficult as possible to get in.

A sense of unease sent spider legs down Evan's spine. He knew what this was: one of her infamous 'tests'. There had been many in his childhood. His mother would declare Evan in need of being taught a lesson, then devise some sort of creative torture for him. Evan's father would administer the lesson as she presided over them both, grim satisfaction etched into her round face. Evan would plead, beg and bargain, all to no avail.

'Now, what kind of mother would I be if I didn't teach you what you needed to be taught?' she'd always say.

Over time, Evan stopped pleading, begging and bargaining. As he became a teenager, his sheer bloody-mindedness grew in accordance with his body.

His mother would make her demands for the smallest of infractions, real or imagined. In return, Evan would withstand even the most ingenious and unpleasant tests his mother could dream up. He let his father push his face into cow shit or make him eat it. He reached his whole arm into a deep pot of boiling water without flinching. Evan withstood his mother's disgust when he won and glee when he failed. The pain was never worse than when she crowed about how useless Evan was.

Sighing, Evan grabbed his phone off his car dashboard. Opening the door, drizzle soaked his face and hair; his feet sank in the mud. Twenty years of town living meant the only torch he had was his phone. His designer trainers were not fit for the great outdoors.

They would have to do.

He set his phone to torchlight and shut the car door. The darkness rushed in at him, but his sights were set up ahead. Grasping his phone in his mouth, he clambered over the gate as gingerly as he could. The bite of steel wire pierced one of his palms; another spiked his knee through his jeans. He didn't care. He jumped down, triumph surging through him.

1 – Evan; 0 – Mum.

'Hello?' He hollered into the darkness.

Evan had felt certain his mother would be waiting on the other side of the gate. She'd loved to watch from the side-lines, arms folded as his father visited her punishment on their only child. In all of his childhood, Evan had never heard his father argue mercy for his son. He'd only ever capitulated to whatever dark and twisted need his wife exhibited.

The mud sucked at Evan's trainers. Cold water seeped through, making his toes go numb. He swept the phone's torchlight left to right, trying to regain his bearings. He thought the farmhouse was closer, but it appeared as if his memory was playing tricks on him.

'Mum? Dad!'

His shoes found concrete; he stubbed his toe. Swearing, he staggered forward, kicking at something metal. It was another abandoned *KEEP OUT* sign, but this time it was an official one: *POLICE: FOOT-AND-MOUTH AREA STARTS HERE.*

That sense of unease upgraded itself to actual fear. Evan could recall the foot-and-mouth outbreak almost too well: it had come the last year he'd been at home. He remembered the lowing of terrified cattle; the sound of the bolt gun; the slaughtermen in their rubber aprons wading through rivers of blood. Later came the huge pyres of dead carcasses, black plumes of smoke spiralling into blue skies. Hell on earth: the fragrant, innocent smell of summer mixed with death and burned meat. Evan's mother made him kill his favourite puppy that year, the runt of the litter.

That was when Evan realised he should protect others by never truly loving anything ever again.

He could feel his mother's dark influence on him via her blood in his veins. It was why he'd told Jenny he didn't want to have children. He couldn't risk their child being a girl, or worse: that a latent sadistic streak would rise in Evan and compel him to do to his kids what had been done to him.

Evan pushed the memory from his psyche and trekked doggedly on.

The moon finally appeared from behind cloud cover, illuminating the courtyard in its pale light. The farmhouse was revealed, its single-pane windows facing the courtyard with a mournful expression like broken eyes. A faded *FOR SALE* sign boarded up one of them. The front door hung off its hinges. It did not look like anyone was home or had even lived there in decades.

Ghost farm.

'Mum ...?'

Confused, he stopped and stared at his childhood home, shock making his mouth slack. Evan had assumed his mother had dragged the old police sign out of storage to freak him out. It was just her style. She knew how upsetting he'd found that period of their lives. Yet seeing the house abandoned and wrecked, he wondered if something more sinister was at work.

No. This was part of his mother's test.

It had to be.

Evan crept towards the broken-door front door and slipped inside the farmhouse. Like many old cottages, it was dark and labyrinthine. The floor was red tile, the walls white stone. The hallway had a variety of pictures hanging; a grandfather clock that had stopped long ago; a small table beside it with an old rotary telephone.

There was thick dust on the table, but the phone had none

on it. As he squinted in the gloom, he noted that it had been left off the hook. That made sense; his mother had called him only a few hours ago. As he passed, he replaced it in the cradle. It gave a little discordant ring as he did so.

'I'm back.' He forced an authority he didn't really feel into his voice. 'Mum? Dad!'

The air smelled stale and damp; there was also something else Evan could not place. He opened the kitchen door, expecting to see his mother at the sink, or by the aga. There was no one there. The Welsh dresser was covered in his mother's old trinkets and ceramics, thick cobwebs dancing between decorative boxes and figurines. The countertops were covered in rotting vegetables and pots and pans full of thick sludge.

He moved from the kitchen to the next room, a mouldering old parlour. A dull *creak* sounded from somewhere, drawing his attention to the filthy window. The glass was so thick with grime he could not make out anything. Next to him an old crusty armchair erupted with mice that ran for cover as his shadow fell on it.

'What's going on!' Evan yelled into the lifeless house.

He no longer cared if he'd passed his mother's stupid test or not. He had already begun to fill in the gaps in his mind. It was obvious. After the financial strain of the '90s followed by that deadly disease, his parents must have lost the farm after all. It had probably happened just after he'd left home.

That's why his mother hadn't spoken when she called; she'd wanted him to make the decision to come back to the farmhouse himself. After her only child's escape and so many years out in the world, his mother would have decided to have something special planned when she finally brought him home. She wanted to rock him to his very foundations as a final act of revenge. Seeing the wreckage of his childhood home was designed to do this.

It was clear to Evan now that this was his mother's masterpiece, her magnum opus, her *pièce de resistance*: this 'test', as repugnant as it was, had been decades in the making.

She had always been a patient woman.

There was just one thing Evan didn't understand. Where was his mother? She had always delighted in his suffering when he was a boy. She was the ultimate voyeur, directing his father's cruelty for her own enjoyment.

There was a part of Evan who hated his mother more for that, even though she'd never laid a hand on him. He downgraded his father's monstrous actions because it seemed clear to Evan his father was nothing but an automaton, a malevolent puppet. Evan had always felt sure that in a parallel universe somewhere, his mother was loving, his father never did anything awful to him and Evan was happy.

All of it was all down to her.

Creak.

Evan's heartbeat fluttered in his ribcage like a trapped bird. Though he'd taken care not to touch the cobwebs, that sense of being watched crawled all over the surface of his skin. Absent-minded, he scratched at his neck and cheek as he picked up the pace, almost running from the parlour to the living room. As he crossed the threshold, his wet trainer touched something on the threadbare carpet, drawing his attention.

A shotgun.

The two barrelled weapon was covered in dust too. It had been his father's. Evan had watched his father lumber out across the fields many times, a roll-up in one hand, the cracked shotgun hanging off his elbow. He'd been an eagle-eyed shot before arthritis had made his knuckles seize up. Nothing had given his father greater pleasure than shooting down the crows that circled overhead, waiting to feed on the eyes of baby lambs.

Evan was about to lean down to pick up the shotgun when he saw them.

On the sofa, the two of them. Their hands touched like two lovers, yet there was nothing romantic about them. Though Evan recognised the dirty dungarees on the first, the flower print dress on the second, neither looked like they once were. Now they gazed upon him via eyeless sockets, their jaws slack. That cloying, sweet smell Evan had detected in the farmhouse: decay. The wastage of many years meant their wizened skin had given way to bone, with just scraps of hair and cloth hinting they were ever human at all.

Not that they ever treated Evan as if *he* were human.

Twenty years of denial broke apart inside Evan. He had spent two decades holding all his memories in separate frames like a hall of mirrors, daring not to scrutinise them for fear of what he might discover.

Now he recalled the evening before he left in vivid detail: how his mother hadn't just cried when he wanted to go to university, she'd instructed his father not to let Evan go. He recalled how he'd gone to the gun cabinet, breaking the lock off it. How he'd not waited for them to plead, beg or bargain.

Evan had pulled the trigger and felt nothing but relief.

He'd dropped the weapon where it lay now, collecting his little suitcase and walking all the way into town to catch a bus, then a train, then another train. He had not returned.

Evan had made no attempt to cover up his crime; only blind luck had concealed it. First quarantine, then the seasons had claimed the farm back. His parents had always kept themselves to themselves; they loved it out in the middle of nowhere. They had no friends and lived off the land. With all the animals already dead due to the foot-and-mouth outbreak, of course no one had come looking.

Confronted with what Evan had done all those years ago, it was like the mirrors smashed. A tsunami of emotions flooded through him: triumph, followed by sorrow, then fear.

He'd got his own back on them, finally.

(*It served them right*).

How could he have done this?

(*Because of what they did to him*).

So, who the hell had called him?

That was the one question he could not answer.

Creak.

That noise again. Evan looked sharply to the two skeletons on the sofa, but neither had moved. Even so, he felt compelled to turn on his heel and rush out of the house, back into the courtyard. He gasped for breath, even though he hadn't been running fast; his chest was tight, panic constricting his throat.

Creak.

The sound was louder now, to his left. He looked towards the old decrepit barn and stopped in his tracks, frozen by the hideous sight before him. He was unable to make sense of what it was at first; his rational brain refused to decipher the image in front of him. He could only take it in piece by piece.

Horns and discoloured bone, large bovine eyes and face. Scraps of rotten flesh hung off its rib cage. It was nothing but skeleton, but more terrifying for it. It didn't have all its pieces: its back legs were missing.

This did not stop it: the creature dragged itself through the mud and onto the concrete of the courtyard. As it made it, the beast uttered a low, mournful bellow despite the noticeable impediment of it having no lungs or vocal cords.

The noise of the creature set Evan in motion.

He tore his eyes away from the grisly spectacle and took off across the courtyard, out towards the darkness of the fields beyond. It felt as if the land itself was fighting him. Pain worked its punishing way through his legs, hips, pelvis. He fought his way through the mud, up towards the headland and the small outcrop of rocks at the top.

The weak torchlight of his phone bounced on the ground. That rational part of his mind reminded him he needed to be careful; he did not want to run straight off the end of the cliff. Though he'd left the skeletal creature far behind him, Evan's panic was no less; he was not sure where he was in the dark, or how he could find his way back to his car. He knew the fog of fear in his brain was the problem, but there was nothing he could do to clear it. His heart banged in his chest so hard it hurt.

Feeling safe enough to stop at last, Evan stood still, attempting to catch his breath. As his breaths rasped in and out, he found himself zoning out from the chilling wind up on the headland; from the pain of the cold in his extremities; from the darkness surrounding him. He had to gain his bearings and find his car.

There up ahead – light.

He blinked, uncertain he could believe his eyes. Yet up ahead was a pillar of light, dancing on the horizon. Evan wasn't sure what it was, but he figured it had to be better than walking straight off the headland onto the sharp rocks below.

His limbs aching, Evan dragged himself step by punishing step towards the source of the light. As he grew closer, he could hear the crackle of flames; he could see the massive pile of kindling beneath it.

A bonfire.

He sent a silent prayer up to the heavens or whatever was looking out for him. Wherever there were controlled fires were people.

'… Hello?'

The heat leapt out towards him, touching his cold, clammy skin. Embers rose in the sky like fireflies swirling in concentric circles. He closed his eyes for a moment, standing still and allowing the warmth to sink into his flesh.

'Evan.'

His mother's voice seared through his thoughts, as clear as if she'd spoken aloud. His eyes snapped open, expecting to see her standing next to him.

She wasn't.

Relief surged through him again, but it did not last. As his gaze fell upon the bonfire, realisation thudded through his chest.

The bonfire was not made of kindling, but the bones of cattle.

It was one of those horrific funeral pyres he'd built that summer twenty years ago. Evan had helped his father drag the carcasses, pushing and pulling them with the tractor. He'd poured gallons of petrol on to the dead cattle, thrown the burning torches onto the pyres. He had stood and felt the heat of the burning bodies, tears streaming down cheeks that were black with soot. Then Evan and his father had returned to the cattle sheds and done it all again, day after day after day.

As Evan watched, the pyre began to collapse. He saw the bones of the cattle move. Like the one in the courtyard, they started to drag themselves towards him, reaching for him, their long, bovine jaws opening and closing like traps.

Unlike in the courtyard, Evan was unable to run. His feet were frozen where they were: from fear or by the mud. It didn't matter.

He was powerless to stop what was happening.

Agony burst through him as the first skeletal creature grabbed him, pulling him into the flames with them. Heat seared through Evan's own flesh in an instant, engulfing him. He opened his mouth to scream, but the sound was snatched from his scorched lungs before he could even make it. He could smell his own burning hair and flesh like he had the doomed animals of two decades ago. Even as he tried to fight the creatures, they held him fast.

As Evan succumbed to the pain amongst the bones, he glimpsed two shadows through the dancing flames. He didn't need to set his burned eyes upon them to know who they were: his parents. They'd visited their vengeance upon their only child for his one act of defiance from beyond the grave. Evan knew too he would be joining them in the broken-down farmhouse, trapped with them forever. He'd spent a lifetime on the run from what he'd done, refusing to allow himself to be loved and cared for. Though Evan had walked away back then, he'd never left.

He was back home, where he belonged.

HOUNDS OF HELL

'A hound it was, an enormous coal-black hound,
but not such a hound as mortal eyes have ever seen.'

So wrote Sir Arthur Conan Doyle when describing the main antagonist in his 1901 Sherlock Holmes novel, 'The Hound of the Baskervilles'. It's a classic tale, still one of the most famous horror stories of all time, sending Holmes and Watson to the vast, rugged emptiness of Dartmoor, and pitting them against an unknown madman who terrorises the wealthy but isolated Baskerville family by staging the reappearance of a legendary demonic hound.

You may recall that this hound had first been summoned into existence at the time of the English Civil War by the bestial ne'er-do-well, Sir Hugo Baskerville, who, for the entertainment of his dissolute friends, had kidnapped a buxom village girl, and who, when she escaped from Baskerville Hall, determined to pursue her, swearing that he'd give his soul to the Devil. The girl died that same night, hunted to her death by the evil landowner, who was then chased across the moor himself by a huge and devilish hound, which caught up with him and tore him to pieces. Ever since that day, the spectral beast, a true Hound of Hell, had haunted the Baskerville line, none of whom were ever advised to go out on the moor alone at night.

Arthur Conan Doyle did very well out of 'The Hound of the Baskervilles', but was always quite open that he'd been inspired to write it by genuine tales of devil dogs that reach far back into ancient West Country lore. In fact, not just the West Country. Anyone interested in Britain's mystical heritage will already know that the populations of many rural areas in these isles have been unnerved at one time or other by stories that sinister, supernatural canines were scouring their nighttime neighbourhoods, seeking to tear out the souls of the unworthy.

And this is the main gist of it.

The old British hellhounds, from the Cŵn Annwn in Wales, to the

Dandy Dogs in Cornwall, from Black Shuck in East Anglia to Hairy Jack in Lincolnshire and Trash or Striker in England's Northwest, from the Barguest of the Northeast to the Gabriel Ratchets of the Midlands, are seemingly compelled to hunt down sinners, and once they've destroyed their bodies, carry their souls off to the infernal realm.

Probably nowhere, though, was this legend more pronounced, nor more widely believed than on Dartmoor in Devon, an untamed region, which even today plays host to rumours of unexplained beasts (though in the 21st century, these tend to be big cats). One certain reason why Dartmoor will always be king of hellhound history is because of the presence in the middle of it of Wistman's Wood.

A high altitude oakwood, the wind-stunted trees of Wistman's Wood are tangled together intricately, possess fantastically twisted trunks and branches, and emerge from inexplicable heaps of boulders, which could only have been placed there by giants. The stones and the trees themselves are so thickly coated in bright green moss that they surely belong in Oz or Middle Earth rather than the English West Country. It's a proven archaeological fact that druids once worshipped here, while all kinds of ghost stories are attached. It should also be no surprise that, according to local tradition, Wistman's Wood kennels the infamous Wisht Hounds or Yeth Hounds, supposedly the souls of children who died outside baptism (which is a pretty disturbing notion in itself, if you consider it). The demonic pack is said to emerge from the wood to roam the moor on Sunday nights. In accordance with the other tales, anyone they encounter who is undeserving will die a most terrible death, their soul then condemned to Hell. (Though just to add spice to the myth, anyone who even hears the pack baying as they romp across the moor will die very shortly, whether he/she be a sinner or not).

Once known as Satan's Hounds, or Odin's Hounds (which indicates how old this story actually is), the origin of the Yeth Hound myth is as obscure in Devon as in all other regions of the country. 'Yeth' derives from the word 'yell', which is an understandable term in this context. But it's interesting that the word 'Wist', as used in Wistman's Wood, is an old local word for 'ghost' or 'haunted', and when you look at the wood, you can understand why it would be so christened.

Folklorists feel strongly that hellhound mythology is a Christian adaptation of the Wild Hunt myth. You'll probably already know that the Wild Hunt, which is mainly associated with Britain and Europe in pagan times, holds that on certain winter nights, a powerful and vengeful god – Cerunnos of the Celts, Woden of the Saxons, Odin of the Vikings – would ride the storm-wracked skies, seeking out unbelievers and setting his ferocious packs upon them, though in these early days the Wild Hunt packs comprised monstrous versions of ravens, eagles, he-goats and wolves, as well as dogs, though it's the 'pack' factor that is key.

It's not atypical Dark Ages overkill that a literal horde of such monsters, particularly, the Yeth Hounds, would burst out of their wooded confines and ravage victims wherever they could find them.

In contrast, when Arthur Conan Doyle got hold of the tale, he decided, with typical Edwardian English restraint, that he needed only one.

CERTAIN DEATH FOR A KNOWN PERSON
Steve Duffy

On the whole my life has been pleasant, but unexceptional. Honestly, you wouldn't pay to read my autobiography, apart from a couple of odd occurrences; or actually just the one occurrence, the beginning of a chain of events which seems, twenty-three years on, still to be working itself out. The rest of it – school, university, work – is everybody's story, and I shan't bore you with it. As for the incident in question, this is what happened:

It was my first term at the University of Exeter, where I shared a room with a bloke called Dave Masters. We're good friends still, and meet up every year or so if it's possible. Both of us were West Country boys: I was from Weston-super-Mare, and he was from a small village to the north of Dartmoor called Inwardleigh ('Really?' I asked him when we first met, and made him show me in the road atlas). He used to go back home for the weekend with a big bag of laundry under his arm – both his and mine, God love him – and leave me the digs to myself. He had a girlfriend at home, and they were both anxious to make sure the relationship didn't fizzle out. They've been married twenty years now, Dave and Cathy, so I suppose it was worth the effort.

One weekend towards the end of the first term, Dave suggested I come back with him: it was Cathy's birthday, and there was a party at her house. Why not, I thought? So come Friday we took the bus from Exeter to Okehampton, then walked the couple of miles to Inwardleigh, where Dave's folks lived. We stopped for tea (dropping off our washing in the process – students, eh?) and then Dave's dad drove us the twelve miles or so to High Thornhays, Cathy's parents' place up on Dartmoor.

It was a big old house that stood on its own on a shoulder of the high moorland. Inside, it was a real rabbit warren, all corridors and staircases, the sort of place it takes a week to find your way around. They needed a big place: besides Monica and Tom, Cathy's mum and dad, there were four Headley children, all daughters. Cathy was the eldest at eighteen, then there was Emily, then Fiona, then Trish. They filled up that crossword puzzle of a house between them: I remember there always being laughter round each corner, as I tried to find my way from one room to another. I liked it very much; I liked the Headleys, too.

At first sight it all might have been a bit intimidating, but the warmth of the Headleys' welcome put me completely at my ease. While I was still trying to get everybody's name right, they were already treating me like an old friend, showing me where I'd be sleeping and asking me if I'd eaten yet. It helped me get over the other stumbling blocks, to do with class and money and my ingrained inferiority complex concerning both those things. I'd never been the guest of anyone as well off as the Headleys, nor of anyone who lived in a house like High Thornhays. It was all a learning curve for me, and it was all good.

That first evening Monica and Tom went out, so Dave, the girls and I had the house to ourselves. I remember us all listening to records in one of the many odd rooms in High Thornhays – I mean, one of the rooms whose original purpose it was hard to guess. You came across them all through the house; half-a-dozen steps, a narrow corridor, then a strange little space like an architect's afterthought, largely unclassifiable. I did ask at first, but the answers I got: 'Oh, it was the muniment room,' or 'this used to be the back receiving parlour' only left me more confused. I forget the name of the room we were in, but it was long and narrow, and the girls used it as a sort of downstairs den. There was a TV and a stereo, and all along one wall mullioned windows looking out over the moor. There were curtains to the windows, but nobody drew them shut. I remember thinking at some point in the evening how we must have looked to anybody outside in the dark and the cold and the constant wind, how enviably comfy and cosy. But of course, there was no-one outside. There were no casual passers-by at High Thornhays. If you were out on the moor at that time of night and you were anywhere near the house, then you probably had business with the Headleys; in which case, you wouldn't waste your time hanging around outside the windows, would you? That whole curtains thing was just a hang-up I had. It came, I suppose, from spending my formative years feeling the glare of constant observation back in our suburban semi in Weston-super-Mare.

So there we were in the long room, Dave and I already making inroads into the booze meant for tomorrow's party. I remember being quite witty, and surprising myself in the process, though I expect this had more to do with the good nature of our hosts than with any latent charisma I might have possessed. They were so perfectly apt to be charmed, even the Elephant Man might have made a good impression.

Really, they were terrific, the Headley girls. Just looking at them made you feel slightly sub-standard in comparison. Do you know what I mean? Those well-bred, well-educated, well-to-do young ladies that just seem so … wholesome? Cathy, for instance, all honey and rose-hips and coltishly long in the bone: I could have gone seriously stupid over Cathy, but of course she was Dave's girlfriend, so no way. Even little Trish, at thirteen the youngest of the pack, was so playfully vivacious, an absolute stunner-in-waiting – though obviously she was even farther out of bounds than her eldest sister, before you get the wrong idea. Fiona, the second youngest, was adorably earnest; she wore specs, and was hugely bookish, so we hit it off straight away. I might as well admit it, I even fancied Monica, their mother. (Later on that first evening, after the girls had gone to bed, I caused Dave to snort beer down his nose when I drunkenly described her as a – wait for it – as a 'mumsy vixen'.)

And then there was Emily, a year and a half younger than Cathy: Emily, for whom it was impossible not to fall, if you were the falling kind. I remember asking Dave how old she was, and thinking *sixteen isn't that young. Not really.* Like that wasn't a clue right there.

It was all in her smile; when she smiled, you felt personally singled out for commendation, as if someone had leaned down from the gods and trained a spotlight on you. One glance, and your whole being was illuminated, you felt the glow of her friendliness all toasty on your face. Your flushed, inebriated face, you understand – your half-wit's phizog, with its stupid goonish leer.

Did Emily notice this; that she was being ogled by a cretin? I hoped not: if she had, it would have been scaldingly embarrassing. Looking at it objectively, with the benefit of hindsight, I doubt whether my gruesome fixation even registered on her radar. Why should it have? I was nineteen and … shall we be kind, and say unpolished? Whereas she was sixteen and a half, improbably, cartoonishly enthused still by everything she lit upon, thrilled by the vividness of her own response. She wanted for nothing, everybody loved her, and she had the natural grace not to let it ruin her. Life had thrown no setbacks into her path, so far, everything had been good, and nothing had hurt. She was in a magic bubble, and it was slightly heartbreaking to think that one day it would have to break, because none of us gets through wholly unscathed, do we? Nobody gets a clear run at it.

Over breakfast the next morning, scratchy and hung-over, I remember squinting through bloodshot eyes at Emily rough-and-tumbling with Jess, the family Labrador, in her basket, and feeling old for the first time in my life. Not just old*er*, you understand, as in a mere two-and-a-half years older, but actually *old*; that feeling I know only too well now on the long slope down to the big five-oh. Creaky, rusting in the chassis, fundamentally unserviceable. I felt it first in the kitchens at High Thornhays, gazing at Emily as she straightened up from playing with the dog and shook her strawberry blonde hair off her face. 'Have you looked outside?' she wanted to know. 'It's just begun to snow!'

Which it had: big fat flakes that soon gave way to a thick and steady whiteout. Bad news for that evening's party, of course, but what with snowballs and snowmen and all the rest of it, there were compensations. Nothing like a snowball in the face to tackle that hangover. All through the afternoon, people who'd been invited to Cathy's eighteenth were phoning up with apologies, *sorry, can't risk it if it stays like this.* Everyone thereabouts knew better than to take a car out in this sort of weather. Naturally enough, Cathy was a bit upset, and Dave took her up to her room, trying to cheer her up. Meanwhile, I helped Tom bring more logs in from the stable block, and we got all the fireplaces banked up and roaring, just in case.

Around dusk, when the snow had stopped falling and all of Dartmoor lay under several feet of drift, I was looking out of the diamond-leaded windows in the long room round the side of the house. The wind had driven a gap in the clouds, and the snow looked quite blue beneath the hard and brittle stars. Around the windows the lamplight from inside shone out through the stained glass, colouring the closest of the snow-banks a cheerful harlequin pattern. Away beyond that, the slopes of the high tors looked picturesque, yet forbidding. I shivered, and wandered back through to the kitchens, the warm hospitable heart of the house.

There, Monica and the girls were getting on with the arrangements for the party despite everything. You never know, said Monica, more in hope than expectation, and sure enough a handful of people braved the conditions – local folk, mostly, people from Chagford and Gidleigh and Lettaford. Nobody from further afield than Okehampton was risking it.

Cathy was great: she smiled and made the best of things, and I was more than a little envious of Dave as I watched them both chatting to the neighbours. You had to be, because they were so clearly made for each other. (It took me the best part of twenty years to find a Cathy of my own; they don't grow on trees.) Inwardly I sighed, and went to look for Emily. Just for a chat.

Annoyingly, she'd found someone her own age to talk to: a girl from school, Pippa or something, all gosh-and-golly, and they were deep in conversation about boys and pony club and stuff I can't even imagine. 'Hiya, Mike,' she said brightly, seeing me loitering by the door to the hallway, glass in hand. 'You all right? Hey, I think Fiona was looking for you just now!'

'You setting him up, Em?' the other girl wanted to know. They giggled, and I joined in the laughter, just so they'd know it was all a perfectly splendid joke but I was totally in on it, yeah. Ha-ha, yeah, right. Fiona. *Don't push it, girly*, I thought.

Tipsily aware of the need for dignity and poise in all things, I strolled through to the front parlour, where Fiona wanted to know which I preferred, Alan Garner or Tolkien. Well, this is the thing about being a bookworm. When romantic expectations fizzle out, you can always spend a good couple of hours debating the merits of Middle-Earth over Elidor. By the time we'd decided that Jenny Agutter should be the girl if they ever made *The Owl Service* into a film, most of the other guests had gone home, and I was into my ninth or tenth pint, and feeling no pain.

Soon after midnight Tom and Monica went upstairs, leaving us young folk to it. 'Don't burn the house down,' said Tom. He may have been looking at me; I may have been one or two over my limit by then. I didn't take it personally. Then again, I may not have fully understood what he was saying at the time. Conversation was getting difficult, mostly because of the seven-second delay newly developed between my brain and my organs of speech. But it was okay. It was fine. I remember all of us sitting in the long room where the record player was, the funny long room, and I was saying how this was a funny room, because it was all long, and we all laughed, because that was funny in itself ... and then I remember there being no electric lights on any more, only the firelight all flickering and magical, and someone was reaching around me, tucking a tartan car blanket around my shoulders ...

'Emily?

'All right, Mike?' she said, her voice kindly as ever. 'How you doing? You were nodding off then.' I was sprawled back into a corner of the sofa, and she was leaning over me with that heart-melting smile of hers. Very close; close enough to kiss, if I dared go for it. Solicitously she removed the pint glass from my unresisting hand. 'Just put that down there, out of the way. Are you going to be okay here, then? Or shall we try and get you up to bed?'

'Fine here,' I assured her. Suave to the core, I was going to point out there was plenty of room for two if she cared to join me, but by the time I'd figured out which order the words should go in, she was gone; and very shortly after that I was gone as well.

I don't know what time it was when the ferocity of my own snoring brought me round. I'm not even sure that I came round all the way, so strictly speaking I don't know whether what I'm about to tell you actually happened, or whether it took place only in some abnormally detailed dream-version of reality. I know what I believe to be true, but you'll judge that for yourselves. This is what I remember:

It was night outside, but the fire in the grate was still in, banked down to a glowing bed of embers. That helped me realise where I was; that and the starlight, reflected off the snow outside and streaming through the still uncurtained windows. The room was dark but not inky black. You could make out shapes, and even a measure of detail; you could probably have found a book, but you wouldn't have been able to sit down and read it, not without turning on a light.

I wanted no light; I wanted only about another twelve hours or so of sleep, and the soothing hand of a beautiful woman on my brow, and possibly a cup of tea, if there was one going. I was thinking in an aimless way about getting back off again, when I realised I wasn't alone in the room.

Someone was sitting in one of the armchairs over by the windows. You could see a head, silhouetted against the gleam of the snowfields outside, but no features, none of the detail; the firelight was too low for that. I must have caught my breath in surprise, or grunted or something, because the figure raised a hand in silent acknowledgement.

Who was it? I assumed it was somebody else sleeping over for the night, one of the neighbours who'd maybe had one over the eight. Had I been introduced? Well, that was anyone's guess. Aloud, I yawned and said, 'All right?'

'Fine, thank you. Nice of you to ask.' A man. I didn't recognise the voice – no, that's not it, exactly. I *thought* I did; I just couldn't put a name to it. He spoke a cultured RP English with just the slightest edge; that cool sardonic humour that comes with the assumption of unbounded and perpetual pre-eminence. The sort of voice that built the Empire, and left half the world wishing we'd stayed at home instead.

'What time is it?' I would have told him how *I* was, but he hadn't asked.

The other – the guest – shifted a little in his seat, glanced over his shoulder through the window. I still couldn't see his face, but I thought I saw a glint of something red as he turned his head; he may have been wearing glasses, and they may have caught the firelight. 'It's very late. Or very early still, depending on which way you look at it.'

Well, that was helpful. 'Have you got a watch on?'

'… I don't have any *use* for watches,' admitted the guest, politely amused at the notion. 'I'm always on time, you see, wherever I arrive.' And modest with it. Clearly, a prince among men.

'No? Well, doesn't matter.' I was quite prepared to leave it at that. Very, very tired, remember; a bit drunk still, I dare say; not in the mood for late-night conversation. I was settling back on the sofa, when the guest spoke again.

'Nice party.' Not inflected one way or the other; an open-ended statement, or a polite enquiry.

'Yeah. Yeah, it was great.' Had I said anything? Had I done anything? Spilled my drink over him? Come on to his wife? Couldn't remember.

'All the young people enjoying themselves.' Again without discernible inflection. A pause, then: '*You* were certainly having a ball.'

Oh Christ. I had done something. What?

'Talking to Emily, I mean.' Friendly on the surface; but no further. Underneath that? You wouldn't want to look.

'They're great ... all the girls.' I so didn't want to be having this conversation. 'Really nice family. Nice people.'

'Yes, but Emily is your favourite, isn't she?'

Oh, no way. No way had I made it that obvious. 'I wouldn't say —'

'That's because you think this is an ordinary conversation.'

Could there be anything more calculated to make you throw your brakes on? In the end I just didn't know what else to say: 'Isn't it?'

'No,' said the guest, so categorically that it seemed to leave no space for an answer. After a little while, during which time I'd almost decided that the whole thing was actually just an extremely weird dream, he resumed: 'No, it isn't. Encounters such as this, they don't happen every day, you see, Mike.'

That sounded ominous. Was it a sex thing? You heard about these posh people. Aloud, I said, 'Encounter?'

'Rendezvous. Rencontre. Whatever.' He waved a hand, as if granting me the freedom to fill in the synonym of my choice. 'You see, my role here tonight – my purpose – was primarily to observe. Nothing more for now. And then when I saw that we were both *observing* the same thing ... well, it seemed only polite to consult, so to speak. One aficionado to another.'

Sometimes when he spoke there was the slightest pause before the noun, as if there were other names for everything – secret names some of them – and he had to be careful which names he used. Careful, because his choice would determine how much he might reveal of his true intent – of his true nature, maybe.

'What do you mean?' It was hypnotic, the dance of the language, but treacherous as well. A snake will dance and weave before it strikes.

The guest sighed, and leaned forwards. Clasping his hands, he rested the point of his chin on the extended tips of his index fingers. Still his face was indistinguishable in the dark. 'The matter of Emily,' he said, and a shudder passed through the room, passed all the way through me. I swear it did.

'Little Emily,' savouring the words. 'So special – but you saw that straight away, didn't you? I noticed you noticing. Such a lovely girl. So … vivacious.'

I wanted to stop him right there, before he went any further. Our parents' generation had that phrase, it sounds absurdly dated now, but it expressed exactly what I felt: *I don't like the tone of your voice.* But he was speaking still:

'*Vivacious.* I wonder, is that exactly the word I was looking for – I mean, in terms of its etymology? Ah, though, I was forgetting: I doubt that sort of thing is covered in college any more. Lively, tenacious of life; long lived.' He tutted, like a Sunday painter who'd selected the wrong colour. 'What do you think?'

'I know what vivacious means,' I said sullenly. I wished I knew the word that would get him to piss off, though politely.

'But is it appropriate to the matter at hand? Is it apposite? Is it correct?' With that last word, a hard flinty quality came into his speech: the *k* sounds practically knapped sparks off the edges of the air.

'Eh? What are you getting at?' For the first time since my arrival at High Thornhays I was on the defensive. Old habits born of inadequacy coming to the fore; truculence, sullenness … and just the beginnings of fear. The man with no face there in the armchair: I was already afraid of him. Not nearly as afraid as I ought to have been, not yet. But soon; very soon.

Already I had that sick black-hole sensation of sliding towards something awful, the kind of feeling we associate only with bad dreams, because we're conditioned to believe that such things never happen in real life. Then why do they seem so familiar in our dreams? And why did I feel as though I knew this man, when I'd never to the best of my recollection met him? Why could I already sense what he was going to say, when I asked him: 'What do you mean?'

'I mean, she *looks* healthy enough,' began the guest; and

there it was. It was that odd dreamy foreknowledge of his answer that made me panic, as much as what he said. 'She *looks* healthy enough, I grant you that. But how could you know, just from looking? How could you possibly be sure?' He spread his hands wide. 'How could you know what's inside?' The word fell very heavily in the darkened room. Absurd as it sounds, I was already thinking, *yes, exactly, how* can *you know*?

'I mean, what about leukaemia?' said the guest, pronouncing that tricky first syllable to a nicety. 'Hyperplasic transformation of leucopoietic tissue. Half of all cancers in teenage children. Or meningitis: presents as a headache and irritability. Well.' He tittered. 'Irritability, in teenagers? How could you even guess, until it was far too late? So many forms; so many causes. Viruses, fungi, bacteria, carcinomas …' A languid flourish of his hand, sketching out a process of infinite regression.

'Carcinomas? What do you mean?' There was a tremor in my voice I didn't like. 'Nobody's got cancer.'

'Ah, well, cancer.' He might have been describing an old bad penny of a friend, a mischievous roué impossible to dislike. 'I suppose there's always that moment, isn't there, when the first cell divides in a slightly different way? And you don't know it, but inside you something is already changing – the traitor cell, the Judas tissue? And it starts like *that* – at the snap of a finger.' A dry clicking of cold bones.

'Cancer. Limbs of the crab. And there are so many places it can hide. Have you ever stopped to consider this? The body is infinitely tolerant in this respect, Mike, infinitely welcoming. All the major organs, of course – but the big toe? The humble hallux, this-little-piggy-went-to-market? Cancer in your big toe? Look it up in the textbooks. And while you're there, try cancer of the rectum. Cancer of the womb. Cancer of the tongue – even cancer of the *eyeball*. Imagine that, Mike!'

How could I not? I wonder: did he know that anything to do with eyes terrified me, ever since that playground fight when I'd nearly lost the sight in my right eye? I think he probably did; I don't think there was much he didn't know. He wanted me terrified, you see. He wanted me to panic. And there was no stopping him, he was off again.

'Or the neurodegenerative diseases! It's a list as long as your arm, all the Herr Doktors jostling for immortality in the medical texts. Sandhoff, Spielmeyer, Kreutzfeld-Jakob, Pelizaeus-Merzbacher, Schilder and Pick. Body dementia. Corticobasal degeneration. Spinocerebellar ataxia. All of it lying in wait as you grow old, and you never know. Neurons deteriorating, connections broken all across the cortex, until all of a sudden you're sitting in the day ward in incontinence pants, crying because you've dropped your sippy-cup. It could happen to anyone. To Emily, even – why not?'

'Are you a doctor?' It was all I could think of to say. I hoped it might distract him.

He chuckled, softly and disagreeably. 'A doctor? Let me see. What would be the *opposite* of doctor, do you think? A doctor; no. No, I'm afraid not, Mike – but I could have a look at it for you, if you like?' Again that creepy chuckle, hardly aspirated, pent up jealously in his throat. 'Isn't that how the old joke goes?'

'I don't understand –'

'In the context of Emily? Why not? Why not, Mike? Just because you're besotted with her after what? – a day? – that won't save her. She can't be sheltered from the world indefinitely, you know! Nothing protects a person forever. All the love in the world weighs less than a new strain of flu – remember that. The love of the poets may be constant and unchanging, but viruses mutate. Viruses win in the end.' I knew he was smiling; I knew how hideous that smile would be. 'You're smitten; how sweet. But that won't save her. Bear that in mind, while you consider all the possibilities.'

How desperately I wanted this filth to stop; this madness, this indecency. Suppose I simply left the room, got up and walked out? Either the dream would be over and I'd wake up, or I'd be out in the hallway at least, and hopefully he wouldn't come after me. But before I could shift a muscle he said, 'No, wait,' as casually as that, almost absentmindedly, the way you'd invite someone to take a seat …

… and there I was, pinned against the cushions. I couldn't move; tried, but found myself rooted in the chair. Again, it was that feeling we get in dreams, when we're trapped in the grip of the monster, unable to escape. That was the point at which I lost it, in retrospect, the point at which I came to believe that the shape in the armchair was something other than a commonplace pervert or sadist, something other than conventionally wicked, or conventionally insane. The fear was racking up inside me, mounting in an exponential clamour, as he spoke again:

'I mean, accidents! We haven't even mentioned accidents yet, have we? That road down to Tawton, for instance. Monica takes it far too fast, you know, that sharp right-hander near the junction with the A30. She drives Emily and Trish down to pony club each Sunday. Trish goes in the passenger seat, but Emily's in the back, without a seatbelt. Now, what if one fine day in … May, shall we say? May 23, next year? Just for the sake of argument. Now, suppose on that bright May morning, something were to be coming the other way along that lane. A Land Rover, say – or better still, a tractor. A big Massey Ferguson, with a tank full of silage behind it. Both going a bit too fast, neither of them concentrating … and poor Emily in the back, without a seatbelt, remember? No protection; no chance. Massive head trauma, a grievous insult to the brain – that's what the doctors would say at the post-mortem. It could happen. *I could make it happen.*'

So calm, so matter-of-fact, but such a terrible depth of malice and psychosis behind every word he spoke. Such a wicked joy in destruction. I was so scared now; so scared, you wouldn't believe it. Dream or not, I knew I was trapped in the presence of a very bad thing, maybe the worst thing of all, and I didn't dare imagine what it wanted with me.

'Or suicide.' I must have tried to say something, because he raised his voice insistently: 'Yes. Suicide. It would take longer, quite a while longer, but in the end there is nothing more sure. You see, deep in every human heart there is a place with no way out – you might not believe it, Mike, but it's true, it's true, it's so terribly true. And I could find that place. I could take her by the hand and lead her there, and then vanish with a puff of smoke – like that!'

He raised his closed fist to his mouth, blew it open to show nothing. And behind his spread fingers, the nothing where his face should have been.

'… Why are you *saying* this?' I was almost sobbing. I'd tried to get up again, tried to run away like a child; but I couldn't. I was rooted to the chair. He had me fast. 'Why are you telling me these things? What do you *want*?'

'What do I want?' He sounded positively jovial. 'Well, Mike, I want to ask your opinion on something. I'd like you to make a choice.'

Somehow, I'd known he was going to say it; feared that he would. Aloud, I said, 'I don't understand,' but I'd known before he even spoke, the way you do in dreams. And of course he was having none of it.

'Yes you do. Don't play the innocent, Mike; don't waste my time. You're a part of this now. Look it up in your Schrödinger: the presence of an observer necessarily affects that which is observed.' He emphasised each beat with a tap of his finger on the chair arm, like an impatient lecturer pointing out the relevant passage in a textbook. 'You stuck your nose in at a critical juncture. Don't complain now when you get it nipped.'

I heard his teeth click together as he suited the action to the word. It was a silly thing to do, a childish thing, beneath his dignity really; but it scared me more than I can ever hope to tell you. From then on, the notion of his teeth simply paralysed me with fear. I was terrified of how they might look, if I could only see them. How long; how sharp … how many.

'This is the very essence of free will.' He was back in control now, any momentary irritation suppressed. He knew he had me where he wanted me, after all. 'A god-given gift, the measure of man. You ought to be glad of the chance to use it – I mean really slam it on the table for once, that existential joker. Isn't it exciting? Isn't it … stimulating?

'Look! Here's our little Emily, tripping through the maze,

tra-la. The paths fork ahead of her, and at the end of each path lies death. Those are the rules. This path is long and meandering, with primroses growing in the borders and bluebirds singing. *This* path is the shortest of short cuts.' A chop of the hand; final. 'And at the fork, we stand together, you and I. Our job is to send her this way, or that. So, again: I would like you to choose. How shall it be? How shall it happen? Which path? What will come to pass?'

'You can't do this,' I said, sobbing almost; but he didn't even dignify that with an answer. He *could* do it: of course he could. That was his job, and I was co-opted. I knew it, and he knew I knew.

There followed a gap – I have no way of judging how long it lasted. It seemed like hours, and I couldn't say anything. The fear was so complete, like a ball of molten glass blown all around me, leaving me perfectly, hermetically trapped. In the space of a few minutes I'd been subtracted from the world of chance and accident and scraping through, and thrown screaming into the awful arena of first causes. Five minutes' conversation in the dark. It had the skewed and brutal logic of a nightmare, the worst you could ever have. It might even have *been* a nightmare, except for the wetness of the tears on my face. The tears at least felt real.

And all the time he waited, the guest with only shadow for a face. He sat with steepled fingers and waited for me to betray myself. Eventually, he leant forward: 'Poor Mike. It isn't easy, is it? But I'm afraid I'm going to have to press you, you know. Time's a-wasting, and we haven't got all night.'

Hanging there between us was a threat – a threat every bit as real as a drunken skid on the motorway or a sharpened razor's edge; the crumbling edge of a precipice without a bottom, the ground giving way beneath your feet. Again he spoke:

'So?'

I knew I had to say something. 'Not her,' I managed, just. 'Not her.'

'Not her?' Such disappointment in his voice; such contemptuousness. 'Is that it? Is that the sum and aggregate of your deliberations? *Not her*? T'ch. I think someone isn't trying.'

'Do it to someone else.' It was all I could think of to say.

'Michael! But we were supposed to decide!' Almost petulant. 'The garden of forking paths, remember?'

'Do it to somebody else.' I was actually sobbing now; my face was absolutely drenched with tears. 'It doesn't have to be her.'

'Really?' the guest asked, as if this was an aspect of it that had never struck him until now. 'You think not?'

'No! Do it to someone else! Anyone!'

'Anyone?' He sounded shocked. 'Oh, not to anyone, Mike. Those aren't the rules at all. We aren't the agents of blind chance, you know. Don't think that for a moment. No, if it were to happen – I only say *if*, mind – then it would have to be someone else further down the line. One of the other branches of the path, you understand. That's the only way it could happen. The repercussions otherwise ...' He spread his hands, sketching an immensity of disruption.

'Do it to someone else, then,' I begged. It was the only way out that I could see.

'You're sure?' He seemed disappointed. It was horrible. 'You're absolutely sure?'

'Yes,' I said unhesitatingly.

'Oh, very well,' he said. 'If you insist. Now, who?'

'*Who*? I don't know!'

'It has to be somebody, Mike. Not just anybody.' He was explaining the rules of the game, very patiently, to an idiot. 'You are choosing certain death for a known person, not just throwing a coin off the top of the Empire State Building. I have to have a name.'

'I – I – I don't know ...' He'd blocked off my escape. Again, I could feel myself sliding down into total, suffocating horror.

'Do you want me to help?' Kindly, yet at the same time inexorable. 'Is that it? Shall I narrow it down for you?'

I couldn't speak. I just nodded, and he inclined his own head. 'After all,' he said, 'I suppose I have the advantage in some respects. When you can see a little further along the forks, then you have the ability to make an aesthetically pleasing choice – and that is important, Mike. It's important to have standards.

'Goodness!' He sighed. 'Let me think. Something equivalent, something … something fitting. There is a balance in all things, Mike, though it may not be immediately apparent. Interconnections, synchronicities. One woman wakes up well, and half a world away another feels the lump in her breast and tries to decide whether to bother the doctor with it.

'I'm prevaricating. A name, a name. How about … oh! How about *Alethea Kakoulis*? I don't think you know her, do you?'

The name meant nothing to me, nothing whatsoever, so of course I seized upon it, like a man in a shipwreck grabbing a lifebelt out of the hands of another survivor. 'Her! Yes! Whatever you said. Do it to her. Do it to –'

Without warning, the room exploded into light, sharp bright searing white, and I threw up my hands to guard my eyes. 'Do what?' said a voice at my elbow. 'Christ, Mike, you all right? You sounded like you were having a right go at someone, there.'

It was Dave, come down to check on me. The armchair over by the window was empty. There was no-one else in the room.

He said he'd heard a voice from out in the hallway, so he'd come in and switched the light on, thinking I was already awake, that there was someone in there with me. But I was on my own. Clearly, I'd been talking in my sleep. 'You'd better not make a habit of that,' he told me, 'or else I'll be putting in for a new roommate. Jesus, Mike, you were screaming like your throat had been cut!'

Quite. Anyway, Dave fetched me a glass of water and led me upstairs to my bedroom, but even there I couldn't shake the feeling it was all still happening, that I hadn't woken up at all – or that I'd never been asleep. I remember sitting propped up against the pillows with my arms around my knees, bedside lamp switched on, thinking no, it couldn't have been a dream, it couldn't …

… and then, the next thing I knew, it was Sunday morning,

and High Thornhays was coming to life once more. The rumble of Victorian plumbing, the clattering of feet on wooden floorboards, the high clear laughter of the girls through all the passageways. Nothing drives away your fears quite like the rising sun over gleaming snowfields. It's white magic, proof against all the terrors of night.

Going down to breakfast I was already well on the way to sublimating all my memories of the long room: a bad dream, nothing more. I couldn't look Emily in the face over the breakfast table, though, not quite. That much at least had changed. But nobody noticed – and hey, I was entitled to be a little quiet that morning, after my drunken-eejit stumblings of the night before. By mid-morning we'd dug out the driveway, and the snowplough was labouring up the main road to meet us; by teatime Tom Headley was driving us back to Exeter in the car.

First of all, let me set your mind at rest, and tell you Emily got through all right – she survived, she's alive to this day. She and her husband live in Poole, where they run a gallery. As for myself, I visited High Thornhays on several more occasions during my time at college, but nothing extraordinary ever happened. I never bagged myself a Headley gal, and I never met anyone worse than myself, as the old saying goes. I made a special point of inviting myself up to Dartmoor the following spring, on May 23 – I took my dream, or whatever it was, that seriously, at least – but as luck would have it, Emily had knocked pony club on the head by then. In fact, she'd started going out with a boy from Newton Abbot, and we saw very little of her that weekend. She was there to wave me off on the evening of my departure, as cheerful as ever.

Once that particular date had passed, and the charm had been broken, I rarely if ever thought about the man in the armchair again. Life has a way of filling in the empty places, if you let it. I'm one of those people who hardly ever remember their dreams, and those I do remember haven't featured the party guest, not for a long time now. Life settled into its everyday groove, which was fine by me. I wasn't looking for anything deeper. As Bertolt Brecht said, in a poem I once knew off by heart, but seem to have forgotten most of now: nothing could be harder than the quest for fun.

In 1984 the quest took me from Exeter up to London, where I made good use of my 2.2 in English lit playing roadie for a shambling indie band called the Stellar Gibbons. Off the back of that I got a job in a rehearsal studios near Clink Wharf, and within ten years I was running the place -- not bad for someone with my essentially adolescent approach to career-building. It was there I first met Lee Oliveira.

Lee came highly recommended from the temping agency, and even though I'd already filled the vacancy, her interview lasted twice as long as the woman's who actually got the job. She was interested in music, and I was interested in her; one thing led to another, and we've been together the best part of a decade now. We have our own place in Islington, and Lee's expecting at last. All those years of sperm tests and fertility clinics, and then everything fell into place a month or two ago quite naturally. We were knocked out. Lee's folks came over from their retirement pad on the Algarve, my mum and dad drove up from Weston, and there was a get-together. It was nice.

Lee's second scan was on the morning of July 7. I'd been up all night in the studio with a band getting ready for their first big national tour, but there was no way I was missing that appointment. I met her in the doctor's waiting room at half eight; I held her hand while they moved the sensor across her belly and we watched the magic images on the screen. Afterwards, she went into work and I caught the bus home.

The doctor's was in Munster Square, near Regent's Park. I walked as far as Euston and jumped on a number 30. No sooner had I sat down than I was fishing my copy of the scan out of its manila envelope. The woman next to me saw me holding it up to the light (now, which bit is the head again?) and smiled before popping the buds of her Walkman into her ears. I fished out my own iPod and followed suit, thinking to listen through some live-in-studio rehearsals from the night before. The first track opened on amplifier hum and the plugging-in of jacks. But then instead of the drummer's count-in there came a voice:

'A significant proportion of birth defects don't necessarily show up on scans, Mike. The really nasty ones, too. Should they do an amniocentesis, be particularly sure to ask —'

That was all I heard. I'd already ripped off my headphones and lurched up out of my seat. The grey daylight of a mild July morning in London was overlaid with a flashbulb burst of white, and for the first time in over twenty-three years I remembered the fleeting impression, that blood-red retinal afterimage that I'd blinked away, that night in the long room at High Thornhays when Dave turned on the light. The man in the armchair, the flicker of glowing coals in his eyes, the terrible tiger's smile …

The bus was just pulling up at the next stop, and without thinking I barged my way off. I couldn't stay in that confined space, not now the panic had sunk its hooks so deep into my crawling skin. My iPod – an engraved present from Lee – was still on the seat, along with the ultrasound scan of our unborn baby. The police returned them to me later, when they allowed me to leave the scene. Because this was exactly 9.45 am on Thursday July 7, 2005, near the junction of Tavistock Square and Upper Woburn Place, and not two minutes after I'd got off the bus an eighteen-year-old on the top deck, Hasib Hussain from Leeds, set off the explosive device in his rucksack, killing thirteen of my fellow passengers. Across London, more bombs were already being detonated.

The rest of that morning was a blur, really, the bad news filtering through from across the capital while we waited behind police cordons to be told what to do. Mobile phone networks were all down, and we had to make do with rumours and Chinese whispers and whatever the coppers would let on, which wasn't much at first, and all the time we were smelling it on the air: Death, in a leafy London square. The simplest things – buses, tube trains – stood revealed as agents of potential chaos. Everything had the capacity to harm you. Everything you thought you knew.

I wasn't scared for me, not really; only for Lee, and the baby. She, of course, was horrified, and there was a lot of crying and pledging of love that evening, when I finally got home. As we lay in bed hugging each other, I remember her saying, 'This feels like such a turning point for us, Mike; it's like a second chance. Like we've been spared. We've been so *lucky* – first the baby, and now you getting off that bus at exactly the right time.' Of course, I hadn't told her *why* I'd got off the bus. How could I? 'I just feel –' she wiped her nose on a tissue and squeezed my arm '– I just feel as though it's time to do all the things we've ever wanted to do – do them *now*. There's no point in putting anything off any more -- don't you feel that way? We should just go for it, full-on, live each day as if it's going to be our last. Don't you think?'

I agreed with her, and squeezed her back and told her I loved her. I believe I also told her everything was going to be all right, which is a thing we all do, I suppose, a lie we all tell. In times of crisis we crave parental reassurance, an order of protection unavailable in the grown-up world. Somehow or other we got off to sleep, and the panic went away for the space of a few hours. No dreams – not that I remember – but on waking it was his words that were running through my head, the voice that had cut through my headphones on the bus. Without thinking I reached across and laid a hand upon Lee's stomach.

It wasn't until teatime that next day that Lee told me the first of the things she was planning to do, the one big thing she'd been putting off for God knows how long. It was so important to her now, she said, now that she was going to have a child of her own. I was uneasy even before she told me, and afterwards … this was when the panic kicked in, for real this time; and it's never gone away, not once, in all the days and weeks since.

Lee was adopted, you see; she never knew her birth parents. The Oliveiras had shortened her birth name to Lee, and when she'd asked what the full version had been her parents had told her, 'Never you mind.' Now, she did mind; she felt it was a necessary step towards self-knowledge. She didn't want to involve her folks, so instead she was going to get hold of her adoption file from the council. Already she'd been in touch with the General Register Office, and they'd told her what to do, who to see, what forms to fill out. She told me all this over dinner that Friday evening, and ever since then I've been waiting in a kind of daze for the axe to fall.

It's August now, a hot brassy afternoon heavy with the threat of thunderstorms and downpour. I've been home from work since lunchtime; I had a feeling it would have arrived, and of course it had, punctual as any bad news and as impossible to ignore. It was waiting on the doormat with the flyers and the junk mail, a big white envelope with the council's logo on it, for the personal attention of 'Lee Oliveira'. I haven't opened it; it's lying in front of me on the kitchen table. I know what it'll say. I know the name inside -- I never forgot it. Lee for Alethea; seems all too obvious. Poor Mrs Kakoulis; though I doubt she was a Mrs, somehow. Did he visit her as well, the uninvited party guest, the bad man in the dark? Which of the forking paths did he push her down, to which dizzy cliff-edge?

And now, as the clock ticks on against the wreck of the day and the last assurances of rationality fall behind like flotsam on a sea deceptively calm for the time being, I sit at the kitchen table with no protection from my nightmares and wait for Lee to come home. Our baby, too -- our gorgeous, impossible baby girl -- nestled inside her and growing, getting bigger every day. In my head there's the ringing of static, the numbing feedback whine of blank horror and tireless malevolence. I don't know what I'll say to her, when she opens the envelope and tells me what's inside. I don't know what I can say. There is only one question I have, and I can't ask it of any living being, Lee least of all:

Will it be before the birth, or afterwards? When will it happen?

When?

THE BLOOD-PRICE

In Anglo-Saxon England, there was a thing called wer-geld, which literally meant blood-price. In purely practical terms, it was a 'murder fine'. In other words, any person who slew another, whatever course of action the law took with them, was bound to pay compensation to the bereaved kinfolk. But there was another more philosophical aspect to the concept of 'blood-price', which predates Dark Age England by many centuries and harks back to the earliest days of civilisation. It is the notion that justice is, or should be, reciprocal, and that whatever is visited on an innocent party, will also, or should be, visited on the perpetrator at some point.

It was a comforting notion to many, because at its heart lay the idea that natural justice prevailed. But others found it sinister, as it implied that if a felon were to evade such penance at the hands of Man, he might still find it at the hands of the deities.

Which brings us to the story of St Indract, a saint almost unheard of in the modern world, even among religious folk, but one whose violent and untimely death was said to have generated a fearsome supernatural response.

Indract, an Irish saint, was venerated throughout the Middle Ages at Glastonbury in Somerset, where it is said, he and his nine companions, including his sister, Dominica, were laid to rest in the Old Church of St Mary, alongside the bones of St Patrick, though there is no trace of the mass tomb now as that building was demolished in 1938.

The story holds that Indract, a deacon and the son of an Irish king, had been on pilgrimage to Rome, and while heading home, opted to visit England, so that he could pay his respects to St Patrick, whose relics lay entombed at Glastonbury Abbey (though this latter detail is strongly contested by historians). During the course of the journey, the party, who were humbly clad but carrying bags filled with food and staffs tipped with brass, caught the attention of a local thegn called Husa, who was not just a ruthless, avaricious man, but a pagan with no respect for the Christianity now resurging in Britain.

It was May 8 that year when Husa, on hearing that a wealthy party was in the district, organised an ambush in woodland on a property owned by the bishopric of Wells, in Somerset, at a place now called Huish Episcopi. However, on being attacked, the pilgrims were found to possess no treasure. Even the brass-tipped staffs – the brass having been incorrectly reported to Husa as gold – were worthless. Enraged, the thegn ordered the party slain, and all subsequently fell to the blows of swords and axes.

A short time later, King Ine of Wessex, a powerful monarch and a recently-converted Christian, heard rumours about the atrocity, and sent his men to locate the bodies. It seemed hopeless, but an eerie light is said to have drawn the search party to a site where the ten dismembered corpses were found half-sunken in a bog. All were taken to Glastonbury, where the king planned to have them interred with great reverence. At the time, no one knew who was responsible for the crime, but Husa and his hearth-men, as local nobility, were expected to attend the grand ceremony.

They did so reluctantly, feeling inexplicably but increasingly frightened as the remains were placed in their caskets. At the very height of the Mass, a curious light fell upon Husa and his party, and one by one the murderers commenced howling and gibbering, and then brutally attacked each other. The congregation watched aghast, unable to intervene, as the raving men, who were unarmed and therefore fought with claws and teeth, tore savagely at each other's flesh and eyes until all of them, Husa included, lay dead and horribly mutilated in the church.

King Ine, a grim onlooker, declared that Husa was clearly responsible for the outrageous murders, and that he and his followers had paid the only blood-price possible.

Modern scholars are unsure whether the St Indract of this story ever existed. They point to a possible confusion with Indrechtach ua Fínnachta, the Irish abbot of Iona, who was similarly martyred in England, possibly during a Viking raid, in 854. However, there are many references to this version of the St Indract story in medieval documents, and it was believed so widely up until the 16th century at least that he remained a popular subject of prayer and pilgrimage, especially on his feast (and death) day, May 8.

Even today, tradition holds that if an undiscovered murderer ever visits the site where Indract's relics lie, he'll be picked out clearly by an eerie and inexplicable light.

Whether he then rends his own flesh and plucks out his own eyes is up to him.

KNYFESMYTHS' STEPS
A K Benedict

'No inflatable dicks, no cock lollipops and no knob straws,' I said when we'd all settled into our table seats on the train. 'Is that clear?' Prosecco was being poured into plastic glasses. Crisp packets split open so we all could share. Out the window, the Somerset landscape blurred past in varied shades of green.

'What about a willy wand?' Natalie asked. She waved her hand in the air, eyes wide in amazement as if demonstrating the magical power of a staff shaped like a stubby stiffy.

'Nope. At the first sign of any penis-related paraphernalia, I'm going home.'

'You'll wear a veil, though, right?' Izzy glanced at her rucksack, suggesting she'd brought a lace monstrosity with her.

'Is it black?'

'Course not,' Izzy laughed. It was if she didn't know me at all.

'Then no. I don't need net curtains – I'm not a suburban widow.'

Fern leaned into me and whispered: 'Window.'

I stared at her, confused.

'You said "widow". I think you meant "window".' Fern was my best friend, my wingwoman. She had my back and I had hers.

'Ah, well. I'd need to get married before I could be a widow.'

'Don't even say it out loud,' Natalie said. 'You'll make it happen.'

'That's not how the world works,' I replied.

'How do we really know what goes on under the surface?' Natalie looked around the carriage as if the Illuminati was lurking under the tables or hiding in the toilets. She had always been superstitious. When they were growing up, Natalie had never dared step on pavement cracks, and crossed herself on seeing black cats. Lone magpies were as worrying to her as hen night clichés were to me.

'Good job I don't believe in omens,' I replied.

'How will anyone know it's a hen weekend?' Izzy asked.

'Why do they need to?' I wasn't being facetious, OK, I wasn't *just* being facetious, although that was one of my favourite states of being. From my point of view, it was enough that I was having a hen weekend, I didn't need to broadcast the fact by being or waving a dick.

Izzy opened her mouth, then her forehead furrowed as she tried to find a good reply. Not finding one, she closed it again.

Fern stood and rootled in the rack above my head. 'I anticipated you feeling like this,' she said. She then whipped black ribbons from her bag and handed me one. It was a silk sash with writing in grey, gothic font:

BRIDE OF FRANKENSTEIN-TO-BE-OR-NOT-TO-BE

I couldn't help smiling. She'd managed to combine my interests in horror and indecisive men. 'Clever. I like it.'

She then placed another black sash over her head so that its words swung across her body:

CHIEF BRIDESMAID TO BRIDE OF FRANKENSTEIN-TO-BE

'You don't have to wear it or anything.' I put mine on in lieu of a reply. Fern grinned and gave Izzy and Nathalie their own sashes.

Izzy held up her drink. We cheers'ed each other, plastic flutes dinking. 'To Jess!'

'To me,' I said.

'Where we heading?' the driver asked when we got into the taxi at Bristol station.

'Christmas Steps, please,' Fern said. She was organising the whole weekend, had booked the accommodation, restaurants, activities – everything.

'Right you are,' the driver replied. Her Bristolian accent was as strong as the suspension bridge, reminding me of my mum's voice. Eighteen-year-old grief caught in the back of my throat like aged whisky.

'Sounds a bit festive for Jess,' Natalie said as we got into the taxi with the gangly lack of co-ordination that too much Prosecco brought.

'You know why it's called that, don't you?' The driver looked at us through the rear view mirror. From where I was sitting, only her eyebrows were visible. Her question was clearly rhetorical as she didn't give time for any of us to answer. 'They think it's 'cos of the old word for the cutlers that lived in the area.'

The others looked to me as the one with the PhD in English, never mind that it was in Gothic literature, not linguistics. I tried to dredge up information from my old medieval English language classes like a body from the canal. Nothing. I blamed the booze, weighing it down. Fern was on her phone, probably trying to find the word to help me out. At last a word bobbed to the surface. 'Knyfesmyths?'

'Exactly. And that was hard to say so it slid into Christmas.' The driver's eyebrows dipped as she nodded, as if language shift could be so easily summed up.

'Nothing says the season of goodwill like knives,' I said.

'Not much goodwill on the Christmas Steps, not in the olden days,' the driver replied.

'And which olden days are these?' I asked. 'The 1950s or the 1750s?'

'Jess,' Fern said, in her warning *don't be a supercilious twat, Jess* voice. Which was fair enough.

The driver, though, raised her head so that I could see her eyes. They were serious, carrying their own warning. 'There's always been trouble on the Christmas Steps. And there are still enough myths about it that I wouldn't hang around the Steps at night.'

I laughed. She didn't.

Bristol was not a town for the unfit or pissed. If, like me, you were both, then the city's hills were already against you. 'How far up is it?' I asked when we'd got out of the taxi and stood at the bottom of the Christmas Steps. The steep stone stairs went up and up, their summit out of sight.

Fern looked at the booking confirmation on her phone. 'Near the top.' When I groaned, she said, 'But our apartment is supposed to be haunted.'

I picked up my case. 'Good. If I'm doing exercise, I'd better get a load of ghosts.'

The first set of steps felt, if not easy, then manageable. The further we got, though, the more my lungs and legs protested. The heat didn't help, settling in a haze that gave a summer sheen to everything but made me want to lie down on the cool stone. No chance of even a quick sit down, though, there were tourists dawdling in front of us and pressing up behind.

I took my mind off the climb by concentrating on all the tiny shops that lined both sides of the narrow street. The cider shop next to a Chinese takeaway, the art gallery, milliner's, teeny cinema … I made a mental note to look in the bridal section at the lingerie shop. Get myself a garter.

I had little breath left by the time we reached our accommodation. It was worth it. Our apartment was in the Fosters Almshouse, built in 1483 to house Bristol's poor and converted into residences only two decades ago. My room, large and filled with sunlight, looked out onto the courtyard and its too-green-for-August lawn. From my bed, I could see the other wings of the Three Kings Court in the Almshouse through the window; their red bricks were broken up by black crosses, as if wishing away the plague. I felt myself breathing more deeply, as if I too were protected.

I flicked through the black information folder left on my dressing table. Alongside the plastic wallets filled with takeaway leaflets, tourist brochures and boiler instruction manuals, there was a short printed history of the Almshouse itself. I was hoping for a ghost story or two, seeing a woman in grey on the winding stairs etc, but it was all a little dry, giving details such as how John Foster insisted that the twenty-six people who lived there, thirteen men and thirteen women, should all be English, unmarried and over fifty. And poor. Interesting, but not haunting.

Then I turned the page. Someone had scrawled on the back:

Do not linger on the Knyfesmyths' Steps after dark, and never pick up the knife.

Despite the heat, I shivered.

I tried to FaceTime Oliver, my fiancé, but it just rang out. He was off on his stag night soon. His 'best' man, Stevie, had winked at me the week before when I'd asked him to look after Oliver. 'What goes on tour, stays on tour,' he'd said.

'You're going out in Slough, not Las Vegas,' I had replied.

Stevie just tapped the side of his nose and walked away. A stab of jealousy twisted in my stomach at the thought of what Stevie had planned. I trusted Oliver with my life, otherwise I wouldn't have been marrying him, but he couldn't stand up to Stevie. I shook it off. I'd been wrong before and would be again.

I sent Oliver a message, wishing him a great time and saying in exactly one week we'd be getting married. And that's what this weekend was about, celebrating the transition from being two individuals to one stitched together. We'd be our own creature, forever.

Once we'd settled into our rooms, we all gathered in the huge living room that backed onto the Christmas Steps. A window let in a warm breeze, tourist chatter and flies. We each had a sofa and a bottle of bubbly complete with (non-penis shaped) straw. Everyone else had a tiny bottle. Fern had given me, the bride-to-be, a jeroboam. I didn't drink much usually. But I needed to that day.

I was about to tell them about the message in the folder

when Fern stood up, clipboard in one hand, phone in the other: 'Today we're taking it easy, just cocktails, dinner, karaoke, then a bar crawl, topped off with a ghost tour of Bristol.'

Taking it easy? That was more than I'd done in the last year. 'Maybe we could stick with one or two of those? The ghost tour and dinner, maybe?'

Fern consulted her spreadsheet. 'I suppose we could do the pub crawl tomorrow, when we get back from Bath.'

'What's in Bath?' I asked, 'Other than sulphur, buns and Austen?'

'The Mary Shelley House of Frankenstein exhibition. We're doing a hen night escape room thing and, assuming we get out, then we've got an hour to drain their Gothic bar bone dry.'

'Perfect,' I said, and meant it.

'I knew you'd like it,' she said, ''cos I love it. I think I'm looking forward to all this more than anyone.' We shared a smile, just as we shared so many likes and dislikes. It was what drew us together. Fern told people that we met while both reaching for the only copy of Julia Briggs' *Night Visitors: Rise and Fall of the English Ghost Story* in the university library. It wasn't true, not quite, but the truth lay in the same Dewey Decimal section, and it made for a good story.

'Will they keep us there if we don't solve it?' Izzy asked. She had an enviably naïve view of the world for a twenty-five-year-old.

'I'd've thought they'll let us out, as long as we pay,' Fern replied.

'Although they might keep one of us, as an example to others. In which case, it'll probably be you, Iz.' Natalie had a cruel streak thicker than the blue one in her hair.

A handbell rang out from the Steps, echoing up and down the narrow passage. A loud voice, rich as plum pudding, soared through the window. 'Take a breather here and consider yourself fortunate. This is the place where many took their last breath.'

'That's the ghost tour we're taking later,' Fern said. 'It ends by coming up the Christmas Steps, so it'll basically bring us back home ready for bed. It'll be pitch black by then, proper spooky. I don't know how people can go on ghost tours when the sun is still shining.'

I got up and went over to the window. Directly below me was a man in a cape and top hat, waving a cane. Below him, a crowd looked up at him, rapt.

'Condemned criminals were made to climb these to the top where the gallows loomed on St Michael's Hill, after which this street was, for a while, named. As they died, their screams were trapped in the stone beneath your feet. Some say their blood was used to bless the street and bring fortune to the quarter. Bristol's riches, they say, are built on blood but the Christmas Steps still drink it in.'

The man in the top hat looked up, then, and saw me. His face was handsome, skeletally shaded with chalk-white cheek, brow and nose bones, with dark carved hollows on his cheeks and around his eyes. He grinned at me, waved a hand tipped with black nail-polish. I looked away.

'You said that people died right here, though,' a woman said. 'Not at the top.' There was hunger in her voice. Desire. I understood her need to be fed more horror.

'I was just getting to that,' the ghost tour guide said. Irritation choked his voice. 'Colonel Henry Lunsford died on these very stairs while fighting in the Civil War Siege of Bristol, alongside less celebrated soldiers who also lost their lives but did not, if only briefly, get some steps named after them. And, as I said, this street was once lined with pubs and brothels to service the sailors who came into port. It was dark and steep and full of sin. Knife makers made a fortune. Can you even imagine the numbers who have died here? Death stalked this thoroughfare, and still does.' The guide then rapped his cane three times on the stone. 'Time to climb as the criminals did to St Michael's Hill where our tour shall end, as did their lives.'

The crowd followed him up the rest of the Christmas Steps, some pausing to take pictures sitting on the seats carved into the Chapel of the Three Kings opposite the Almshouse. I craned my neck, watching the guide lope ahead of his tourists. He stopped and looked back towards me and waved again. This time, I waved back.

Fern's phone beeped. She looked at it and smiled. 'Cake time,' she said. She loved an itinerary with beeping reminders. 'Tell me you want some, 'cos if you don't, none of us can have some.' Fern was standing behind me, at the long kitchen table. Natalie and Izzy were looking over with pleading faces.

'When have I ever turned down cake?' I asked.

'What if it was a special hen night cake?' Natalie asked. 'In the shape of a cock?'

'Fern wouldn't do that to me,' I replied.

'No. But close,' Fern replied. 'Just one extra letter.' She then flipped open the lid of a cardboard box on the work surface. Inside was a large cake decorated to look like a clock face. In swirling, Gothic handwriting it said in the centre: *Still time to back out and marry us instead!*

Fern opened a drawer and took out a knife with a shabby wooden handle. 'Not a cake knife but it'll do.' The words in the information folder came back to me – *never pick up the knife*. But it's not like you could just stop holding all knives. Avoiding knives would have been almost as ridiculous as avoiding cake.

'A big slice for me, please,' I said. I closed the window but I could still hear the ghost tour guide's cane, tapping against stone.

Late afternoon was laced into evening, and evening into night. Wearing our black sashes, we stalked the streets for fun: had Indian food that made Natalie gasp with its flavours. Drank more fizz, then countless spirits, mixed into a hooch that had Izzy hurling before we'd even got to karaoke. We sang until our throats hurt and our hearts swelled, then ate chips by the canal.

I sat on the edge next to Fern, our feet swinging in time over the water. 'Thank you,' I said, leaning into her.

'I just want you to be happy.' She turned to me then. 'You are happy, aren't you?' she asked. 'With Oliver?'

'Of course,' I replied. 'Just as you are with Rob. Oliver is so kind and loving. Clever. He really knows me. It's like he's unpicked my stitches.' I suddenly felt too exposed and felt the urge to cover up. 'And he makes a great lasagne. Who could want more from a husband-to-be?'

She nodded, slowly, then reached for my face. She held it between her palms, eyes looking at my features like hands sweeping over a clock. Then our eyes stopped on each other. I thought she was going to kiss me. Maybe I wanted her to. What goes on tour ... Then she dropped her hands back into her lap and folded up her chip paper. The grease smears looked like fallen tears.

As Fern stood to take the rubbish to the bin, I checked my phone. Oliver had left a pissed and happy sounding voicenote – 'I'm having an alright time, thanks, sweetheart. We're in a club and Stevie's buying and that never happens so I'm making the most of it. I know this is my stag do but I wish you were here. Now, I want you to have the best time and have loads of stories to tell me when you get home. I love you.'

I felt the urge to get on a train there and then, go back to him. But there wouldn't have been any at that time of night. And, anyway, it would be a weird, stalkerish fiancée who turned up at her fiancé's stag do. And I had my own fun to have.

Fern's phone beeped. 'It's eleven,' she called over, 'time to find some ghosts.'

Bristol Cathedral glowered in uplit orange as we waited with ten others for the tour to start. The sky was purple with no stars. The air was still warm, but I felt the same chill I did earlier, this time laced with anticipation.

'Are you ready?' The guide's voice seemed to come from nowhere.

And so did he. His hand appeared on my shoulder.

The woman next to me shrieked and clapped her hands together. 'But you weren't there!'

'And yet here I am, Madam,' he tapped her very lightly on

the arm with his cane. He was taller than I expected and candy cane thin. He smelled of thyme and fresh tobacco. 'This is my last ghost tour of the evening, and the one I love the most. We shall, of course, be passing through the witching hour, when spirits surge and the undead make themselves known. Some of you,' and he whirled round me then, using me as a maypole, twirling as he spoke, making me feel dizzy and sick. 'Such as this bride-to-be here, may have an affinity with the spirit world. If so, I'd advise you to keep your head down.' He stopped dead, right in front of me. He placed his palms either side of my face and slowly lowered my head. I let him. It felt good to not be in control. 'Do not interact with the spirit world unless you know what you're doing.'

He raised my head again and stared down at me. His gaze was sharp, metallic. A charge stitched us together.

I followed him, head hazy and already starting to ache. My footsteps echoed his. The others, too, fell into line behind him. We shadowed him across the city centre as he told us of the restless spirit of a monk in St Augustine's Abbey, the ghostly keening of a dying bear in Haymarket, a spectral couple whose arguments are repeated every night. The guide danced, as light on his feet as I felt booze leaden in mine. His words echoed in my head as if it were a stone passageway and I never wanted them to stop.

It was midnight when we reached the bottom of the Christmas Steps. I could sense something. It was as if the dark was thickening. Preparing.

The guide gathered the group into a semi-circle facing the steps and stood facing us. 'Like all of us, Christmas Steps has taken many forms in its lifetime. It was originally called Queene Street, after Elizabeth I's visit to Bristol, and was once a treacherous, muddy, steep track that plunged into the river where you're standing right now.'

Fern looped her arm through mine and rested her head on my shoulder. I squeezed her arm.

'The actual steps were built in the seventeenth century,' the ghost tour guide continued. 'Around that time it was known as

Knyfesmyths' Street and there would have been enough inns and brothels on and around the street to fell even the most hardy stag do. Of course, where there's drink, there are fights, and where there are fights, and knives made by cutlers nearby, lives are lost. Lots of them. Which is why there are so many ghosts to meet on Knyfesmyths' Steps.'

The guide beckoned for us to follow. His eyes, though, were following me. His face glowed white in the Victorian-style lamp light.

Fern's phone beeped again.

'Don't tell me you've got something else planned?' I said, smiling.

Fern shook her head. 'I must have programmed another reminder by mistake.'

'Yeah, right,' I replied, laughing, as we began to climb. 'Go on, show me.'

Fern tightened her arm into mine. 'Ssh, you'll spoil the atmosphere.'

She was right. Something was different. Something wrong.

Shadows that should have been still were moving. Spreading. Becoming more solid.

I felt sickness rise in my throat, and tried to put it down to booze and food, not fear. I looked at Fern. Her eyes were ice-cube shiny. She was gripping her phone with both hands as if that was something to hold onto.

Part of me wanted to get into that big soft bed in the Almshouse, another part wanted to chase down the danger. I wanted to peel the skin from the night.

The ghost tour guide was now further up, looking down at them all. 'Blood has run down these steps, feeding myths and rumours and stone. Because even cities need to eat.'

Nervous laughter from the crowd.

'What ghosts are here, then?' the woman who had shrieked earlier asked. She looked around her as if she could see them.

'I could give you names, dates of birth, national insurance numbers if that's what you're after. But do you really want to know?' the guide said, his face now very close to hers, skeletal

335

teeth bared.

'I, I don't know,' the woman said.

Izzy crept up next to me. 'I want to go back to our flat,' she whispered. 'I don't like this anymore.'

Natalie appeared next to her. 'Yeah, let's just go ahead. The skelly jester here will be too busy trying to scare people to notice.'

Fern nodded, as did I. I was going to listen to the part of me that wants a cup of tea and bed.

Beep. Fern's phone agreed, too.

The guide twisted round at the sound, staring at Fern. 'Someone's got a message.'

'It's just a reminder,' I said. 'Fern's arranged everything for the weekend.'

'Then let's see what's so important.' He grabbed the phone from Fern and looked at it. His eyes glinted. 'Who's Oliver?'

'Jess' fiancé,' Izzy said. Behind her, the sign for the cider shop tipped back and forth in a non-existent wind.

My first thought was that Fern was reminding herself to do something for the wedding – ask Oliver about his gift for the bridesmaids or something. The guide, though, was staring at me with something near pity. Then he handed me the phone.

Oliver had sent Fern a message. 'Sorry you're having to handle her. I'll make it up to you, I promise. It's not for much longer. I love you.'

It felt like I was tipping too, in a non-existent wind. Solid shadows moved, pressed into us. Some had a slant of a face and could only move in an ooze. Others were mirrored, showing only ourselves. They flitted through the gaps between us like silverfish between floorboards. They were gaining strength, pushing harder. My skin was alive with the dead.

I grabbed Izzy's hand. 'We've got to run,' I tried to say, but the words wouldn't form. They were glued to my tongue, buzzing, unsaid.

I headed up, as quickly as I could. The feeling of stone beneath my feet felt like the first real thing to happen in too long. Izzy and Natalie were alongside me. Fern was somewhere behind, shouting after me, saying words that stuck to the ones on my tongue.

The shadows were moving quicker now, becoming person-shaped. So many of them. They walked and ran as if broken, dragging almost legs. Holding once arms at wrong angles.

Izzy's hand grew limp in mine, and sweaty. Worried that she'd fainted, I turned to pick her up but Izzy was no longer there. I was holding the hand of a wet shadow. It turned its oval to me and opened a mouth. A curdled sound echoed against stone.

I couldn't see Izzy, Natalie or the guide. The crowd dawdled in front and pressed behind me but I couldn't tell if they were real, or if they ever were.

I knew I had to keep going. Get up to the Almshouse and into the flat. It was the Christmas Steps that had the problem, not me. It was infested.

Step after step, I kept climbing. I caught a glimpse of the lingerie shop and knew I'd reached a certain point, saw the little cinema sign and knew I didn't have much further to go.

But the steps didn't stop rising in front of me. My lungs blazed, my legs ached, and I knew I should be back at the Fosters Almshouse by now, but I couldn't see it or the chapel. The shop signs were the same. It was as if I were on the step machine at the gym, going up but going nowhere.

'Jess.' Fern's voice, from behind me. I walked on and up. Didn't look back. My heart felt like it was being sliced into portions. 'Please, Jess.' She was breathing heavily, I could feel the shadows being pushed out of her way and into me. They felt like burnt marshmallow skin.

Fern joined me, at my side again. 'We can talk when we get back,' I hissed.

'We're not going to get back.' Fern's breath was asthma-cracked. Even after what she'd done, I still felt worried for her. And fucked off at myself for caring.

'What do you mean?'

The shadow in front of me made a sound that was half laugh, half scream.

'The guide gave me this when he took my phone.' Fern held up the knife she'd used to cut my cake. 'I don't know how he got it. But he handed it to me and said that someone must die by this on Knyfesmyths' Steps tonight. The ghosts demand it.' She looked around at the shadows that moved around us.

Of course he had the knife. It somehow made more sense than some things she had seen that evening. It was always going to happen, from the moment they arrived. But she could divert the path they were heading up. No one had to die. 'They can demand as much as they like, they're not getting it. And if you don't use the knife, we'll all be fine. Simple.' I didn't know how I was still picking up my feet. They felt like stone. We marched up and up. To take my mind off the climb, I concentrated on counting, but lost track once I'd got to twenty thousand.

'Jess, please, I have to explain. About Olly.'

'Olly? You've never called him Olly before.'

She said nothing then, and I knew she'd been calling him Olly for a long time. Part of me didn't want to know how long. Another part of me wanted to know that and much more: when it started, how many times, what they did in bed and out of it, when they fell in love, and when were they going to tell me.

I felt something tear inside me. I turned, and pushed her, hard.

She teetered, her chest falling backwards, but her legs kept climbing. 'What the fuck is happening?' she screamed.

A long way ahead, the guide laughed.

I tried again, pushing her sideways this time into the swarming shadows. She fell through a shade at once dense and not there, retching. She covered her eyes with her hands but her feet continued to walk uphill.

And still the steps kept coming for me.

Time marshmallowed: stretching and oozing, crisping at the edges. I no longer knew how long I'd been walking for. I may have fallen asleep as I walked. 'Why can't we get anywhere?' My voice ricocheted, buffeted the ghosts.

Fern's voice was faint, unfurling. 'The guide said, "the Steps will not stop until your heart stops". I think it means that we will never stop climbing until the knife is used.'

I was about to say that was stupid, that we couldn't climb forever, and then I saw a reflection of us in the cider shop window, arms pumping backwards and forwards, knees rising and falling, going nowhere. 'Why us?' I asked. 'Why me?'

Fern shrugged. 'Wrong place, wrong time? I don't know. But he meant for you to find out. Showed you the phone.'

'He wants me to kill you?'

'Or the ghosts do. Or maybe I'm to kill you, he gave me the knife, after all.'

I looked across at the person I thought I knew so well we didn't even have to talk. And now I didn't even know if she was going to kill me.

She handed me the knife, carefully, handle first. 'You should say that they mugged us on the Christmas Steps, came at us with a knife.'

'No,' I said. 'This is not happening.'

'What else are we going to do? Keep climbing till both our hearts give out?' She then placed her hands either side of my face, still walking backwards up the hill, leading me. She then kissed me. Her lips tasted of chips, salted with tears.

The ghosts with something of a face were watching us. Crowding in. Some sniffed, some tried to lick. Others sobbed.

Fern placed her hands round mine as I held the knife. 'You tried to stop them, but they stabbed me.' She jerked forwards, onto the knife. Her blood streamed onto our black sashes and the stone. The ghosts rushed to it and swayed as one shadow, bobbing and bowing and something like a strangled song came out of half-sewn mouths.

Fern's legs still climbed behind her. 'Make it stop,' I screamed, but we only stopped climbing when her breath had gone, and her pupils were fixed and dilated.

I held her body and the shadows sang of Fern, my wingwoman. Both she and the knife lay on Knyfesmyths' Steps. And her ghost must walk upon them.

LONESOME ROADS

Fear of phantom hitchhikers is nothing new. There seem to be infinite numbers of such stories in Britain alone, but it isn't just confined to the United Kingdom. Ghostly hitchhiker rumours, or variations thereof, have been reported in lands as far apart as Korea, Russia and Hawaii, and they continue to be reported even to this day.

For the uninformed, the traditional story, or at least the modern version of it, involves a lone motorist, usually a man (though not always), travelling a considerable distance at night through an unoccupied landscape, and feeling so concerned when he sees a lone pedestrian by the side of the road that he stops and offers them a ride. The pedestrian, usually a young woman, is often very grateful but also distracted: tired, cold, wet, upset by some problem she won't disclose. The motorist chats amiably as he drives, perhaps a little disconcerted, but attempting to be cheerful and behave as if everything is normal. When they arrive at the passenger's destination, they find it's a graveyard or mausoleum, and when the driver looks questioningly at the young woman, she is no longer there, the passenger seat empty except for some token left behind, which will inevitably indicate that she died many years before.

For all that many countries can report legends of this kind, it is, as I say, most often found in the ghost lore of Britain. And nowhere, perhaps, is it more frightening than in the West Country, where there are two particular stand-out examples, though both have notable variations on the main theme.

The first one comes from Somerset and takes place on the road between Frome and Nunney, and was widely reported in the local press at the time. It was 1975, and a driver travelling late at night saw an elderly, heavy-set man in a chequered jacket waiting alone by the roadside. Even from inside his car, the driver could see that the man was in distress, and stopped to offer assistance. The man explained that he was very cold and very tired, and accepted a lift, climbing into the back seat, which the driver found a little unnerving as he then couldn't keep an eye on him easily.

The driver attempted to open a conversation, but the passenger simply repeated that he was very cold. They drove on, the driver still trying to talk, when he suddenly noticed that the man was no longer visible in the rear-view mirror. Stunned, the driver realised that the car's back-seat was empty. He'd never slowed down once since picking the lone figure up, so the only conclusion was that the man had jumped out while the car was moving. Shocked, the driver drove back along the road but saw no sign of a body or anyone lying injured. He then proceeded to Nunney, where he reported the incident to the police, who also searched but found no indication that anything untoward had happened (and kept a copy of the report they made, which can still be read today). They also checked the day's bulletins, and no one had been reported missing locally who matched the description of the man in the chequered jacket.

However, two years later, the same motorist was following the same route, and at roughly the same spot saw the same man again, still wearing his chequered jacket, only this time he was standing in the middle of the road. The motorist jammed his brakes on, skidding off the blacktop and hitting a tree. The police again searched and found nothing, but this time the story caused a sensation, as this was 1977 and Nunney was planning a big party for the Queen's Silver Jubilee celebrations. Not wanting any problems, a posse of volunteers searched the woodlands lining the road at the point where the crash had occurred, in case a living person was actually trying to cause accidents.

They found no one, but a Nunney haulage company owner later gave an interview to the press, claiming that his drivers had reported odd occurrences in that spot as far back as the 1940s, spectral figures attempting to interfere with passing wagons.

Historians have pointed to the rumour that several hangings occurred along this stretch of road after the Duke of Monmouth's unsuccessful revolt in 1685, but that has never been proved, while the motorist concerned always maintained that his eerie tormentor was wearing a modern jacket.

Cut from a similar cloth, but perhaps even eerier, is the case of the 'Hairy Hands of Dartmoor', which must surely qualify as one of the most bizarre and inexplicable tales of West Country horror.

It has been attested to by many that on the road now known as the B3212, which runs across northern Dartmoor between Postbridge and Two Bridges, motorists and bikers have suddenly found themselves wrestling for control of their vehicle with a disembodied pair of large, hairy hands. The heyday of this legend appears to have been in the 1920s, when a number of vehicles screeched off the narrow, twisting road, some drivers complaining afterwards about the phantom hands, though others, the majority in fact, simply saying that their steering wheels or handlebars had jolted out of their possession unexplainably, causing them to crash onto the verge.

Whatever the reason, on several occasions the outcome was fatal.

In June 1921, the medical officer of Princeton Prison on Dartmoor lost control of his motorcycle on the same stretch of road and was killed. A few weeks later, at more or less the same spot, a bus was also misdirected onto the verge, a number of passengers suffering severe injuries. A few weeks after that, the national press became interested when a soldier was thrown off his motorbike in the same place, afterwards reporting that a ghostly pair of hands had grabbed his handlebars and twisted them out of his grasp. Not long after this, a diary entry by a recently deceased journalist called Rufus Endle was published, in which he described a similar incident at the same place.

'A pair of hands gripped the driving wheel and I had to fight for control,' he wrote. It was later revealed that, though he'd told friends about the incident, he'd begged no one to repeat it as he was fearful that people would laugh at him.

Similar occurrences have been reported along that same stretch of road until as recently as the 1970s, though perhaps the scariest story of all dates back to the 1920s again and doesn't even involve a vehicle in motion.

It was 1924, and a woman from London was camping with her husband in a caravan on the moor, very close to the location of the previous accidents. In the middle of their first night there, she awoke to see what she at first took to be an unnaturally large spider on the outside of the nearest window, picking at the cement in the frame as though attempting to force its way in. On looking closer, the appalled holidaymaker was then even more appalled to see that it wasn't a spider, but a single, very hairy human hand. Terrified beyond belief, the woman uttered a prayer and made the sign of the cross, and the hand dropped from view.

When she and her husband plucked up the courage to look outside, there was no trace of the abominable thing.

Over the years, various solutions have been offered to this mystery, from the rational to the truly bizarre. Most believe the unusual number of accidents on the Dartmoor stretch of the B3212 is down to reckless driving in poor conditions. It's an up-and-down road with many sharp turns, while there are sheep on the moor too, who often stray into the carriageway, and at night, even in summer, it can be thick with mist. Others are somewhat less prosaic; the unique geological structure of Dartmoor creates confluences of dangerous magnetic forces; or it's the result of witchcraft, or the revenant of a man who died during a pony-and-trap accident in the 19th century.

The most popularly ascribed-to ghost theory blames the spirit of a worker at the nearby Powder Mills Factory, of which no trace remains today because it was destroyed during a cataclysmic explosion in the 1850s, when the employee in question entered the premises wearing hobnail boots, struck a spark and ignited the powder.

All that supposedly remained of him was his hands.

Umpteen studies have been made of the general phenomena of ghostly hitchhikers.

Parapsychologists, psychologists and folklorists have proposed a range of possible explanations, ranging from local idiots playing pranks on lost travellers to forgotten deities seeking to lure Godless wanderers back to sacred places. My own take is that anyone travelling alone through night-time emptiness is going to feel vulnerable, even enclosed in a car – the number of urban legends involving serial killers being picked up in the middle of nowhere, even though it's almost never happened in reality, is testament to this – and yet none of us, even then, knows how we'd react if we saw someone struggling by the wayside. Most people are kind, even though they know full well that it's a weakness in the eyes of predators.

The Phantom Hitchhiker is the ultimate terror tale in this regard. The ultimate nightmare. The ultimate warning. It's just that in the West Country, not atypically, the variations on this theme are more extreme than anywhere else.

SOON, THE DARKNESS
John Llewellyn Probert

Something was standing at the crossroads.

As he drove closer David Taylor still couldn't make out what it was. The on-again off-again drizzling rain that had persisted since he had left Taunton didn't help. He knew the giant looming figures on either side of the road were actually winter-bare trees, their arching branches threatening to block out the thick grey cloud cover that was allowing little enough light on this miserable winter's day, but that didn't make them seem any less threatening. Even though it was just after lunch David had needed to put the headlights on. Right now the beams picked out droplets of moisture that hung in the air, their only seeming intent to make it even harder for him to see where he was going.

And, of course, to work out what that thing at the crossroads was.

David pulled the car over, less to confront the shadowy figure and more to recheck his directions. He picked up the hand-drawn map he had scribbled as he had pursued Mr Robertson on his way to the operating theatre following the morning ward round. He had assured the senior consultant that yes he was happy to cover the vascular surgeon's afternoon peripheral clinic for him, yes he would apologise to the patients and explain that Mr Robertson had a difficult aneurysm repair and fem-fem crossover graft to perform, and no he would have no trouble finding the clinic as his mobile had SatNav installed.

'I doubt you'll be able to find Kempton Hospital with that thing,' had been the reply, accompanied by a knowing wink as Mr Robertson had disappeared into the changing rooms. And his boss had been right. Any attempt to bring up the area in which David was now driving simply produced a patchwork maze of tiny backroads and country lanes that made no sense at all. Some led nowhere, while others circled back on themselves. Now, perhaps predictably, there was no signal at all for his phone to navigate with. He switched on the car's interior light and peered at the map, scrawled in dark blue biro on the back of an X-Ray request form. 'Good old paper,' his boss had said after handing him the card to write on. 'More reliable than computers, certainly more than the wretched system this institution has deemed fit, or rather cheap enough, for us to use.'

There was no crossroads on the map.

Shit.

He left the engine running and got out of the car. Maybe the thing he had seen at the crossroads was a road sign and it could set him back in the right direction. As soon as he was outside the damp air tickled his throat, triggering a coughing fit so severe it made his eyes water. He was still wiping tears away as he approached the small mound that marked where the roads crossed. Now he could see what the thing was.

It wasn't a road sign, although it was tall enough.

It wasn't a person, but it was person-shaped.

Looking up at the stick-thin effigy, its body and limbs presumably constructed from the branches of nearby trees, David could only think of one word to describe it.

Terrifying.

The head was the worst. David presumed it must have been carved from an oversized turnip, the yellowing flesh roughly hacked at to form a rudimentary horse's head, or perhaps a bull's. After all, horses didn't have horns, did they? And this thing definitely did, if that was what the sticks protruding from the 'skull' at awkward angles were supposed to represent. Holes had been poked for eye sockets. The blackened lumps of something moist that had been pushed deep within the ragged cavities now regarded him soullessly. It was the kind of weird nonsensical thing that under normal circumstances would be funny but here, in this desolate place, with the chill and the damp worming their way between the folds of his clothes, the idea of some mutant horse-thing hobbling across the landscape on its hind legs wasn't remotely amusing. For a moment David forgot he had somewhere to get to. What was the point of this thing? Halloween had been several weeks ago. Had it been here since then? Longer?

A lot longer?

When he finally found Kempton Community Hospital he resolved to ask if it was part of some sort of local tradition. If he ever managed to find the place.

He got back into the car, remembering the advice Linda Belgrave, who had been Mr Robertson's previous surgical registrar, had given him.

'Every now and then they'll ask you to cover some clinic in the middle of nowhere. Half the time I was late because no matter how good you think the directions are the roads in Somerset all conspire to get you lost. My advice is to just keep driving round and round and eventually you'll either find whatever godforsaken tiny district hospital you're supposed to be at, or you'll find the house of someone who knows where it is and can give you directions.'

Linda was up in Bristol now, working at the lovely big clean new teaching hospital free from terrifying tree-things, and certainly not one in the shape of something you'd see some mountain tribe sacrificing people to on a Netflix show.

Well you'll be up there next year, he told himself as he resolved to follow her advice and trust to luck. Turning left at the crossroads felt it would take him back the way he had come, so instead he turned right and found himself driving down a lane even wetter and gloomier and narrower than the one he had just come off. The road curved round to the left and soon began to degenerate into a single lane so bereft of its gravel surfacing that it began to resemble a rutted track.

He must have gone the wrong way.

Time to turn round.

No space to turn round.

Shit.

Now the dirt track was curving even further to the left. It was also getting narrower, dry dead branches of the closest trees clicking and scraping against the car's paintwork, sounding for all the world like fleshless fingers scrabbling to gain purchase on the car's bodywork and the fleshy prey it held within.

And then, suddenly, David was out of the darkness and entering a broad, paved area with car parking spaces painted on it. To his right was a large Victorian building, set back in its own grounds. Directly opposite, a broader road led away back into the trees and was presumably the road he had been supposed to come in on.

Idiot.

David parked the car. The sign beside the main doors read 'Kempton Community Hospital' in no-nonsense blue lettering on a white background. A heavy rumble of thunder accompanied his dash to the entrance, and he was inside just in time to avoid the ensuing downpour.

'You made it, then?' The plump receptionist's beaming moon-face was shiny grey in the fluorescent tube glare. Behind her, the patient waiting area was already half-full.

'I've come to do Mr Robertson's clinic,' David said by way of introduction.

'We know.' The voice came from behind him. David turned to find himself confronted with a woman who could have been the twin of the receptionist, only shorter and stouter and wearing a navy blue sister's uniform. 'Your consultant's secretary rang ahead to let us know.'

David felt self-conscious as he peered at the tiny text on her name badge. 'So you guessed I might be a bit late, then?'

'Oh you're right on time, David.' Sister Lowndes (at least that was his best guess) led him to a corridor. 'We've had to put you right at the end.' They passed flaking-varnished oak-panelled doors that exhibited all the faded grandeur of what must have once been a lavishly appointed building. The stuck-on plastic nameplates (*Mr B Parkinson – Gynaecology, Miss A Molina – Oral Surgery*) looked all the more incongruous for the apparent lack of expertise with which the black misaligned lettering had been applied to the white plastic. The corridor ended in the door to the vascular clinic. Mr Robertson's name was still on it.

'Don't worry, we'll soon fix that.' The sister took a piece of paper from her pocket and Blu-tacked it to the door. Now the sign read 'Registrar' in blue biro so poorly scrawled it looked more to David like 'Regain' or even 'Rebirth'. 'Now the patients will know,' she said as she turned the brass meringue knob.

David had expected to suffer the usual junior doctor's fate of being assigned the tiniest cupboard in the building in which to see the patients. That, plus the less-than-extravagant replacement nameplate for the door did nothing to prepare him for the large room in which he found himself. A smart oak desk with a swivel chair faced the door. Behind it large bay windows opened out onto lawns, which extended as far as the woods beyond. Despite its distance from the building the tree line still managed to look menacing, as if an army of skeletal creatures had lined up for battle and was now merely waiting for the command to advance.

To the left of the desk was the examination couch – one of those old leather affairs rather than the electronic ones David was used to back at the hospital. There was no curtain to pull round and David felt moved to point it out.

'Don't you worry about that.' Sister Lowndes nodded towards the woods. 'There's nobody out there who'd be interested in what's going on in here. Not right now, anyway.'

That was an odd way of putting it. 'But what if one of the patients complains?'

'They won't. We're not in the big city here, David. People are grateful for the help they receive.' And judging from the pile of notes to David's right it looked as if quite a few people were hoping to receive it today.

'How many patients are on the clinic?'

'Oh you'll get through them. I'm sure Mr Robertson had confidence you'd get them all done in time, otherwise he wouldn't have sent you.'

'Done in time?'

'All done and dusted by five.' The sister turned to leave. 'That's what we like. You don't want to be driving home in the dark, do you? Not from here.' She paused for a moment, as if allowing that to sink in. 'Ready for the first one, then?'

Shit, no he wasn't. 'Hang on.' David grabbed the top set of notes and sat down to flick through. Mr Jarvis was a seventy-six-year-old man attending for a post-op check of his left below knee amputation. 'Okay send him in.'

Sister Lowndes, her face still turned away from him, made what David thought was an approving sound and went off to fetch his first customer of the afternoon.

Afternoon. David swivelled the chair to gaze out of the window. It already felt like it was the middle of the night. That comment about driving back in the dark had struck a nerve. It had been difficult enough finding the place by daylight. He didn't fancy ending up having to negotiate dirt tracks like the one he had found himself stuck on once the sun had gone down. He looked at the printed patient list on the desk in front of him. Twenty of them. Would he get through that lot before dark? It was already after two, and patients with amputations and poor circulation weren't exactly known for being quick on their feet, those that still had them. And they'd given him the room furthest away from the waiting area.

The door opened again, providing merciful release from his mounting anxiety. The nurse who wheeled Mr Jarvis in was younger and far less stern-looking than Sister Lowndes and she flashed David a smile as she manoeuvred her charge next to the desk.

'Here you go, sir. It's Dr Taylor to see you today. Or is it Mister?'

David returned her smile. 'It's actually Mister but I don't mind.'

'Fine. I'm Becki.' She locked the brake on Mr Jarvis's chair. 'Sister's given me your clinic to do. Are you okay with him here?'

No. 'I actually need him up on the couch so I can check his

wound.'

'Sure.' Becki put her hands on her hips. 'Which bit is it we need to look at, then?'

Mr Jarvis looked down at his absent right leg and then up at the nurse. 'Obvious, 'innit?' he said in the rasping tones of someone who has enjoyed a long-term relationship with tobacco.

'In that case why don't we just roll that trouser leg up so doctor can take a look.' Becki checked that David was happy with that. He gave her a grateful nod. 'Right then, let's see what we've got.'

Or rather what he didn't have. Mr Jarvis' right lower limb ended just below the knee. The muscular flap that had been fashioned to cover the stump, brought up over the anterior aspect of the bone, appeared to be healing nicely.

Or was it?

On initial inspection the suture line looked healthy, but when David looked closer some of the dried scar tissue looked … wrong.

'Let's get him up on the couch.'

'Everything all right, doctor?' Mr Jarvis spoke with a heavy Somerset burr but David had spent enough time in the area to be able to decode the accent.

'I'm sure it is.' Becki didn't look too happy about having to help Mr Jarvis up either. 'I just want to have a good look at it.'

The couch came with an overhead lamp which would have been of tremendous help in the encroaching gloom of the clinic room if it had worked properly. David rattled the head and eventually an unhealthy glow bathed Mr Jarvis' stump. David drew the lamp close to get a better look.

The scar tissue was dark brown and patchy. It was also extremely tough and resisted David's attempts to lever up a small piece with a metal probe. Jarvis winced as David did so.

'Careful, Doctor!'

'You're hurting him,' said the nurse, unnecessarily.

But David was too engrossed in Mr Jarvis' wound to pay too much attention. Instead of covering healthy tissue beneath, the piece of thick brown scar tissue David was now gently tugging at appeared to be growing into the flesh.

Or emerging from it.

'You haven't been sticking anything into this, have you?'

'You what?'

It was always worth asking. Patients had been known to do funny things with surgical scar sites, prodding them with everything from their own fingers to foreign objects that could be distinctly more traumatising.

'Well, it looks like ...' David was searching for a way to describe it. 'Have you been gardening recently, or anything like that?' Because now he thought about it that was what it reminded him of. It looked as if a twig was emerging from Mr Jarvis's stump. Several twigs, in fact. All of different sizes, all emerging along the suture line.

'I stays in me cottage, Doctor. Ain't been near the garden since you took my leg.'

'Does it hurt?'

'It bloody well did when you pulled on it.'

'Yes, sorry. Well I'm not quite sure what it is but if it's not causing you any trouble, I guess we can just keep an eye on it.'

By the time Mr Jarvis was back in his chair David had filled out the paperwork. 'We'll see you in three months but if it starts to get painful or looks infected we'll see you sooner, okay?'

'Right you are, Doctor.' Mr Jarvis aimed a shrug at Becki who responded with a reassuring smile. 'Might see you later, then.'

Next was Mabel Parsons, eighty-years-old and resistant to the idea of removing the dead tissue her poorly-controlled diabetes had caused her right foot to become. David read in the notes that his consultant had made it clear there wasn't much else that could be done but they were keeping an eye on her in case she changed her mind.

'I think it's a little better, don't you?' she said.

David found it difficult to agree, partly because he had not seen the patient before but mainly because, once the battered fur-lined slipper and stained grey woollen sock had been removed to allow him to examine her, he found it difficult to believe that the purple foot, the toes black with necrosis, could have possibly improved since her last visit.

'It doesn't hurt at all.'

David wasn't surprised. The nerves would have gone ages ago. 'Well it doesn't look very healthy to me,' he said, checking for the pulse that should have been palpable over the front of her ankle. Her flesh was icy to the touch and unsurprisingly there was no suggestion the dorsalis pedis artery was still patent. David didn't see much point in applying pressure to Mabel's big toe to check the capillary refill time as Mabel's toe capillaries had most likely been consigned to history many moons ago, but as his finger hovered she seemed to want him to.

'Go on,' she said. 'I'm sure it's better than last time.'

David made sure he was wearing a glove before he applied pressure. It was like pushing against cold, wet, clay. The tissue yielded a little but had no elasticity. The imprint of his thumb would no doubt remain for many hours. Or at least it would have if at that point Mabel's leg hadn't gone into involuntary spasm and she had jerked her foot towards him.

And his thumb had sunk in further.

And the blackened flesh of her big toe had fallen away too reveal the bark-coloured bone beneath.

'Oh I'm sorry about that.' Mabel straightened herself in the chair. 'My GP thinks its restless legs but those tablets she gives me make no difference, no difference at all.' She peered at David's shocked expression. 'Is everything all right?'

Unable to resist, David prodded at the exposed bone. Like Mr Jarvis' scar tissue it, too, felt almost like a piece of wood, only thicker and more resilient – a small branch or root rather than a twig. 'Can you feel that?'

Rather than provoking the expected reaction of shock and quite possibly pain, Mabel Parsons' reaction was a beaming smile.

'I can. You see? I told you I was getting better.' As if to back this up Mabel attempted to wiggle her toes. David could tell because the other blackened digits, the flesh dead, the nails virtually slipping from their attachments, moved slightly as well. So she still had some muscle control down there. But what were the tendons attached to? Normal bone or more of what her big toe now resembled? What lurked beneath that necrotic tissue, perhaps seeking egress to make Mabel feel 'even better'?

David shook his head and blinked. Where had that thought come from?

'I think Mrs Parsons would benefit from having that dressed, doctor.'

David was grateful for the interruption to the silence. 'Yes. Thanks Becki. I think that would be a very good idea.'

Mrs Parsons was whisked from the consulting room with remarkable speed. David guessed he would have a few minutes before his nurse was ready to bring in the next patient and, keen to eradicate the memory of what he had just seen he turned his attention to the view from the window behind him.

Was it his imagination or had the tree line moved closer?

The day had got darker as well. Somehow that didn't surprise him. The sun set so early this time of year. Combine that with shitty weather and thick forest and the people round here probably lived half their lives without sunlight.

He wondered if they ever got scared, if they ever let their imaginations run away with them, fancying they could see shapes moving amongst the trees, deeper blacknesses that leapt between the higher branches or crawled along the ground, all slowly but inexorably assembling in preparation for the coming of something infinitely larger, infinitely more powerful.

Infinitely darker.

The noise made by the clinic door opening made David start. Where the hell had all that nonsense dropped into his head from?

'I've taken Mrs Parsons to the clinic room for dressings.' Becki didn't seem to notice how high David felt he had jumped. 'She'll be fine.'

David wasn't at all sure about that. 'I was thinking we really ought to get her over to Musgrove Park. She can't carry on like that.'

'I think you'll find she'll refuse any such suggestion, just like she always does.'

So others had tried before. 'But does she not understand what a risk she is at of life-threatening sepsis?'

It seemed as if this had all been gone through many times. 'Oh yes. But she carries on, like so many of them do. Like we all do, down here.' Her words were accompanied by a rumble of thunder, as if the brittle bones of some long-forgotten god were being crushed in the firmament above. Did the nurse smile because of the sound? Or because of what she had just said?

'You mean being this far from …'

'Go on, you can say the word.' When David didn't come straight out with it she said it for him. 'Civilisation. That's what all you doctors who come here and visit think. You all come from cities, and even if you don't then you were educated in cities, and you can't wait to get back to them, and you think those of us who don't live anywhere near a motorway are so much poorer off for being distanced from the place you think is so much better.'

That was quite the outburst, and her upbeat delivery and smile as she came out with it did nothing to quell David's sense of unease, or help him come up with the most appropriate response. In the end he just said, 'We come here to help.'

'Of course you do. No-one would say otherwise. And we know you mean the best for everyone here. It's just that sometimes you people forget that we're a little bit different to you.' David's expression led to a ripple of laughter. 'Oh look I'm sorry. I promise I'm not trying to scare you and we're not all weirdos down here or anything, but I've been trying to work out the best way to explain something to you that's going to happen in about ten minutes.' She looked at the clock. 'At 3pm. Every twelve months we have a tradition and it just so happens that this year it's fallen on a weekday afternoon. Nothing serious or major. Have you heard of the hobby horse that they have over in Minehead?'

Actually David had. A friend of his had been over there on

May Day and witnessed the spectacle of the three large boat-shaped and beribboned wooden horses converging on the town centre from different directions. Something to do with bringing good luck. He nodded.

'Well here we have something that's a bit like that. The image of good fortune is carried by those who have been appointed and it visits all the important sites in the area.'

'And this hospital is one of them?'

She beamed. 'That's right. They bring it in and knock on every door. All you have to do is say the right thing and it's good luck for the community for the coming year.'

'And they're going to knock on my door are they?'

'Not them,' she said, looking as if he hadn't understood anything. 'The Luck Spirit.'

'Okay.' Best to go along with it, he thought. 'And the Luck Spirit is going to knock on my clinic door?'

'Yes.'

'And you're going to say the appropriate words to it?'

'Oh no.' Suddenly she seemed very serious. 'You are.'

'I am?' What had he found himself in the middle of? 'Why me?'

'The words have to be spoken by a figure of authority, that's why we always get the doctors to do it if they're here.'

'I'm not sure if I …'

'Oh it's easy.' She came over and took his hand. Her skin was much drier than he had expected it to be, her bony fingers like sticks wrapped in paper. 'They say a few words, you say a few words, and then they go on their way and everyone's happy. You wouldn't want to spoil the tradition, would you?'

David certainly didn't want to be known as the surgical registrar who upset an entire region of Somerset. If nothing else it would look bad on his end-of-year training report. 'No of course not.'

That seemed to make it all better. 'Good. Now, when you open the door you'll hear a voice say "The Awaited One is coming".'

'"The Awaited One is coming".' David repeated to show

willing.

'Yes. Good. But you don't repeat what they say. You have to reply with "The Expected One is here".'

'"The Expected One is here".' What harm could it do?

'Good! Great! Do it just like that and everything will be fine.'

'And after that we can get on with the clinic?'

The nurse didn't reply and instead gave David a sympathetic look he wasn't quite sure how to take.

He also didn't know what to do for the next ten minutes. Anywhere else he would have suggested squeezing in another patient, but this wasn't anywhere else, so instead he looked out at the view again.

To see that the world outside was now almost completely obscured by the worsening downpour.

Were the locals seriously going to carry on with things in weather like this? Perhaps they would wait until things calmed down. But no, what was that, approaching to the left? David had to press his face against the glass and bring both hands up to make out the flickering torch held high and the procession that followed. And at the back, bringing up the rear like some monstrous totem was … something. No matter how hard David squinted he couldn't tell what it was. A man on another's shoulders? Someone holding some sort of effigy up high? Whatever it was its head seemed so much larger than its body, causing the figure to sway from side to side as it walked, almost as if it was a little drunk, or perhaps suffered from some disorder of poor coordination.

'Can you see them?' Nurse Becki sounded almost breathless with excitement.

'Yes.' David's voice was a croak. 'I think I can.'

And then he couldn't, partly because of the rain and partly because the procession had disappeared around the side of the building where the entrance was. Even down here at the end of the corridor, David fancied he could hear them knock on the main door.

And then, suddenly, it all went very quiet.

Clinics always have a background hum. Patients coming and

going, equipment being fetched, the hustle and bustle of administration. It was the kind of thing you never tended to notice under normal circumstances. Not until it was gone.

And now it was.

It was so silent all David could hear, even standing right next to the door of his clinic room, was the sound of his own breathing. For a moment he was convinced he was alone but when he looked Becki was still there, standing behind him, almost on tiptoe with anticipation. He was tempted to flash her an 'isn't this all a bit daft' grin until he realised she was no longer paying attention to him. She was listening for what lay beyond the door.

The silence persisted. What could they be doing out there? And was it really keeping all those patients waiting to be seen in such rapt attention that they weren't making a sound? David imagined them all sitting there in the waiting area, eyes wide, mouths agape at the jigging and posturing of some silly bloody farmers waving their Morris dancing sticks.

The sound of something large and heavy being thumped against a wooden surface shook David from his attempts to relieve his mounting anxiety. A moment later it came again, and then again.

There was the sound of a door being opened, presumably the first one in David's corridor, the one being used by the Gynaecology Clinic.

'The Awaited One Is Coming!'

It sounded like no voice David had ever heard. In fact it hardly sounded like a voice at all, more like a scratching squawk being wrung from a throat that was nothing but bone, or paper. Or dry sticks, David thought with a shudder. He fancied he heard a mumbled reply but it was so indistinct that it was impossible to make out individual words or even guess at it being similar to the response he had been asked to provide. Then all was silent once more.

Why?

Why could he not hear the procession coming down the corridor? If they were still standing in the doorway of the

357

Gynaecology Clinic why could he not hear whatever exchange must be taking place?

Thump. Thump. Thump.

They must have reached the second door, now, even though David had heard no footsteps, no creaking of floorboards, no general commotion from what had looked like a significant number of individuals making up the procession he had seen. Perhaps they were all gathered in the waiting area while just the person carrying the 'Lucky One' as Nurse Becki had called it, came down the corridor with the lightest of footsteps.

'The Awaited One Is Coming!'

It really did sound as if every word was being pronounced with a capital letter, once again in the horrible, dry, creaking, croaking voice, only louder this time, and more piercing.

If there was a reply David didn't hear it. All he could think about was that he was next. Why the whole situation bothered him so much he couldn't explain, and as he attempted to calm his rapid breathing he once more tried to distract himself by turning and looking out of the window.

Beyond the glass there was nothing but darkness.

That made no sense. It was a miserable day and the lights were on in the room but he should have been able to see something. He went over to the middle window and cupped his hands around his face, staring into the void.

No lawn. No trees. Nothing.

Thump. Thump. Thump.

The door, the heavy oak door of his clinic, shuddered under the pressure of each blow.

David remained over at the far side of the room.

'Answer it!' The nurse's barked command made him jump.

'That's okay.' All David wanted to do right now was stay as far away from that door as possible. 'Let's just pretend I'm somewhere else for a minute. If I'm not here they'll have to move on.'

'But you are in here.' She didn't look happy. 'You are in here,' she said again, this time loudly enough for anyone … anything … poised just outside to be able to hear. 'And you're going to answer the door or you will spoil everything.'

David turned back to the windows, searching for a catch, a handle, anything that would allow him to escape. Even that threatening void of nothingness seemed preferable now to whatever was waiting for him to answer that door.

'You *will* answer it.' Becki's voice was cold, almost commanding. 'You have no choice.'

He didn't. Despite all his efforts to remain where he was, David felt his legs twitch, then an invisible force began to move him towards the door.

He held his breath, heart pounding in his chest, as his hand was moved to the doorknob to twist it. To his ears the sound of the clunk of the door mechanism was almost deafening, as was the creaking sound as it slowly opened.

Something was standing in the doorway.

Something eight feet tall.

Something he had seen before, at the crossroads, only this was much, much worse. Because this something was alive. As it towered over him with malicious intent the last remaining rational part of his brain kept telling him it had to be a man dressed up, an impossibly thin man with a body no thicker than a telegraph pole on which was balanced the most immense head made of some yellowish, pulpy substance with coal-black eyes and sticks for horns. Maybe it was a puppet, his scrabbling brain thought desperately. But if it was then that telegraph pole body would not be breathing, emitting a dull creaking sound he could hear as the torso expanded and relaxed, and those twig-thin fingers couldn't possibly move with such dexterity as they reached for him. Most of all, that head couldn't possibly create that expression of lust and hate and desire as it looked down at him. It drew in a rusty, moist breath and prepared to bellow its hideous herald.

'The Awaited One Is —'

That was all David heard as, with the last vestige of voluntary movement remaining to him, he pushed past the towering, tottering thing. He could not help but draw breath as he did so and the stench of wet decay that filled his nostrils and lungs was so choking it almost stopped him dead.

'No!' Did that hideous screech come from Becki or the thing? It didn't matter. David stumbled up the corridor. The dim hospital lighting was intermittent now, plunging his progress into darkness with every few steps he made.

The other clinic doors were open.

As he passed he could not resist looking inside. In the first room, the one closest to his, Dr Molina, the oral surgeon, was in the grip of something unholy, her entire head encased in a mesh of what resembled a fungal network, its mycelial threads glistening greenly in the pale light. The threads themselves had all emerged from the mouth of the patient she had been examining, a mouth that was now too large and gaped too widely to belong to any normal human being. The harder she struggled the more the threads increased in number, springing from her patient's oral cavity with whip-like movements.

David hurried past, only to be confronted with further horrors in the Gynaecology Clinic, where the specialist appeared to be delivering something made of thorns and splintered sticks from between the bloodstained thighs of a woman far too old to be of childbearing age. His fingers had become fused to the wriggling thing and now appeared to be a part of it.

'It … won't … let … me … go.' The desperate words were spoken in a horrible, dry twig-like scraping tone that suggested that it was not just the man's fingers that had become part of it.

And then the ground shook.

Was it an earthquake? David braced himself and made for Reception.

The shapes in the waiting area were now just that – rudimentary forms of what had once been human beings. Now they more resembled bundles of knotted brambles, bereft of foliage but rich in thorns ready to tear and penetrate, nature at its nastiest, ready to cause the worst kind of traumas and infections.

And as he stood there regarding this new horror so they, too, turned their bristling 'heads' to regard him.

The ground shook again. And then again.

The heads swayed towards the door. From throats that could not be came rasping sounds like nothing David had ever heard, and yet somehow he understood the roughly-formed words.

'The … Expected … One … Is … Here!'

Another shake, accompanied by a sound so loud it could have been thunder but David knew it was not.

'The Expected One Is Here!'

David had presumed the main doors would be locked but he pushed through them easily. It was dark outside. although not quite as black as he had imagined. He could just about make out the grounds, the car park, the lawns, and the tree line with the sky above it.

The sky had changed colour.

It had been a dark day before, with a lot of cloud cover. Now that cloud had cleared, but the normal sky seemed to have been cleared with it, as if a great hand had wiped across the heavens, leaving nothing but a strange, silvery blankness. As David's eyes began to adjust he found he could see more of his surroundings.

Including the thing on the horizon.

It towered so high over the rest of the landscape that at first he thought it was an electric pylon. Then it took a step forward. And another, and another. Each step was accompanied by that shaking of the ground, that boom that was now so intense David could feel his eardrums bleeding. By the time the immense creature was close enough to make out in more detail, David already knew what it was, striding across a land it had waited so long to make its own, its stick-like, stilt-like feet leaving huge sinkholes where it trod, its huge head filled less with malice and rather with a very different idea of how its new world should be, preparing to fashion it in its image from the life that had existed long before man had dared to encroach upon its realm.

David could no longer hear, but he spoke the words anyway. It was all he could do before he bade farewell to the world he knew, before he, too, became as those back in the clinic. Part of a different world. Part of a better world? The words were difficult because his throat was no longer designed to utter such things, but he did his best, hoping they would be heard one last time by the thing that had come for him, and for all of them.

'The Expected One Is Here.'

SOURCES

All stories in *Terror Tales of the West Country* are original to this anthology, with the exception of *Objects in Dreams May Be Closer Than They Appear* by Lisa Tuttle, which was first published in *House of Fear* (2011), *Bullbeggar Walk* by Paul Finch, which was first published in *Inhuman #1* (2004) and *Certain Death for a Known Person* by Steve Duffy, which was first published in *Apparitions* (2009).

OTHER TELOS TITLES
YOU MAY LIKE

PAUL FINCH
Cape Wrath & The Hellion
Terror Tales of Cornwall
Terror Tales of Northwest England
Terror Tales of the Home Counties
Terror Tales of the Scottish Lowlands

RAVEN DANE
THE MISADVENTURES OF CYRUS DARIAN
Steampunk Adventure Series
1: Cyrus Darian and the Technomicron
2: Cyrus Darian and the Ghastly Horde
3: Cyrus Darian and the Wicked Wraith

Death's Dark Wings
Standalone alternative history novel

Absinthe and Arsenic
13 Horror and Fantasy Short Story Collection

HELEN MCCABE
THE PIPER TRILOGY
1: Piper
2: The Piercing
3: The Codex

GRAHAM MASTERTON
The Djinn
The Wells of Hell
Rules Of Duel (with WILLIAM S BURROUGHS)
The Hell Candidate

DAWN G HARRIS
Diviner

SAM STONE (S L HOWE / SAMANTHA LEE HOWE)
KAT LIGHTFOOT MYSTERIES
Steampunk Adventure Series
1: Zombies at Tiffany's
2: Kat on a Hot Tin Airship
3: What's Dead PussyKat
4: Kat of Green Tentacles
5: Kat and the Pendulum
6: Ten Little Demons

THE COMPLETE LIGHTFOOT
Hardback limited-edition compendium of all Kat Lightfoot books with bonus extras.

THE JINX CHRONICLES
Dark Science Fiction and Fantasy, dystopian future
1: Jinx Town
2: Jinx Magic
3: Jinx Bound

THE VAMPIRE GENE SERIES
Vampire, Historical and Time Travel Series
1: Killing Kiss
2: Futile Flame
3: Demon Dance
4: Hateful Heart
5: Silent Sand
6: Jaded Jewel

Zombies In New York And Other Bloody Jottings
Horror Story Collection

TELOS PUBLISHING
www.telos.co.uk

Printed in Great Britain
by Amazon